TUMULT IN THE CLOUDS

The British Experience of the War in the Air 1914–1918

Nigel Steel and Peter Hart

Hodder & Stoughton

First published in 1997
by Hodder and Stoughton
A division of Hodder Headline PLC

British Library Cataloguing in Publication Data

Steel, Nigel, 1962–
Tumult in the clouds : the British experience
of war in the air, 1914–1918
1. World War, 1914–1918 – Aerial operations, British
I. Title II. Hart, Peter, 1955-
940.4'4'941

ISBN 0 340 63845 1

Typeset by Hewer Text Composition Services, Edinburgh
Printed and bound in Great Britain by
Mackays of Chatham PLC, Chatham, Kent.

Hodder and Stoughton
A division of Hodder Headline PLC
338 Euston Road
London NW1 3BH

TUMULT IN THE CLOUDS

To

James McCudden VC

and

Edward Mannock VC

'A Working-class Hero is Something to Be', John Lennon

'Nor law, nor duty bade me fight,
Nor public men, nor cheering crowds,
A lonely impulse of delight
Drove to this tumult in the clouds.'

'An Irish Airman Foresees his Death', W. B. Yeats

Contents

List of Illustrations	ix
Preface	xi
Map of Western Front	xv
1 The War in the Air	1
2 The Dawn of Aviation	3
3 1914	23
4 1915	40
5 Training	77
6 1916	101
7 Zeppelins	140
8 Naval Aviation	174
9 1917	200
10 Dawn Patrol	240
11 Gothas	260
12 On the Ground	286
13 1918	306
14 Aftermath	348
Source References	353
Bibliography	364
Index	370

List of Illustrations

All photographs have been taken from the Imperial War Museum's Photograph Archive and the authors would like to thank the Keeper and the Museum's Trustees for their permission to reproduce them. IWM negative numbers are given in brackets after the brief captions in the following list.

S F Cody (Q85173)
A BE2 at an early air review in May 1913 (H(AM)1671)
Lanoe Hawker VC (Q61077)
Albert Ball VC (Q69593)
James McCudden VC (HU71314)
Edward Mannock VC (Q73408)
Cockpit of an SE5 A scout (Q67871)
Officers and SE5 A scouts of 85 Squadron (Q12049)
Maurice Farman Longhorn (Q67057)
BE2 A (Q54985)
Sopwith Camels of 44 Squadron (Q67903)
DH4s of 27 Squadron (Q12015)
Oswald Boelcke (Q58027)
Max Immelmann (Q58026)
Fokker EIII as flown by Boelcke (Q58037)
Manfred, Freiherr von Richthofen (Q58028)
Werner Voss (Q63127)
Aerodrome of Jasta 12 (Q23907)
Combat report written by James McCudden (HU71313)
RE8 pilot photographed by his observer (Q91437)
RE8 observer photographed by his pilot (Q91438)
Aerial photograph, 1915 (Q85216)
Diagramatic key to the aerial photograph (Q85216a)
BE2 C fitted with a camera for aerial photography (Q33850)
Map being assembled from aerial photographs (Q34027)

Demonstration of a CFS bombsight (Q60869)
Loading a bomb on to an FE2 B (Q11551)
Submarine Scout (SS) airship (Q48034)
Sopwith Camels on HMS *Furious* (Q96599)
Devastated homes in east London (H013)
Bomb damaged London bus (Q70238)
William Leefe Robinson VC (Q66934)
Naval Zeppelin L70 (Q58479)
Gotha bombers (Q73552A)
Letter of sympathy to the parents of a schoolgirl wounded in June 1917 (HU71312)

Preface

The first great air war, fought in the skies of Europe between August 1914 and November 1918, changed the world for ever. The development of flight in the preceding decade had extended the scope of warfare, projecting it into a new dimension. Now it could reach out to threaten what had previously been the safest of places. Reserve lines, headquarters, dockyards, factories, even houses far from the battlefield, all fell within the thrall of aircraft. Nowhere was safe. The ubiquitous eyes of the enemy probed into every corner, watching, waiting, as he prepared to swoop like a hawk out of the blinding halo of the sun on to his helpless prey. The story of the development of aviation during the First World War is a powerful and inspiring subject. Over the course of four years, driven by the supreme catalyst of battle, aeroplanes advanced with amazing speed, from slow and stable machines such as the BE2 C and Aviatik through to fast and agile scouts like the SE5 and Fokker DVII. Able in the first instance to do little more than shake their fists at the enemy, or wave if they felt more courteously inclined, within four years pilots could attack each other with deadly precision using sophisticated automatic weapons. Bombing too developed apace. In 1914 bombs consisted simply of adapted grenades or artillery shells which could be wantonly dropped either by airships or heavier-than-air machines. By 1918 formations of specially designed versions of both were conducting massed raids on military and domestic targets. Reliable methods of carrying out reconnaissance through aerial photography and guiding the fall of artillery shells to greater accuracy using the clock code also gradually revolutionised the conduct of individual battles until, by the date of the Armistice, the air services had become an integral part of the way wars were fought.

Tumult in the Clouds examines the experiences of both the British airmen at the Front and the civilians who remained at home as these cataclysmic events unfolded. Incorporating wherever possible the actual words of the participants, taken either from oral interviews or contemporary documents, it allows them to speak for themselves. Detailed recollections set down later in life, combined with letters and diaries written at the time, are used both to reveal factual information and to evoke a sense of how life changed as the apparently theoretical concepts of aerial warfare suddenly became a fearful reality. In attempting to provide a comprehensive account of such a vast subject in this way, it is inevitable that some technical details have been omitted. Aircraft developed so quickly, with each new generation spawning multiple variations, that it would be impossible to refer to them all. This is not to suggest that the absent machines were unimportant, simply that it has not been possible to include them. Likewise, as the flying services mushroomed to keep pace with the rapid expansion of the war, new units were formed at breakneck speed. Clearly not all the squadrons of the RFC, RNAS and RAF have been mentioned. But hopefully those that are featured will stand in for those that are not and provide a common strand of experience. Military ranks have been given as accurately as possible in line with the position of the 'speaker' at the time of the event being described. However, given the fast turnover of flying personnel, promotions were rapid and occasionally there may be an anachronism.

The key, chronological chapters of the book focus on the campaigns that were fought along the Western Front. This is now accepted as the most important area of confrontation where the lion's share of resources were expended. As a result, it was here that most of the crucial developments in weaponry and tactics first appeared and, although 'side-shows' such as Gallipoli, Palestine and Mesopotamia included aerial elements, on the whole they tended to follow the trends already set closer to the heart of the global conflict in France and Belgium. Partly in reflection of the sources available in this country, events have been predominantly presented from a British perspective. The archival resources of the Imperial War Museum stand second to none in the breadth and diversity of choice that they offer to students of this country during the First World War and, as in *Defeat at Gallipoli*, one of the principal aims of *Tumult in the Clouds* has been to utilise one small part of these unparalleled riches. There is also a more profound reason. With the advent of wholesale bombing, for the first time civilians were exposed to a new and unprecedented form of warfare. Beginning in the early months of 1915, it was in Great Britain that this wanton violation from the air of the traditionally enjoyed right to safety and security was most keenly felt and enjoyed its greatest impact. The experiences of the men, women and children of Great Britain in all walks of life stand as a testament to their courage and strength of character as they faced the unknown threat of the war in the air. It is right to tell their story.

During the course of the past three years we have been greatly assisted by many people without whose freely given contributions this book could not have been completed. We are, however, particularly grateful to our work colleagues at the IWM. In the Sound Archive, Margaret Brooks, Kate Johnston, Laura Kamel, Rosemary Tudge and Conrad Wood have been a collective tower of strength in amassing a fantastic treasure store of oral recordings for those willing to use it. The former Keeper, David Lance, must also be thanked, for it was under his auspices in the early 1970s that the Archive undertook its project on aerial warfare during the First World War. In the Department of Documents, Rod Suddaby, Penny Bonning, Wendy Lutterloch, Tony Richards, Simon Robbins, David Shaw, and Stephen Walton have attained a miraculous efficiency in running a huge and complicated archive and, although not technically part of the Department, as he makes his 'mess' there, Malcolm Brown must also be included among their number. Within other departments of the museum we would like to acknowledge Brad King of the Film Archive, our inspiration and 'mentor' right from the start, and Neil Young of the Research and Information Office, whose practical advice is always soundly rooted in Yorkshire common sense, as well as Chris McCarthy and Paul Cornish of Exhibits and Firearms, Bryn Hammond of Information Systems, and David Parry, Gordon McLeod, Richard Bayford, Allan Amesbury and Paul Coleman of the Photograph Archive.

Beyond the bounds of the Museum we would like to thank all those people who have given us permission to include extracts from the documents quoted in the text (Mrs J Anderson, Mrs L M Anson, G R E Brooke, Lady Campbell, Mrs A Chacksfield, Miss B Coombs, Mrs E C R Fawcett MBE, Mrs V M Greene, Mrs S Halliwell, Mrs D E Keates, Mrs J Keeling, J S Luxford, Miss E Rowell, Dr P M Smith, P Stevenson, A T Wilkinson and J V C

Wyllie DFC) and those veterans who, over the past twenty-five years, have allowed their recollections to be recorded on tape. All the written and oral sources used have been listed in detail in the source references and bibliography. We would also like to thank the Trustees of the Royal Air Force Museum for allowing us access to their archives and in particular to Peter Elliott whose public service skills must have been tested to the limit by Peter Hart's research! On an entirely personal note the writing of *Tumult in the Clouds* has been radically different from *Defeat at Gallipoli*, principally because we have been tackling a wholly new subject. Although along the way we have had to resist many distractions and encountered several surprises, it has been an overwhelmingly rewarding experience, something that we hope we have been able to convey through the text. Alas, it has simply not been the same without either Polly the cat or George the dog.

Nigel Steel and Peter Hart

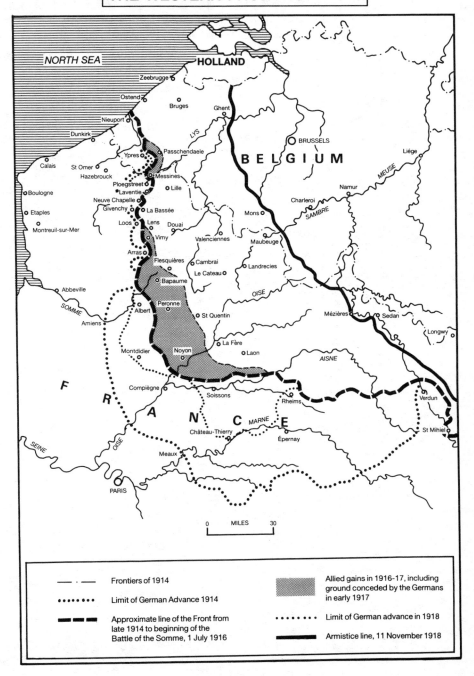

THE WESTERN FRONT 1914-1918

NORTH SEA

HOLLAND

Zeebrugge

Ostend

Bruges

Ghent

Nieuport

LYS

BRUSSELS

Liége

BELGIUM

MEUSE

Ypres

Passchendaele

Calais

St Omer

Hazebrouck

Messines

Namur

Lille

Boulogne

Ploegstreet

Laventie

Charleroi

Neuve Chapelle

Etaples

Givenchy

La Bassée

Mons

SAMBRE

Loos

Lens

Montreuil-sur-Mer

Douai

Vimy

Valenciennes

Maubeuge

Arras

Flesquières

Cambrai

Landrecies

Le Cateau

OISE

Abbeville

Bapaume

SOMME

Peronne

Albert

Amiens

St Quentin

Mézières

Sedan

Montdidier

Noyon

La Fère

Longwy

Laon

AISNE

F

Compiègne

R

Soissons

Rheims

Verdun

A

N

C

MARNE

E

Château-Thierry

St Mihiel

Épernay

SEINE

OISE

Meaux

PARIS

0   MILES   30

Frontiers of 1914	Allied gains in 1916-17, including ground conceded by the Germans in early 1917
Limit of German Advance 1914	Limit of German advance in 1918
Approximate line of the Front from late 1914 to beginning of the Battle of the Somme, 1 July 1916	Armistice line, 11 November 1918

CHAPTER ONE

The War in the Air

In January 1908 the first parts of a new serial entitled *The War in the Air* appeared in *Pall Mall* magazine. Although fictional, the underlying purpose of the story was serious. Written by H.G. Wells, it was intended to provide a stark warning of the possible consequences of a vast international conflict fought through the embryonic medium of aviation. Depicting the aggressive use of both aeroplanes and airships, it described scenes of widespread devastation and pointed towards a menacing future in which the very fabric of civilisation was rent asunder by the uncontrollable forces of destruction released by the war. It was a cataclysmic vision, written with deliberately unrestrained panache that fuelled the growing anxieties of many people about the awful potential of aerial warfare. The central episode included a graphic description of an attack on New York by a fleet of German airships. Through a series of unfortunate mishaps, this event was witnessed at first hand by the story's protagonist, a young British civilian called Bert Smallways, who stood transfixed in disbelief on the observation deck of the leading ship as the first bomb was released.

It hit the pavement near a big archway just underneath Bert. A little man was sprinting along the sidewalk within half a dozen yards, and two or three others and one woman were bolting across the roadway . . . The little man on the pavement jumped comically – no doubt with terror – as the bomb fell beside him. Then blinding flames squirted out in all directions from the point of impact, and

1

the little man who had jumped became, for an instant, a flash of fire and vanished – vanished absolutely. The people running out into the road took preposterous clumsy leaps, then flopped down and lay still, with their torn clothes smouldering into flame. Then pieces of the archway began to drop, and the lower masonry of the building to fall in with the rumbling sound of coals being shot into a cellar. A faint screaming reached Bert, and then a crowd of people ran out into the street, one man limping and gesticulating awkwardly. He halted, and went back towards the building. A falling mass of brickwork hit him and sent him sprawling to lie still and crumpled where he fell. Dust and black smoke came pouring into the street, and were presently shot with red flame . . . [Bert] clung to the frame of the porthole as the airship tossed and swayed, and stared down through the light rain that now drove before the wind, into the twilight streets, watching people running out of the houses, watching buildings collapse and fires begin. As the airships sailed along they smashed up the city as a child will shatter its cities of brick and card. Below, they left ruins and blazing conflagrations and heaped and scattered dead; men, women, and children mixed together . . . and it came to him suddenly as an incredible discovery, that such disasters were not only possible now in this strange, gigantic, foreign New York, but also in London . . . that the little island in the silver seas was at the end of its immunity, that nowhere in the world any more was there a place left where a Smallways might lift his head proudly and vote for war and a spirited foreign policy, and go secure from such horrible things.[1]

CHAPTER TWO

The Dawn of Aviation

Looking back, 1908 can be seen as a pivotal year for aviation. A number of important initiatives that had been underway since the turn of the century came to a head and by the close of its final month there could be no doubt that the world had embarked upon a new era. The first flight had taken place five years earlier on 17 December 1903 when Wilbur and Orville Wright had guided their innovative heavier-than-air machine off the earth and flown it through the air. Their success at Kitty Hawk, North Carolina had been the result of a series of methodical annual experiments which had been carried out on the same site since 1900. The Wrights believed that the key to powered flight lay not in the application of force to drive a heavy object through the air but in the delicate harnessing of the wind and its skilful manipulation by the pilot to keep his machine aloft. Following these beliefs, they had slowly worked their way up from the construction of a man-carrying glider to a fully-fledged aeroplane. Once they had finally succeeded in making this work, they gradually enhanced their machine near their home town of Dayton, Ohio until by the autumn of 1905 they could fly distances of several miles, with the longest flight of that year on 5 October covering twenty-four miles at a speed of around thirty-eight miles per hour. Naturally cautious about allowing observation of their work, few people realised just how much the Wrights had achieved and when in August 1908, having been invited to France by a syndicate of businessmen, Wilbur Wright demonstrated his machine at Hunaudières near Le Mans its grace and dexterity completely overwhelmed the watching French pioneers.

For the previous two years the French had also been engaged on research into the development of a practical aeroplane. The first spluttering flight had been made in France in September 1906 and from that point on a small but dedicated band of French enthusiasts had made steady progress. Unlike the Wrights, however, these men flew in public and knowledge about successful developments spread quickly. Unaware of what had already been achieved in the United States, they mistakenly claimed world records for distance and duration of flights, as well as for basic manoeuvres such as turns and circuits, and it was inevitable that when they finally realised how far they still had to travel they were disappointed. German aeronautical research, meanwhile, was not focused on aeroplanes but on dirigible airships and it was led by Count Ferdinand von Zeppelin, a retired General whose first ship had been flown at Friedrichshafen near Lake Constance in July 1900. Although Luftschift Zeppelin or LZ1, as it was termed, had made a successful flight, it prompted little official response and it was not until the development of aviation began to accelerate in France that the German authorities started to take a closer look at his work. In November 1907, encouraged by both the army and navy to build a much larger vessel, construction commenced on von Zeppelin's fourth, LZ4. At 446 feet in length and thirty-two feet in diameter, it was of mammoth size compared to the tiny aeroplanes that had flown such short distances and this difference was starkly accentuated when, during its maiden voyage on 1 July 1908, it flew a staggering 240 miles in twelve hours. This long flight was greeted with popular acclaim by the German people and prompted the identification of airships with Germany while the aeroplane became more closely associated with France.

In Great Britain the development of successful aeroplanes in France and dirigibles in Germany led to a growing sense of public unease. For centuries the English Channel and the power of the Royal Navy had protected Britain from the threat of invasion and the effects of the periodic wars that had swept across northern Europe, only a relatively short distance from her shores. Now, as H.G. Wells so emphatically pointed out, the years of complacent insularity appeared to be over. Britain would no longer be able to stand safely in the background while conflicts were resolved out of sight. Before long the new dimension of aviation would allow airmen to reach Britain directly, drawing the country for the first time into the centre of the action.

This sense of anxiety was most widely propagated through the empire of newspapers and magazines owned by Lord Northcliffe, in particular his leading title the *Daily Mail*. Having witnessed some of the earliest aeroplane flights in France, Northcliffe had immediately become convinced of the massive potential of aircraft and the threat they would pose to Britain. He believed that the country had already started to fall behind and on 17 November 1906, in an attempt to counter this trend, he announced a prize of £10,000 to be awarded to the first person to fly from London to Manchester. Although at the time this goal was unattainable, and the idea was widely ridiculed by journalists, the size of the sum on offer dramatically drew attention to the fact that one day it would be possible. In a deliberate attempt 'to make the nation air-minded', Northcliffe made use of the *Daily Mail* at every opportunity to stress the advances that were being made in aviation.[1] When Wilbur Wright took Europe by storm in the summer of 1908, Northcliffe worked out that if his longest flights were executed in a straight line they could easily carry him across the Channel. To make this point, on 5 October 1908 he offered a new prize of £500, later doubled to £1,000, to the first airman to achieve this feat. For the British the crossing of the Channel by aeroplane represented an event of momentous significance and when, on 25 July 1909, Louis Blériot, a Frenchman, finally achieved it in a flight of just thirty-seven minutes from Calais to Dover, although he was enthusiastically greeted on his arrival, many people were also deeply unsettled. Northcliffe's two-year campaign had been vindicated and the apparently exaggerated claim with which he had begun it was found to be true. Britain was indeed 'no longer an island'.[2]

It was not just in his mainstream newspapers that Northcliffe highlighted the threat of aviation. He also published a number of titles aimed at young people, particularly boys, in which this was a regular theme. The originator of this genre had been Jules Verne who had published a novel in 1886, *The Clipper of the Clouds*, in which both the malevolent as well as the beneficial power of dirigible balloons had been vividly described. This and other works by Verne prompted a wave of derivative stories which by the middle of the first decade of the new century had seized the imagination of a whole generation of energetic, inquisitive young men who were to come to maturity in time for the start of the Great European War in 1914. To them the use of air power in war was a concept they had literally grown up with and one which they readily accepted. With the publication in book form of *The War in the Air* these themes were brought to the attention of a more mature reading public and compounded the factual reports which appeared so regularly in the national newspapers.

The extent of the influence of such predictive fiction can be gauged by the fact that the Chancellor of the Exchequer, David Lloyd George, brought *The War in the Air* to the attention of Parliament through the Aerial Navigation Sub-committee. Established in October 1908 under the auspices of the Committee of Imperial Defence by the Prime Minister Herbert Asquith, the committee carried out the first concerted political investigation into aviation by weighing up the dangers posed by aircraft and deliberating between the two types that had been developed, airships versus aeroplanes. After interviewing a number of expert witnesses, in January 1909 it concluded that, since aeroplanes were still at an experimental stage and unable either to rise to significant heights or to carry feasible weight, they posed little threat as a military weapon. Although acknowledging that they would inevitably become more dangerous once these factors had been overcome, the committee recommended that the tests which the army had been carrying out into this type of machine be discontinued and instead 'advantage . . . taken of private enterprise in this form of aviation'.[3] Airships were considered more favourably, with the success of Zeppelin and others already proving them to be capable of performing a number of useful functions, including the collection of intelligence through reconnaissance and the bombing of terrestrial targets. The committee decided that fully-rigid dirigibles might well be of value to the Royal Navy for observation at sea, as well as defending naval installations on land, and suggested that the senior service begin experiments into their construction. Semi-rigid airships, which could be deflated and transported across land, were also considered potentially helpful to military observation and the army was told to concentrate on these in lieu of its work on aeroplanes. As research into both kinds of airships was deemed too expensive to be funded by the private sector, the sum of £35,000 was allocated to the Admiralty and £10,000 to the

War Office. In comparison with what was already being spent by most other leading countries on aeronautical research, these amounts were paltry and the generally complacent outcome of the sub-committee's investigations dismayed those already closely involved in Britain in the field of aviation.

By spring 1909 balloons had been employed by the army in varying capacities for over thirty years. In 1885 a balloon detachment commanded by Major (later Colonel) James Templer had been used for the first time in the eastern Sudan and proved its value by observing the enemy's movements. In 1894 Templer was appointed Superintendent of the Balloon Factory which together with the individual Balloon Detachments (later called Sections) made up the formal Balloon Establishment and under his supervision balloons gradually expanded their role to include directing artillery fire and even experimental photography. On the outbreak of the South African War in 1899 four Balloon Sections joined the military forces and, together with man-lifting kites which were used when the wind was too strong for balloons, they provided useful assistance in observation, signalling and gun control during the initial phase of the war. But despite their successful deployment, financial cutbacks in the aftermath of the conflict prevented any further developments from being pursued. Following the announcement of the Wright brothers' trials in 1903, attention turned away from balloons to the consideration of heavier-than-air craft and in October 1904 Lieutenant Colonel John Capper RE, who commanded the Balloon Sections at Farnborough, visited the Wright brothers at Dayton after being sent to the United States to attend the St Louis Exhibition. Although he did not witness their machine in flight, his meeting with them convinced him of the importance of what they had achieved.

Less than two years later, Capper replaced Templer as Superintendent of the Balloon Factory and in June 1906, in conjunction with Lieutenant John Dunne, he began research there into heavier-than-air craft. Together they were determined to match the Wrights' achievements and believed themselves capable of developing a British aeroplane before too long. Completely underestimating the extent of the Wright brothers' advances, Capper's confidence was such that on two occasions he had previously provided the War Office with advice which led them to reject offers from the Wright brothers to buy their aeroplane.

Capper's attitude, which arose from a combination of patriotism and ambition, was by no means unique and was matched in equal measure by all other countries that the Wright brothers approached. Believing that it would make observation easier and so enhance its military value, Capper and Dunne intended their aeroplane to be inherently stable, unlike the Wrights' which needed to be constantly manipulated to keep it in flight. By early 1907 Dunne's first full-sized glider was produced as the basis for a machine and in July a prototype was tested at the secluded Scottish estate of Blair Atholl. Despite Dunne's high expectations and confidence, it was a complete failure and even when a powered glider was launched downhill to gain additional momentum, no flight was achieved.

In parallel with these aeroplane experiments, Capper had also been working at the Factory to produce an airship with Samuel Franklin Cody, an anglicised American who had been appointed Chief Kite Instructor to the British Army in 1906. The ironically named *Nulli Secundus*, 120 feet long and only thirty feet in diameter, and with a maximum speed of just sixteen miles per hour, made its first public flight at Farnborough on 10 September 1907 and less than a month later, on 5 October, flew in deliberate ostentation over the metropolitan sprawl of London. However, when a strong wind blew up Capper and Cody were forced to land their ship at Crystal Palace and were frustrated in their hope of returning home in triumph. The press lauded the demonstration both as a long awaited indication of Britain's commitment to aviation and an example of the vulnerability of London to attack from the air. Unfortunately, five days later, with *Nulli Secundus* still marooned at Crystal Palace, another storm wrenched the ship from its moorings and, fearing that the ship would be seriously damaged if it continued to crash about in the wind, a corporal cut the skin of the balloon and deflated it. Once back at Farnborough, despite this precipitate action, it was discovered that the structure of the ship had been irrevocably damaged. It was an ignominious end to Capper and Cody's earlier adventure and showed that in terms of navigation and control of the ship they were both out of their depth.

The reconstruction of the airship as *Nulli Secundus* II was one of three initiatives pursued at the Balloon Factory in 1908. Although it was completed and flown, it was deflated again in August before being placed in storage and proved to be of little long-term significance. Dunne returned to Blair Atholl for another series of tests on his machine and fared a little better. In December he achieved a short run of 120 feet but, despite Capper's unfailing support, he was still unable to accomplish anything compared to work in either the United States or France. It was the third project that reaped the greatest rewards. Independent of Dunne's work and in addition to his involvement with *Nulli Secundus*, Cody had also been designing an aeroplane, heavily influenced by reports that he had received of the Wrights' aeroplane. The first trials at Farnborough were disappointing but, after adjustments, on 16 October he flew for a respectable twenty-seven seconds, covering a distance of 1,390 feet and lifting himself thirty feet off the ground.

Despite this limited success, as a result of the deliberations of the Aerial Navigation Sub-committee, both Dunne and Cody were dismissed and forced to continue their work privately. Capper had little to show for his years in command of the Balloon Factory but this was perhaps as much a reflection on the meagre investment made by the authorities during this time as his own capabilities. By April 1909 Germany had invested around £400,000 in military aeronautics and France about £47,000, but in Britain the Government had spent just £5,000. The Secretary of State for War, Richard Haldane, who had taken a close interest in Capper's work, had been convinced for some time of the need for a more rigorous scientific approach to aeronautical research and in May 1909 through Parliament he succeeded in establishing the Advisory Committee for Aeronautics. In October he also replaced Capper as Superintendent of the Balloon Factory with a civilian, Mervyn O'Gorman, and removed the Factory from the military hierarchy by placing it directly under the control of the Secretary of State. Left only in command of the Balloon School, a year later Capper returned to the Royal Engineers and, although during the war he eventually rose to command the 24th Division, he was never again directly involved with Britain's air services.

From the beginning of 1910 the rate of aeronautical development in Great Britain escalated rapidly and by the time war broke out in August 1914 the naval and military air services were unrecognisable from the tentative, embryonic units in existence at the start of the decade. The extent of this transformation was reflected in the way the Government felt unable to rely on private enterprise for the production of its military aeroplanes as it had anticipated but turned increasingly to the Balloon Factory, renamed first the Army Aircraft Factory in 1911 and then the Royal Aircraft Factory a year later. Denied official custom through this change of policy, the private firms were only saved by the more imaginative interest of the Royal Navy. But as its requirements were much more limited, the pre-war aviation industry in Britain remained very small and encountered significant problems when demand exploded once hostilities began. Although the predominance of the Factory made political sense, it severely restricted the choice of machinery available to the burgeoning army air service. The Factory's huge expansion under O'Gorman between 1909 and 1916, with the numbers employed increasing from 100 to 4,600, resulted in a solid but slow-moving organisation that lacked both the innovative spark of genius which the private designers were able to offer and, as an experimental institution, the capacity to produce machines at the rate required in wartime. Nevertheless, the Factory did play a highly valuable role in developing military aviation and under O'Gorman's management a stable of designers was collected drawn exclusively from an engineering background. Perhaps the best known was Geoffrey de Havilland who joined in December 1910 and was responsible for many of the best features of the early Factory aeroplanes. Like Capper and Dunne, these designers sought inherent stability in their machines and in 1911 they produced the first in a long series of aeroplanes each distinguished by a set of initials. The Blériot Experimental or BE was a 'tractor' biplane with the engine and airscrew, or propeller, fitted at the front facing the direction of travel. In contrast to this the next machine, called a Farman Experimental or FE after another of the French pioneers, was a 'pusher' biplane, with the engine positioned behind the pilot and the airscrew facing towards the rear. In time two more types were produced known as the Scouting Experimental, or SE, and the Reconnaissance Experimental, or RE. Variations of these four lines were to form the basis of the Factory's production until the end of the war.

A wider public interest in aviation also began to take root. At first this was largely confined to those who looked on it as a sport and it often coincided with an enthusiasm for the relatively new pastime of motoring. In spring 1910 the management of Brooklands, the famous motor-racing club, persuaded the motor club's committee to allow an aerodrome to be built in the middle of the track. In time it became one of the most famous centres of British aviation and attracted some of the best-known pioneers of those early days including A.V. Roe, the first man to fly in Britain in a triplane of his own design on 8 June 1908, the British and Colonial Aeroplane Company, better known as the Bristol Company, the two designers Martin and Handasyde who produced the eponymous Martinsyde aeroplanes and Vickers, the great armaments company. Another famous aerodrome grew up at Eastchurch on the Isle of Sheppey, founded near the aircraft factory built by the Short Brothers, which over the course of time became recognised as a centre for scientific innovation. In 1911 the first groups of naval officers, including Lieutenant Charles Samson RN, were taught to fly there. This began an important link between Eastchurch and the senior service and eventually in 1917 when the Shorts factory closed it became an official naval establishment. A similarly close relationship was formed between the army and Larkhill on Salisbury Plain where the first aeroplane sheds were built in 1910. At the end of that year the Bristol Company established a second base there and subsequently opened the Bristol School of Aviation, principally to teach army officers to fly. The proximity of Larkhill to Salisbury Plain did much to interest the large numbers of nearby soldiers in aviation and it was there during the army manoeuvres of 1910 that the actor Robert Loraine, who was a great air enthusiast, succeeded in sending the first wireless signal from an aeroplane to a position on the ground.

To the public at large perhaps the best known venue for flying was Hendon in north London which had been established as a business venture by Claude Grahame-White in 1911. He and his business partner built stands and accommodation for visitors and started to promote aerial displays specifically for public excitement. For one key event on 11 May 1911, Grahame-White invited over two hundred MPs and among those who came were Asquith and Haldane. In the two years leading up to the war, it was at Hendon that the thrill of flying was first conveyed to thousands of day-trippers who made their way out to the grandly styled 'London aerodrome'.

Set some way in from the fence were a number of pylons
– open structures gaily painted with numbers on. These

were the circuit for racing. The pilots would take off and have to do so many circuits. They used to fly very close to the ground – the best pilots would fly with their wing-tip three feet from the ground and three feet from the pylon as they went round the corner on pretty steep banks. This of course made very spectacular flying especially as the pilot was sitting out in the open and you could almost see the expression on his face; you could see him peering over his shoulder to see where the next fellow was. Then they'd dodge over the man in front when they overtook. They would get behind the chap, try to get in his blind spot, climb up behind him, then dive down in front of him – frighten the daylights out of him so that he swung out of the circuit and you took his place. But although it was so spectacular and apparently dangerous I don't ever remember a crash.[4] Eric Furlong

Hendon also provided a rare opportunity to fly in an aeroplane and, as their showmanship contributed significantly to the popularity of the ride, the pilots made sure their passengers had a good time!

Clarence Winchester was a free-lance pilot with his own aeroplane giving joy rides to people for something like £1 a time. He used to put the passenger in the aeroplane and then start frightening them by telling them that they musn't touch this, that whatever they do, they were not to lean against that, that wire was absolute death if they got tangled up in it . . . By the time they took off they were jelly. When we asked him why he did this he said, 'Well they think they get their money's worth if they're really frightened!' This was his technique all along![5] Eric Furlong

The rapid advance of aeroplanes to a position of almost equal importance and capability with airships forced the military authorities to recognise that this new form of navigation would shortly have to be more formally incorporated into the army's structure. On 28 February 1911, a Special Army Order created the Air Battalion, Royal Engineers from 1 April. Superseding the Balloon School, it was placed under the command of Lieutenant Colonel Sir Alexander Bannerman, who had replaced Capper as Commandant in 1910. Officers would be eligible to join the Air Battalion from any branch or arm of the army, but the Warrant Officers, NCOs and other ranks would be drawn from the Royal Engineers. In addition to Battalion Headquarters, there were to be two companies, the first concerned with balloons and the second with aeroplanes, neatly reflecting the equal significance then accorded to both types of machine. Shortly after its formation, 2 (Aeroplane) Company moved to Larkhill where part of its purpose was to train prospective pilots. As the cost of this was too great for the battalion to bear, officers who wished to join first had to obtain a civilian certificate from the Royal Aero Club, or one of the other internationally recognised bodies, at their own expense. On joining they would then be given a statutory £75 compensation. The examination itself was relatively straightforward.

> As far as the Aero Club's certificate was concerned one had to do two flights of five figures-of-eight observed by two qualified pilots – usually two of the instructors from one of the other flying schools. At the end of each flight one had to land within 50 metres of a specified point – which was the two observers themselves. Then came the *pièce de résistance* – the height test. One had to fly up to a height of 50 metres, cut off one's engine and land again within 50 metres of the observers. Often, if it looked as if the pupil was about to land short, the instructors would walk slowly towards the spot where they thought it would be the defined distance! I do not recall a single pupil being 'ploughed' for not landing within the specified distance.[6] Donald Clappen

The qualities judged necessary for a good pilot included experience of aeronautics, medical fitness, clear eyesight, age under thirty, good at map reading and sketching, mechanically inclined and weighing less than eleven stone seven pounds.

In August 1911 the Air Battalion was detailed to take part in that year's army manoeuvres in Cambridgeshire and to reach them it was decided that 2 Company would fly there from Larkhill via Oxford. Unfortunately navigation proved difficult, with few maps available and one officer had to rely upon his Bradshaw's railway guide. An even greater obstacle that ambushed them *en route* was the weather and during the second stage of the journey a thunderstorm struck the beleaguered planes, throwing one officer not just off his course but also literally out of his seat.

> The tail of the machine was suddenly wrenched upwards as if it had been hit from below, and I saw the elevator go down perpendicularly below me. I was not strapped in, and I suppose I caught hold of the uprights at my side, for the next thing I realised was that I was lying in a heap on what ordinarily is the under surface of the top plane. The machine in fact was upside down. I stood up, held on and waited. The machine just floated about, gliding from side to side like a piece of paper falling. Then it over-swung itself, so to speak, and went down more or less vertically sideways until it righted itself momentarily the right way up. Then it went down tail first, turned over upside-down again, and restarted the old floating motion. We were still some way from the ground, and took what seemed like a long time reaching it . . . Fortunately I hung on practically to the end, and according to those who were looking on, I did not jump till about ten feet from the ground.[7] Lieutenant H.R.P. Reynolds, 2 Company, Air Battalion, Royal Engineers

The onlookers turned out to be two bathers whose nudity passed relatively unnoticed in the excitement. Only two of the Air Battalion's planes succeeded in reaching Cambridge successfully and on arrival they discovered the manoeuvres had been cancelled owing to a lack of water in the area where they had been due to take place.

By the following winter a lack of clear organisation had become apparent in the Air Battalion and in November the desire to place the unit on to a more suitable footing prompted Asquith once again to request the Committee of Imperial Defence 'to consider the future development of aerial navigation for naval and military purposes'.[8] In contrast to 1908 the committee came to a quick and decisive conclusion. In a radical step they recommended the formation of a unified aeronautical service to be called the Royal

Flying Corps (RFC) which was to include both a Naval and a Military Wing, as well as a Central Flying School at Upavon to train pilots for both. The RFC was to liaise closely both with the Army Aircraft Factory and the Advisory Committee for Aeronautics. In turn a permanent parliamentary body known as the Air Committee was to co-ordinate the separate requirements of the RFC's two wings and provide guidance on relevant aeronautical questions. These outline proposals were discussed in detail over the course of the winter and finalised by the end of February 1912. On 13 April a Royal Warrant was issued to provide for the constitution of the RFC and a month later on 13 May it came into being.

Instrumental in seeing through the proposals were a trio of officers at the War Office. The most senior was Brigadier General David Henderson, the Director of Military Training, who enjoyed a good reputation as an able staff officer with an open, direct personality which made him respected by soldiers and politicians alike. This trait placed him in sharp contrast to the second of these figures, Captain Frederick Sykes, a visionary and energetic advocate of military aviation, who had the unfortunate disadvantage of making people dislike him. There was some ineffable trait in his character that appeared to make him untrustworthy and as a result he was frequently treated with suspicion, particularly by other army officers. Yet, despite this, later in the year he was appointed the first commander of the Military Wing and the following January given the temporary rank of Lieutenant Colonel. The third member of this informal administrative body was Major Duncan MacInnes, who eventually rose to be Director of Aircraft Equipment in 1916. The committee continued in operation until June 1913 when it was disbanded and replaced in the following September by a Directorate of Military Aeronautics which assumed responsibility for all matters of policy, equipment and procurement relating to the army's aviation activities. Henderson was appointed Director-General of this new body and in recognition of his position as Britain's senior military aviator was knighted the following year.

The army had already drawn up plans to send to the continent in the event of a major European war a British Expeditionary Force (BEF) comprised of seven infantry divisions. To this it was intended that the RFC's Military Wing would ultimately be able to offer a strength of 131 planes organised in seven companies, subsequently renamed squadrons, with a further company of balloons – a significantly different balance from that envisaged at the inception of the Air Battalion less than two years before. Each aeroplane squadron was to be comprised of three flights of four machines each, with the balloon squadron containing two airships and two flights of the increasingly redundant kites. For the aeroplanes, in addition to pilots, experienced observers would also be needed and to provide sufficient numbers of trained personnel, as well as to form a reserve to make good any casualties, the complement of the defunct Air Battalion would clearly have to be greatly increased. This would be done through the new Central Flying School which was to be established at Upavon Downs on Salisbury Plain.

The organisation of the complementary Naval Wing was never worked out in such detail. From the beginning, despite the Committee of Imperial Defence's intention that 'the British aeronautical service should be regarded as one',[9] the Royal Navy remained distanced from the new body. It chose to continue on the more independent path that it had already established at Eastchurch through the Naval Flying School, believing that it alone could understand the unique requirements of maritime aviation. The Naval Wing's title was quickly dispensed with and in its place the name 'Royal Naval Air Service' was adopted. By July 1914 this unilateral act had been officially recognised and, as this in turn made the title Military Wing redundant, the name of the Royal Flying Corps was ultimately left entirely to the preserve of the army. No attempt was made by the Air Committee to repair this rift and through this failure an expensive and ultimately deleterious competition for resources was allowed to begin between the two air services which was not resolved until 1917.

During the winter of 1911–12, with the question of reform already under consideration, the development of the Air Battalion was effectively suspended and by the date of the RFC's formation the Military Wing had only eleven aeroplanes in active use, with eight more being adapted or repaired at the headquarters workshops in Farnborough. Those planes that were in service were still very basic with no altimeters and maximum speeds of just sixty miles per hour. In the search for higher quality machines, in August 1912 the War Office held Military Aeroplane Trials on Salisbury Plain and in a welcome vindication of his work since 1906 the winner was S.F. Cody. As befitted a man whose whole life had been a challenge to convention, Cody possessed an ebullient personality that made him popular with all those who met him:

> Oh, I thought the world of him. He was deliberately dressed like his cousin Buffalo Bill Cody – cowboy hat, little beard and moustache – we expected him to produce a lasso at any moment! He was an awfully nice chap and he had a look at the big scale model I was making of an Antoinette Monoplane that I rather liked. As he was looking at my ailerons – balanced ailerons, one went down and the other up he said, 'No, no, my boy. Warp the wings, warp the wings! Imitate the birds, my boy, imitate the birds!' I didn't know that quite soon every aeroplane would have balanced ailerons – I liked them because they were easier to make![10] Graham Donald

To win the prize in August 1912, Cody needed a stroke of luck to fulfil all the criteria.

> All the hangars were built by the Government and they wanted a machine for the Royal Flying Corps. There was about 15 sheds built. A.V. Roe had one, Martinsyde had one, we had one and Cody had one. He had a machine there and I used to do him a bit of work, true it up for him now and again. He used to take me up and explain to me the joy-stick wasn't on its right position when he was flying. Of course that's a sign that a machine wants truing up. You alter a flying wire and you alter a landing wire to pull that machine right dead level. Then you go up again and test it – in fact it's done in about ten operations. His machine was a pusher type with the prop behind and we used to call it the Cathedral because it was so huge. I sat on a bicycle seat with my hand on his shoulders. The trials were the altitude test, a flight test and every test of the day that the machine required. One was that you landed on a ploughed field and you got off on the ploughed field. The only thing was that every machine that landed on that ploughed field never got off. They kept on landing and they were all trying to get off and they were raking this field up so much. Every time you

landed an inspector came along to test the tank – you were only allowed so much and they used to take about half an hour before you attempted to get off. I think Cody was the last one to land and his son Charlie was with him and I was there too. Cody was sitting up on top of the machine while the inspector was testing his tank and all of the controls. Charlie called out and said, 'Dad, look!' When he looked there was a space in that field that was nearly bare with the roughage of the previous machines. They'd flattened it down, smashed it down as if a steam roller had been over it. Charlie pointed out the place, Cody opened up his engine, revved and away he went – he got off. I do believe that if Cody had landed first he wouldn't have got off that ploughed field.[11] Coppersmith Charles Tye, Handley Page Aircraft Company

Despite its victory, Cody's plane was not taken up by the army and, although prevented from actually entering the trials, it was a machine produced by the Factory, the BE2, that made the longest lasting impression through its most famous variation the BE2 C. As was the case with so many aviation pioneers, Cody was tragically killed when his plane broke up in an accident on Laffan's Plain in August 1913.

Cody took up a passenger, a man that came from Reading. Leon Cody and I were watching and all of a sudden the machine started wobbling and we could see quite clearly that the passenger was grabbing hold of Cody's shoulders, which I am sure caused the crash, and both were killed.[12] Air Mechanic Edward Bolt, Military Wing, RFC

In September 1912 the Military Wing successfully participated in that year's army manoeuvres during which a Red team under the command of Lieutenant General Sir Douglas Haig were to attack a position defended by a Blue team led by Lieutenant General Sir James Grierson. An air force comprised of seven aeroplanes and one airship was attached to each team. One of the flight detailed to serve with Grierson's force was a machine flown by Lieutenant Arthur Longmore RN, an instructor at the Central Flying School, with Major Hugh Trenchard, the School's Adjutant, as his observer.

On the first day of the manoeuvre Longmore and Trenchard had only been airborne for a short while when they spotted Haig's troops deploying *en masse* and quickly deduced the direction of their advance. Returning immediately to the Blue team's headquarters they explained to Grierson in person what they had seen. His cavalry had already started to move in a different direction but Trenchard and Longmore volunteered to fly revised orders to them so that they could prevent the enemy's advance. The airmen's precipitate actions placed Grierson in a hugely advantageous position and helped him, against all expectations, to carry the day. Grierson also demonstrated a firm grasp of the danger posed by aerial reconnaissance to his own troops and ordered half of his infantry to lie low during the day, making as much 'like toadstools as they could', to avoid detection[13]. Both sides also made good use of their airships which had been fitted with wireless telegraphy sets and by the end of the manoeuvres the value of aircraft for reconnaissance – the role that the Military Wing had been designated to undertake in wartime – had been demonstrated beyond question.

> The impression left on my mind is that their use has revolutionised the art of war. So long as hostile aircraft are hovering over one's troops all movements are liable to be seen and reported, and therefore the first step in war will be to get rid of the hostile aircraft. He who does this first or who keeps the last aeroplane afloat will win, other things being approximately equal.[14] Lieutenant General Sir James Grierson, GOC Eastern Command

As the Military Wing slowly developed its tactical position within the army, the naval air service followed a more experimental pattern. Its aviators were less concerned with establishing themselves as an integral part of the way the Fleet operated as exploring new ways in which aircraft could be used. At Eastchurch, command of which Samson had assumed in March 1912, tests were begun into the attachment of floats to the underside of planes in place of wheels and some of the first primitive seaplanes were produced. Devices for dropping bombs and other explosive missiles of increasing size were also tried out in order to allow naval planes to attack specific targets such as surface ships and even submarines. But the real aerial threat identified by the naval authorities, including the First Lord of the Admiralty, Winston Churchill, was German airships. These were felt to be capable of making a direct strike against targets in Britain and, as many naval establishments were naturally spread along the coastline, they appeared to be particularly vulnerable. A chain of air stations was consequently set up along the east coast to provide a defensive shield of both planes and airships. Trials were also undertaken in mounting some form of machine-gun in a plane to provide a defence against Zeppelins but the limited performance of the available machines meant that they were inconclusive; similar attempts by the army over the winter of 1913–14 met with the same fate and it was not until after the war had started that a practical means of achieving this was devised.

These two different approaches helped to stress the diverging characters of the two air services. The ambition of the Military Wing's Adjutant, Lieutenant B.H. Barrington-Kennett, was that 'the corps should combine the smartness of the Guards with the efficiency of the Sappers.'[15] One important way in which this was to be done was through the high standards of education and achievement that the Military Wing expected. Trenchard, who was appointed Second in Command of the Central Flying School in August 1913, instituted firm discipline and stressed the need for everyone, including himself, to have a detailed academic grasp of the science of aeronautics. At times a fierce martinet, whose manner of speech earned him the onomatopoeic nickname of 'Boom', he sometimes found it difficult to express himself either on paper or in person. Nevertheless, his integrity and strength of character inspired a deep loyalty and respect in many of those who served under him.

The second in command, Major Trenchard, was always on the aerodrome. He used to do a lot of flying and the officers were very much afraid of him. We were all a little bit scared of him because he was very severe and his manner was quite frightening. I was often picked to be his orderly – he used to call you to him and tell you what you had to do: 'Now, you'll follow 20 paces behind me wherever I go. If I go in a doorway and I want you to come, I'll beckon you. If not wait at the doorway until I come out. If I call you, you'll come at the double to receive your orders.' That was carried out strictly and he never said anything that was unnecessary. If he growled, 'Orderly!' you jumped to attention, flew up and stood stiffly to hear what he had to say. Then you went off at the double to obey. One day he said to me, 'There's an aeroplane over there that has just landed, go over and tell the pilot to report to me immediately!' It landed and I went over to him and said, 'Major Trenchard wants to see you, Sir!' The pilot looked very anxious, 'Do you know what he wants, Orderly?' I said, 'No, I'm afraid I don't . . .' I followed him respectfully as he went up to Major Trenchard. Amongst other things I heard Trenchard say, 'You will catch the train back to your unit and I shall send your report afterwards . . .' The officer said, 'But, Sir . . .' He said, 'That'll do. I'll send your report in!' No wonder they were frightened of him. Evidently this man had done something wrong in flying and he was just being turned down.[16] Air Mechanic Cecil King, Central Flying School, Upavon

Often these judgements were based as much on instinct as hard evidence but they were almost always correct. From the start Trenchard believed that the senior officers in the Military Wing should qualify as pilots at some point in their career in order to establish an empathy with the men they commanded. He struggled against many factors including his large, ungainly physique and his age, to gain his ticket in 1912 when thirty-nine and undoubtedly this later helped him to understand more clearly what he was asking his pilots and observers to do when he assumed overall command of the RFC in the Field.

The men who were recruited into the rank and file were also of the highest standard. Because they had to undertake a range of complex mechanical tasks upon which lives literally depended, they needed to be both intelligent and reliable. To maintain the delicate early machines, experienced tradesmen of many different callings were required including carpenters, mechanics, smiths, riggers and wheelwrights.

All us recruits in the RFC had some kind of training or apprenticeship and we actually had to pass a trade test to get in. Therefore we considered ourselves a bit superior to the others. We also got a bit more pay than they did![17] Air Mechanic Cecil King, Central Flying School, Upavon

Throughout the Military Wing both officers and men soon became proud of their reputations. They were modern men. The public's fascination with aviation meant that it was indeed something to be a member of the Royal Flying Corps.

In June 1914 Sykes ordered the whole of the Military Wing to concentrate at Netheravon, the new aerodrome built near Larkhill, to assess how far it had progressed towards its goal of providing the BEF with a satisfactory air capacity. Over the twenty-four months of the RFC's existence the army's aeronautical arm had advanced a long way. The slightly ramshackle, disorganised appearance of the Air Battalion, RE had now completely disappeared and in its place a new, purposeful body had emerged imbued with a justifiable sense of self-confidence. The original plan for seven squadrons, one each for the infantry divisions of the BEF, was well underway but by the date of the concentration it had not yet reached fruition: 2, 3, 4 and 5 Squadrons were all complete and fully operational, but 1 Squadron, originally based around the Air Battalion's Airship Company, had continued to work with dirigibles until the end of 1913 and had only begun its conversion to an aeroplane unit on 1 May 1914. The remaining 6 and 7 Squadrons had also only been formed earlier in the year and although by June the former was well underway, the latter was still only at an embryonic stage. By the summer of 1914 the Military Wing of the RFC had, therefore, not yet reached full strength. But given the fact that the sums provided for military aviation in the Army Estimates of 1912 and 1913 were still relatively small, although much larger than had been allocated in the initial pioneering years, to have advanced so far so fast was a considerable achievement. Like the BEF itself, tiny in comparison to the resources prepared by both France and Germany, the Military Wing stood as a fine testament to the energy and determination of all those who saw the vital need for a British air force once aeronautics had been released from the heavy world of theory into the intoxicating ether of reality. Hampered by politicians and senior officers who did not share their vision, these men had been forced to swim against a strong tide of obduracy and ignorance to make sure that when the call came the RFC was ready.

CHAPTER THREE

1914

Having gathered over the Balkans since the end of June 1914, the storm clouds of war finally broke over Britain on 4 August and unleashed a torrential deluge that was to sweep away the best part of a generation. For many ordinary citizens the sudden eruption of hostilities came as an arresting shock, but closer to the centre of power the authorities had been preparing for this moment for many years. After committing themselves to war, the Germans put into operation an amended version of the Schlieffen Plan which had first been conceived in 1905 and envisaged their armies sweeping through the neutral Low Countries in a massive right wheel to attack France at its most vulnerable point along the border with Belgium. Its ultimate goal was to encircle Paris and isolate it from the French armies deployed further east along the heavily fortified German border. Having had almost ten years to consider this possibility, the French had decided to parry the German thrust by delivering an ambitious counter-attack in the region of Alsace-Lorraine and, to protect the extreme left flank of their armies as they undertook this, they had reached an agreement with the British that the BEF would move into a covering position beyond Maubeuge just inside the southern corner of Belgium.

The plans for the deployment of the BEF had been drawn up for almost a decade and during that time new developments, such as the creation of the Royal Flying Corps, had obviously been incorporated into them but they had not had as much time to mature as the older elements. As a result the way in which the RFC was mobilised caught its senior officers by surprise. All had naturally hoped to go on active service straight away but some inevitably had to stay at home. Hugh Trenchard was one of the latter. 'It was only on 3 August that I was told I would not be going to France with the Expeditionary Force, but to replace Sykes as commandant of the Military Wing'.[1] With almost the entire stock of serviceable machines at the Farnborough headquarters ordered abroad as a reserve for the front line squadrons, his nominal command was rather limited but his disappointment was assuaged by promotion to Lieutenant Colonel. In addition he was given the task of training new pilots and observers to replace casualties and forming a series of new squadrons to meet the demands of the RFC as they inevitably expanded. Colonel Sykes, who had guided the formation of the Military Wing over the previous two years, was appointed chief staff officer to the overall commander, a position that he had hoped he would occupy himself. But for this role the Army Council selected the most senior military figure within the RFC, Brigadier General Henderson. Both his personal qualities and position as the head of military aviation appeared to make him an ideal candidate to command the RFC in the Field.

When it departed from Britain for its first taste of active service the RFC consisted of its headquarters, the four completed aeroplane squadrons and an aircraft park to act as a mobile base for the supply and repair of the front line units. The mobilisation plans called for 2, 3, 4 and 5 Squadrons to fly from their peace time stations to a single rendezvous at Dover from where, as a massed aerial flotilla, they would cross to France before moving up to their forward position near Maubeuge. The squadrons' supporting logistical services, such as their transport and ground crew, were to cross by sea shortly after and meet them at their aerodromes, while the aircraft park was to be based further back at Amiens. By the start of mobilisation, although 2 and 4 Squadrons had been equipped with one standard aircraft, the BE2, lack of time and resources meant that the other two squadrons and the aircraft park contained a multitude of different types of aircraft acquired over the previous years, including Blériots, Henri Farmans, Avros, BE8s and Sopwith Tabloids.

The mobilisation and embarkation began on time and by 12 August, 2, 3 and 4 Squadrons had all arrived at Dover. With such a large movement of aircraft, keeping with a set timetable, some accidents were perhaps inevitable, and as 3 Squadron began its departure from Netheravon one such tragedy occurred involving Second Lieutenant Robert Skene and Air Mechanic Keith Barlow. Having swung the prop, Air Mechanic James McCudden watched the aircraft take off. He had originally joined the Royal Engineers as a Boy Bugler and transferred to the RFC, in which two of his brothers were already serving, as soon as he reached the age of eighteen in April 1913. Over the next five years he was slowly to work his way up to become one of Britain's top wartime aces, receiving a succession of gallantry medals along the way including the Victoria Cross, an achievement that stands in sharp contrast to his apparent sensitivity on the very first day of his war.

We then heard the engine stop and following that the awful crash, which once heard is never forgotten. I ran for half a mile, and found the machine in a small copse of firs, so I got over the fence and pulled the wreckage away from the occupants, and found them both dead . . . I shall never forget that morning at about half past six kneeling by poor Keith Barlow and looking at the rising sun and then again at poor Barlow, who had no superficial injury, and was killed purely by concussion, and wondering if war was going to be like this always.[2] Air Mechanic James McCudden, 3 Squadron RFC

Despite these local set-backs, which affected 5 Squadron most of all and caused a forty-eight-hour delay in its departure, the bulk of Britain's first aeronautical armada reached France successfully. The first to arrive was the high-spirited Lieutenant Hubert Harvey-Kelly of 2 Squadron who landed his BE2 at Amiens on 13 August after a two-hour flight. Behind the aircraft, in common with the whole of the BEF, the men bringing up the transport and supporting vehicles received an ecstatic reception from the French people as they moved towards the border.

The station workshop, which was heavily loaded, got stuck in the mud at the side of the road. There was quite a to-do then – everybody had to turn out to push this thing and dig it out. We were all covered in mud. Robert Loraine, well he was helping us on with language if nothing else. He had the most vivid flow of

language I have ever heard. This went on for a long time
– practically the whole way up we were getting vehicles
stuck in the mud. But the French people were absolutely
marvellous. They assembled along the road and gave us
terrific cheers and we were loaded up with wine, bottles
of wine were everywhere – the lorries had more wine in
than equipment I think! As a result of that in fact I have
never drunk wine since![3] Air Mechanic James Gascoyne,
3 Squadron RFC

When the mobilisation was completed the four squadrons total-
ling 105 officers and 755 other ranks were successfully concentrated
at Maubeuge and preliminary reconnaissance flights were launched
on 19 August. The aircraft were vulnerable to attack from the
ground, particularly when flying at low altitude. The RFC's first
battle casualty occurred on 22 August when Sergeant-Major David
Jillings of 2 Squadron was wounded through the seat of his cockpit
while flying over the German lines as an observer. But at least the
shot which hit him had been deliberately fired. For many others
the dangers arose not from the enemy but from their own side, an
occurrence described in modern parlance by the ironic euphemism
'friendly fire'. The enthusiasm of the troops of all nations for the
fine sport of aircraft target shooting revealed itself even before
hostilities commenced as the British infantry were still moving
up to their forward positions.

We were rather sorry they had come because up till
that moment we had only been fired on by the French
whenever we flew. Now we were fired on by the French
and English . . . To this day I can remember the roar of
musketry that greeted two of our machines as they left
the aerodrome and crossed the main Maubeuge–Mons
road, along which a British column was proceeding.[4]
Captain Philip Joubert de la Ferté, 3 Squadron RFC

Despite the risks the reconnaissances continued and over the
coming weeks were able to follow the movements of the huge
German armies as their strategy unfolded. Unfortunately, even
though the ability of aircraft had been clearly demonstrated in
the pre-war army manoeuvres, the value of the intelligence they

gathered was still only as good as the use to which it was put by those who received it. When one observer returned in great excitement with valuable information which revealed a significant change in the direction of the German advance, he was sent straight to the Commander-in-Chief, Field Marshal Sir John French, only to discover that he was apparently one of those senior officers who had not yet been persuaded of the importance of aerial reconnaissance.

I started out that morning from Maubeuge and we were told to go to a given area – east – and we were told we should see advancing German troops. We were very, very excited as we looked for them. You were very limited in your facilities, you had a map strapped on one knee and a pad with a pencil on the other and it was rather wobbling about. As soon as we got over our area, instead of seeing a few odd German troops I saw the whole area covered with hordes of field grey uniforms – advancing infantry, cavalry, transport and guns. In fact it looked as though the place was alive with the Germans. My pilot and I were completely astounded because it was not a *little* more than we'd been looking for – it was *infinitely* more. The main roads of Belgium were *pavé* in the centre with two areas of a yard or two of dry earth, which in the winter were chewed all up, but which in the summer you could use. The Germans had their guns and heavy transport on the pavé to give them foundation, infantry walking along on this soft earth and on the field on either side in many cases there were cavalry. We very busily covered the area, made marks on the map, made notes as much as we could. After a little while we went away. I was completely horrified. We came roaring back and we landed whereupon I was put into a motor car by my squadron commander and taken off to GHQ which was in a château some miles away. As we arrived we were ushered in and we went into a room with a lot of elderly gentlemen covered in gold lace and all the rest of it. All these senior generals, it was Sir John French's own personal conference that was going on. Somebody announced us and he said, 'Well here's a boy from the

Flying Corps, come here and sit down!' I was put to sit next to him then he said, 'Now, where have you been? Have you been flying? What have you been doing?' He called up to some man, 'Come here and just look at this!' I showed him a map all marked out. He said, 'Have you been over that area?' and I said, 'Yes, Sir!' I explained what I had seen and they were enormously interested. Then they began reading the figures that I had estimated, whereupon I feel that their interest faded – they seemed to look at each other and shrug their shoulders. Then French turned round to me and said, 'Now, my boy, tell me all about an aeroplane. What can you do when you're in these machines? Aren't they very dangerous? Are they very cold? Can you see anything? What do you do if your engine stops?' I couldn't bring him back to earth because obviously he wasn't interested. I again tried and he looked at me and said, 'Yes, this is very interesting, what you've got, but you know *our* information – which of course is correct – proves that I don't think you could have seen as much as you think! Well, of course I quite understand that you may imagine that you have, but it's not the case.'[5]
Lieutenant C. E. C. Rabagliati, 5 Squadron RFC

Yet, even in the face of such scepticism, the cumulative weight of the reports brought in by the RFC during the opening days of the war was such that they could not be ignored for long and soon they came to play a central role in the way French and his corps commanders, Lieutenant Generals Haig and Smith-Dorrien, deployed their forces.

The British army's concentration at Mons, completed by 20 August, was unknown to the Germans and, as they attempted to execute their right wheel, instead of finding open space beyond the French they found the BEF. There, on 23 August the German juggernaut finally ran into the British barricade and, after being temporarily brought up short, inevitably sent it reeling. The intelligence from the RFC as to the strength and nature of the German advance did help to persuade French that the withdrawal of the BEF was inevitable if it was not to be completely overwhelmed and by the end of the day the British had begun their long, frustrating retreat to the Marne.

Meanwhile, the first direct contact between the Royal Flying Corps and its German counterpart actually occurred on the day before the retreat from Mons began. In a seemingly trivial episode, a German pilot flying an Albatross biplane had bearded the RFC in its den at Maubeuge. The keen and energetic response of the British aviators, many of whom had already devoted considerable efforts to placing deadly armaments in their machines which mostly consisted of either rifles or revolvers but with others preferring bombs, showed that even then only the technical limitations of the aircraft prevented a fight from taking place and it was clear that as soon as these had been overcome combat would ensue.

> We all turned out armed with rifles and about six machines got ready to go up in pursuit. Mr Joubert, who stood near me, remarked that he thought it was a 'Loehner' biplane. All the machines which went up were loaded with hand grenades, as the intention then was to bring a hostile aeroplane down by dropping bombs on it. The German easily got away, although it looked at one time as if Captain Longcroft would be able to intercept him on a BE2 A. About half an hour after the German had departed a Henri Farman of 5 Squadron, fitted with a machine-gun, was still climbing steadily over the aerodrome at about 1,000 feet in a strenuous endeavour to catch the Boche.[6]
> Air Mechanic James McCudden, 3 Squadron RFC

The pilot of this well meaning, but tardy, aircraft was Second Lieutenant Louis Strange. Despite the inconclusive nature of the pre-war experiments into how to mount a machine-gun on an aircraft, he retained ambitions in that direction and on his own initiative had equipped his observer with what he considered to be an appropriate weapon. 'The Lewis gun was an idea of my own . . . I was ready to back my opinion to any money that before long all the aircraft on both sides would carry machine-guns.'[7] Unfortunately this moment had not yet arrived and it soon became apparent that the weight of the machine-gun was too great for the already limited performance of his aircraft.

> I set off in my Henri Farman, with Lieutenant Penn Gaskell to work the Lewis gun . . . The enemy machine made off

while we were still climbing up over our aerodrome, and I imagine its occupants must have enjoyed a good laugh at our futile efforts. But my disappointment was increased when I landed, because our CO came to the conclusion that I should have a better chance of coming to grips with any aerial invaders if I lightened my machine by dispensing with my Lewis gun. He therefore promptly ordered me to unship both it and the mounting I had been at some pains to devise for it, telling my observer he would have to manage with a rifle in future.[8] Second Lieutenant Louis Strange, 5 Squadron RFC

To engage an enemy aircraft with a single shot weapon of this kind was a very difficult task but not an impossible one. Three days later another officer from 5 Squadron successfully achieved a hit and the preceding duel between the two machines underlined the often unrecognised fact that on both sides the desire to attack and kill enemy aviators was present from the earliest days of the war.

One morning just after the Mons retreat had started we were flying at a height of about 3 or 4,000 feet when my co-pilot and I came across a German aeroplane which to our intense joy didn't remove itself as German aeroplanes always did. I think they'd been told they musn't stay and fight and that their job was reconnaissance. Anyway, this chap stayed and we immediately joined in and manoeuvred around. I was using a .303 service rifle and the German was using a Mauser pistol with a shoulder stock. We manoeuvred ourselves one against the other. Sometimes we'd be extremely close, it seemed to be almost touching, other times we'd be out of range. We couldn't shoot through the propeller in front so we had to shoot sideways. We knew nothing whatever about the question of lay off. Not only was the other aeroplane going fast but our own aeroplane from which I was shooting was also going fast. None of us knew anything about how much to lay off, it was a purely hit and miss effort. We fired a great many rounds – I fired over 100 – and then suddenly to my intense joy I saw the German pilot fall forward on his joy-stick and the machine tipped up and went down. I knew that either I'd hit him or something had happened. We were of course completely thrilled. We'd had our duel and we'd won! We watched him going down, we circled round and he finally crashed.[9] Lieutenant C.E.C. Rabagliati, 5 Squadron RFC

The RFC's first move began during the morning of 23 August when it withdrew to Le Cateau.

The German advance moved much more rapidly than anyone thought and they were dropping shells actually in the aerodrome, so we were ordered to retire. The squadrons moved off in different directions. They set fire to the stores and petrol and everyone took to the lorries and began to retire. We never stopped doing our usual work of keeping the aircraft going with the pilots taking reconnaissance views of the advancing Germans and retreating British. But when we got onto the roads there was real confusion – French units mixed with British units, refugees on the roads. Those narrow French roads were made of cobbles and if our lorries got off the cobbles onto the side the wheels would go into the soft mud. The bridges were very narrow. Well, coming up that didn't worry us very much, but when we had to thread through refugees and units of the British and French Army it was very, very different and slowed us down.[10] Air Mechanic Cecil King, 5 Squadron RFC

In order to be able to maintain their reconnaissance flights and monitor the advancing Germans, it was essential that the squadrons stay on the move and in the chaotic circumstances that prevailed during the retreat it was a great achievement that they did so.

We were never dependent on any static apparatus of any kind. We just put our squadron equipment into Leyland lorries and the light stuff in Crossley tenders. So the move from place to place was not as difficult as one might think because everything was planned to be mobile.[11] Air Mechanic Cecil King, 5 Squadron RFC

The sight of the bitter fighting on the ground was crystal clear and the pilots and observers were able to see minute details of even local actions.

The whole sight was wonderful. It consisted of a fierce artillery engagement for the most part, but we were getting the worst of it . . . I watched one battery of ours put out of action. It had only just opened fire when it became the target of the enemy's artillery. Shell after shell burst over it and in between the guns, and then there was silence except from one gun. Then another bunch of shells burst over this gun also, and then everything became quiet until more men, probably, were sent up and the battery opened fire again . . . The town of Le Cateau was partly in flames. One could see red patches on the ground round the guns showing what an awful hell this battery had gone through. But we also gave them a very bad time and in numbers they lost more then we. Their cavalry and infantry nearly always advanced in masses and, offering as they did a splendid target, got mown down by the score.[12] Lieutenant William Read, 3 Squadron RFC

From Le Cateau, as the retreat continued pell mell, the aircraft hopped from one makeshift landing ground to another, stopping at St Quentin, La Fère, Compiègne, Senlis, Jilly, Serris, Pezarches and Melun. As Read discovered when he returned from his reconnaissance, the landing fields were often unsuitable which led to many minor accidents which tested the patience of both pilots and ground crews who were kept busy making minor repairs to keep the machines in flying condition.

There was not a suitable place to land, although the Engineers had put out a landing 'T' which they had put down across wind. In landing, we skidded and as soon as we touched ground the landing chassis gave way and [the] Henri [Farman] pitched on his nose. Jackson was thrown out about 10 yards ahead and I was left in the machine. Neither of us was hurt – only shaken.[13] Lieutenant William Read, 3 Squadron RFC

The frustration of other officers on suffering such an ignominious landing was sometimes more colourfully expressed.

Gordon Bell landed in a cabbage field, as a result of which the Bristol Bullet turned up on its nose with its tail sticking up in the air. He was coming along the road, making for Brooke-Popham who was Quarter Master General. Popham saw Bell and said, 'Oh, Bell, where's your machine?' To my surprise Bell turned round and said, 'Over in that b-b-b-blasted field of f-f-f fucking cabbages!'[14] Air Mechanic James Gascoyne, 3 Squadron RFC

For fourteen days the British and the French outstripped the Germans who doggedly followed them until they reached the river Marne. There, from 6 to 11 September, the allied forces finally turned and began to push the severely extended Germans back along the same track towards the border. In turn the Germans retreated until they too were able to make a solid stand, from 13 to 25 September, along the river Aisne. There then began a series of clumsy movements to the north-west as the opposing armies attempted to outflank each other, slowly lurching closer and closer to the Channel coast. At the start of October the BEF moved north to Ypres where, between 19 October and 11 November, it faced the final German attempt to break through. The skill and resolution of the regular British soldiers devastated a much larger body of German troops, mostly conscripts, and brought the three month war of movement to an end. Facing the onset of winter and bewildered by the unexpected stalemate, both sides proceeded to dig in where they had come to rest.

The continual shifting of sites, each bringing new hazards and leaving insufficient time to prepare them for the aircraft, began to place a serious strain on the resources of the RFC. By the time the BEF moved to Belgium forty machines had been lost, principally as a result of the strain of keeping pace with the meandering army. Only after the BEF's peregrinations came to an end at Ypres were more satisfactory sites able to be chosen and adequately prepared.

About the end of November No. 3 Squadron moved to an aerodrome at Gonneham, near Choques. We arrived here, and found the proposed aerodrome was a beet field. Some Indian cavalry had a roller and were attempting to level the uneven ground, while every available man in the Squadron turned out to be marched up and down the field to harden the ground and press down the beet roots. We spent a whole afternoon doing this, and although the ground was very soft it was good enough to land upon when we had finished.[15] Air Mechanic James McCudden, 3 Squadron RFC

It was not only the difficulties of bringing the machines down safely that plagued the RFC during these early days. The weather too threatened the delicate fabric of the aeroplanes and caused the hard-pressed ground crews endless headaches.

These aircraft in peacetime had always been kept in hangars and, as you might say, petted and coddled but on active service they were out in the open all the time. Our great enemy was the wind. These aircraft used to stand in fields and we just used to put a block behind them – a picket but not very serious. One night a heavy gale came along and tore the aircraft away from the pickets – one or two were destroyed. So all the men actually working on the aircraft were hauled before the Commander who said, 'You men must guard these aircraft with your lives. Without these aircraft the Army is blind. We are the eyes of the Army and if it's between you and the aircraft, the aircraft comes first. We've got plenty of men but we can't get aircraft.' After this ticking off we had to take a lot more trouble in picketing them out. We always put them head to the wind and got long pickets, great big stakes driven into the ground. Even then some of the aircraft came adrift till we got to the point where we had to dig holes in the ground, make a ramp and run the aircraft into the hole so that the wind couldn't get under the plane. We had Henri Farman aircraft and they were so light that they were very vulnerable. Many a time we used to be all turned out to stand by the machines all night. It didn't matter if it rained or what happened – those machines were more valuable than we were.[16] Air Mechanic Cecil King, 5 Squadron RFC

When the wind reached its peak they literally had to hold down their lightweight aircraft as they sought to tear themselves away on one last, unpiloted flight to destruction.

All the Blériots were picketed out using only screw pickets and ropes. There was a terrific gale and rain storm and at about eight o'clock at night the whole squadron was turned out and we stayed there all night – five or six people to every aircraft hanging on to the wings and tailplane – holding it down so it wouldn't be lifted away. As a result we saved the lot and they were able to fly again next day.[17] Air Mechanic James Gascoyne, 3 Squadron RFC

Although the ground crews' bodies may have been feeling somewhat frail after their heroic efforts, they were still definitely capable of protesting at their lot in life!

Rain pouring in torrents, wind howling like mad, and all the hangars level with the ground flapping about the machines. To make things more cheerful, there were deep ditches around the hangars to catch the water, and every minute or so one heard a loud splash, to the accompaniment of curses and oaths, as some unfortunate mechanic fell into one of these drainage pools.[18] Air Mechanic James McCudden, 3 Squadron RFC

The reconnaissance flights continued over the embryonic trench lines that marked the boundaries of the Western Front. The aircraft were usually unable to fly high above the trenches due to their own performance restrictions and often came under heavy ground fire from all sides. On 26 October the seriousness of what on occasions had seemed like only a light-hearted pastime was finally brought home.

> Hosking and Crean – a Captain in the Northamptons – were killed yesterday in a BE, both shot in the machine by our own troops, being mistaken for a German. The machine caught fire in the air and they were both burnt. I hope the poor fellows were killed outright by the bullets. It is a great shame as our troops have had orders not to fire on any machines at all – unless they are absolutely certain.[19] Lieutenant William Read, 3 Squadron RFC

The obvious solution to this problem was to mark the underside of the wings with a distinctive symbol which could be clearly seen from the ground. After some experimentation this was eventually standardised late in 1914.

> At first we had no distinguishing marks on our aircraft. The Germans hit on a very good plan for marking theirs – they had a big black cross on a white ground – but we had nothing. So our infantry if there was an aircraft come too low over their trenches they'd fire at it whether it was British or German. They did a lot of damage that way and something had to be done about it. We tried to decide on some kind of mark for our own. Well the first thing was they painted Union Jacks on the underneath of the plane and flew off with it but that just looked like a smudge. Then they tried painting a bar but that didn't seem much. Then we painted the target, as we used to call it, and the aircraft were sent up. The staff officers decided that was a good thing. After the roundels were painted on there was no more firing at our own machines.[20] Air Mechanic Cecil King, 5 Squadron RFC

Throughout the whole campaign, aircraft were quick to launch bombing attacks against targets on the ground, with the swirling formations of German troops proving a favourite with British pilots. Initially the bombs were merely simple hand grenades which were carried in the cockpit and thrown over the side of the aircraft at the appropriate target.

They had these grenades which they hung on the nacelle of the aircraft. The pilot would take them out of the rack and they had a plastic cap at the top. He used to undo the cap, put the detonator on and throw them to the ground. The tail of these bombs was too short – it was about a quarter of an inch iron rod about six inches long – they wanted to extend this to, say, twelve inches so that it was better to hang on to the machine. They took the bombs without detonators and gave them to the smith. He had a little portable forge and he actually welded a piece of metal on to the live bomb. He was careful to keep it cool all the while with water! When that job was on we gave him a very wide berth and he would say, 'Well what are you chaps walking right over there for? What's the matter?' So he merrily did a great pile of these bombs![21] Air Mechanic Cecil King, 5 Squadron RFC

Another improvised petrol bomb, a primitive precursor of napalm, was also unofficially tested by some pilots in an illustration of the fact that the Germans did not have a monopoly on 'frightfulness'.

We had one kind of bomb which hung in the undercarriage of the Henri Farman. It contained two gallons of petrol and in the nose was a Verey light cartridge. If this bomb was dropped the cartridge used to explode and set fire to the petrol – it was a primitive fire bomb.[22] Air Mechanic Cecil King, 5 Squadron RFC

The principal role of the RFC continued to be one of reconnaissance, but as opportunities for strikes against the ground became more frequent the airmen worked hard to improve the sophistication of their bombing methods. Most experimentation was undertaken on personal initiative and was potentially very dangerous if something went wrong – which it often did.

When we were operating from the Aisne in September we were served out with various kinds of bombs which we used to carry in our machines and drop on likely targets whenever we found any. I and my co-pilot were using a French shrapnel bomb, it was a contraption about four inches wide and about eight or ten inches long. We used to dump it over the side hoping that you wouldn't hit one of your own wires or your wheels as it went. I thought we could improve on that and I made, in the squadron workshops, a metal tube which I put through the floor of my seat right down and fastened it on to the central skid of my Avro machine. We could drop bombs right through it without entangling ourselves with anything. On that day I dropped two, and all went well. I dropped the third – but it wasn't apparently the same size as the others and to my horror it stuck in the tube. Not only did it stick in the tube but it stuck with the detonator of the bomb lower than the level of my wheels – which was a bit exciting. We tried everything we could think of and I couldn't get it out. I even tried to climb out over the side but I couldn't. I passed a note back to my pilot telling him what had happened and I watched him read it and I watched his face – it was a sight! We flew round for a long time. Then we came back to the squadron, came very low and I wrote a message. I put it in a message bag and dropped it down in front of the hangars telling them what had happened and saying that when we landed to keep well away, because obviously the whole thing was going to blow up. Then we landed right away at the far end of the aerodrome – as far away as we could possibly get – we were for it but we didn't want to blow up the whole squadron as well! I suppose my pilot was a bit scared and he landed much faster than usual. We skimmed along at practically ground level and the edge of the aerodrome was covered in uncut corn so that it was quite high. The stalks of corn wrapped themselves round the detonator of the bomb and had wrenched it right out of the bomb so that when we finally landed we had no detonator and it did nothing. You can imagine the feeling of touching the ground, drawing your feet and knees up – knowing perfectly well that that was the end – and suddenly there was a bounce, then another bounce, then you began running along. Your reaction? All I know is I leapt out of the machine when it was still running and I gather my pilot did too, because when it finally came to a stop there we were lying with complete silence. I got up to try and go to it whereupon my pilot called out, 'For God's sake stay still, you've done enough damage for one day!'[23] Lieutenant C.E.C. Rabagliati, 5 Squadron RFC

Although not officially encouraged, such undertakings did much to contribute to the reputation of the RFC as an unconventional military unit where men could indulge their senses of adventure and ambition. Yet in doing so it was essential they remained aware that other men's lives were often closely linked to theirs. A good commanding officer was one who was always ready to point out to those under him exactly where they stood in the pecking order of life and it was not always where they expected it to be.

We were rather fond of Major Higgins, we felt he really was a commander who looked after his men. Once I'd been on a flight with Lieutenant Rabagliati and he made a very bad landing – he half slid and half landed into the aerodrome and knocked the undercarriage off. Major Higgins came running up and said, 'If you want to kill yourself, you can, but don't kill one of my men!' I thought that was very good of him![24] Air Mechanic Cecil King, 5 Squadron RFC

CHAPTER FOUR

1915

By the end of November 1914, the war of movement across northern France and western Belgium had finally come to an exhausted end. Events had not unfolded as either the Germans, or the British and French allies, had planned and already the conflict had grown to a size that very few had expected. The widely held belief that the war would be over by the end of the year had been harshly exposed as unfounded and instead the Governments of all the belligerent nations had been forced to re-examine their positions. At the centre of the action the petrifaction of the conflict finally allowed the commanding generals to take stock of their situations and reorganise their forces accordingly. The BEF was now much larger than envisaged in the original plan for its engagement and at the end of December Sir John French rationalised his command structure by forming two new armies to direct the numerous army corps that had collected in France; the First Army was to be commanded by General Haig and the Second by General Smith-Dorrien. In Britain, to support what he foresaw would be a continental clash involving armies of millions, the prescient Secretary of State for War, Field Marshal Lord Kitchener, had issued his famous call for volunteers and begun the process of forming the thousands of men who came forward into a series of New Armies.

In keeping with this, the rapid expansion of the RFC also became a key priority for those left behind at Farnborough and the War Office. The decision to appoint Brigadier General Henderson to command the RFC in the Field without replacing him as Director-General of Military Aeronautics placed a heavy burden of administrative responsibility on the Assistant-Director, Major Sefton Brancker. In effect he was forced to assume Henderson's position and, although a capable, clear thinking officer, he was severely hampered both by an understandable lack of experience and his relatively junior rank which made dealings with senior officers and politicians much more difficult. With the establishment at Farnborough reduced virtually to the point of extinction, Colonel Trenchard was able to concentrate on his additional duties in building up the manpower of the RFC and he was able to provide considerable assistance to Brancker. In the face of intense competition from the other branches of the army they began a co-ordinated campaign to attract new recruits into the RFC. They needed not just trainee pilots and observers, but skilled technicians as well, including riggers, fitters and mechanics, without whom the fliers were helpless. Acting before they received official authorisation to do so, they offered higher rates of pay to suitable men and had soon enlisted over one thousand. Experienced instructors also had to be found and, acting expeditiously again, civilian pilots were signed up and commissioned as officers. To absorb the new recruits, training establishments were formed all over the country. The Central Flying School was doubled by the incorporation of Netheravon and the pre-war civilian airfield and hangars at Brooklands were bought up lock, stock and barrel, the local public house and all its contents being included in the deal!

However, these successes in increasing the size of the RFC did not address the fundamental problem of where the aeroplanes were to be found for the new pilots to fly. As the previous plans for the RFC had concentrated on supplying a preordained number of squadrons to support the BEF, no contingency had been drawn up to allow for an expansion under wartime conditions. As a direct consequence of the myopic pre-war policy of leaving the private aviation companies to fend for themselves without government investment or support, in contrast to the attitudes of the French and German Governments, the British aviation 'industry' was totally unsuited to the steady production of large numbers of aeroplanes. The firms that had been established were accustomed through necessity to dealing with individual, private customers who placed very small orders and it was impossible for them suddenly to increase their levels of production. The Royal Aircraft Factory was largely an experimental institution and was also not suited to producing *en masse* the aeroplanes that it designed. They had to be manufactured elsewhere, but the location and instruction of suitable new companies was likely to take some time. Manufacturing problems were most acute with regard to engines. Only a very small proportion of pre-war aero engines had been made in Britain and instead the private aircraft designers had relied largely on those made in France. But with the French gearing their aero industry towards an expansion of their own air service, spare capacity for exports to Britain was likely to be scarce.

As early as 10 August 1914, Brancker was ordered by Kitchener to begin preparations for the formation of five new squadrons, almost doubling the size of the RFC before it had even embarked for France. The dislocation in the administrative direction of the RFC caused by Henderson's removal prevented Brancker from giving serious consideration to a more ordered programme until much later in the year and it was not until the beginning of December that he was able to draw up an estimate of what he believed the future strength of the RFC should be. Holding that there should be a squadron attached to the headquarters of each new army and each corps within it, as well as six more working direct from RFC Headquarters, he concluded that a minimum of fifty squadrons would be necessary. In his inimitable style, Kitchener disagreed and instructed him to double this to 100.

In an attempt to ease the logistical difficulties of the expansion it was recognised as desirable that one aeroplane should be selected from the many available as the standard RFC machine. Firstly this would reduce the amount that both pilots and ground crew would have to learn during their training. Secondly it would be easier to help firms who had no previous experience of building aircraft to switch to this kind of work if a single, common standard existed. At that time, as it had been before the war, the overriding requirement was for a stable, two-seater aircraft that would facilitate the most effective reconnaissance. The leading candidate was the latest model in the Factory's BE series, the BE2 C. It was, however, already clear that the BE2 C was not in any way a fighting machine and could not be converted to this purpose. It was so stable that it would be difficult to manoeuvre in a fight and as a tractor aircraft, before the development of a mechanism to synchronise the forward firing of a machine-gun through the propeller arc, it could not be effectively armed. Brancker preferred the Henri Farman, a pusher which, as Strange had shown, could have a gun mounted in the forward nacelle or cockpit for use by the observer. Unfortunately though, the overall performance of the Henri Farman was not sufficiently powerful to make it an acceptable alternative, particularly after the BE2 C was fitted with the Factory's new ninety horse power engine, the RAF1, and as the question of a machine's suitability for combat was not the primary concern, the BE2 C was adopted.

Partly in anticipation of the new units that would be produced as a result of these changes, and partly in reflection of the way existing squadrons had started to work much more closely with individual corps headquarters, in November Henderson decided to reorganise the structure of the RFC both overseas and at home. In future squadrons were to be collected together to form wings which would be allocated specifically to work with designated corps. In France two wings were formed, with Trenchard finally receiving the call to leave Britain to assume command of the First Wing and Lieutenant Colonel Charles Burke, erstwhile commander of 2 Squadron, appointed to lead the Second Wing. When the corps were reorganised into two armies the following month the RFC's wings fitted this new structure perfectly. The home establishment was also divided up. The RFC's Headquarters at Farnborough was split into two to form an Administrative Wing, including the two training squadrons, under Lieutenant Colonel Edward Ashmore and a Fourth Wing at Netheravon commanded by Lieutenant Colonel Josh Higgins to incorporate the still uncompleted 1 and 7 Squadrons. The way in which the Third Wing, formed in the New Year, arrived in France in March showed how this new structure was intended to absorb the squadrons formed under Brancker's plans by sending them to join the overseas forces as ready formed wings.

Over the course of the winter, with the armies on the ground frozen in two opposing networks of trenches that grew more complicated every day, the RFC was able to devote considerable time to developing its tactical role. Mostly this was done by increasing the efficiency and competence with which it carried out its original tasks, such as reconnaissance and spotting for the artillery, but new applications also emerged. After assuming command of the First Wing, Trenchard immersed himself in the technicalities of aerial warfare and quickly built up a clear understanding of what it had to offer the army as a whole. On 16 February he had his first meeting with Haig, the GOC First Army to which the First Wing was attached, and during their discussions he conveyed his ideas on the potential military role of aircraft.

> I tried to explain what I thought they would do in future besides reconnaissance work, how our machines would have to fight in the air against German machines and how we should have to develop machine guns and bombs. He was interested. Then he said he was going to tell me something that only three or four people in the world yet knew; in March, somewhere in the vicinity of Merville and Neuve Chapelle, we were to launch an attack on the Germans. I was not to tell anybody. He asked: 'What will you be able to do?' I explained rather badly about artillery observation, reporting to gun batteries by Morse and signal lamps, and of our early efforts to get wireless going. On the map I showed him the position of my squadrons and said what their several tasks could be . . . When I'd finished he said: 'Well Trenchard, I shall expect you to tell me before the attack whether you can fly, because on your being able to observe for the artillery, and carry out reconnaissance, the battle will partly depend. If you can't fly because of the weather, I shall probably put off the attack.'[1] Lieutenant Colonel Hugh Trenchard, Headquarters, First Wing RFC

The Battle of Neuve Chapelle, fought between 10 and 12 March 1915, was a disappointment, despite the careful thought and innovation that went into its planning. In an attempt to overcome the strong, semi–permanent defences which opposed the selected area of attack, Haig decided to launch a concentrated artillery bombardment followed by a strong infantry assault. After an initially good start, which included the capture of Neuve Chapelle itself, the battle petered out and was unable to regain its early momentum. From the perspective of military aviation it provided an important demonstration of how much things had moved on since the autumn of 1914 and fully justified Haig's recognition of the vital need for air support in future operations.

Reconnaissance remained of prime importance, but since the early days of the war, when both sides were still engaged in tactical movements, its nature had changed. Initially, observers were required to interpret the significance of what was happening on the ground. But after the end of the First Battle of Ypres this was no longer required. Yet although the degree of military skill needed to understand what had been seen may have diminished, the overall importance of reconnaissance had not. After the establishment of apparently impregnable German trench lines, only aircraft were able to probe beyond them to uncover the minute changes which indicated activity of either tactical or strategic significance. They could identify strongpoints and expose weaknesses. Tiny adjustments to the pattern of trench lines might indicate the position of a new machine-gun post and it was soon found that it was impossible to conceal effectively the signs of fresh digging from the air. Further behind the lines unusual concentrations of rail or road traffic provided evidence of movements which offered vital information as to a possible future offensive in that locality or of a strategically significant switch of men and material to another front. News of apparently trivial changes that occurred overnight could often be of great significance and was enthusiastically welcomed at divisional and corps headquarters by generals who were increasingly aware of the value of aerial reports.

Went out with Leighton in a Blériot to sketch trenches at Messines. Very cold. Got a sketch with difficulty owing to intricacy of the lines of trenches . . . Came down after 2½ hours. Took a tracing to Brigadier General Furse. He was delighted with the information contained in the sketch as it showed some saps and a parallel being pushed out by the enemy which they did not know of. I was thanked by the general and he said the information was most important and sent me off at once to report it to the OC 3rd Division, General Haldane, at Scherpenberg, and to General Morland, commanding 5th Division, at St Jean Capelle. The Staffs were very interested and General Haldane said he would give orders to have the

parallel knocked out at once.[2] Captain Harold Wyllie, 4
Squadron RFC

Even though the information that was required may have
changed, the means by which it was recorded was still the
same – verbal reports of what had been seen by the naked eye,
supported by scribbled notes and rough sketch maps drawn on a
message pad where possible. But as the front–line trench systems
became increasingly complex, it required more and more time to
note and draw the changes that had appeared. A photograph, which
could then be studied on the ground at leisure, seemed to offer
the obvious solution. The first experimental photographs taken
from aircraft during the Battle of the Aisne were, not surprisingly,
blurred and of little help. But the pioneers were not discouraged and
gradually results improved, especially following the establishment
of an experimental Photographic Section under the aegis of the
First Wing.

We used a big, heavy, clumsy box camera. You exposed
the prints by pulling a slide away and changed them by
hand. You had the box camera on your knee and on
either side of your cockpit you had a little canvas bag.
It was of course essential for the pilot to fly dead level
when you were photographing. So you yelled at the pilot
when you were going to take a photograph so he kept the
machine quite level and didn't tilt the angle of the camera.
One took photographs through a circular hole cut in the
floor. It was quite a difficult job because first of all you
had to look through the hole to see the target you were
photographing. Then you lost sight of it as you put the
camera in position between your knees and pressed the
trigger to take the photograph. I became rather the star
photographer being very small and able to bend down
and adjust the camera which one had to hold in one's
hands. One only took about six plates which one had
to change by hand. On landing after taking photographs
one took them straight to Moore-Brabazon's office where
they were developed. One waited there while they were
developed because 'Brab' might wish to make comments
on the fact that one had been inaccurate in one's pointing

of the camera. One day unfortunately 'Brab' had forgotten to change the film in his camera and superimposed on all my pictures was a beautiful white horse of someone who'd come to lunch![3] Lieutenant Archibald James, 16 Squadron RFC

Despite such comical set-backs, the hard work and ingenuity of men like Lieutenant J.T.C. Moore-Brabazon of the Photographic Section, holder of the Royal Aero Club's licence No. 1, meant that a special 'A' Type box camera was developed for use in the air. But without any sort of control or plate-changing apparatus the taking of photographs could be an extremely painful job in icy weather, made even colder by the altitude.

Taking the photographs was a very pleasant job in the summer time but in the winter – not very funny! Our camera gear was slung over the outside of the aircraft. It was a one plate camera, no repeats at all. To work your camera you had to take your slide out of the box – with your glove off of course – get it into the camera, then wriggle your way through the Archie bursts over your target. Take your photograph, away from the Archie bursts, close up the plate. Take the slide out of the camera, back into your box. By that time your hand was so cold that over and over again I've known my hand lose the plate as I took it out of the camera. I've cried with numbness and the pain in my hand – and exasperation at losing the repeated photographs that I've been trying to get. I've known myself cry and the tears freeze on the side of my face in the cold blast of the propeller.[4] Second Lieutenant Charles Chabot, 4 Squadron RFC

The first organised use of these new techniques was in the production of a photographic 'map' by the First Wing of the whole of the German trench system in the Neuve Chapelle area. The exact details of the web of German fortifications were traced on to 1:8000 maps and these were then used not only in the planning of the attack, but also by the leading infantry battalions so that on going over the top they could identify their objectives quickly.

Another factor first revealed at Neuve Chapelle was the vast improvement that had occurred over the winter months in both the theoretical and practical use of aeroplanes to help the British artillery destroy specific targets. The value of aerial observation in registering long-range gun fire had been recognised since the early days of military ballooning and, continuing this established practice, aeroplanes had been used for this purpose since the beginning of the war. Initially the airmen had employed a simple system of firing Very lights to correct the guns. By firing flares of different colours they had been able to indicate whether the shot had to be adjusted to the left or right, made shorter or extended. The practice had worked well as long as the weather was good but when this deteriorated it became increasingly unreliable. By flying at a previously agreed height over a set location, other batteries had tried using the aircraft itself as a ranging device. The risks involved in this soon outweighed the advantages! The real answer lay in another piece of modern technology that was emerging almost as rapidly as the aircraft themselves. If taken aloft a spark radio could be used to send wireless communications to gun positions to convey the corrections needed to guide the shells exactly on to the targets. During the 1912 Army Manoeuvres the airships of 1 Squadron RFC attached to both teams had done some good work with the wireless sets that they carried but, despite the first wireless signal having been sent from an aircraft in 1910, the poor performance of the available machines meant that it remained impractical for them to carry radios, which weighed around seventy-five pounds, until after the war had begun. Later in 1915 this conundrum was eventually solved by the development of the relatively light Sterling radio which weighed only twenty pounds.

Having overcome the technical problem, a method was then needed by which the relative positions of aircraft, artillery battery and target could be accurately established. If this could not be done, it would not be possible to make corrections to the shot. The first step was the introduction of squared maps which were lettered and numbered so that any point on the ground could be clearly identified. Next a code was developed based on the concept of a 'clock'. The target was considered to be at the junction of the hands and twelve o'clock always pointed true north. From this starting point the relative position of each shot could be accurately communicated to the gunners.

The day before the bombardment we got in touch with the battery commander and had a chat as to how the thing was to proceed. We fixed up the time and everything. We also brought our wireless operator with his equipment which consisted of a copper net about fifteen by two feet wide and his aerial. On our aircraft we also had an aerial – a piece of copper wire with a weight on it wound round a drum. When we wanted to call the battery we dropped this down and it hung from the aircraft. Then with the aid of a Morse signal we were able to contact the battery. If they heard us distinctly they put out a white ground sheet. On the day of the bombardment, at the time arranged, we'd take off from the airfield and go over the battery again and just send down the battery call. If the wireless operator got it alright, he'd put out the piece of white sheeting. When we acknowledged it, he'd take it in. Then we went over the target. The battery commander had the target on the map and of course we had it – so we worked on the clock code. The target was the centre of the clock and then we used clock figures to give him what direction he was in. There were also imaginary circles drawn around the centre of the target which we knew as Ack, B, C and Don. 'Ack Ack' was the signal for the battery to get ready to fire immediately we told them; 'G–G' was the signal to fire, so that they fired one gun. We arranged it so that when we were flying towards the gun we gave the 'Ack Ack' signal, then we manoeuvred in such a position that we were near enough the target to see where the shot fell. Then we came back and told the Battery Commander where it was. By saying it was 'B Three', that'd be fifty yards to the right. He corrected all his guns to that. We went back again to the target and had another look and repeated this until we gradually got him right on to target. As soon as we got that we sent the signal, 'OK', he loaded all his guns at the same range and just poured as many shots as we thought necessary into it.[5]
Air Mechanic/Observer S.S. Saunders, 1 Squadron RFC

The first use of the clock code was during the preparations for Neuve Chapelle where it was a crucial part of Haig's plan that the

German artillery batteries and strongpoints should be effectively engaged by the British guns either to destroy them or to prevent them from opening up on the advancing infantry. Unfortunately many of the batteries were still very inexperienced in working with their new observers in the sky and sometimes corrections were either inaccurately applied or, worse still, ignored. It was clear that with additional training the situation would certainly improve and the senior officers of the Royal Artillery quickly came to realise that these new methods of registering their guns were not just an optional extra but an integral part of their arsenal. The clock code was an extremely successful system that was to remain in use throughout the war.

Bombing was another development given concrete expression at the time of Neuve Chapelle. Although the German troops in the front line were by definition well dug in, and thus at least partially protected against assault from the air, immediately behind the lines lay a wealth of tempting opportunities and the RFC was never short of targets within a reasonable range. All the support services, without which the infantry could not function, were extremely vulnerable to this kind of attack. Further behind lay other key installations, such as railway stations and bridges, the destruction of which would seriously disrupt German transportation. By spring techniques for dropping bombs from aircraft had advanced since the previous autumn, with simple bomb racks developed for individual machines.

> We'd made some light racks up that we could fit on the fuselage bottom of the Moranes just by fitting four pins in position. We had a wire going round each bomb so that when the wire was pulled the bomb dropped down. We had to fuse these bombs with fulminate of mercury detonators. They came in a box, half a dozen at a time wrapped in cotton wool. We had no instructions so we got the bombs, unscrewed the top and when we wanted one of these detonators I'd just say 'Chuck us a detonator, Charlie!'[6] Air Mechanic/Observer S.S. Saunders, 1 Squadron RFC

These devices were still extremely primitive and inevitably accidents happened. One such incident occurred when the ground crew were loading the bombs aboard the Morane Parasol of Captain Reginald Cholmondley at Henge on 12 March 1915 in readiness for a raid on the Don railway station.

> We were using ordinary army shells, converting them with a fuse cap which exploded on contact with the ground. These bombs were inserted into aluminium tubes made in the station workshops and a pin was pushed through to hold the bomb in position. When the pilot wished to drop the bomb he leaned over the side, pulled the pin out and away went the bomb. On this particular occasion Captain Cholmondley was in his aircraft, the mechanic was busy putting the bomb in and he thought the pin was there. Instead the bomb came down the tube. He was within a foot of the tube, put his knee under it to stop the bomb and the whole thing went up.[7] Air Mechanic James Gascoyne, 3 Squadron RFC

As he went about his duties, James McCudden, who had reached the rank of Corporal, had barely walked past the machine when the Melinite bombs exploded behind him.

> I had just got to my flight sheds when 'crump-crump' came two explosions in quick succession, and I distinctly felt the displacement of air. I turned round and saw Captain Cholmondeley's Morane on fire from wing-tip to wing-tip. Two bombs had exploded during the loading process. I ran over to render assistance and found about a dozen men lying around the Morane, all badly mutilated. Owing to the Morane being on fire and still more bombs being in the machine we got away the wounded quickly.[8] Corporal James McCudden, 3 Squadron RFC

This simple accident killed twelve men but it was found that, despite the force of the explosions, somewhat perversely some of the bombs had not gone off.

> Major J.M. Salmond, the commanding officer of No. 3 Squadron, forbade any one to go near the aeroplane that evening. Next morning we found some of the wreckage

had been cleared and the remaining bombs removed and buried. Major Salmond had done this himself at daybreak.[9] Captain G. F. Pretyman, 3 Squadron RFC

Before Neuve Chapelle bombing had been of a casual, opportunistic nature, but subsequently it was increasingly directed at specific targets and aimed at interfering as much as possible with German troop movements. On 22 April the Germans launched a major offensive to the north of Ypres preceded by the first use of poisonous gas. Alerted by intelligence to the dispatch of German reinforcements to support the attack, GHQ ordered 7 and 8 Squadrons of the newly arrived Third Wing to bomb the trains that were carrying them and inflict further delays by destroying stations and junctions along their route. The raids were a failure but such was the importance ascribed to the task that the First Wing was ordered to repeat them on the following day. A small force of just four aircraft from 2 Squadron, each armed with only a single 112-pound bomb, was detailed to carry out the attack. However, only two of the machines reached their targets and despite dropping their bombs the effect on German communications was negligible. The size of the bombing force and the inadequacy of their payload meant that it was never likely to be anything else. These two factors highlighted the difficulty inherent in any attempt to undertake effective tactical bombing in 1915.

The raid also embodied the underlying ethos that had already become firmly established in the RFC. The impossibility of a task was not considered to be sufficient grounds for not attempting it. One of the targets attacked on 24 April was the railway junction at Courtrai, thirty-five miles inside the German lines, and the pilot detailed to hit it a twenty-five-year-old New Zealander called William Rhodes-Moorhouse. Determined to reach his destination despite the known severity of its defences, Rhodes-Moorhouse attacked it from just 300 feet and consequently was heavily hit by ground fire. Mortally wounded, he returned to his aerodrome at Merville and submitted his report before dying shortly afterwards. He was awarded the Victoria Cross, the first awarded to an airman during the war. His actions were the epitome of Trenchard's characteristic dictum which in essence stated that no call from the army must ever find the RFC wanting.

The impact of the German gas attack at Ypres was such that for a short while the British line became disrupted. Several gaps and weakly held areas appeared which for a brief period were exceedingly vulnerable to further German thrusts. In these circumstances, hamstrung by the lack of reserves to throw into the line, it was absolutely vital that reconnaissances should be carried out to maintain a picture of what exactly was happening. Flying low over the battlefield and drawing considerable German fire as a result, one pilot in particular made a strong impression through the accuracy of his reports.

> We still clung on to that part of St Julien S.E. of the stream which seemed to be forming our line of resistance at the moment. From here the line went N.E. again and I had a very careful look at that bit of ground, circling and going over it again and again till I could make sure of the exact positions we held. It was while flying low over a big farm to the north of this bit that I received a bullet just above my left ankle that solved the problem as to who held the farm! It was remarkably painful at first and I headed for home but as I could use my foot I turned back to deny the Germans the satisfaction of having driven me off, placed the farm carefully on the map and then turned and went home.[10] Captain Lanoe Hawker, 6 Squadron RFC

Such exploits provided the British generals with the raw information they needed to make the maximum use of their defending forces by not wasting reserves on areas that were actually free from immediate threat.

The next step forward for the RFC came in the middle of May when, to support the main French offensive in Artois intended to capture Vimy Ridge, the British launched the subsidiary Battle of Festubert. Both Neuve Chapelle and the continuation of that attack against Aubers Ridge on 9 May had shown the virtual impossibility of maintaining communications between the front-line troops and those conducting the battle once it had commenced. As soon as the attacking troops crossed into no man's land they were inevitably swallowed up by the German trench system and with most of the existing telephone wires cut by the German counter bombardments all track of them was soon lost. Attempts to solve this problem using aerial reconnaissance proved disappointing as the broken ground made it difficult even to see small groups of troops, let alone identify correctly which side they were on. At this stage most pilots, not unnaturally, felt that flying at low altitudes, as Hawker had done, exposed them and their aircraft to unacceptable risks. Therefore at Festubert, which began with the first British night attack of the war, a new method was employed to help the aerial observers when they arrived shortly after dawn to work out how far the infantry had advanced. Three Maurice Farmans of 16 Squadron were given the task of carrying out a patrol above the battlefield and reporting back by wireless what could be seen.

> I was sent out to observe the progress of the battle, so far as I could from 5,000 feet. It had been arranged that, in order to let those in the air see how far they'd got, the most advanced troops would from time to time put out white strips of cloth about eight foot long and a foot wide. To my astonishment when I arrived at almost first light the whole of the battlefront was covered with white strips. What in fact had happened was that the methodical Germans had lined their trenches with wooden boards. Our bombardment when it hit a trench blew out a number of planks which scattered round and were quite indistinguishable from the white strips the troops were supposed to put out.[11] Lieutenant Archibald James, 16 Squadron RFC

In fact the success of the infantry assault varied and the intermittent nature of the advance meant that few markers were laid down and what little detail of the battlefield could be discerned from 5,000 feet meant that the observers' reports were as imprecise as before. As a result, this early experiment in what was to become known as the 'contact patrol' was considered a failure.

By the end of the first year of the war, it was clear to everyone that artillery was the real master of the battlefield and that it was now inextricably linked to the air. Neither side could afford to allow the other to move freely across an undefended sky identifying targets and then guiding shells on to them to ensure their destruction. From as early as September 1914, specially adapted artillery pieces had been used to deliver anti-aircraft fire to protect vulnerable sites. The Germans seemed to be particularly adept at deploying this type of defence, to the frustration of many airmen.

> The Germans are getting awfully energetic with their anti-aircraft guns. Their zeal is worthy of much praise and it is not for want of trying that they have been unsuccessful in bringing any of us down with shell fire so far. They will get somebody soon with 'Archibald' as their shooting is improving every day. We ought to have some anti-aircraft guns also. All we have is a miserable pom-pom which is no use for putting the fear of God into one, in the way 'Archibald' does. 'Archibald' can reach you at 10,000 feet, and belches forth dirty yellow and black smoke and chain shot, and the noise of the shell bursting is almost enough to make one stall the machine with fright. The pom-pom shell on the other hand only bursts on percussion, and its maximum height of smoke trail is only 4,500 feet.[12] Lieutenant William Read, 3 Squadron RFC

In a characteristic display of sang-froid, the RFC had nicknamed the German anti-aircraft fire 'Archibald', or more simply 'Archie', after a popular musical-hall song of the time. After returning from a patrol during the Battle of the Aisne a pilot was asked if he had been fired at and immediately responded with the refrain of the song, 'Archibald, certainly not!'

At first the weight of the shells and the inexperience of the German gunners meant that although discomforting the fire represented little real threat. But as it continued it inevitably became more accurate and soon also began to take a toll on the pilots' mental equilibrium, particularly when it forced them to recognise the limited performance of their machines. By the end of October 1914, Read was beginning to feel the strain.

> I wonder how long my nerves will stand this almost daily bombardment by 'Archie'. I notice several people's nerves are not as strong as they used to be and I am sure 'Archie' is responsible for a good deal. I would not mind quite so much if I were in a machine that was fast and that

would climb a little more willingly. Today we both had a good dressing down by 'Archibald' and some of the shells burst much too near and I could hear the pieces of shell whistling past – and they have to burst very close for one to be able to hear the shrieking of loose bits of shell above the noise of one's engine. Well, well, I suppose the end will be pretty sharp and quick if one of Archie's physic-balls catches one. I think I would rather it caught me than crumple up Henri, because one would have too long to think when falling from 4,000 feet.[13]
Lieutenant William Read, 3 Squadron RFC

Read was hit in the leg just over a fortnight later while flying, with Robert Loraine as his observer, in a Henri Farman over Courtrai. He was evacuated to hospital in Britain. Other men were more sanguine and in January 1915 Corporal McCudden was fascinated by the minutiae of how the shells disintegrated during one of his first flights as an observer.

Going north at 8,000 feet over Violanes I heard a c-r-r-r-ump, then another, and another, and looking above me saw several balls of white smoke floating away. The pilot turned to mislead Archie, of whom I was having my first bad experience. However, I can honestly say that I did not feel any more than a certain curiosity as to where the next one was going to burst. Watching these shells burst – they were mostly shrapnel then – the shrapnel bullets each left a thin line of smoke, so that as each shell burst the shrapnel came from each burst in the shape of a fan. These shrapnel shells did not burst very loudly but they had a most effective radius; and I think they were more effective from a destructive point of view than some of the high-explosive shells.[14]
Corporal James McCudden, 3 Squadron RFC

The response to anti-aircraft fire had to be painstakingly learned from experience. If an aircraft flew in a straight line at a steady height, the gunners below would inevitably catch it, making evasive tactics essential. But the decision on how to adjust one's height and direction was a delicate one and instead of moving away from the shell bursts a pilot could easily run on to them, inadvertently bringing disaster upon himself and his observer.

How often did one turn? How long did one wait after turning? And then what? Did one alter one's height just after a shell had burst or just before? 'After' might be too late; but how did one know when it was just 'before'? I wondered if I ought not to try everything at once so as to be on the safe side ... Sudden sympathy for driven grouse came to me; the Twelfth of August appeared as the feast day of aerial murder.[15] Second Lieutenant Duncan Grinnell-Milne, 16 Squadron RFC

Eventually pilots developed the ability to distinguish patterns in the German fire which helped them in their deadly battle of wits.

When flying the Germans used to bracket an aircraft and if one was flying at 4,000 feet one would suddenly hear little 'pops'. You looked up and about 500 feet above you, you would see the three shell bursts. You looked down, and 500 feet below you would be three more shell bursts. After a time the next lot would be only about 100 feet above and below you. That was the time to take evasive action. The only action one could take, as you had no engine power, was to dive as fast as you could go about 500 feet. It was rather amusing to see that the six bursts of the battery would all converge on the spot in which you had been before.[16] Lieutenant F.J. Powell, RFC, 5 Squadron RFC

Although 'Archie' was by no means a toothless beast, it remained extraordinarily difficult to hit a moving target at indeterminate altitude which was engaged in even simple evasive manoeuvres. While direct hits, usually a result of bad luck rather than high skill on the part of the gunners, were invariably fatal, a close miss could still be survived as the apparently frail aircraft were actually extremely resilient due to their lack of rigid construction.

A high velocity anti-aircraft shell burst so close to our left front that the blast cut no less than seven flying wires and drew blood on my face. It shows the extraordinary toughness of the aircraft that it was possible for the pilot to turn, albeit cautiously and get back to the aerodrome, with all these wires flapping and great chunks of fabric torn out of the wings. They were constructed of prime ash main spars and longerons and selected spruce inter-strutting. The wings were covered with fabric, the finest Irish linen with acetone dope to tighten them and give them a smooth surface. The factor of safety was extraordinarily high – they could bend without cracking in a most remarkable way.[17] Lieutenant Archibald James, 16 Squadron RFC

Viewed from the opposite perspective the lethal consequences of German reconnaissance aircraft were clearly understood by the trench-bound British infantry who had nowhere to look but up and whenever they appeared the men in the front line inevitably pointed the finger of blame at the RFC. In practice, however, despite the infantry's understandable desire that their aircraft should be seen to be doing something, there was very little either side could do to interrupt the reconnaissance missions of the other side. Throughout the winter most aviators were still issued only with handguns and rifles both for their own defence and to attack the enemy.

The arms issued to the Royal Flying Corps at that time was a revolver, and we used to take this up in our pockets fully loaded. Standing in the observer's cockpit there was a rifle. The aircraft rigger was responsible and before the aircraft left the ground he had to report, 'One in the breech, five in the magazine and fifteen rounds to spare.' You said, 'Alright', and then stood the rifle up beside you on a little catch so that you could get it out handy. If you saw an enemy aircraft you took this rifle out and if he came close enough, say to within 50 to 100 yards, you would let him have it as best as you could. Beyond that it was a waste of ammunition. You wanted a hell of a lot of luck to hit him! First of all you had to take into consideration where the enemy aircraft was. If he was behind you, you undid your belt, sort of stood up and knelt on your seat – watched to see where he

was. You had to be very careful not to shoot any of the controls away. If he happened to be below you on the port or starboard side, then you would just lean over the side and if you could get your gun on him try it that way. If he was directly below you there was nothing you could do so you had to try and get your pilot to manoeuvre into a certain position to get your gun to bear on him. After flying with one pilot on several occasions you had a sort of way of communicating with him without actually telling him and you worked as a team. You manoeuvred round a bit and if he fired at you from a long distance you knew you had a novice. So you just kept darting about, twisting your aircraft this way and that, trying to get up to a proper position to get close. Then as soon as you got into a favourable position, quite close to him, particularly if you could get under his tail then you just opened up on him. Under the tail was the blind spot.[18]
Air Mechanic/Observer S.S. Saunders, 1 Squadron RFC

To stand any chance at all of a hit it was essential to reduce the distance to the shortest possible range. But even the most expert of shots first had to learn to recalibrate their minds as to what close range actually was in the air in a bucketing aircraft.

I had been a very good rifle shot all my life and had before the war shot a number of stags in Scotland. So I was very confident of my marksmanship. We met a German aircraft at about the same altitude and speed as ourselves so that we couldn't get any closer than 600 yards. I put my sights on the service rifle to 600 yards and fired six deliberate shots – and was miserable that I didn't hit him at all, I've no doubt I was miles away. We had no conception then at what close ranges it was necessary to shoot to have any effect at all. Later we learnt that with the vibrating platform that effective range rarely exceeded 50 yards.[19] Lieutenant Archibald James, 16 Squadron RFC

Yet from these humble beginnings began the race to develop the first true fighting machine. The answer of course lay in the machine-gun. But as Lieutenant Strange had found over Maubeuge, the simple addition of an automatic weapon to an insufficiently powerful aircraft created almost as many problems as it solved. The reduction in performance caused by the additional weight gradually became less of a problem as aircraft improved until finally the lightweight Lewis gun, which Strange had attempted to place in his Henri Farman, could be successfully carried. The mounting of a Lewis gun in a pusher aircraft, which offered a clear, wide-ranging field of fire from the forward nacelle, was relatively straightforward. But in a tractor, it proved to be very difficult to find a position from which the gun could fire in any direction without causing fatal damage either to the propeller or some other vital part of the aircraft.

> The Lewis gun had an air cooled radiator round the barrel, but we took this off and secured the gun direct to the fuselage in such a way that it was pointing at an angle that just cleared the tip of the propeller as it went round. The observer, gunner if you like, he had another Lewis gun – we'd fitted a butt to it like a rifle. But he had to fire this from the shoulder. We had to be very careful because as soon as you lifted the gun up the pressure of the air almost blew it out of your hands, so you had to hang on very tight. Eventually we fixed up mountings behind the observer so we could swing the gun round. This limited our field of fire a bit because we had to be very careful not to shoot away the rudder or elevator controls. It was very difficult if you were firing at an enemy overhead, on your tail, diving at you. You had to crouch down in a very small cockpit and trust to luck as much as anything else.[20]
> Air Mechanic/Observer S.S. Saunders, 1 Squadron RFC

As neither of these impromptu gun fittings was aligned with the direction of the aircraft, each engagement required deflection shooting. To line up a target an allowance had to be made for the relative positions of aggressor and intended 'victim' which were constantly changing. Without standard fittings, even within the same squadrons aircraft would have different gun mountings.

The fastest single-seater aircraft of the early 1915 period were the Bristol and Martinsyde Scouts which were so called because their original role had envisaged them as 'scouts' to fly out quickly to points of interest and report what they had found. However, their speed of over eighty miles per hour made them an obvious choice as a machine to intercept and hunt down German aircraft and one was attached to each of the squadrons. 'Scout' came to be accepted as the term for what in modern parlance would be known as 'fighter' aircraft. In 6 Squadron, Captain Hawker was the obvious choice to fly their Bristol Scout. In the absence of an observer to act as gunner Hawker showed considerable ingenuity in mounting a Lewis gun on the left-hand side of the cockpit so that it fired obliquely forwards past the propeller. This made aiming an extremely difficult proposition as he had to allow for a large 'deflection' to the left. Despite this handicap, Hawker's determination was such that he achieved considerable success as he recorded in the formal language of his combat report after a patrol on 25 July over the Ypres Salient.

[My] Bristol attacked two machines behind the lines, one at Passchendaele about 6pm and one over Houthulst Forest about 6.20 pm. Both machines dived and the Bristol loosed a drum at each at about 400 yards before returning. The Bristol climbed to 11,000 and about 7 pm saw a hostile machine being fired at by anti-aircraft guns at about 10,000 over Hooge. The Bristol approached down-sun and opened fire at about 100 yards range. The hostile machine burst into flames, turned upside down, and crashed East of Zillebeke.[21] Captain Lanoe Hawker, 6 Squadron RFC

As a result of this triumph over adversity and his previous exemplary record Hawker was awarded the VC.

The first effective British aircraft intended primarily to destroy German aircraft was the Vickers Fighter (Vickers FB5), often known as the 'Gunbus', which began to arrive on the Western Front in February 1915. A biplane pusher, it was an enhancement of a pre-war Vickers design, partly based on the Henri Farman, which had a Lewis gun fitted on a pillar-mounting in the observer's front nacelle. Its 100 horsepower Gnome Monosoupape engine generated a top speed of seventy miles per hour at 5,000 feet, to which height it could climb in sixteen minutes and it had an effective ceiling of 7,000 feet; by comparison in October 1914 it had taken Read forty minutes to climb to just 4,000 feet in his Henri Farman. As a French engine the Monosoupape was initially unfamiliar to the British mechanics who had to work with it, an unfortunate problem as it was less than reliable, and wise pilots learned to pay it a good deal of attention themselves.

> With the Monosoupape engine it certainly paid a pilot to listen because he flew entirely from the ear. After I had flown with these engines something over twelve months I could tell – that is hand on heart – I could tell you whether the thing is missing because the mixture was too rich or too weak, or that a plug had cut out, or a rocker arm had broken. I could tell all those from ear. If a rocker arm broke one had to get down as quickly as possible 'cause you only had about a minute before the cylinder on this rotary engine filled up with the oil and then naturally there comes a compression. The only hope was that the piston would break in which case you'd have a con rod flapping round. If the piston didn't break it would come up and push the cylinder out of the crank case. As one flew these pushers with little tail booms behind, a thing like a large shell flying off at eleven hundred revs might cut the tail boom – away goes your tail and you break your neck merely because you didn't listen to your engine.[22] Lieutenant F.J. Powell, 5 Squadron RFC

A landmark event occurred in July 1915 when the first homogeneous 'scout' squadron, equipped solely with Vickers Fighters, arrived on the Western Front. Under the command of Major George Dawes, 11 Squadron joined the Third Wing which, in support of the Third Army, had been sent south to the Somme to the area newly taken over from the French. At this stage the Vickers had a considerable advantage in combat over the German machines it encountered as many were still not armed with machine-guns, as exemplified on 23 August when Second Lieutenant A.J. Insall, flying as observer to Second Lieutenant H.A. Cooper, sighted a pale blue LVG two-seater biplane some 1,500 feet below them.

> As I banged on the side of my cockpit and pointed him out to Cooper, I could see the observer leaning over

the side of his fuselage, studying the ground and quite unaware of our presence above him. He was an absolute sitter. We went down on to his tail in a steep curving dive, and I held my fire until we were as close to him as we dared go without risk of colliding. I saw the observer whip round as we levelled up. He was wearing a black flying-jacket, and appeared to be aiming a rifle at me as I opened fire in a series of short, five-round bursts. At the same moment his pilot pushed his nose right down. I saw two quick flashes from the observer's weapon, and then the enemy machine gave a lurch and Cooper swerved to avoid him, and I seized the opportunity to change drums. We were now both diving again, and the LVG was travelling at a phenomenal speed, with its engine full on. Before it drew away, while it was still no more than 30 or 40 feet from us, I emptied one half of the new drum into him, and at that stage I saw a bright light appear where previously the black figure of the observer had been. Then Cooper, aware of the fact that we had gone down to less than 3,000 feet, came out of his dive.[23]
Second Lieutenant A.J. Insall, 11 Squadron RFC

The LVG was officially confirmed as destroyed. Of strong steel tubed construction and for the time well armed, the Vickers Fighter remained for some time a formidable opponent, even as more modern and heavily armed German aircraft appeared over the lines. On 19 September Powell and his observer, Air Mechanic James Shaw, were on patrol to the east of Ypres.

I saw a Boche Aviatik and I was higher than he was so I dived down towards him, shouted to my gunner and he, being a very good shot, got him. The Aviatik started to swerve down, and down, and down and down, and down and I was naturally anxious to see whether it crashed. At that moment my dear old Vickers Fighter seemed to want to turn and I was fighting it to try and keep my wing out of the way so that I could watch the German to see whether he had fallen to the ground, or not. In desperation I said, 'All right you brute, you want to turn to the right – come round!' I swung round on a bank – and just coming up on my tail was this enormous great aircraft. It had two fuselages, two engines, one at the nose of each fuselage and we never imagined a thing of this size. The pilot sat in a needle positioned in between. It had a crew of three – two gunners, one forward, then the pilot, then the rear gunner. To my mind it was a very formidable thing. I told the gunner to stick his gun pointing upwards and just keep his finger on the trigger and I aimed the machine underneath the nacelle. To my intense delight we must have hit him because 'two tails' went down in a slow spiral, down and down and down and crashed just behind the German lines.[24] Lieutenant F.J. Powell, 5 Squadron RFC

*　　*　　*

While the Vickers Fighters were becoming established over the lines, further up the RFC's chain of command important changes were taking place which were to have a profound effect on the way operations in the air were conducted for the remainder of the war. After struggling against heavy odds to run the Directorate of Military Aeronautics for almost a year and implement the hastily devised plan for the massive expansion of military aviation that had been agreed at the end of 1914, Brancker finally succeeded in persuading Henderson that he was desperately needed in London to provide the RFC with a steadier and more credible sense of direction. In August he stated bluntly that 'the Director-General of Military Aeronautics must be a Major General at least, have a loud voice in the War Office, and if possible, be on terms of equality with the Army Council.'[25] Unable to deny the truth of this argument, Henderson returned to the War Office to resume his duties as Director-General. At first it was not intended he should remain there permanently and in February 1916 preparations were begun to allow him to go back to France. But increased political pressure on the Army Council as a result of public reaction to the first Zeppelin raids on Britain and the escalating conflict with the Admiralty over resources for their respective air services meant that the decision was reversed and instead, after his appointment to the Army Council, Henderson was drawn inescapably into the political maelstrom to act as the champion of military aviation.

Earlier in 1915 he had returned to Britain for a brief period of sick leave and, during his absence, command of the RFC in the Field had been temporarily assumed by his deputy, Colonel Sykes. In ways that are now difficult to identify, Sykes grievously offended Henderson and was commonly held to have intrigued against him in a brazen attempt to secure command of the RFC for himself. As a result Sykes was ignominiously banished to the eastern Mediterranean to command the aerial detachments engaged in the Gallipoli campaign and he was to be denied any further leading role in the military air service until April 1918 when the major upheavals contingent upon the formation of the Royal Air Force led to his appointment as its professional head. With Sykes gone, the only serious candidate capable of replacing Henderson was Trenchard and in August 1915 he was formally appointed to command the RFC in the Field with the rank of Brigadier General. Command of the First Wing was given to Ashmore, Burke was replaced as head of the Second Wing by Lieutenant Colonel John Salmond and Brancker was released from Britain to take over the Third Wing.

The reputation that Trenchard had acquired for his bluff, ruthless approach to the job in hand meant that he was viewed with great trepidation and the manner in which he conducted himself in France had changed little from the way he had first taken the Central Flying School in hand in 1912. Yet, as had been the case there, he managed at the same time to show a great concern for the men under his jurisdiction and by constantly journeying out to meet them he retained their respect, whatever he might ultimately be responsible for ordering them to do on the following day. Once in command in France he was greatly helped in this respect by his ADC, Captain Maurice Baring, who had been bequeathed to him by Henderson on his departure. Disconcertingly well educated and civilised, exquisitely at home in any social circle, Baring was in many ways the complete antithesis of his chief. Yet his memory for detail and ability to take notes equipped him ideally to act as Trenchard's amanuensis.

The General's system of note taking was like this. He visited Squadrons or Depots or Aircraft Parks as the case might be and took someone with him who made notes (for the next four years the someone was myself) of anything they wanted. In the evening the notes used to be put on his table typed, and then he would send for the various staff officers who dealt with the matters referred to in the notes, and discuss them. The first thing he would ascertain was if the matter mentioned in the note had a real foundation; for instance, whether a Squadron which complained that they were short of propellers had not in fact received a double dose the day before. If the need or the complaint or the request was found to be justified and reasonable, he would proceed to hasten its execution and see that the necessary steps were taken. If the requests were found to be idle or baseless, the Squadron or the petitioner in question would be informed at once. But where the General differed from many capable men was in this: he was never satisfied with investigating a request or a grievance or a suggestion. After having dealt with it he never let the matter rest, but in a day or two's time he would insist on hearing the sequel.[26] Captain Maurice Baring, RFC Headquarters

Indeed, Baring's deep understanding of Trenchard's psyche, as well as a ready wit, put him in such a powerful position that eventually it became difficult to distinguish who was the master and who the manservant.

He realised that 'Boom' [Trenchard] was human and, being a philosopher, knew that Humanity is frail, and must perforce be chastised with whips and scorpions of sorts. Therefore he instituted a series of punishments numbered from One to Five X, and varying in that order in degree of severity. Punishment Number One consisted in taking away or hiding 'Boom's' pipe. Punishment Number Five X consisted in breaking the window of 'Boom's' car so that he had to sit in a draught, which he abhorred. As the punishments could only be awarded by Maurice Baring, so could they only be carried out by him. He was judge, jury and executioner.[27] Recording Officer T.B. Marson, 56 Squadron RFC

If Trenchard overstepped the mark in the brusque manner with which he dealt with his subordinates, they at least had the consolation of knowing that the General himself would not escape scot-free if Baring had noted the misdemeanour.

> The aggrieved party was always rung up and informed, 'The General behaved very badly today. He had Punishment Number One all the way home. He almost cried for his pipe; but I was adamant. I had it in my pocket, but I said that I could not think what he had done with it. At dinner he was very penitent, so he was allowed to find his pipe afterwards. I think he is really sorry, and that he will be better now.'[28] Recording Officer T.B. Marson, 56 Squadron RFC

When commanding the First Wing Trenchard had come into regular contact with Haig and from their first meeting before Neuve Chapelle a strong rapport developed between them. Their personalities were, in many ways, similar and this allowed them to deal successfully with each other. By the start of 1916 Trenchard had effectively built upon his early start and convinced Haig of the overriding importance of including aviation in his battle plans. But in the summer of 1915 this position was still some months away and, newly appointed to the senior ranks of command, Trenchard's opinion was little sought in the planning of the coming autumn offensive. His position on the sidelines may also have been a reflection of the fact that despite Brancker's best efforts over the previous twelve months, the attempt to effect a rapid expansion of the RFC had not fared well. Principally as a result of the aircraft industry's inability to grow in line with demand, in the latter half of 1915 the size of the force in France still remained relatively small. By 30 September the number of aircraft had only risen to 185 from the 112 available on 31 March and the strength of the RFC stood at twelve squadrons, just five more than had been present in May.

By mid-summer 1915, despite the frustrated hopes of May and June, both the British and French had begun to consider how best to renew their offensive against the German line in France. Once again it was decided that the selected point of attack would be in Artois but this time the British would fight alongside the French, immediately to the north of the point where their two forces met, around the mining town of Loos. Neither French nor Haig, whose First Army was to make the assault, was greatly enthused by the prospect of what was proposed but for many reasons both recognised that it needed to be carried out. The Battle of Loos began on 25 September and, because the level of available artillery support was too small to guarantee a sufficiently concentrated bombardment, it was preceded by the first British use of poisonous gas, which unfortunately went awry when the wind failed to blow in the right direction. On the first day of the battle some success was achieved but the poor handling of the reserves by French, which delayed their engagement until the following day, meant that what slight opportunities were created simply drifted away overnight. By the middle of the following month the battle had ground to a halt with little tangible gain. Its most significant consequence was the removal of French as Commander-in-Chief of the BEF in December and his subsequent replacement by Haig.

In the battle the First Wing was designated to support the attacking troops of the First Army and the tasks assigned to it were fundamentally the same as those performed by the RFC since the beginning of the war: directing artillery fire, observing and photographing the results, monitoring if possible the advance of the infantry and identifying any fresh German defences which could be targeted in the next bombardment. But the means by which they were carried out were growing steadily more sophisticated. A new 'C' Type camera, fixed to the machine and incorporating a semi-automatic plate-changing device, had been brought into use and improved photo reconnaissance immeasurably, allowing a clearer picture to be pieced together of the German front line. The clock code had proved highly effective and, used in conjunction with lighter radio equipment, had significantly improved the accuracy of spotting for the artillery's guns. Although the offensive itself failed, the RFC performed its observation and artillery co-operation roles reasonably well and, even when an attempt to institute embryonic contact patrols was once again ineffective, it added further lustre to its growing reputation.

The one new development tried out during the period of the battle was the concentration of aircraft to carry out bombing raids on targets beyond the battlefield in an extension of the policy first attempted in April. The earlier raids had been a tremendous disappointment and had only achieved any impact when they had triggered a secondary incident, such as the explosion of an ammunition dump. An analysis of bombing operations carried out between the beginning of March and the middle of June revealed that of the 141 raids on railway junctions and stations, only three had really succeeded. As a result it was decided in future to concentrate resources and increase the co-operation between the RFC and the French Air Service to ensure that squadrons of specially trained pilots could carry out sustained attacks on trains in motion, rather than railway stations. Through this it was hoped the destructive impact and consequences of a train crash would be added to the explosive effect of the bombs.

Emphasis was also placed on the development of more efficient bomb-sights. The dilemma of deciding at what point an aircraft should drop its bomb and from what height in order to hit a target, while allowing for the speed of the aircraft relative to the ground and the effect of the wind, proved difficult to solve. However, a series of special experiments by Lieutenant Robert Bourdillon and a meteorological officer, Second Lieutenant G.M.B. Dobson, both attached to the Central Flying School (CFS) at Upavon, culminated in the development of the CFS bomb-sight. Harnessing a stop-watch to a timing scale, for the first time it allowed a more accurate, scientific approach to bombing and began to reduce the unreliable dependence on instinct. Armed with this new technology, aircraft from the Second and Third Wings began attacks on German troop trains on 21 September. In a new tactic the pilots were ordered to follow each other down from about 500 feet to attack the trains with a series of bombs. Although operations were interrupted by bad weather which made flying difficult or impossible, they were notably more successful than they had been in the spring. Five and a half tons of bombs were dropped between 25 and 28 September and at least five trains put out of action, with others being disrupted as a result. The most impressive incident occurred during an attack on the engine sheds at Valenciennes when a direct hit on an ammunition train caused severe damage. However, the reinforcements sent up to Artois by the German High Command were still only marginally delayed and the overall situation was not affected. Although the tactics and conduct of the raids had improved, they were still being carried out by too small a force, carrying bombs of insufficient weight, to be truly effective.

★　　★　　★

Towards the end of the Battle of Loos a new German aircraft began to make its presence increasingly felt. Earlier in the year a French pilot, Lieutenant Roland Garros, had privately adapted his Morane Saulnier monoplane so that it could fire a machine-gun directly ahead in line with the direction of flight. Working with Raymond Saulnier, the aeroplane's designer, Garros had worked out that only a small proportion of any rounds fired through the propeller's arc were likely to hit it. Those that did could be deflected and prevented from causing any damage by fitting metal plates to the blades. His innovation was an immediate success and on 1 April he successfully shot down a German aircraft engaged in a reconnaissance mission. The achievement was repeated twice more over the coming weeks but on 18 April, when deep over the German lines, his engine failed and he was forced to land. His machine was captured intact and the Germans handed it over to Anthony Fokker, one of their leading aircraft designers.

Fokker, a Dutchman, was technically a neutral citizen. Originally he had offered to work for the British but after being turned down he had turned to the more appreciative Germans. In 1912 he had designed a monoplane similar to the Morane Saulnier and by 1915 the Germans had already put it into service in their military air force. The capture of Garros' machine now inspired Fokker and his team. The German authorities, immediately aware of its immense value, asked simply for the deflector mechanism to be copied. But Fokker went further. Before the war 'interrupter' mechanisms had been developed which could co-ordinate the rate of a machine-gun's fire with the revolutions of a propeller so that when the blade passed through the line of fire, the mechanism stopped the gun from firing; one such device had been shown to the War Office before the war but they had failed to act upon it. Harking back to these developments, Fokker now equipped his monoplane with an interrupter gear and created the first true single-seater fighting aircraft. Known as the Eindecker or E1, it began to make its first sporadic appearances in July. In fact it was not until the late autumn, when sufficient numbers had collected on the Western Front and the Germans had revised their combat tactics in the light of their early experiences, that the aircraft began to realise its full potential.

As they gradually gained in skill and confidence the German

Fokker pilots overcame their paucity of numbers and succeeded in establishing an aura of superiority. By the end of the year they had gained a fearsome reputation and many British airmen considered them to be all powerful. This psychological power added considerably to their material advantage. The tactics adopted by the select band of Fokker pilots, such as Leutnants Oswald Boelcke and Max Immelmann, were simple but remarkably effective in exploiting the three key advantages of the E1: the ability to shoot through the propeller and hence aim the machine-gun in line with the aircraft, a high altitude ceiling and wonderful diving characteristics derived from the strong metal-tubed frame around which the machine was built. The pilots would fly high until they saw their 'prey' and then, after waiting patiently for precisely the right moment, swoop down at great speed to attack from behind, preventing their victim from returning fire. The BE2C was particularly vulnerable. Unable to manoeuvre or run away it had to stand and fight a contest it was almost bound to lose. Even the redoubtable Vickers Fighter had met its match.

I had just climbed to 3,500 when I saw an enemy airman fly over the lines by Arras and make for Cambrai. I let him fly on eastward for a while. Then I took up the pursuit, hiding behind his tail all the time. I followed him for about a quarter of an hour in this fashion. My fingers were itching to shoot, but I controlled myself and withheld my fire until I was within 60 metres of him. I could plainly see the observer in the front seat peering out downward. Knack-knack-knack . . . went my gun. Fifty rounds, and then a long flame shot out of his engine. Another fifty rounds at the pilot. Now his fate was sealed. He went down in long spirals to land. Almost every bullet of my first series went home. Elevator, rudder, wings, engine, tank and control wires were shot up. The pilot (Captain C. Darley) had a bullet in the right upper arm. I also shot his right thumb away. The machine had received 40 hits. The observer (Lieutenant R.J. Slade) was unwounded. His machine-gun was in perfect working order, but he had not fired a single shot. So complete was the surprise I sprung on him.[29] Leutnant Max Immelman, 62 Section, German Air Service

Hit or miss, the Fokkers would continue their dive, thus slipping away from possible retribution. If their target had survived then they would immediately regain sufficient altitude to have another go. To accelerate the whole process Immelmann devised his eponymous 'turn' to give him another bite at the cherry without losing altitude during the manoeuvre. He realised that if he pulled steeply out of his dive and began a loop, when he reached the zenith he could simply roll his aircraft to regain an upright position from which he would be able to manoeuvre into a favourable position to resume the attack.

Speed was of the essence and even if a British observer or pilot spotted Immelmann swooping down on them, it was often too late. On 15 December Second Lieutenants Alan Hobbs and Charles Tudor-Jones were sent in a Morane LA on a long-range reconnaissance over Valenciennes, always a risky mission due to the density of the defences there. Immelmann's attention was attracted by the German anti-aircraft shells bursting in the vicinity of the British machine, and as he gained precious altitude he flew towards it. When he was spotted by the observer, Tudor-Jones, the pilot, Hobbs, commenced a murderous game of aerial chess.

When he saw me, he did not fly southward, as was probably his original intention, but bore away from me in an eastward direction. I went into a turn and flew alongside him, although still much lower. He tried to reach the salvation of the lines by a right-hand turn. I promptly flew towards him, although still somewhat lower and so unable to attack. I had climbed to 2,600 by then, but he was at 2,800. The feint attack I made on him misled him into abandoning his westward course and flying further south-east. Again he tried to reach his lines, but with a similar lack of result. Now we were both at the same height, but I nevertheless let my machine climb a bit more. He did the opposite for he put his machine down and thus obtained such a great speed that he almost disappeared from my view. I could only see him as a faint grey smudge on the distant horizon. He certainly hoped I had lost him, because he went into a right-hand turn and headed for Douai. I was now 3,200 metres up, while he might have been 2,600–2,700. As his line of flight was now about perpendicular to my own, my great height enabled me to approach him at a very fast speed. When we were still 500–600 metres apart, he opened a furious fire on me. The distance was too great for him to have any chance to succeed. He fired at least 500 rounds while I was coming up from 500 to 150 metres of him. Then I too began to shoot. First I gave him a series of 40 rounds. The enemy flew gaily on; why not? Now there was only 100 metres between us, then 80 and finally 50. I saw the enemy observer fiddling at his machine-gun. Probably he had a jam. I had to use the moment. Without allowing the pause of even a fraction of a second, I let off 150 rounds. Suddenly the enemy monoplane reared up; with its propeller pointing skyward and its steering surfaces earthward, it stood on its tail for several seconds. Then it turned over by the right wing and whirled down in a nose dive.[30] Leutnant Max Immelmann, 62 Section, German Air Service

Immelman flew on while the deceased losers dropped out of the sky. Tudor-Jones, whose machine-gun had in fact been smashed by Immelmann's bullets, had suffered multiple head and neck wounds. As the aircraft plummeted, his corpse was flung out and impaled on the branches of a tree before it dropped to the ground. Hobbs had head, chest and leg wounds and after his Morane smashed into pieces against the side of a house, his body was found in the wreckage.

Trenchard believed that the RFC's losses were relatively slight compared to the thousands of deaths suffered by the infantry but they were nevertheless extremely serious. Although numerically small they were difficult to replace. Each aircraft destroyed meant that it would not be available for further operations and a new machine would be required to take its place. Pilots shot down by a Fokker in seconds took months to train, even if they arrived in France with just a few hours' flying time, and the experience and skills that could only be gained on active service would have to be learned under threat of constant danger. Many would inevitably be killed first. But the reconnaissance missions still had to be made and in an attempt to ameliorate the effect of the Fokkers a policy was introduced of flying groups of aircraft together to achieve a degree of mutual protection. Four days after the death of Hobbs and Tudor-Jones, a formation of three aircraft set out to complete their mission over Valenciennes. Observing in one of them was McCudden, who had moved another stage forward in his steady rise through the RFC.

We were by now about five miles east of the lines, and were flying E.S.E when my pilot pointed to his left front and above, and looking in the direction he pointed, I saw a long dark brown form fairly streaking across the sky. We could see that it was a German machine, and when it got above and behind our middle machine it dived on to it for all the world like a huge hawk on a hapless sparrow. I now saw the black crosses on the underneath surface of the Fokker's wings, for a Fokker it was, and as it got to close range, Mr Mealing, the pilot of this middle machine, turned, and thus saved itself, although the Fokker had already hit the machine. The Fokker had by now turned and was coming towards our machine, nose on, slightly above. I stood up, with my Lewis gun to the shoulder, and fired as he passed over our right wing. He carried on flying in the opposite direction until he was lost to view. We were by now over Douai Aerodrome, and, looking down, I could see several enemy machines leaving the ground. I watched them for a while, and then noticed the Fokker climbing up under our tail. I told my pilot to turn, and then fired half a drum of Lewis at the Fokker at 300 yards' range. The Fokker seemed rather surprised that we had seen him, and immediately turned off to my left rear as I was facing the tail. After this he climbed about 300 feet above us, and then put his nose down to fire. Having been waiting for him, I opened fire at once, and he promptly pulled out of his dive and retired to a distance of 500 yards, at which distance he remained, for every time he came closer I fired a short burst, which had the desired effect of keeping him at a distance. By now we had reached Valenciennes, and were circling round, obtaining the desired information, which consisted in finding out how much rolling-stock was in Valenciennes station . . . The Fokker had remained at a respectable distance and was doing vertical turns and such tricks. As soon as we left he followed us, just like a vulture, no doubt waiting for one of us to fall out with engine trouble. By now we were approaching Douai on our homeward journey, and the Fokker went down into Douai Aerodrome, as he had no doubt finished his petrol . . . It was assumed that the Fokker pilot was most likely Immelmann . . . I was very thankful indeed to return from this outing . . . I had imagined that if once Immelmann in his Fokker saw us there was not much chance for us. However, we live and learn.[31] Sergeant James McCudden, 3 Squadron RFC

Such actions demonstrated that formations of determined pilots with skilful gunners were not necessarily 'Fokker fodder' and learning from such experiences Trenchard issued an order on 16 January 1916.

Until the Royal Flying Corps are in possession of a machine as good as or better than the German Fokker it seems that a change in the tactics employed becomes necessary. It is hoped very shortly to obtain a machine which will be able to successfully engage the Fokkers . . . In the meantime, it must be laid down as a hard and fast rule that a machine proceeding on reconnaissance must be escorted by at least three other fighting machines. These machines must fly in close formation and a reconnaissance should not be continued if any of the machines become detached. This should apply to both short and distant reconnaissances. Aeroplanes proceeding on photographic duty any considerable distance east of the German line should be similarly escorted.[32] Brigadier General Hugh Trenchard, RFC Headquarters

The consequence of this pragmatic change of tactics was soon felt. By requiring more aircraft to go out on each operation it inevitably reduced the total number that could be carried out. Unable to accelerate the increase in its overall size, the RFC had to concentrate its resources more tightly and by the beginning of April 1916 Trenchard was wistfully forced to point out to Henderson, 'I have cut down the work, in my opinion enormously. I have dropped bombing, no long-distance reconnaissances are done, and jolly few short ones, and these are just over the line.'[33] This change of practice, so alien to Trenchard's philosophy, was perhaps the most important achievement of the Fokkers. In comparison with earlier casualties suffered in the air, which by June 1915 had still not reached one hundred, the numbers lost to this deadly German innovation were proportionately high but still smaller than the losses the RFC was to suffer later in the war. Yet the sudden growth in the casualty rate and the unfounded myth of invincibility that became associated with the Fokker had an indelible impact on wider public opinion. They became seen as a sinister force and were referred to in tabloid newspapers such as Northcliffe's *Daily Mail* as the 'Fokker scourge'. The real answer lay in better, faster British aircraft with a more powerful armament and within weeks of Trenchard's complaint to Henderson they had started to arrive. But the spectre of the Fokker continued to linger long after its real threat had been removed.

CHAPTER FIVE

Training

As the size of the armies on the Western Front grew, so too did the air forces needed to support them. Beginning with Brancker's and Trenchard's efforts in the late summer of 1914 and continuing unabated through the whole of the following year, the RFC eagerly tried to attract the brightest and the best to join its ranks. There was an unfortunate conflict between the number of recruits that were needed, as new roles emerged for aerial warfare demanding ever larger numbers of aircraft and aircrew to operate them, and the number of pupils with which the trimmed-to-the-bone training establishments could cope. Hence, although casualties began to occur in increasing numbers and needed to be replaced quickly, the speed with which the replacements could be trained placed restraints on the rate at which both the RFC and RNAS could grow and in defiance of demand it remained difficult to join either.

Many recruits joined straight from civilian life attracted by the public image of the RFC and RNAS while others, already in the army, and saddled with the far greater discomforts and risks of the trenches, looked up in their few leisure moments and saw a vision of what their future might be.

> For the first time in my life I found I was covered with lice. It was that that really made me think that trench warfare was not for me! I used to look up with great envy at these aircraft flying round about. So I immediately put in an application to join the Royal Flying Corps.[1] Donald Clappen

Although increased comfort, the opportunity of living for most of the day out of danger and the sheer spiritual attraction of flying like a bird had their attractions, the risks of fighting surrounded by petrol thousands of feet above the ground were also apparent.

My brother officers said, 'Good Heavens haven't you seen enough planes come down in flames?' I said, 'Yes, but haven't you seen enough death in trenches?' That was one way of dying that was all. The real reason was I wanted to fly and with flying it would soon be over if you'd come to the end of your life. You didn't have to sleep in mud, night after night, day after day, in mud and water.[2] T.E. Rogers

Many would-be flyers found it difficult to obtain permission to transfer from their superior officers who resented losing some of their brightest and best to the RFC. Donald Clappen was a pre-war pilot who had joined the London Scottish in a flush of enthusiasm on the outbreak of war. His change of heart was not popular.

My Colonel was not very keen as he was losing a lot of his personnel for commissions. So he instructed that he would pass on any application for a commission if the applicant could obtain a signature or application for him from whatever regiment he wished to join. In my case I knew nobody from the Royal Flying Corps. So when we were resting behind the trenches I went up to Auchel. With great envy I was watching these people flying. There was a staff car and emerging from the office was a brass hat – two of them in fact. As he stepped into the car, acting on the spur of the moment, I said, 'Please Sir, may I speak?' He looked round, astonished and didn't say anything. I pulled out my application papers and told him my story – that I was a qualified pilot and wanted to join the RFC, had some difficulty in getting anyone to apply for me, that I had already applied and heard nothing more about it . . . In a very deep voice he told his second officer, also a brass hat, 'Make a note of that; make a note of that . . .' and so forth. He said, 'Well I'll see what we can do.' In the meantime he called to one of the airmen and said, 'Is there a transport going back towards the trenches – if so make sure this soldier gets a lift back.' With that I saluted smartly and he went off. In the tender I asked the driver, 'Who was that I was speaking to?' He said, 'Blimey, you've got a nerve – that was General Trenchard!!!' I knew his name but I had no idea . . . I still regard that as quite the bravest action I've ever taken in my life!![3] Donald Clappen

Returning to England in November 1915 after a campaign spent marching across most of South-west Africa with the 1st Rhodesian Rifles another young man had also had enough of infantry life but he was able to invoke family influence to secure a transfer into the Royal Flying Corps. It was to have a significant effect on the rest of his life.

We marched from one end of that country to the other, carrying everything we possessed – a generally empty water bottle, a nearly empty haversack, 250 rounds of ammunition and a rifle. We out-marched the Boer commandos who were with us on horseback and one realised the truth of the saying that a man can always, given equal conditions, out-walk a horse. The result was I have never walked a yard since if I could avoid it. I knew it was no good trying to get on to a horse because horses were out – I thought I might try to be a gunner and get a seat on a limber but they seemed to be full up. I went round to the War Office where I was interviewed by a rather supercilious young man. When I said I would like to fly, which I realised was something I could do sitting down not walking, he said, 'So would 6,000 other people! Would you like to be 6,001 on the waiting list?' So I retired rather disgruntled and when I got back my father had just returned from India and when I told him what had happened he said, 'Well why didn't you go and see your Uncle Charlie!' He was just one of my many uncles. I didn't know who or where or what he was but he gave me a note and I went back to the War Office next day. When I handed the note addressed to my Uncle Charlie to the same supercilious

young fellow he said, 'Oh, please sit down a minute, Sir!'
Which was rather a change from his reception the day
before. He came back about ten minutes later and he
said, 'Colonel Elliot is in conference and unable to see
you at the moment, but if you will report to Number 2
Reserve Squadron at Brooklands this evening you can
start flying.' So I did just that![4] Arthur Harris

Step by tentative step Harris, whose career was to lead him to
the highest ranks of the RAF and some degree of notoriety as
the head of Bomber Command in the Second World War, and
many other young men like him commenced on the path which
would turn them from excited pupils into aerial warriors.

For many such would-be pilots their first sight of the machine in
which they were to do their basic training was a little disconcerting.
The Maurice Farman 'Longhorn', in which many of them took
their first faltering steps to a pilot's licence, hardly looked as if it
was at the cutting edge of modern flying technology.

To the uninitiated eye the Longhorn presented such
a forest of struts and spars, with floppy white fabric
drooped over all, as inevitably brought to mind a
prosperous seaport in the heyday of sailing ships, while
piano-wire was festooned everywhere to such an extent
that the wrecking of a few of these machines before the
lines in Flanders would have provided our troops with
an impenetrable entanglement. At the sight of the craft
before us, we put our heads on one side like puzzled
terriers.[5] Duncan Grinnell-Milne, RFC

The new cadets were taken up for an acclimatisation flight with
an experienced pilot or instructor and the eagerly-awaited first
flight offered a trip into a previously unimagined third dimension.
Everything in the air seemed exaggerated and strange and once
carried aloft the cadets were bemused to find that there was no
great feeling of height as they gazed down at the ground.

The funny thing was that I cannot stand heights on
buildings or going up ladders – it really gets me down!
I hate it! But flying made absolutely no impression on

me at all in that respect and I think it's due to the fact that you're not connected with anything on the ground whereas if you look over a high building you have the sensation of being connected with the ground.[6] Gordon Hyams, RNAS

Real flying training began when the trainee pilots were taken up in dual control machines which allowed the instructor to monitor what they were doing or, more importantly, take over the controls if things went wrong. In the early days some of these 'dual' arrangements were extraordinarily makeshift.

The nacelle has two cockpits and the pupil sits just behind the instructor who has the controls. The pupil reaches over his shoulders and by putting his hands on the instructor's hands – or the instructor taking his hands off occasionally – he has control of the machine in the fore and aft and lateral sense. He has no control of the rudder.[7] Charles Chabot, RFC

The first hurdle a pilot had to overcome was the take-off. This was an area of great risk for everyone from the inexperienced beginner to the over-confident 'veteran'. If certain basic rules were not followed then, as the aircraft staggered off the ground, no room was left for recovery and a serious crash was almost inevitable. Duncan Grinnell-Milne was training at Shoreham-by-Sea when he witnessed in horror a much admired, experienced pilot immolate both himself and a passenger after committing an elementary blunder on take-off. Afterwards the squadron commander bluntly expressed his views in a didactic tirade to the shocked trainee pilots.

'With regard to this unfortunate and unnecessary happening,' he began harshly, 'the first and only thing to do is to find out the causes of the accident, to see where the pilot was to blame so as to learn what lessons we may. Now in this particularly stupid case . . .' I thought him terribly callous. But he was not; he was perfectly right. 'A pilot must never turn down wind at low altitude when faced with the possibility of a forced landing. A

pilot in difficulties after leaving the ground must keep
straight on and not attempt to turn back. A pilot in
difficulties must save himself and his passengers first,
not the aeroplane. It is better to smash wheels and
propeller than burn a man to death. A pilot must take
particular care to maintain flying speed when leaving the
ground or after engine failure. The risks of a crash can
always be minimised if the machine has flying speed and
is facing into the wind . . .' Those were the lessons. If the
manner of their teaching was hard, it was also effective.[8]
Duncan Grinnell-Milne, RFC

In the early days of the war many of the trainer aircraft were
inherently unreliable as Graham Donald discovered when flying
an original Wright Biplane during his training at the Beatty School
of Flying at Hendon in late 1914.

I got started training on this dual control genuine
American Wright Biplane with twin propellers, chain
driven – one of them with a cross chain which makes
most engineers shudder. It was completely, inherently
unstable and a lot of people said that if you could fly
a Wright Biplane you could fly anything. Well the fact
remains that it flew. The speed range was about three
knots: it flew level at 43 knots, began diving at 42 and
stalled at 39 or 40. So you hadn't got very much to play
with! The instrumentation was quite simple – there was
a length of fine cords about 18 inches long tied to one
of the struts in front of you. You kept your eye on
these cords, the idea being that if they went sideways
you were side-slipping. If the cord went limp the only
thing to do was sing, 'Nearer My God To Thee!'[9] Graham
Donald, RNAS

On such aircraft when things went wrong there was often little
or no time for the instructor to correct the situation at the low
altitudes at which the typical training flight was undertaken.

We were flying out a bit beyond the Midland Railway
line which runs from St Pancras to the North when the

engine cut completely. The pilot, Jimmy James, grabbed his control stick and immediately put her nose down because the Caudron Biplane had the gliding angle of a brick. We were pointing straight for the aerodrome but there was rather a toss up whether we cleared the railway line. At that moment there were two express trains coming; one heading for Scotland the other for St Pancras. However, he just managed to jerk her up through the smoke and got over the line. By the time we reached the field on the other side we stalled at a height of about six feet up so the Caudron did its sort of normal neat little dive and turned upside down with its wheels in the air – that was the sort of conventional way for Caudrons to land! We both tumbled out and nobody was any the worse.[10] Graham Donald, RNAS

The landing, which determined the manner in which the aircraft and the pilot came back into contact with the ground, was fraught with real and imagined perils. For the beginner it took both skill and courage to surmount them.

Landing is the most difficult thing of all because it's the one thing that matters! If you make a mistake in the air it doesn't matter – if you make a mistake in landing, you're in trouble. Anybody can fly but the whole art is to learn to land – to get down on Mother Earth again! The knack of the landing is that when you come down you've got your gliding height, your engine is off. An ideal landing is that you gradually pull your nose up as you lose flying speed, it stalls your aeroplane and the perfect landing is to have the wheels and the tail skid hit the ground together. That is the perfect landing which happens once in twenty times. A bad landing is when you pull up your nose too early and you're not near enough the ground and your plane then drops. If it drops sufficiently badly your undercarriage is gone![11] Laurie Field, RFC

Sporting metaphors were often used to describe success or failure in achieving a clean, bounce free landing. 'I discovered that a good landing on a new type of aeroplane gives one a much greater glow of satisfaction than the most perfect drive at golf.'[12] While, conversely, to fail was to be totally humiliated in front of one's peers. 'A bad landing was not a thing to be passed over lightly. It was a crime equal to a dropped catch in a first eleven match when the last men of the other side were trying to hold out for the last over.'[13] Shame indeed!

Some of the flying instructors simply lacked the teaching skills needed to impart their own accumulated knowledge in a coherent fashion to their eager pupils. Gerald Livock was 'trained' at the Grahame-White School of Flying at Hendon.

> Most of my instruction was from a Russian whose real name was Ozepanko but was always known as Russell for some reason or other. He not only was very excitable but he couldn't talk English – or very little English. After you'd come down with a bit of a bump he'd bellow in your ear, 'You come down too steep – wheels break!' Which was very useful advice which one knew already – but he never told you how not to come down too steep.[14] Gerald Livock, RNAS

Teaching inexperienced, over-confident or incompetent novice pilots was dangerous and it is no wonder that some instructors saw the pupils as the enemy and even nicknamed them 'Huns' to express their opinions. Unfortunately instructing was often used to give a rest to pilots who had completed a period of active service and some simply could not cope with the extra strain.

> My instructor was a chap whom I'm quite certain had had a bad shaking up and thoroughly lost his nerve because I virtually never touched the controls when I was supposed to be having dual. With the result that when I did go solo I got off the ground all right but I did a mighty bounce on landing and squashed the undercarriage.[15] Christopher Bilney, RFC

Bilney was lucky. There were many cases of pupils similarly rushed through on to their solo flight before they were ready which resulted in a serious or fatal crash. This first solo flight was the final challenge that every trainee had to confront before he could become a fully-fledged pilot. Many individuals had problems but one *ingénu* excelled himself by not even getting off the ground before having his first serious accident.

I had a Canadian instructor and his particular aeroplane was called 'Adanac' which is, of course, Canada written backwards. When my day came for my first solo he said, 'Now look, if you treat this aeroplane very carefully you can do your first solo on my aeroplane.' So I got out into the middle of the aerodrome and my prop stopped. Well of course the normal thing to do is to call for a mechanic to start your prop but with the impetuosity of youth I thought I'd start the prop myself. All the boys on the tarmac were always interested in first solos and they saw me doing this and were yelling words of advice which I didn't take any notice of! So I swung the prop myself and although I had pulled the throttle right back the aeroplane started moving forwards. So I dashed under the plane, tried to get in the seat, I couldn't get in and I fell over. The tailplane hit my head and knocked me to the ground. There I saw this beautiful aeroplane which belonged to my instructor which he treasured so much actually running away from me. Then it swerved to the left and I ran after it but it gradually gained speed until it was beginning to run after me. I fell over, it was just as well that I did because the aeroplane took off over my head flew at about 50 feet up and eventually crashed. In the meantime my instructor of course was going absolutely mad on the tarmac. His invective they tell me was terrible because I'd practically destroyed his lovely machine! I had to go in front of my commanding officer and he told me, 'Pilots are cheap, but aeroplanes are very, very expensive. You made an awful mess of things today.' I thought I was going to be dismissed from the service and I held my head very low and said I was sorry. But he had a half smile on his face as he told me, 'All right, well we'll forget it this time!'[16]
F. Silwood, RNAS

The solo itself was a terrifying mixture of exhilaration, terror, panic and desperate concentration.

When I had done some two and a half hours total flying time, the instructor said to me, 'It's about time you did your first solo flight, isn't it?' I did not agree, but he persuaded me to have a try. What an awful moment! This indubitably is the worst flight a pilot ever makes. He is never competent to fly a machine alone; but by some extraordinary guarding of providence, he will make a successful flight, and then the ice is broken and he makes good headway afterwards. 'Go ahead then!' were the words of encouragement that I got, and I climbed into the old Maurice Farman. The oldest of the MFs is kept particularly for these exciting ventures. The engine was started up and off I went down the Straights into the air in grand style and up over the treetops where I had no business to go. But how could I help it? I didn't mean the machine to go over there but I couldn't stop it – I was a passenger, as they say. Away down to the right of the Straights, over the pond and trees, bound for the Lord knows where. The forward outrigger elevator was my guide, and I kept my eyes fixed on it intently, keeping it in line and level with the horizon. Was I climbing too steeply? I couldn't tell. I hadn't the courage at first to take my eyes off the outrigger to glance at my airspeed indicator; but after a moment's thought, I realised it was imperative that I should, and so, keeping my head perfectly still, I swivelled my eyes on to the instrument board, only to get another fright. The indicator showed forty and a few odd miles an hour, a speed at which Longhorns are not supposed to lift, much less have any grip on the air with their controlling surfaces. Instantly I pushed the controls forward, and as luck was with me, they answered; up went my tail, and in a second or two I was charging downhill with the engine at full throttle, nearly jumping out of the frame. I knew no other way. So I went on, alternately stalling and diving as I went round. When I got down over Laffan's Plain, it was high time for me to turn home. I put on a little left rudder and no bank – I was afraid to put bank on – and the machine turned gradually, slipping outwards as hard as it would go, making a terrific draught on the right side of my head. The perspiration was now rolling off me and my knees were so weak that I could hardly press the rudder controls; but it was nearly over. I was facing the balloon sheds and making for home, fair and square up the Straights again. I now foresaw that I must shortly shut my throttle as I was fairly high (1,000 feet). I had been climbing all the time and would gladly have gone on rather than face the descent. I looked at the balloon sheds. I was still true in line for a good landing. I looked at my left hand on the controls; I looked at the throttle lever. How in the name of all that's crisp was I to leave go of the control with one hand and shut that throttle. This was more than one man could do; and all the time the balloon sheds got nearer and nearer. Well, it's got to be done, and so 'here goes'. I made a dive for the lever without even looking, caught the end of the lever with my knuckles as I made a bold sweep with my arm, and there was dead silence. I had remembered my instructor's last words, 'Put your nose down when you shut your engine off', and I obeyed. The ground was rapidly approaching, and now I only had to do what I had done heaps of times before quite successfully. But this time everything went wrong. I had been higher than usual, and my glide down took longer than usual. All the eyes on the aerodrome were breathlessly watching my performance and of course, in my anxiety to get down, I was gliding far too fast. Quite suddenly I thought I was going to fly right into the ground. I pulled the machine up and flew horizontally for some distance then, starting another glide I made a heavy landing, bouncing like a kangaroo. What a joy, it was all over; and how pleased I was with myself.[17] Robin Rowell, RFC

Shortly after the first solo the pilots would take their Flying Certificate test administered by the Royal Aero Club and still recognised as the register of qualified pilots throughout the war. This was known as 'taking one's ticket'. At this stage the pilots usually moved to the advanced flying training school where they began to fly as often as possible to build up their 'hours', with every flight meticulously recorded in their personal log book. It was important that they quickly developed a relaxed approach to flying and 'stiff' pilots who found their muscles tensing in the air had either to learn to relax or give up.

Flying was very much a manual dexterity. Instruments were virtually not used except for the engine revolution counter which the pilot watched while he was warming up his engine to be able to fly. From the moment he took off the pilot never looked at his instrument again – never! He went by the feel of the joystick, feel on his feet and the wind on his face. It was all manual which was one reason why people who had been good horsemen tended to be good pilots. The same delicacy of touch on the controls as opposed to a grab of jog in the mouth on a horse was what made for good and pleasant flying.[18]
Archibald James, RFC

* * *

Arriving at such a detached state of tranquillity was often difficult, particularly since the unreliable nature of many engines made forced landings inevitable. The feeling of terror and utter indecisiveness which took over when the engine spluttered to a stop was extremely unnerving.

A glance at the altimeter – less than fifteen hundred feet – in alarm I hung over the side, goggling at the earth. Choose? Not so easy. There were innumerable fields, but only a few large enough. I examined these few attentively. Marshes! Or else green mud from which the tide receded . . . Under a thousand feet now. No time to lose. I had been told that, from long periods of sitting still in the air, an airman's chief trouble was constipation. In this business of forced landing I fancied I had found a certain cure; I wanted that field for more reasons than one. And at last just in time I found it.[19]
Duncan Grinnell-Milne, RFC

* * *

As the war progressed an increasing blend of experience and innovation from the instructors began to have an impact on flying training. Major Robert Smith-Barry was an experienced pre-war pilot who subsequently acquired first-hand knowledge of the reality of flying on the Western Front as the Commander of 60 Squadron, RFC in 1916. As a result of his observations he developed an innovative philosophy of training that sought to give the pupils a truly realistic introduction to combat flying. After much harassment Trenchard agreed to give him the chance to prove his theories and sent him home to command 1 (Reserve) Squadron, RFC at Gosport in December 1916.

> One morning I was told that the Commanding Officer wanted to take me up again. This rather shook me because one seldom had any dual control after you'd once gone solo. The C.O. was Major Smith-Barry and I suppose he treated me as one of his early guinea pigs just to try out his new ideas. I enjoyed the few minutes I had with him enormously. He showed me above anything else how to get out of a spin which up to that time most of us regarded as fatal. He was undoubtedly a genius. The confidence that I could always get out of a spin saved my life many months later when I went into a little bit of a spin on purpose when I was chased by Baron von Richthofen and his circus.[20] Reginald Fuljames, RFC

Smith-Barry's early experiments at Gosport were recognised as a success and within a few months he had developed a completely new method of flying instruction. His first priority was to revolutionise the manner in which dual instruction was carried out. Instead of the pupil sitting in the passenger seat and looking over the instructor's shoulders he insisted that the pupil should have a full set of controls and sit in the front – in the position he would be when he came to make his first solo flight. The instructor would then be in the passenger seat and communicate with the pupil by a specially designed set of headphones called the 'Gosport tube'. He also advocated that once a pilot had gone solo he still needed extensive dual flying time in order to familiarise himself with the more advanced manoeuvres of flying, such as sudden turns and spinning, which equipped him with complete control of his aircraft.

> The object has been not to prevent flyers from getting into difficulties or dangers, but to show them how to

get out of them satisfactorily, and having done so, to make them go and repeat the process alone. If the pupil considers this dangerous, let him find some other employment, as whatever risks he is asked to run here, he will have to run a hundred times as many when he gets to France.[21] Major Robert Smith-Barry, 1 (Reserve) Squadron, Gosport

Smith-Barry sought an aircraft that would act as a transitional machine between the slow stable *ab initio* training aircraft and the vagaries of the high-performance scouts. He found it in the Avro 504 series of aircraft of which the most famous was the Avro 504 K. It was the ideal training aeroplane that allowed a novice to experiment in a lively, relatively high-performance machine with a reassuringly reliable pedigree. The Avro, however, was still too 'fast' for less talented pupils who perhaps lacked the mental agility needed to become an effective scout pilot and were probably better suited to duties with reconnaissance or bomber aircraft.

> I was a very slow pupil. I suppose I was a little bit dense. I took eight hours to go solo whereas the average was about three hours and I knew of one person who took only twenty minutes to go solo. It was psychological I think because when I went on the faster machines I was taken up in an Avro by the instructor and put into a spin. He had told me what to do to get it out but when I saw the world turning round on an axis directly below me I absolutely froze on the controls and I couldn't do anything – I was so fascinated by the ground getting closer and closer. The instructor was swearing and cursing and after a while he overcame the pressure on the controls and pulled out about 500 feet from the ground. The instructors thought that I wasn't fit to fly fast machines – single-seater fighters – so I was sent to fly heavier two-seater machines.[22] Frank Burslem, RFC

Occasions such as these helped to identify men such as Burslem at relatively little risk to themselves and allowed them to be shepherded into other flying duties before they encountered single-seater scouts which would undoubtedly have killed anyone who froze at a critical moment. Smith–Barry positively encouraged dangerous flying but only within a structure of theoretical lectures and practical demonstrations with experienced instructors. This combination allowed new pilots to gain a detailed understanding of the exact effect each movement of the controls had on an aircraft in certain situations. Once pilots knew what they were doing, stunting, far from being banned, was encouraged and, as a result of the greater self-confidence that was built up, there was a reduction in fatal crashes. In July 1917, Smith–Barry's success was recognised by the formation under his command of the School of Special Flying at Gosport where he took great pleasure in the expertise and daring of his special instructors.

Captain Billy Williams took up an Avro to practise completely stalled landings. At 500 feet he stalled until the engine and propeller ceased revolving, then glided down slowly at a steep angle, rather like the descent of an auto-gyro, holding his machine balanced by sheer skill as a pilot. In attempting to land from the stalled glide he misjudged the final movement of the elevators and fell heavily the last few feet, crashing the undercarriage. Colonel Smith–Barry stood on the tarmac, and, without a word, watched Williams jump out of the wrecked Avro and order another. The second Avro, too, stalled heavily, near the ground and crashed. Still the Colonel watched unspeaking. Williams, determined to succeed, went up in a third machine, and this time achieved his purpose, making an almost stationary landing in front of his hangar with his engine stopped. 'Good show, Williams,' he said, 'but it's a good thing for you that you didn't stop at number two.' That was Smith–Barry, who believed that the result of successful achievement justified the cost. Failure he would not brook at any cost.[23] Harold Balfour, RFC

The main role of the school became the teaching of instructors to create a cadre who would spread Smith–Barry's methods throughout the country. Gwilym Lewis, who had been serving as an instructor at the Central Flying School, was sent on a special instructors' course. Initially he was fairly sceptical but soon became a convert.

> What really happens here is super instruction. Some clever people down here have devised a very sound system of instruction, and to standardise this in the Flying Corps they train other instructors. It is mostly for dual control. They have got at the theory of the whole thing and instead of flying in the slip-shod fashion that most of us taught ourselves to do, you learn exactly what you are doing, and why you do it, and so you can teach others the same sort of thing. The amusing part of the show is that many others like myself have found out how very badly they really fly, and have settled down to learn again, under the supervision of very critical instructors. Of course there are a number of little tricks thrown in, which were once thought clever, because we knew how to do them without knowing what we were doing, and consequently flying far from perfectly. Some misguided individuals come down here feeling proud, but one can only feel sorry for them. However good you are, you are nearly sure to learn something on a show like this. In fact one individual considered by many the best pilot in the Corps, said that he learnt more about flying in three weeks down here than in the three years previous.[24] Gwilym Lewis, RFC

By 1918, the Smith-Barry method of flying instruction had become the cornerstone of all flying training instruction in Britain. Ultimately it produced a greater number of better-trained pilots who were not fatally surprised when they moved on to the next stage of their flying education in the high-performance aircraft which were used in action.

The relaxation in the ban on stunting meant that a whole series of dramatic aerial manoeuvres could be learnt and rehearsed. Some had minimal practical use in actual combat but all of them played a vital role in honing the flying skills of pilots so that they could do as they willed in the air without hesitation. Complete confidence and instant action might one day save a pilot's life in combat. The loop was one of the more impressive tricks, with the additional advantage of being comparatively easy as long as the pilot kept his nerve.

> The sensation that always struck me as being exhilarating was that, after I'd seen the earth disappear in front of me as the nose went up in the sky, I'd see nothing but sky for a bit, then suddenly the earth came in sight above my head at a funny angle. That always seemed a little bit odd. Then I just pulled the stick a bit harder to make sure that the centrifugal force kept me in the seat when I was inverted.[25] Ronald Sykes, RNAS

The spin was also a gut-wrenching experience but pilots soon worked out how to use it in combat as a means of escaping from a dangerous situation.

> I pulled the Camel up into a stall, then put on rudder and the machine just fell away sideways. The most sickening sensation. It fell towards the earth, one wing tip first, on its side. Suddenly it whipped round, flicked round very quickly into this quick spin, round and round. I was thrown violently to one side of the cockpit with a fierce blast of wind on one cheek. Then you got used to that and tried to straighten everything and bring it out. In my case it usually wouldn't come out very quickly. You just had to put everything central and wait.[26] Ronald Sykes, RNAS

There were many different methods of turning which was probably the most important of combat flying skills.

> I found a vertical bank was a most delightful manoeuvre. You could just move your stick an inch or two over to the side and the Camel would immediately turn over on to a wing-tip. At the same time you pulled the stick back into your stomach and the nose began to whip round the horizon. At the same time you had to put on full left rudder because the gyroscopic forces from the big Bentley engine tended to make the nose climb into the sky on a left turn and the left rudder kept it down.[27] Ronald Sykes, RNAS

There was an unforeseen side-effect to this manoeuvre.

When you do a vertical turn you have to do with your feet what you've previously done with your hands and vice versa. When you turn on your side your rudder becomes elevator and your elevator becomes your rudder. I found it difficult at first but eventually I learnt.[28] Second Lieutenant Laurie Field, RFC

As the pilots mastered these stunts so they naturally revelled in showing them off, to the alarm and consternation of ordinary law-abiding citizens.

We used to go to Brighton and fly along the sea front very often below the level of the pier. Then we'd zoom up over the West Pier, down again, zoom up over the Palace Pier and down again. We'd swing round and fly inland looking as if we were going to fly in the windows of the hotels then we'd zoom up over the roofs. That gave us great amusement but the people of Brighton didn't like it very much![29] Archibald Yuille, RFC

The final stage of a pilot's training came when he joined his squadron on active service. If the operational situation allowed, they would be given a series of flights in the aircraft they would be flying in action although staying behind the front lines. When Sub Lieutenant Ronald Sykes joined 9 Squadron, RNAS his Canadian Flight Commander, Captain Roy Brown, showed him the very limits to which a Sopwith Camel could be flown.

He took me round and into a steep dive to introduce me to just how much a Camel could stand. He went over fairly quickly, down nose first – I was following. Very soon we were going down vertically with engine full on. The airspeed indicator was round to its maximum 180 knots and everything was making a terrific din – the wires, the wind in the struts – everything was shaking and howling. We went down for thousands of feet. When he came to come out of the dive first of all his speed dropped slightly when he throttled back the engine. I throttled back mine and the speed dropped a little bit. Then moving the stick just about an eighth of an inch at a time we came out of the vertical. With every little movement you could feel the centrifugal force pushing right down into your shoulders, pushing your body down on the seat. When the speed got down to 150 it handled quite well and we continued to pull out. It just seemed that above 150 it had to be handled in a very sensitive way otherwise the canvas and wood would have broken up.[30] Flight Sub-Lieutenant Ronald Sykes, 9 Squadron RNAS

As the war progressed so the training reflected the increasing complexities of the aerial fighting on the Western Front. Successful pilots were brought back from the Front to teach others what they had been lucky or skilled enough to learn without getting killed. Through lectures and demonstrations they tried to convey some of the tactics that had been developed. In 1917, F.J. Powell was made Chief Fighting Instructor to the Northern Training Squadrons.

My responsibility was to see that fighting instructors were actually instructing the pupils in the art of fighting: the method of attack; keeping the sun behind you where possible; always attacking from underneath and behind an aircraft. It struck me as being so ridiculous to ask a man to instruct a pupil – who is standing on the aerodrome – in the art of flying. Just to go up and fly about oneself and do a few acrobatics wasn't teaching the pupil on the ground anything at all. One might as well expect anybody who paid half a crown at Hendon to watch a flying display to come away from the aerodrome a fully qualified pilot![31] Chief Fighting Instructor F.J. Powell, RFC

Gradually the training programme was revolutionised with the establishment of Special Schools of Aerial Fighting where the pupils could practise the skills they would need in the air. Such establishments at least gave the tyro pilots a taste of what they would face on the Western Front.

Many of the instructors, drawn to the Front like moths to a flame, fretted in this relative inaction, hoping only to be sent back. Powell was one such, and he set a different kind of example to his pupils in attempting a difficult stunt through a mixture of bravado and boredom. It was to be a salutary lesson that even the best could become careless and over-confident.

That night I was lying in my bed and I thought, 'Now, I'll do something nobody else has ever done – tomorrow morning I will loop off the ground.' My Bristol Bullet had a maximum speed level of about 70 miles an hour but I thought that if I held it down just over the top of the grass until I was going flat out then I could go up in a very big loop, when I got to the top, pull the joystick into my tummy, whip the tail over and then gravity plus the engine would pull me round. Next morning I went off and tried this – I pulled up in the loop, flipped it – and realised I hadn't enough room! I think my life was saved by some sheep grazing at the far end of the grass airfield. They all started to run out star fashion away from me and I was so interested in the sheep that I didn't stiffen myself up. There was a bean field at that corner – the beans were about two feet high. When the crash came I went straight into the deck at about 150 miles and hour straight into the earth in the bean field. I shot through the front of the aircraft, my belt broke, I hit my head on the instrument board and was knocked out. My legs had shot through the rotary engine and another quarter of a turn and I would have lost both my legs. As it was I finished with the engine in my crutch. The only thing I could see of the aircraft above the bean field was the very tip of the rudder. The ground was hard and not one bit had sunk more than a few inches into the earth – it was flattened like a pancake. My CO, seeing this, stopped everyone from running out because he knew it was going to be a nasty mess. So he strolled slowly across to the crash and when he got there he found me singing the latest song of the time which was:

> 'Sprinkle me with kisses
> A lot of loving kisses
> If you want my love to grow.'[32]

Chief Fighting Instructor F.J. Powell, RFC

It is commonplace to insinuate that the flying skills of the 'aces' who emerged in the later years of the war were in some way a negligible factor in their success but James McCudden demonstrated his skill and nerve when he successfully achieved what Powell had failed to accomplish by looping his Sopwith Pup straight from take-off during a period on home service as an instructor in 1917.

He was a brilliant pilot, absolutely outstanding. I saw him do the most hair-raising stunts round the aerodrome when he was demonstrating what a Pup could do. His favourite was to loop directly off the ground when he was taking off and continue looping! Once he looped thirteen times from take-off and when he finished he was 500 feet high. A wonderful piece of flying. Or he would go up to about 1,000 feet, turn the machine upside down and just go round the airfield till the engine stopped – then he'd go on gliding. Next thing he'd roll it out, get the engine going again and away he'd go. He was absolutely marvellous – there wasn't a thing that he couldn't do with that machine.[33] J.C.F. Hopkins, RFC

The increasing complexity of the war was reflected in the various different disciplines that had to be taught. Pilots had to learn to fly at night – something that had been almost inconceivable at the start of the war.

At the start it was very unnatural. You go to bed at night usually! The lack of a horizon to go by – everything was black. Even in your cockpit you couldn't see your instruments. Your feel of balance was quite different to what it was in the daytime and flying was all a question of balance when all's said and done.[34] C. Gordon-Burge, RFC

Gradually, hard-earned experience in night flying meant that a reasonably safe training method was established.

A flare path was laid out consisting of empty drums filled with waste soaked in petrol. These were lighted and they were in the form of an 'L'. We took off parallel with the long arm towards the short arm. I went to the starting point and a search light was put down which lit up the ground. I followed the normal routine: revved up the engine, started off and flew along the flight path till I got sufficient speed to take off. Our main instruction was to keep everything central – rudder, elevators – until the actual take-off took place. After we left the ground coming out of the light of the flares into the darkness there was no horizon at all – it was just like flying into a black blanket. That moment was very unnerving. After we'd climbed a matter of 100 feet or so, only a few seconds really, then the light that's always present at night manifested itself and the horizon became a clear line in front. Having got the horizon I was able to trim the machine – your sense of balance was restored and in those days you had to rely on your sense of balance to fly.[35] J.C.F. Hopkins, RFC

The specialised training of reconnaissance, artillery observation and bomber aircrew was absolutely crucial since these disciplines remained at the heart of the role which the RFC had established for itself on the Western Front. All observers had to qualify as aerial gunners to defend their two–seaters against attacks from the rear. To save on ammunition and to allow the instructors to judge the pupil's accuracy camera guns were developed which recorded what the gunner was aiming at whenever he pulled the trigger. Howard Andrews found the experience more than a little embarrassing.

It was an ordinary machine-gun with a camera strapped on the front and every time you pressed the trigger you took a photograph. We were taken up in the air, flown round and every time we saw an aeroplane on the ground or in the air we took photographs of it. The first time I went up with this gun of course I didn't know anything – I didn't know which was ground and which was sky! The Canadian pilots were a bit of devils and the aeroplane went round like a drunken caterpillar. I looked round and I couldn't see aeroplanes anywhere. The pilot swore at me and pointed at the ground – I saw one on the ground so I took a photograph and gave it up! He screamed at me, 'Where do you want to go?' I said, 'I'd like to go to Hastings!' He said, 'All right!' We got to Hastings and he went right round the pier – I thought it looked nice so I took a photograph of it! I thought to myself, 'I've done myself now – I can't get this off.' We came back and landed. The squadron leader came racing over to the pilot ticking him off as apparently he wasn't allowed to go anywhere near Hastings and not thinking I'd pressed the trigger. The next day they read out that somebody got six aeroplanes, somebody got five and he said, 'Stand up, Cadet Andrews!' I stood up and he said, 'You've got one photograph of an aeroplane, very nice, one of Hastings Pier and one of the Squadron Leader – and he doesn't like it!'[36] Howard Andrews, RFC

Likewise, the routine of helping the artillery range on to their targets had to be perfected in the most efficient manner possible.

They had little model villages and stretches of land down below and we were up in a balcony. We looked down on this model landscape and they would have bursts of shellfire – minute little thing – puffs of smoke came up out of the ground. We had to look at this miniature landscape and compare it with a map and get the exact map points that the burst had occurred when ranging the gun. It was very, very good. The one great failure was the fact that we were not given enough training or time to assimilate the Morse code because I know that when first I went out to France the gunner on the ground reading my Morse was having considerable difficulty in doing so until I'd been there at least two or three weeks.[37] T.E. Rogers, RFC

Bombing was diligently practised and the results assessed to judge the level of competence achieved and to allow improvement to be made.

I practised bomb dropping by day and night in all kinds of weather, into and with the wind, and from all heights up to two thousand five hundred feet. In the centre of the aerodrome a large circle had been painted in chalk;

an 'OK' consisted in dropping the bomb so that it fell anywhere within this circle ... After a week's constant practice most of us became fairly proficient in the art of bomb dropping. Sometimes one or other of us would be deputed to stand out on the aerodrome and 'mark' for another observer who was doing his tests. This was a rather trying job. We used to call it 'death dodging'. You would take your scoring card with its bull's eye and concentric circles marked upon it, and proceed to the spot as near to, or as far from, the target as your temperament dictated. Some fellows would stand in the geometric centre of the ring and allege that they felt safer there; others would hang about near the edge of the field, and with the fall of each bomb would dash forward, measure roughly its distance from the bull's eye, then retreat once more to the comparative security of the hedge ... The bombs employed were dummy fifteen-pounders – practically the same bombs as those used in France, but minus charge and detonator. They always hit the earth with a sound which can only be described in words as a 'concentrated wonk', and generally buried themselves several inches in the ground.[38] W.J. Harvey, RFC

The training programme that nurtured and harvested the British pilots, observers and gunners who fought in the First World War was at first riven with mistakes and misconceptions. The arts of flying, bombing and observation were in their infancy in 1914 with the only hope of piercing the veil an unscientific combination of guesswork and primitive experimentation. Yet the needs of the BEF on the Western Front were paramount and so, by hook or by crook, pilots and observers were produced and sent off to active service where all they had between themselves and an early grave was what knowledge they had gleaned from their haphazard training. In the hot-house of war, so the technical expertise of the mechanics of flying and all the related disciplines grew. Finally, as crystallised in the Smith–Barry training revolution, it became a science – still in its relative infancy – but with a known system of cause and effect which could be taught quickly and effectively.

CHAPTER SIX

1916

The failure to achieve a breakout in 1915 by thrusting through the German lines on the Western Front, as exemplified by Neuve Chapelle and Loos, led General Haig and the French Commander-in-Chief, General Joseph Joffre, to develop a theory of attrition to wear down the German reserves until the *coup de grâce* could be administered. In the summer of 1916 they agreed that the BEF would take the predominant role in the first joint offensive to this end which could then be followed by a decisive French thrust once the German Army was judged to have been terminally weakened. However, before this plan could be implemented, it was pre-empted by the unexpected eruption of a massive German assault on Verdun beginning on 21 February 1916. Foreshadowing the British and French strategy, the Germans also intended to wear down their enemies by picking a battleground that for reasons of national pride the French could not afford to abandon. Left with little option the French accepted the challenge but as the severe fighting at Verdun dragged on, they were forced to ask the British to adopt an ever greater role in the forthcoming summer offensive around the Somme and to bring forward its starting date.

The learning curve of 1915, coupled with the accelerated expansion of both the RFC and BEF, had made it apparent that a higher formation than the wing was required to co-ordinate the diverging work of the army's air force. By July 1916 the fighting strength of the RFC on the Western Front had expanded to twenty-seven squadrons from the twelve present at Loos the previous September. But a dichotomy had arisen between the regular local reconnaissance work, photographic mapping and artillery observation, which was required by each one of the army corps and the longer range reconnaissances that were of more interest to the army commanders. As a result, in early 1916 a major reorganisation of the RFC created three new brigades out of the existing wings. First Wing and Tenth Wing, together with an aircraft park and a kite-balloon section formed a complete aerial unit known as I Brigade under the command of Brigadier General Ashmore; similarly Second and Eleventh Wing were combined to form II Brigade under Brigadier General John Salmond; while Third and Twelfth Wings formed III Brigade under Brigadier General Higgins. Shortly after a Ninth Wing was formed for special strategic work under the direct control of General Headquarters, BEF. Trenchard himself was promoted to the rank of Major General.

At the root of this reorganisation was a new aerial offensive doctrine which Trenchard had been formulating with the French Air Commander, Commandant Paul-Fernand du Peuty. At the centre of Trenchard's philosophy was the unwavering belief that the RFC was a part of the army and entirely subordinate to its needs and wishes. No risks and no casualties were too great to prevent reconnaissance, artillery observation or bombing raids from being carried out if that was what was required. In turn the Germans had to be stopped from carrying out their own reconnaissance, artillery observation and bombing raids. In order to satisfy the expectations of other parts of the army a delicate balance had to be struck but the coveted prize was the overall mastery of the air.

If the RFC yielded too much to the demands for the defensive deployment of their resources then they would hand the initiative to the Germans. No matter how many aircraft were assigned to defensive patrols along the line, or covering artillery observation machines, it was just not possible to prevent enemy aircraft from breaking through. The secure and impregnable front line on the ground could not be reflected in the sky. Attacking aircraft moved and manoeuvred too fast. There were too many limitations on the amount of time defensive aircraft could patrol in the air, too much cover in the shifting mountains of cumulus cloud and constantly changing local weather conditions. No air force could guarantee that a determined and skilful aircraft would not get through, a fact succinctly recognised by the subsequent official history of the war in the air: 'Aeroplanes cannot be distributed like policemen across the face of the earth. The air service must carry the war into enemy territory and keep it there. The air war becomes a test of nervous endurance. The nation which keeps a stiff upper lip, and whose air service adheres to its determined offensive, of course will, in the end, secure the greatest measure of protection from the air for all its various activities.'[1] In rugby union terms this would be considered the equivalent of playing as much of the game as possible in the opponents' half and accepting the occasional breakaway try in return for overall domination and the inevitable points that would ensue from controlling most of the field.

The French experiences in the air during the Battle of Verdun in spring 1916 showed that if scout aircraft were pre-eminently deployed to protect reconnaissance and artillery observation aircraft as they went about their duties, then they would not be attending to their own work of clearing the sky of German aircraft. Therefore the 'working' machines must fend for themselves in times of trouble or the situation would only get worse. It was here that a strong nerve was required in the face of possibly severe casualties. In accordance with this theory the British concentrated all aircraft that would be needed to dominate the battlefield and its hinterland through offensive action into 'army wings'. The remaining aircraft were collected into 'corps wings' that would be free to reap a rich harvest of reconnaissance and artillery observation unmolested. In time it was believed this would prove the moral superiority of British aviators and would demoralise the Germans.

The first step in promoting this policy was the elimination of the Fokker scourge. The initial response of the RFC was far from impressive. In searching for a solution it devoted little time to the development of an interrupter mechanism of its own, the obvious answer, and instead investigated every other alternative imaginable.

Ideas for new gun-mountings, guns on the wings, guns on the top-plane, new schemes of attack, new aeroplanes – everything save the solution to the real problem to which, it seemed, our scientists refused to apply themselves. With characteristic British skill at compromise, our designers went so far as to produce an extraordinary craft which in their fertile brains did away with the problem altogether. It was called the B.E.9, but the reason for its unofficial name – 'The Pulpit' – was all too obvious. A little three-ply box projected from the Front of the machine, a box supported from ball-bearings running on an extension of the propeller shaft. The wretched man in this box had indeed an unrestricted forward view, but just behind his head revolved the four deadly blades of the propeller. There was no communication possible between front and back seat; if anything happened, if the pilot was wounded, or even if nothing more serious occurred than a bad landing in which the machine tipped over on its nose, the man in the box could but say his prayers; he would inevitably be crushed by the engine behind him. One of these machines was attached to the Squadron in which I served, but by the merciful dispensation of Providence it never succeeded in defeating an enemy craft. Had it done so I have no doubt that the brains of the Farnborough Factory would have rejoiced in their war-winning discovery, hundreds of 'Pulpits' would have been produced and in a short while we should not have had a living observer in France to tell the experts what it was like in that little box – for I feel sure that no civilian expert ever risked his own life in it.[2] Second Lieutenant Duncan Grinnell-Milne, 16 Squadron, RFC

One of the innovations which circumnavigated rather than solved the problem was the top wing Lewis gun mounting which offered many of the advantages of the interrupter gear.

We had a Flight Sergeant Fitzgerald with us who was absolutely mad on guns and he was a very good mechanic. He devised a scheme whereby you could put a Lewis gun on to the top plane of our Morane machines. When the gun was anchored in this position it fired straight ahead but just cleared the propeller tip as it was revolving. The gun was also mounted in such a way that when the ammunition was exhausted, the observer could reach up his hand, lower the gun, put on a new drum of ammunition and re-set it. Then the pilot could use that drum – he was able to aim the aircraft at the enemy whereas previously he had to fly at an angle and fire at about 60 degrees to his line of flight. You really aimed the aircraft at the enemy instead of trying to aim the gun – it was synchronised with the centre of the aircraft.[3] Air Mechanic/Observer S.S. Saunders, 1 Squadron RFC

Although the mounting developed by Fitzgerald was a success, it was another similar mechanism invented by Sergeant R.G. Foster of 11 Squadron that was officially adopted by the RFC and used on many British scouts right up until the end of the war. Yet, despite the effectiveness of top wing mountings, the Lewis gun had a limited rate of fire and the difficulties in changing the ammunition drum meant that it was better as an ancillary weapon rather than the main armament. It did not address what Fokker had proved to be a relatively simple mechanical problem.

Early in 1915 a new, multi-purpose 'pusher' aircraft, the FE2 B, had been produced by the Royal Aircraft Factory based on the pre-war Geoffrey de Havilland designed FE2 A which had incorporated many features of the ubiquitous Maurice Farman biplane. Unfortunately attempts by the Factory to get the machine into mass production had been beset by difficulties. Although the first FE2 B had reached the Western Front by May, it did not arrive in strength until January 1916 with the embarkation of the homogeneously equipped 20 Squadron. The FE2 B's 120 horsepower Beardmore engine generated a speed of seventy-two miles per hour at 7,000 feet and it could reach its service ceiling of 9,000 feet in forty-two minutes.

In the FE2 B the pilot was behind the observer in front of the engine and the observer was in the front nacelle or cockpit. In that cockpit I had three clips for the gun mounting to be assembled in. One for nose firing down, one firing to the right and one firing to the left. If you wanted to use the left gun the mounting used to be pulled out of its clip and it was swivelled round on to the left-hand clip. When you fired you had to put your knee against the mounting otherwise it would blow out with the explosion. In the rear you had one gun firing over the top plane on a movable mounting, a plunger arrangement where you just pressed the plunger underneath and the gun used to go as high as possible to fire over the back plane. In the cockpit you had spare drums and it was one of your duties to make certain that when you were firing the Lewis gun to see that you carry out all the necessary things for safe flying. For instance if you changed a drum you had to get hold of the drum on the gun, hold it very tight, take it off the gun, bend down and lay it very carefully in its compartment as an empty drum. We also had on the Lewis gun an ejector bag where the empty cartridge cases fell into. On one occasion my clip on my cartridge case gave way and all the rounds were whisked through the propeller in the windstream. The observer's job was in the main to keep his eye on enemy aircraft and if necessary to ask the pilot to move the plane into position if they spotted an enemy plane to make sure that he could get into a position to fire at it.[4] Sergeant Harold Taylor, 25 Squadron RFC

Although as a two-seater on its own it was still not much of a match for the Fokker, in formation the FE2 B could generate considerable firepower. On being attacked FE2 Bs would quickly form a circle in which each covered the tail of the machine in front and together they mustered a strength far greater than the sum of the individual parts. Any Fokker attacking a 'circle' of FE2 Bs was taking a severe risk and most did not bother.

The RFC's real answer to the Fokker was finally found in another Geoffrey de Havilland machine, the DH2. By the beginning of the war de Havilland had joined the Aircraft Manufacturing Company based at Hendon as Chief Designer and in mid-1915, before the Fokker had even made an impact, he built the first DH2. It was another 'pusher' biplane, like the Vickers Fighter and the FE2 B, but this time it was a single-seater and a true 'scout'. Despite the natural 'airy-fairy' appearance of pusher aircraft, the DH2 was sturdily constructed and mounted a 100 horsepower Gnome Monosoupape engine behind the pilot who had a Lewis gun in front of him normally fixed to fire straight ahead in the direction of flight. Despite having a smaller engine capacity than the FE2 B, the lesser weight that the DH2 carried gave it a better overall performance, with a speed of eighty-five miles per hour at 7,000 feet, to which height it could climb in just fourteen minutes, and a service ceiling of 14,000 feet. Although the pusher now seems an anomaly, in these early days it had many advantages in combat and its demise did not yet seem inevitable.

The pusher, with the engine behind, was to my mind the best form of aircraft in that you had visibility. What's the good of sending a fellow up in an aircraft where he is supposed to do observation, if he can only do about a quarter of it because he can't see out? His wings are always in the way! That's why I always thought the pusher was the finest form of aircraft and I couldn't understand why they were dropped – except that for the manufacturers and designers it was much easier to make a really fine tractor aircraft. You got better speed, better performance – it was very difficult to streamline a pusher.[5] Lieutenant F.J. Powell, 5 Squadron RFC

The DH2's main rival was the essentially similar FE8, again produced by the Royal Aircraft Factory, but the persistent production difficulties experienced there meant that the DH2 had a far greater impact on the war over the Western Front.

At first the DH2s arrived in penny packets and were generally allotted to those pilots who were considered best able to make use of their potential. These men were naturally keen to keep them exclusively as 'their' aircraft – partly to preserve their status and partly through fear of what other, ham-fisted pilots might do to them.

It was the prize for any pilot in the squadron to call himself the 'Scout'. At that time in the war an aeroplane and its pilot were indivisible. They weren't swapped about and no pilot flew another pilot's aircraft – they were guarded as jealously as one's girlfriend – not shared at all. You can imagine the excitement of young fellows in their teens all wanting to be the squadron scout pilot.[6] Lieutenant F.J. Powell, 5 Squadron RFC

Combat techniques evolved through the usual mixture of trial and error and the new British scouts found they could visit death on the German reconnaissance machines just as the BE2 Cs had suffered from the Fokker.

> You always got underneath the other fellow's tail because with his guns placed as they were he couldn't hit you but you could write your initials with your gun on the bottom of his fuselage. You had all the time in the world. The machines we were up against were these heavy Aviatiks which took a long time to turn round on a bank. If you were in a little Scout you had a much more adaptable machine – you could do quicker turns. You were manoeuvrable where these heavy cumbersome Aviatiks with Merc engines were so heavy in the nose that they had a job to dodge and swing and swivel.[7] Lieutenant F.J. Powell, 5 Squadron RFC

The first complete DH2 unit, 24 Squadron, arrived in France in February 1916. It was commanded by Major Lanoe Hawker VC who had instilled in his pilots his air fighting philosophy and pinned an admirably concise tactical order on the Squadron noticeboard, 'Attack everything'. When combat with the Germans finally began the DH2 showed conclusively that it was faster and more manoeuvrable than the Fokker. With the central advantage of its armament removed, the German aircraft's otherwise mediocre performance was ruthlessly exposed and by the time 32 Squadron, commanded by Major Lionel Rees, reached the Front in late May 1916 the DH2s had really begun to make their mark.

> If a Hun sees a De Hav he runs for his life; they won't come near them. It was only yesterday that one of the fellows came across a Fokker. The Fokker dived followed by the De Hav but the wretched Fokker dived so hard that when he tried to pull his machine out his elevator broke and he dived into our Lines; not a shot was fired.[8] Second Lieutenant Gwilym Lewis, 32 Squadron RFC

The Fokkers fought a more equal duel with the slower and less manoeuvrable FE2 Bs and both sides suffered casualties. The nature of the fighting was illustrated by the skirmish which took place on 31 May when four FE2 Bs and two Martinsyde Scouts on a reconnaissance mission were attacked by three Fokkers over Marquion.

> The Fokkers evidently worked on some prearranged plan as they were firing small white lights before swooping down. After the first attack which was made between us and the sun, the enemy showed much more caution in approaching near. It was in this first attack I think that Cairn Duff was shot down. Allen had his observer (Powell) shot dead as he was firing back and I rather think he got his man too as three of us saw one Fokker going down anyhow, side slipping and nose diving. Anyway Powell had his gun right 'on' as the bullet grazed his trigger finger and struck him in the eye. He fell back in the nacelle breaking one of his legs in the fall. Allen was now defenceless and in spite of the fact that the machine was shot to 'bits' just managed to scrape back over the lines, when his engine stopped. He got back into the aerodrome. While all this was going on Solly was making his notes in the most cool manner. I got him to man the after gun two or three times when I saw a Fokker coming up behind, but the escort kept him . . . Unfortunately Allen completely lost his nerve, and told me today that he could not go on flying. It was a terrible time for him as besides the fact of the engine gradually going worse and worse and finally stopping over the lines, the machine was in a dreadful state, covered in blood.[9] Captain Harold Wyllie, 23 Squadron RFC

Gradually the Fokkers began to respect the combined firepower that the seemingly cumbersome FE2 Bs could generate.

> Went on reconnaissance. Unfortunately the camera jammed. Five Fokkers hung on our tails but did not close in to fighting range. The wind was strong against us coming back. We were lucky not to have another running fight. Perhaps they realised we carry a sting in our tail.[10] Captain Harold Wyllie, 23 Squadron RFC

Indeed, one of the greatest German Fokker pilots was finally brought down to earth by the FE2 B. On 18 June, Immelmann was killed during a dogfight with Second Lieutenant G.R. McCubbin and his gunner Corporal J.H. Waller of 25 Squadron. Although there is some question as to whether Immelmann was actually shot down or, as the Germans claimed, crashed as a result of a catastrophic engine failure, the result was the same – the 'Eagle of Lille' was dead.

Other new aircraft continued to arrive during the first half of the year. The French developed a superb aircraft in the single-seater Nieuport Scout, examples of which came into service in some RFC squadrons in March 1916. Powered by the 110 horsepower Le Rhône engine it could achieve 107 miles per hour and had a ceiling of 17,400 feet. Its rate of climb was such that it could reach 10,000 feet in just over ten minutes. Its armament was the ubiquitous Lewis gun secured to the top wing firing safely over the propeller. Finally in May 1916, the British acquired their first tractor aircraft fitted with an interrupter gear to facilitate forward firing. The Sopwith two-seater known irreverently as the Sopwith '1½ Strutter' was a multi-purpose aircraft armed with a fixed Vickers machine-gun which had originally been devised for use by the RNAS.

Throughout 1915, as both the naval and military air services had expanded their roles and developed new areas of specialisation, bitter competition had arisen between them for the limited resources of the British aviation industry. In many ways this struggle was epitomised by the aeroplanes manufactured by Tom Sopwith, one of the pre-war pioneer designers who had constructed his first machine in 1911. It was eventually bought by the Admiralty and from that time on a close association had developed between them. Unhampered by the War Office's policy of preferring military aeroplanes to be developed by the Royal Aircraft Factory, the RNAS was able to foster the talented private sector through its basic requirement for a lesser number of more versatile machines. Following the outbreak of war, when the RNAS began to undertake a wider variety of operations and needed more machines to facilitate this, it was able to draw on a less constrained procurement network and found it easier to place its orders than the more heavily centralised organisation of the RFC.

Major General Henderson's return to the Directorate of Military Aeronautics in August 1915 was intended to help the RFC overcome this central problem and to accelerate the rate at which it could expand to meet the escalating demand by the army for air support. But once back at the War Office he discovered how great the logistical difficulties were in trying to keep up with the ever-growing calls from France for more men and machines, a need given even greater urgency by the rise in the casualty rate linked to the appearance of the Fokkers. Theoretically, the RFC in the Field was subordinate to the Directorate of Military Aeronautics and Henderson reigned supreme over both. But in reality, with the decline in the Directorate's influence resulting from Henderson's departure for France in August 1914, this position had become reversed. The required strength of the RFC was now determined solely by the size of its commitment to the BEF rather than a more realistic policy which took into account what Britain's industrial base could provide. Henderson had acquired the tricky job of solving this dilemma and in March 1916 he reorganised the Directorate by establishing clearer lines of responsibility. Brigadier General Brancker was brought back from France to become Director of Air Organisation and Brigadier General MacInnes, one of the original triumvirate who had drawn up the scheme for foundation of RFC in 1912, was appointed Director of Air Equipment, in charge of co-ordinating all aspects of the RFC's procurement.

In November 1915 Henderson had predicted that within six months the front-line strength of the RFC would be doubled from eighteen to thirty-six service squadrons. But as the overall size of each squadron was simultaneously to be increased from twelve to eighteen aeroplanes, the remaining twenty-four squadrons needed to bring the RFC to the desired establishment of sixty squadrons would not be available before the end of 1916. In the end, even this modest timetable slipped behind schedule. The main fault lay in the embryonic nature of the country's aero-engine industry. Having relied so heavily before 1914 on engines imported from France, few British companies had any experience of their manufacture and those that had produced them were generally used to making French engines under licence. These had been mostly rotary engines, in which the engine revolved around the crankshaft, but some had been in-line, in which fixed pistons drove a moving shaft. Despite the urgent need to create an aero-engine industry practically from nothing, by the end of 1916 imports still accounted for almost a quarter of those used by British aircraft manufacturers. The difficulties of procuring sufficient quantities of engines to meet the rising demands of the RFC in the Field were exacerbated by the burgeoning competition with the RNAS, which also needed engines for the aircraft it had ordered.

By January 1916 Henderson was deeply concerned that this unco-ordinated, simultaneous demand might seriously compromise the RFC's ability to maintain its expansion programme and he raised this point with the War Committee, which since November 1915 had exercised overall responsibility for the strategic conduct of the war on behalf of the Cabinet.

There is only a limited amount of aeronautical material available for both services, particularly with regard to the supply of engines. I do not anticipate serious difficulty in providing aeroplanes of suitable design and in sufficient quantity: but the question of high-powered engines is serious, and is at present chiefly affecting the military service . . . The Royal Flying Corps is now suffering from a lack of suitable engines for its necessary daily work, while it is understood that the Admiralty is using a large number of the most suitable engines for land work.[11] Major General Sir David Henderson, Director-General of Military Aeronautics

In addition to the problem of the small number of engines being made available, the Directorate was anxious about their capacity. Most of the licensed French engines were between 80 and 100 horsepower. But the new generation of faster, more effective planes now being produced needed better engines to deliver their superior performance. With no earlier models of their own on which to base new designs, British industry would have to design prototypes and put them into production from scratch and, although by the end of 1916 over 5,000 engines had been produced in Britain, as opposed to 1,720 in 1915, their quality was highly unpredictable. Unfortunately this fact was often not discovered until large orders had already been placed.

★   ★   ★

S F Cody, the pioneer pilot and aircraft designer, beside his biplane which triumphed at the Military Aeroplane Trials of 1912.

A BE2 flying past General Sir Horace Smith-Dorrien and his staff at an early air review in May 1913.

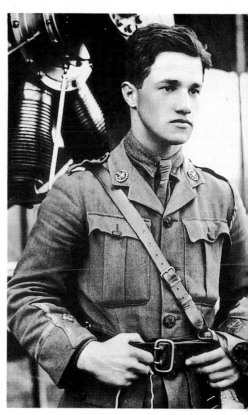

Four British scout VCs (*clockwise from top left*): Lanoe Hawker, Albert Ball, James McCudden (photographed when an Air Mechanic in 1914) and Edward Mannock.

'The Office' – the cockpit of an SE5 A scout showing its primary armament (*left*), a Vickers .303 machine gun, and (*right*) an Aldis sight through which the gun was aimed.

Officers and SE5 A scouts of 85 Squadron, RAF at St Omer, 21 June 1918.

The Maurice Farman Longhorn, employed as a reconnaissance aircraft on the Western Front in 1914, it became familiar to many pilots as a two seater training aircraft.

The BE2 A, the first of the BE2 series of aircraft which formed the mainstay of British reconnaissance right up to 1917. The pilot of this aeroplane, Hubert Harvey-Kelly (*seen casually smoking against the haystack on the right*), was the first British airman to land in France following the outbreak of war.

The Sopwith Camels of 44 Squadron at Hainault Farm deployed to meet the Gotha menace in the summer of 1917. The Camel remains possibly the best known First World War aeroplane.

The DH4s of 27 Squadron at Serny, Pas de Calais on 17 February 1918.

Oswald Boelcke (*left*) and Max Immelmann (*right*), with (*below*) the Fokker EIII flown by Boelcke showing his machine gun and interrupter gear which allowed the gun to fire through his propeller arc.

Manfred, Freiherr von Richtofen (*left*) and Werner Voss (*right*).

The aerodrome of Jasta 12 in Belgium.

Form: W3348. Army Form W 334.

Combats in the Air.

Squadron: 56.

Type and No. of Aeroplane: S.E.5. No B.4891.

Armament: Vickers and Lewis.

Pilot: Capt. J.B.McCudden.D.S.O.,M.C.

Observer: None.

Locality: E of Oppy.
Nr Cherisy.

Date: 26/2/18.

Time: 10 21.. 11.30 a.m.

Duty: Spl Mission.

Height: 17,000ft.
15,000ft.

Remarks on Hostile machine :- Type. armament. speed. etc.

E.A. Rumpler.

E.A. Albatross Fighter.

— Narrative. —

Left aerodrome at 10.am. and at 10 30 engaged a L.V.G. over
Gonnelieu from 14,000 down to 10,000 ft, firing 200 rounds at
varying ranges. E.A. fought skilfully and at last got away E
apparently alright. Now saw 4 S.E.'s of 84 Sqdn engaging 3
Albatross scouts above me. I climbed and joined in the fight and
the E.A. were driven down East. Went N climbing and at 11.20
attacked a Rumpler at 17,000 over Oppy as he was recrossing his
lines. Opened fire at 200 yards and fired until E.A. burst into
flames and then fell to pieces, the wreckage falling E of Oppy at
11.21. Went S and attacked an Albatross fighter who was escorting
a D.F.W. over Cherisy at 15,000 at 11.30. Opened fire at 200 yards
and continued firing until E.A. fell to pieces, the wreckage
falling near Cherisy. (This machine had the double tail plane
and is known in this Sqdn as an Albatross Fighter, bearing a
close resemblance to the scout of that name, only it is a
2-seater).

Went N climbing and at 12 a.m. attacked a Rumpler
at 18,000 ft over Fresnoy. Opened fire at 300 yards range with
both guns and pieces fell off E.A. resembling maps or perhaps
plates. Vickers now finished ammunition and Lewis gave a Stoppage,
so had to leave E.A., who went down steeply but flattened out
later, and I last saw E.A. at about 15,000 ft at 12.5 p.m. over
Beaumont, N.W. of Douai under control. Returned 12.20.

J.B. McCudden

2 E.A. destroyed confirmed by A.A.

2 Brought down
(Nor'e)

56. SQUADRON
ROYAL FLYING CORPS
NO.... DATE 26/2/18

Combat report written by James McCudden in February 1918 at the height of his
career.

In France artillery observation work by the RFC was expanding at a phenomenal rate in an effort to keep pace with the equally staggering increase in artillery units coming on-stream and into line. The methodology of air observation and effective communication between aircraft and battery underwent constant reviews. Procedures and equipment that had seemed reasonably efficient at Neuve Chapelle in March 1915 were plainly inadequate when required to cope with the grind of day-to-day operations twelve months later. Demand for up-to-the-minute photographs of the front-line areas had also mushroomed. Corps staff gave their requests directly to 'their' attached squadron who would take the required photographs and have them developed and printed in their own small photographic sections. Photographic interpretation developed into a new field of expertise as the effects of contour configuration, light sources and shadows were studied to reveal the shape and size of the smallest features and to reveal such vital information as the position of trench mortar-emplacements, unit headquarters and new barbed-wire concentrations.

Technical developments meanwhile had reduced the weight of wireless equipment and minimised the effects of 'jamming' caused by too many airborne wireless operators signalling in close proximity to each other. Zone calls had been developed whereby limited areas of the battlefield were deemed the responsibility of specific batteries and the aerial observer could call down fire on a 'target of opportunity' without convoluted prior arrangements. Simply by broadcasting the target zone call sign the relevant battery would swing into action and the results of their fire could be corrected in the normal way using the clock code. The nature of the co-operation between the RFC and the Royal Artillery was under constant scrutiny but inevitably there was occasional friction as they attempted to define the limits of their symbiotic relationship. Such problems could only be resolved through the exercise of patience and both sides recognising the operational difficulties that the other faced. This was not always forthcoming.

The real crux of the controversy is that the artillery have a profound distrust & contempt for the Flying Corps, and have a terror of 'allowing their guns to be run by the Flying Corps'. This is the phrase which is always produced in such controversies. As a matter of fact there are many cases when the Flying Corps are the only people who can run the artillery, & if they are not even allowed to have priority in the use of one gun they are practically wasted. The artillery are apt to exaggerate their accuracy when firing without aerial observation I think. Both sides lost their tempers.[12] Recording Officer Lieutenant Thomas Hughes, 1 Squadron RFC

In anticipation of the summer offensive new methods were devised to establish the position of the leading waves in the infantry attack using small flares and reflective triangles fixed on to the backs of soldiers to catch the sunlight. Aircraft would furthermore try to fly much lower to ensure that they could actually see what progress the infantry was making. Here again there were some problems in trying to harmonise the requirements of the infantry in action with the contact aircraft.

Major Lumsden of the 5th Corps also arrived with a couple of umbrellas, ordinary umbrellas, painted half white, in sections. His idea was that the infantry should indicate their position to an aeroplane by opening & shutting their umbrellas. I think he was rather offended when I laughed. I did not gather whether it would be the Colonel who would leap over the parapet with a joyous shout & lead the charge brandishing his umbrella.[13] Recording Officer Lieutenant Thomas Hughes, 1 Squadron RFC

Bombing was also gradually increased in both quantity and scope. Individual aircraft were used to provide a constant dribble of bombs on to the German side of the lines – partly for the sheer nuisance value of such activities and also to help keep the aircrews 'up to the mark'.

All machines that flew up to the lines and across had to always carry two 20-lb bombs and drop them on any target they thought was worthwhile. The object of this was to make quite sure that the pilots did cross the lines and go over enemy territory. Very often they rather shirked that through nerve tiredness – they preferred not to do it. Across the lines is always more dangerous than your own side. They had to get across the lines to do it and choose some railway station or whatever it might be that they thought it might be useful to bomb. Not that they ever hit them so it didn't much matter but still they dropped the bombs and got across the line which was the object of the exercise.[14] Lieutenant Alan Jackson, 5 Squadron RFC

The FE2 B squadrons were maids of all work and were frequently assigned to bombing raids.

Standing by to drop bombs on railhead. Ordered to attempt it, wind blowing up from West about 50 to 55 mph and could not climb well on account of extra weight of bombs. Nearly had a bad smash getting off as got a bad bump which stalled the machine and she crashed back on one wheel – a horrid moment with four bombs in the rack. Could only get to 8,500 in 1½ hours. Went across and dropped bombs, on railway at Fampoux. Got heavily shelled coming out. One nearly got us with a direct hit and burst above. No machine hit for a wonder, as 20 mph is no speed to dally over Archie with.[15] Captain Harold Wyllie, 23 Squadron RFC

Night bombing raids were seen as an important future development and preliminary trials were held in the still largely uncharted area of night flying.

We only went out on bright moonlight nights. We used to fly over to some important railway junction and drop a couple of 112-lb bombs and then come home again. We were supplied with signal pistols to fire on our way home, with given codes so that we would know if the ground was clear for us to land. If we lost our way and we wanted to find our aerodrome we would fire red lights, and all the aerodromes would send up their different coloured rockets. This scheme worked wonderfully until Brother Boche tumbled to it; and on one moonlit night he came over with several machines, fired some red lights, which were answered at once by all our squadrons, and then bombed the lot, and went home again laughing. After this episode codes were adopted.[16] Lieutenant Robin Rowell, 8 Squadron RFC

*   *   *

By early summer 1916 the steady haemorrhaging of French resources at Verdun meant that the great Anglo-French offensive planned by Joffre and Haig to straddle the river Somme would, for the first time, be a predominantly British affair, with the BEF fielding twenty-two divisions in comparison to a smaller French force of just eight. Haig's intention was to advance his line along either side of the Roman road which ran from Albert to Bapaume until he had captured the Pozières Ridge. This initial success would then be exploited by a reserve force of cavalry and infantry who would move rapidly to the north and roll up the German line. The central British attack on an eighteen-mile front was eventually set for 1 July. In the main part it was to be carried out by the Fourth Army under General Sir Henry Rawlinson who ordered a massive preliminary bombardment to increase the chances of achieving a rapid thrust during the opening phase. The troops were told that this alone would destroy the German defences enabling them to move forward with relative ease. In the event, despite it being the largest bombardment ever fired by the British Army prior to that date and expending 1,700,000 shells, it failed to destroy the deep defences that the Germans had built over the previous two years. When the moment came for the British troops to leave their trenches the enemy were waiting and massive casualties were inflicted on the assaulting infantry.

To support the operations of the Fourth Army during the battle a new RFC unit, IV Brigade, was formed under the command of Brigadier General Ashmore who had been transferred from I Brigade. Of its two component wings, the Third was to be responsible for the 'corps' operations of artillery observation and photographing the German defences, while the Fourteenth was placed under the direct control of Fourth Army Headquarters. All the squadrons of both formations had recently been increased to the new standard establishment of eighteen aircraft working in three flights. The Ninth Wing from RFC Headquarters was also moved to the Somme to be directly responsible for strategic reconnaissance, as well as undertaking the brunt of the planned effort to sweep the German Air Service from the skies. In addition the Fourth Army had the artillery observation services of 1 Balloon Squadron RFC which was comprised of five kite-balloon sections. Since the middle of 1915 kite balloons, through their steady 'eye in the sky', had offered yet another weapon in the artillery war but necessarily static in nature, they lacked the flexibility of observation aircraft.

During the first weeks of June, Cecil Lewis, a young scout pilot, watched in fascination as the artillery batteries began to concentrate in the Somme area. Once they finally began their bombardment in earnest on 24 June, he found the sky to be literally full of shells.

The batteries were being piled in night after night – the roads were roaring with the traffic going up as the guns went into position. This enormous feeling of the build-up of a big offensive. The day was peaceful, there wasn't a thing on the road. As soon as dusk came it started and it went right through the night. Our billets were right on the road and one had a tremendous feeling of war and what it meant. When everything was in position they began to build up to the main bombardment which lasted for about a week before the actual offensive took place. We used to go out and photograph and these jobs were among the most terrifying that I ever did in the whole war. By that time we were flying very much lower – down to 1,000 feet – and when you had to go right over the lines you were mid-way between our guns firing and where the shells were falling. The intensity of the bombardment was such that it was really like a broad swathe of dirty-looking cotton wool laid over the ground so close and continual were the shell bursts. When you looked on the other side, particularly in the evening, the whole of the ground beneath the darkening sky was just like a veil of sequins which were flashing and flashing and flashing and each one was a gun. One knew that these things were coming over all the time. The artillery had orders not to fire when an aeroplane was in their sights – they cut it pretty fine you know! One used to fly along the Front on those patrols and the aeroplane was flung up with a shell that had just gone underneath and missed you by two or three feet; or flung down when it had gone over the top. This was continuous so the machine was bucketing and jumping as if it was in a gale but it was shells. You didn't see them – they were going much too fast but this was really terrifying. One had the sort of feeling that they were flying at us – it's us they wanted to get – this was extraordinarily ridiculous but quite terrifying. At last, having finished the photos and got out of the buffeting I thought, 'Well heavens alive I've come through that!'[17] Second Lieutenant Cecil Lewis, 3 Squadron RFC

On one occasion Lewis was particularly lucky when he saw a howitzer shell pass his machine in mid-air.

Out of the corner of my eye, when I wasn't really looking, I saw something moving like a lump. I didn't really know what the devil it was. It was a mystifying sort of effect. Then I looked again and focused and about 100 yards ahead there was the business part of a 9-inch howitzer shell right at the top of its trajectory – just about 8,000 feet. It had come up like a lobbed tennis ball and right at the top it was going quite slowly and it was a pretty hefty bit of metal, turning end over end before it gathered speed again and went off down to the ground again. The battery was evidently firing and we saw two or three shells and once you had caught them you could follow them right down to burst.[18] Second Lieutenant Cecil Lewis, 3 Squadron RFC

The bombardment reached its crescendo as the infantry prepared to surge over the top at seven thirty a.m. on 1 July. Lewis had a spectacular view of the explosion of the La Boiselle mines which immediately preceded the initial assault.

When the zero hour came I was on the first patrol on the northern part of the salient from Pozières down to Fricourt. They'd put down two enormous mines right on the front-line hoping to clear the whole of the front-line with this enormous burst. This was what we were looking for. We had our watches synchronised. We were up at about 8,000 feet and really it was a fantastic sight because when the hurricane bombardment started every gun we had, and there were thousands of them, had all been let loose at once. It was wild. You could hear the roar of the guns above the noise of the aircraft like rain on a pane. Extraordinary this roll of thousands of guns at the same time. Then came the blast when we were looking at the La Boiselle Salient. Suddenly the whole earth heaved and up from the ground came great cone shaped lifts of earth up to 3,000, 4,000, 5,000 feet. A moment later we struck the repercussion wave of the blast which flung us over right away backwards, over on one side away from the blast.[19] Second Lieutenant Cecil Lewis, 3 Squadron RFC

Lessons had been learnt from the failure of the contact patrols in 1915 and there were high hopes that the new methods would be more successful in providing accurate information about the forward locations of the attacking infantry. Unfortunately, as the infantry launched themselves 'over the top', Lewis was soon made all too aware of the difference between successful exercises in training and their execution under battle conditions.

We had all our contact patrol technique perfected and we went right down to 3,000 feet to see what was happening. We had a klaxon horn on the undercarriage of the Morane – a great big 12-volt klaxon and I had a button which I used to press out a letter to tell the infantry that we wanted to know where they were. When they heard us honking at them from above they had little red Bengal flares, they carried them in their pockets, they would put a match to their flares. All along the line wherever there was a chap there would be a flare and we would note these flares down on the map and Bob's your uncle! It was one thing to practise this but quite another thing for them to really do it when they were under fire and particularly when things began to go a bit badly. Then they jolly well wouldn't light anything and small blame to them because it drew fire of the enemy on to them at once. So we went down looking for flares and we only got about two flares on the whole front. We were bitterly disappointed because this we hoped was our part to

help the infantry and we weren't able to do it.[20] Second
Lieutenant Cecil Lewis, 3 Squadron RFC

As Hawker had found during the Second Battle of Ypres in April
1915, the desperate fliers were forced to fly ever lower to try to
determine where the infantry were by the actual colour of their
uniforms and, more alarmingly, whether the troops in question
opened fire on their machines or not! The contact aircraft were
shot about but none was actually brought down. The resulting
reports were of mixed value: some were over–optimistic; some
just plain wrong and some valuable reports were ignored in the
chaotic nature of events.

Throughout the day 22 and 24 Squadrons maintained a continuous series of patrols to prevent any interference by German
aircraft above the battlefield. One observer in an FE2 B had a
dreadful experience.

I was with Captain Webb and we went about 4 or 5
miles over the German lines in his machine on 1 July
at 11 am. We saw eight German machines approaching
from south-west – they were higher than us, and we
flew towards them to attack. Two passed over our heads
together about 300 yards or so apart, and I opened fire on
one. They both replied together. I gave the signal to Webb
to turn so that I could fire at the other machine behind
us, but he put the machine's head down. I turned to see
what was the matter, and he pointed to his abdomen and
collapsed over the 'joy stick'. He died in a few seconds I
think, but his last thought was to save his machine. The
machine at once began turning towards the German side,
and I had to get back to my machine-gun to fire at a
machine diving at us. This happened again and again,
but my fire always prevented them finishing the dive.
Other machines fired from above all the time. I only had
time to get the machine pointing towards our lines when
I had to get back to the gun. I never got the chance to
pull Webb out of the pilot's seat, so I had to steer with my
hand over the windscreen. I didn't expect to get off alive,
but tried to put up as good a fight as possible, and tried all
the time to keep her towards our lines, but having to man

the gun so often made it impossible to make progress, but the erratic course the machine flew probably saved it. At last, still being fired at, I got right down near the ground and proceeded to make a landing, as it was all I could do. I saw a lot of men with rifles, and realised that I might get shot before I could set fire to the machine, so I, at the last minute, put her nose down in order to crash. One wing tip hit first, the whole machine was destroyed, I was hurled out and escaped with a bruised and paralysed side and broken ankle and rib.[21] Lieutenant W.O. Tudor-Hart, 22 Squadron

Although they suffered losses these patrols distracted the German scouts from their real target – the British corps artillery and reconnaissance aircraft.

From their unique viewing platform, buffeted about by passing shells, the pilots watched the tragedy of failure unfolding below them. Although some ground was gained in the Montauban and Mametz sectors, in most areas along the whole battlefront the infantry were cut down as they attempted to cross no man's land. During the first day alone British casualties totalled 57,470 killed, wounded and missing. This successful German resistance did not daunt the British High Command who continued the offensive by launching a series of determined attacks. Through the high summer and autumn Haig's New Armies were led through the mincing machine of his own creation. In such a battle the artillery observation and reconnaissance duties performed by the RFC were invaluable. As German artillery reinforcements arrived it was vital that they were located and deluged with shells as soon as possible, or they would do the same to the British batteries. At a tactical level it was also crucial, but extremely difficult, to identify exactly where the often isolated pockets of British and German troops were in the chaos of the shell-spattered battlefield. The third main facet of RFC operations was the bombing of significant targets previously identified behind the German front line.

The bombing raids had the usual mixed results, with some direct hits being scored on trains and stations, but in order to achieve these results casualties were initially very heavy. The main cause of this was the trial introduction of the policy of 'distant escorts' as opposed to 'close escorts' to the bombing formations. It was felt that close escorts, who actually flew with the bombers, were not necessary for raids within thirty miles of the front-line and that any aircraft generally on patrol in that area could act as a deterrent to German aircraft, thus forming a distant escort. Since, even with this second-hand protection, the bombing aircraft were deemed 'escorted', no observers were carried in their heavily-laden BE2 Cs. In the event distant patrols were easily breached by the Germans leaving the bombers almost defenceless and in the first two days of the offensive the RFC lost eight aircraft with many others badly shot up. This was not acceptable even to Trenchard and close escorts were immediately reintroduced.

The main tactical targets for bombing were the villages known to be used as troop billets or supply dumps. These were relentlessly pounded day and night. This not only resulted in casualties and material damage but it severely affected the morale of German troops many of whom were already at the limits of their endurance from their experiences during the intense ground fighting. Attacks were also launched against German airfields, with the intention of crippling their air strength when it was lying helpless on the ground. The key strategic targets remained the train lines which linked the Somme battlefield area with the rest of the German railway system. Three of the key junctions were at Marcoing, Epehy and Velu and titanic battles developed, with the German scout formations fighting hard to prevent successful raids. One such raid against the junction at Marcoing was carried out on 30 July by seven Martinsydes of 27 Squadron escorted by four Sopwith 1½ Strutters of 70 Squadron.

The patrol seemed to break up just as we were crossing the lines. As I didn't see any signals to return and as I still had a Sopwith with me I went on to Marcoing and dropped my bombs both of which fell in the village – I turned quickly round and almost ran into an LVG, I gave him a drum and at the same time I heard a machine-gun behind me, looked round and saw three Rolands on my tail. I was hit in the leg almost immediately, but managed to give them a drum of my side gun and they went away, my engine started spluttering and I saw a hole in my petrol tank – my engine stopped so I started gliding down thinking I should have to land – petrol flowing

all over my left leg so I put my left knee over the hole in the petrol tank. It struck me that by pumping I might be able to get up a little pressure, by this time I was about 200 feet up – the engine started and I was then about 15 miles from our lines, I kept pumping hard all the time and just managed to keep enough engine to keep going – I thought I should have to land three or four times.[22]
Second Lieutenant R.H.C. Usher, 27 Squadron RFC

Usher was lucky because, although harassed by ground fire, he was not attacked by any more German scouts and he just regained the British lines. Despite being expensive in terms of men and machines, the bombing raids did damage installations, material and men and the efforts of the German Air Force were forced on to the defensive depriving their hard-pressed infantry of even basic support.

As the battle raged one pilot became increasingly influential within the RFC. Albert Ball achieved a string of successes in shooting down German aircraft while flying a Nieuport Scout first with 11 and then 60 Squadrons. Where Ball made his greatest impact was in his sheer vigour and panache. Whenever there was even an inkling of an opportunity to shoot down German aircraft he pursued it. Often spending hours in the air on solo patrols, always seeking combat, never heeding the odds against him, he was the very spirit of *l'offensive*. Ball had developed a combat method perfectly adjusted to his own skills, temperament and aircraft. Unfortunately his personalised method of fighting made it impossible for less accomplished individuals to follow his example.

To surprise his enemy he made clever use of the Lewis gun mounting on the Nieuport Scout. There was a curved rail down which the gun had to be run to change drums. By exerting pressure on one side of the stock of the gun, he held it rigid when nearly down and pointing upwards at about 80 degrees. By skilful manoeuvre – and incidentally by pluck and determination – he was able to zoom up beneath his intended victim; then, by a slight oscillation of the control stick to cause his gun to rake the target fore and aft, at a range of 30 feet or so . . . I found that my own efforts to emulate Ball in reaching a favourable position beneath a Hun so irritated it that a mêlée ensued in which I soon lost any idea of what was its 'underneath' and what was its 'top'.[23] Second Lieutenant Roderic Hill, 60 Squadron RFC

Ball had a particular reputation for attacking large formations without any hesitation but again his own advice, although well intentioned, cannot have been reassuring to novice pilots.

NOTE RE ATTACKING FORMATION WITH A LEWIS GUN AND FOSTER MOUNTING. If a scout attacks a large formation of HA [Hostile Aircraft], I think it is best to attack from above and dive in among them, getting under the nearest machine. Pull gun down and fire up into HA. If you get it, a number of HA will put their noses down and make off. Don't run after them, but wait for the HA that don't run, and again take the nearest machine. If they all run wait for a bit and look out for a straggler. One is nearly always left behind. Go for that & give it a drum, at the same time keeping your eyes as much as possible on the other machines, as they may get together and get round you. If fighting on the Boche's side (as you mostly are), never use your last drum, unless forced to do so. Keep it to help you on your way back. A Hun can always tell when you are out of ammunition and he at once closes with you, and if they are in formation, you stand no chance. Keep this last drum and when you want to get back, manoeuvre for a chance to break away, and if they follow you, as they mostly do, keep turning on them and firing a few rounds at long range. When this is done they nearly always turn and run. This gives you a chance to get on the way home.[24] Captain Albert Ball, 60 Squadron RFC

An idea of the nature of his commitment to attack and refusal to retreat unless absolutely necessary can be seen in his advice as to what to do in the event of the Lewis gun jamming in action.

I do not think it advisable to give up a scrap on account of a small jam. If you are faster than HA and he is a

scout like yourself, and you have a small jam, don't give up the flight, but try to keep on his blind side, and at the same time correct your jam. You don't get a chance for a Hun every day so don't give in when the slightest bit of trouble arises. He won't know you have a jam, but will think you are holding fire to get a better position or a better chance. If you cannot correct jam, then, naturally, you must break away, but don't break away at once. Manoeuvre until you get a favourable chance.[25]
Captain Albert Ball, 60 Squadron RFC

Ball was granted a roving commission to fly as he desired and his 'score' of victories mounted rapidly. By the time he returned home for a rest at the beginning of October 1916 he was credited with thirty 'kills', and had been awarded both the Military Cross and the Distinguished Service Order with two Bars, the first soldier to achieve this. Such 'scores' and decorations were, and are, extremely difficult to assess and it is perhaps safest to treat them as a guide to effective performance rather than a method of grading individual abilities in a profession governed by a thousand random factors. In a sense Ball was the first real British 'ace', though the term was rightly never accepted by Trenchard or the air authorities who considered that such a system of 'recognition' was invidious when the work of others in the less glamorous fields of artillery observation and reconnaissance had equally far-reaching but less immediately obvious ramifications.

The offensive attitude which Trenchard had hoped would be inculcated into all RFC crew was well-understood by most pilots and observers even though they also recognised the danger that it posed to their own longevity by subjecting them to continuous patrols over German territory.

Offensive patrols are well worthwhile, but for the comfort of those directly concerned they are rather too exciting. When friends are below during an air duel a pilot is warmly conscious that should he or his machine be crippled he can break away and land, and there's an end of it. But if a pilot be wounded in a scrap far away from home, before he can land he must fly for many miles, under shellfire and probably pursued by enemies. He must conquer the blighting faintness which accompanies loss of blood, keep clear-headed enough to deal instantaneously with adverse emergency, and make an unwilling brain command unwilling hands and feet to control a delicate apparatus. Worst of all, if his engine be put out of action at a spot beyond gliding distance of the lines, there is nothing for it but to descend and tamely surrender.[26] Lieutenant Alan Bott, 70 Squadron RFC

Bott had his own series of increasingly tight shaves during an offensive patrol acting as the observer to Lieutenant A.M. Vaucour in a Sopwith 1½ Strutter on 24 August 1916. After a clash with a trio of German aircraft, and a severe working over from German anti-aircraft fire, they continued their patrol undaunted.

> Some little distance ahead, and not far below, was a group of five Albatross two-seaters. Vaucour pointed our machine at them, in the wake of the flight commander's bus. Next instant the fuselage shivered. I looked along the inside of it and found that a burning shell fragment was lodged on a longeron, half-way between my cockpit and the tail-plane. A little flame zigzagged over the fabric, all but died away, but, being fanned by the wind as we lost height, recovered and licked its way towards the tail. I was too far away to reach the flame with my hands, and the fire extinguisher was by the pilot's seat. I called for it into the speaking-tube. The pilot made no move. Once more I shouted. Again no answer. Vaucour's ear-piece had slipped from under his cap. A thrill of acute fear passed through me as I stood up, forced my arm through the rush of wind and grabbed Vaucour's shoulder. 'Fuselage burning! Pass the fire extinguisher!' I yelled. My words were drowned in the engine's roar; and the pilot, intent on getting near the Boches, thought I had asked which one we were to attack. 'Look out for those two Huns on the left,' he called over his shoulder. 'Pass the fire extinguisher!' 'Get ready to shoot, blast you!' 'Fire extinguisher, you ruddy fool!' A backward glance told me that the fire was nearing the tail-plane at the one end and my box of ammunition at the other, and was too

serious for treatment by the extinguisher unless I could get it at once. Desperately I tried to force myself through the bracing-struts and cross-wires behind my seat. To my surprise, head and shoulders and one arm got to the other side – a curious circumstance, as afterwards I tried repeatedly to repeat this contortionist trick on the ground, but failed every time. There I stuck, for it was impossible to wriggle farther. However, I could now reach part of the fire, and at it I beat with gloved hands. Within half a minute most of the fire was crushed to death. But a thin streak of flame, outside the radius of my arm, still flickered towards the tail. I tore off one of my gauntlets and swung it furiously on to the burning strip. The flame lessened, rose again when I raised the glove, but died out altogether after I had hit it twice more. The load of fear left me, and I discovered an intense discomfort, wedged in as I was between the two crossed bracing-struts. Five minutes passed before I was able, with many a heave and gasp, to withdraw back to my seat. By now we were at close grips with the enemy, and our machine and another converged on a Hun. Vaucour was firing industriously. As we turned, he glared at me, and knowing nothing of the fire, shouted: 'Why the hell haven't you fired yet?' I caught sight of a Boche bus below us, aimed at it, and emptied a drum in short bursts. It swept away but not before two of the German observer's bullets had plugged our petrol tank from underneath.[27] Lieutenant Alan Bott, 70 Squadron RFC

They were at a height of 9,000 feet and just under ten miles from the British lines when the loss of fuel caused their engine to stop and they began the long glide back desperately calculating whether they could make it. Then, to complete a perfect day, a German scout attacked.

Taking advantage of our plight, its pilot dived steeply from a point slightly behind us. We could not afford to lose any distance by dodging, so Vaucour did the only thing possible – he kept straight on. I raised my gun, aimed at the wicked-looking nose of the attacking craft, and met it with a barrage of bullets. These must have worried the Boche, for he swerved aside when a hundred and fifty yards distant, and did not flatten out until he was beneath the tail of our machine. Afterwards he climbed away from us, turned, and dived once more. For a second time we escaped, owing either to some lucky shots from my gun or to the lack of judgement by the Hun pilot. The scout pulled up and passed ahead of us. It rose and manoeuvred as if to dive from the front and bar the way. Meanwhile, four specks, approaching from the west, had grown larger and larger, until they were revealed as of the F.E. type – the British 'pusher' two-seater. The Boche saw them, and hesitated as they bore down on him. Finding himself in the position of a lion attacked by hunters when about to pounce on a tethered goat, he decided not to destroy, for in so doing he would have laid himself open to destruction. When I last saw him he was racing north-east.[28] Lieutenant Alan Bott, 70 Squadron RFC

All that was left for Bott and Vaucour to do was endure the attentions of Archie, machine-guns and rifle fire as they drifted ever lower – just skating over no man's land – to crash land finally just behind the French lines. Here the French infantry were bemused to find Bott and Vaucour animatedly discussing their mutual misunderstandings. The strain of such operations can perhaps be best illustrated by the fact that Vaucour had an almost identical experience when he was hit by anti-aircraft fire the very next day and this time his observer, Air Mechanic Warminger, died of the wounds he received.

During the Somme offensive Trenchard's offensive policy was particularly effective but the repetitive strain and mounting casualties led some to resent what they considered to be a simplistic and brutal approach.

Trenchard follows the good military principle of repeating any tactics that have not been actually disastrous – and often those that have – again and again, regardless of the fact that the enemy will probably think out some very good reply, until they really are so disastrous that they have to be abandoned.[29] Recording Officer Lieutenant Thomas Hughes, 1 Squadron RFC

In truth, although Trenchard's was a simple plan and apparently expensive in men and machines, it does seem to have been effective in putting the Germans on the back foot and forcing them to utilise all their resources in defensive patrolling, an essentially fruitless task that distracted them from the main battle fought on the ground. The German High Command were fully aware of how much the British had gained from their mastery of the Somme skies.

The beginning and the first weeks of the Somme battle were marked by a complete inferiority of our own air forces. The enemy's aeroplanes enjoyed complete freedom in carrying out distant reconnaissances. With the aid of aeroplane observation, the hostile artillery neutralised our guns and was able to range with the most extreme accuracy on the trenches occupied by our infantry; the required data for this were provided by undisturbed trench reconnaissance and photography. By means of bombing and machine-gun attacks from a low height against infantry, battery positions and marching columns, the enemy's aircraft inspired our troops with a feeling of defencelessness against the enemy's mastery of the air. On the other hand, our own aeroplanes only succeeded in quite exceptional cases in breaking through the hostile patrol barrage and carrying out distant reconnaissances; our artillery machines were driven off whenever they attempted to carry out registration for their own batteries. Photographic reconnaissance could not fulfil the demands made upon it. Thus at decisive moments, the infantry frequently lacked the support of the German artillery either in counter-battery work or in barrage on the enemy's infantry massing for attack.[30] General Fritz von Below, Headquarters, German Second Army

German anti-aircraft batteries had little impact on the swarms of British aircraft marauding over the German lines, although the occasional unlucky pilot discovered that it was by no means always ineffectual.

> A large group of our machines were going over the enemy lines on some business or other and naturally attracted the attention of their guns. One out of the number of our aircraft was hit and his petrol tank exploded much to the horror of all onlookers. The stricken machine turned over and over and narrowly escaped falling on another of ours, but very soon regained its balance and from that time fell gently down behind our own lines, all the time spinning round and round. We have since heard that beyond rather serious burns the pilot was uninjured.[31] Private Oswald Evans, 2/16th London Regiment

From their worm's-eye perspective in the trenches many of the infantry certainly appreciated the devoted work of the RFC in the skies above.

> Our aeroplanes are magnificent all day and every day. They fly very low over our line, and the Bosch line, and see exactly where we are and what is going on. I should think that the Bosch hate it. I know we should. Any Bosch plane that puts its nose out of port is jolly soon chased back again. Our good work is not easily done, and I'm afraid that we have a steady list of casualties in the RFC, but the work they do is invaluable.[32] Captain Arthur Gibbs, 1st Battalion, Welsh Guards

The German Air Force could not allow this expression of naked air power to go unchecked and they began to flood the Somme area with reinforcements, despite to some extent being hamstrung by their continued commitments over Verdun. On 27 August, this situation changed when Field Marshal Paul von Hindenburg replaced General Erich von Falkenhayn as Chief of the German General Staff. Hindenburg was fully aware of the potential dangers of splitting his resources between two major land battles and as soon as possible he suspended the German offensive at Verdun, although serious fighting continued there as a result of a series of counter-attacks launched by the French to recapture their lost ground. With the pressure eased to the south, the Germans were able to concentrate their troops and aircraft on the Somme. New reconnaissance and artillery observation units were moved up and the increasingly vital fighting scout aircraft were concentrated in separate units for the first time. The resulting Jagdstaffeln or 'hunting squadrons', later known as Jasta, were roughly equivalent in size and purpose to the British scout squadrons. The first, Jasta 2, was commanded by the leading German pilot, Oswald Boelcke, who had spent a great deal of time and effort collecting together a sympathetic body of 'scout pilots' – men suited to the cut and thrust of single-seater fighting. In a clear indication of his ability to spot the right man, one of the men he chose was Leutnant Manfred von Richthofen whom he found flying observation aircraft on the Eastern Front

Boelcke explained and demonstrated to his protégés his new principles of tactical fighting in groups. The German pilots were thus fully prepared when they went into action and they had the ideal weapon with which to put their theories into practice when their long-awaited new aircraft arrived in September. The Albatross D I with which Jasta 2 was armed was a superb fighting machine. Armed with twin synchronised machine-guns firing through the propeller arc it was powered by a 160 horsepower Mercedes engine to a top speed of 109 miles per hour and an effective ceiling of 17,000 feet. With the arrival of the Albatross D Is, the circle of technological supremacy turned again and, although the Nieuports could still hold their own, the older generation of aircraft such as the FE2 B were doomed. The method of circling adopted by the FE2 B pilots to cover each others' tails was no longer sufficient to thwart the Albatross and from this time they ceased to be an effective escort aircraft. On 17 September 1916 Boelcke led a six-strong formation of his new machines on their first patrol and by good fortune they intercepted a bombing formation of eight BE2 Cs from 12 Squadron engaged in an attack on Marcoing rail junction together with their escort of six FE2 Bs from 11 Squadron. The radical superiority of the Albatross was immediately revealed as the novice scout pilot von Richthofen flew into his first combat action.

The Englishman nearest to me was travelling in a large machine painted in dark colours. I did not reflect very

long, but took my aim and shot. He also fired and so
did I, and both of us missed our aim. A struggle began,
and the great point for me was to get to the rear of
the fellow because I could only shoot forward with my
gun. He was differently placed, for his machine-gun
was movable. It could fire in all directions. Apparently
he was no beginner, for he knew exactly that his last
hour had arrived at the moment I got at the back of
him. At that time I had not yet the conviction 'He must
fall' which I have now on such occasions, but, on the
contrary, I was curious to see whether he would fall.
There is a great difference between the two feelings.
When one has shot down one's first, second or third
opponent, then one begins to find out how the trick
is done. My Englishmen twisted and turned, flying in
zigzags. I did not think for a moment that the hostile
squadron contained other Englishmen who conceivably
might come to the aid of their comrades. I was animated
by a single thought: 'The man in front of me must come
down, whatever happens.' At last a favourable moment
arrived. My opponent had apparently lost sight of me.
Instead of twisting and turning he flew straight along.
In a fraction of a second I was at his back with my
excellent machine. I gave a short burst of shots with
my machine-gun. I had gone so close that I was afraid
that I might dash into the Englishman. Suddenly I nearly
yelled with joy, for the propeller of the enemy machine
had stopped running. Hurrah! I had shot his engine to
pieces; the enemy was compelled to land, for it was
impossible for him to reach his own lines.[33] Leutnant
Manfred von Richtofen, Jasta 2

It should, however, be noted that the escorts had in a sense
done their job for the BE2 Cs had been protected and indeed
had managed to drop their bombs on their target. Nevertheless, this was cold comfort for the FE2 Bs who had been
comprehensively outclassed by the Albatross while Boelcke had
categorically blooded his pupils. Following this abrupt reversal
of fortunes, the British soon found that they were still able to
reach their objectives but only given luck or at the expense

of casualties. Even the DH2 pilots noticed the impact of the Albatross.

> I know I felt very uncomfortable with two HA well above me, and in spite of the fact that I climbed to about 13,500 they were still above, which is very demoralising. We shall have to bring out some very fine machines next year if we are to keep up with them. Their scouts are very much better than ours now on average . . . the good days of July and August, when two or three DHs used to push half a dozen Huns on to the chimney tops of Bapaume, are no more. In the Roland they possessed the finest two-seater machine in the world, and now they have introduced a few of their single-seater ideas, and very good they are too, one specimen especially deserves mention. They are manned by jolly good pilots, probably the best, and the juggling they can do when they are scrapping is quite remarkable. They can fly round and round a DH and make one look quite silly.[34] Second Lieutenant Gwilym Lewis, 32 Squadron RFC

Trenchard was sensitive to the new situation and in his report in mid-September he identified the danger but remained robustly confident in the RFC's ability to prevail.

> I have come to the conclusion, that the Germans have brought another squadron or squadrons of fighting machines to this neighbourhood and also more artillery machines. One or two German aeroplanes have crossed the line during the last few days . . . With all this, however, the anti-aircraft guns have only reported 14 hostile machines as having crossed the line in the 4th Army area in the last week ending yesterday, whereas something like 2,000 to 3,000 of our machines crossed the lines during the week.[35] Major General Hugh Trenchard, RFC Headquarters

He urgently requested an augmentation of his scout force by new aircraft to counter the Albatross and his case was put forward by no less than Sir Douglas Haig.

I have the honour to request that the immediate attention of the Army Council may be given to the urgent necessity for a very early increase in the numbers and efficiency of the fighting aeroplanes at my disposal. Throughout the last three months the Royal Flying Corps in France has maintained such a measure of superiority over the enemy in the air that it has been enabled to render services of incalculable value. The result is that the enemy has made extraordinary efforts to increase the number, and develop the speed and power, of his fighting machines. He has unfortunately succeeded in doing so and it is necessary to realise clearly, and at once, that we shall undoubtedly lose our superiority in the air if I am not provided at an early date with improved means of retaining it ... The result of the advent of the enemy's improved machines has been a marked increase in the casualties suffered by the Royal Flying Corps, and though I do not anticipate losing our present predominance in the air for the next three or four months, the situation after that threatens to be very serious unless adequate steps to deal with it are taken at once.[36] General Sir Douglas Haig, Commander-in-Chief, BEF

Both Haig and Trenchard were prepared to accept the inevitable increase in casualties if the air offensive was to be continued in outclassed aircraft and so the twin land and air offensives ground on. Although German resistance to the penetration of their lines by RFC reconnaissance, bombing and artillery aircraft stepped up, British reinforcements arrived in the battle area in a steady stream throughout the autumn but they were merely more of the same. The BE12 fighter improvised from the basic BE2 C design proved a complete failure and had to be withdrawn after only a brief exposure to reality in the Picardy skies. In desperation Trenchard called on the RNAS and their 8 Squadron, formerly based at Dunkirk, was moved south to join the fray. In a mirror of the tension which existed between the War Office and the Admiralty, on the ground inter-service rivalry was also fairly intense, with both RFC and RNAS personnel occasionally adopting entrenched positions, alleging favouritism or accusing each other of wanton incompetence. The triviality of much of this bickering was highlighted when Trenchard and Baring paid the newly arrived naval unit a visit.

> We went to the Naval Squadron which is now attached to us, and which is on the same aerodrome as No. 32. They said they would like the oil used by No. 32 for machine-guns. It was better than their own *naval* oil. We then went on to No. 32. They asked if they might have the *naval* oil, which they said was better than their *military* oil. When the matter was investigated later there was found to be not the slightest difference between the naval and the military oil.[37] Lieutenant Colonel Maurice Baring, RFC Headquarters

For a while Boelcke seemed to be everywhere. Following his arrival on the Somme he shot down no less than twenty aircraft, while Jasta 2 notched up victory after victory. Ironically, Boelcke was finally killed on 28 October in a mid-air collision with one of his own pilots. Although the British DH2 pilots found that the inevitable plusses and minuses of aircraft design equipped the Albatross with greater speed, rate of climb and fire power, they also soon learnt that it was less manoeuvrable in close combat; in particular it lost height when turning. One classic, if inconclusive, dogfight occurred when an offensive patrol of three DH2s of 29 Squadron RFC met six Albatross. One of the British pilots was James McCudden who had graduated from observer to pilot in July 1916 but remained an NCO.

> I saw about six specks east of us. I drew Noakes's attention, and so we made off west a little as we were a long way east of the lines. Long before we got to Adinfer Wood the Hun machines overtook us, and directly they got within range we turned to fight. One Hun came down at me nose-on but then turned away, and in doing so I got a good view of the Hun which I had never seen before. It had a fuselage like the belly of a fish. Its wings were cut fairly square at the tips, and had no dihedral angle. The tail-plane was of the shape of a spade. We learned later that these machines were the new German 'Albatross D I' chasers. By now we were fairly in the middle of six

of them and were getting a fairly bad time of it, for we were a long way east of the line, so we all knew that we had to fight hard or go down. At one time I saw a fat Hun about ten yards behind Ball absolutely filling him with lead, as Ball was flying straight, apparently changing a drum of ammunition, and had not seen the Hun. I could not at the time go to Ball's assistance as I had two Huns after me fairly screaming for my blood. However, Ball did not go down. Noakes was having a good time too, and was putting up a wonderful show. The Huns were co-operating very well. Their main tactic seemed to be for one of them to dive at one of us from the front and then turn away, inviting us to follow. I followed three times, but the third time I heard a terrific clack, bang, crash, rip behind me, and found a Hun was firing from about ten yards in the rear, and his guns seemed to be firing in my very ears. I at once did a half roll, and as the Hun passed over me I saw the black and white streams on his inter-plane struts. This fellow was the Hun leader, and I had previously noticed that he had manoeuvred very well. By now, however, we had fought our way back to our lines, and all three of us had kept together, which was undoubtedly our salvation, but I had used all my ammunition and had to chase round after Huns without firing at them. However, the Huns had apparently had enough too, and as soon as we got back to our lines they withdrew east.[38] Sergeant James McCudden, 29 Squadron RFC

It had already been shown how aircraft that were intrinsically weaker than their opponents could survive if they adopted the disciplines of formation flying and interdependency. Thus formations of BE2 Cs had withstood attacks from the Fokker E1. The circling FE2 Bs had protected each other and now the DH2s found in a similar way they could survive against the superior Albatross. Yet once separated, their slower speed and relatively gradual rate of climb meant that they could no longer choose when to initiate and terminate combat. This point was cruelly illustrated in a fight on 23 November when Hawker VC led three DH2s across the German lines on an offensive patrol.

The patrol was split up and Hawker came face-to-face with von Richthofen, who had emerged as Boelcke's greatest pupil and his natural successor. Both Hawker and Richthofen were great pilots but the pupil took his revenge for his teacher's death in a way that cruelly demonstrated how in single combat the ability to turn in tight circles could not save a pilot trapped miles behind the lines. The encounter symbolised the end of the DH2s' brief period of supremacy and represented one of very rare occasions when two aces fought each other to the death. It was, of course, the victor who passed his version of the fight on to posterity.

So we circled round and round like madmen after one another at an altitude of about 10,000 feet. First we circled twenty times to the left, and then thirty times to the right. Each tried to get behind and above the other. Soon I discovered I was not meeting a beginner. He had not the slightest intention to break off the fight. He was travelling in a box which turned beautifully. However, my packing case was better at climbing than his. But I succeeded at last in getting above and beyond my English waltzing partner. When we had got down to about 6,000 feet without having achieved anything particular, my opponent ought to have discovered that it was time for him to take his leave. The wind was favourable to me, for it drove us more and more towards the German position. At last we were above Bapaume, about half a mile behind the German front. The gallant fellow was full of pluck, and when we had got down to about 3,000 ft he merrily waved to me as if he would say, 'Well, how do you do?' The circles which we made around one another were so narrow that their diameter was probably no more than 250 or 300 feet. I had time to take a good look at my opponent. I looked down into his carriage and could see every movement of his head. If he had not had his cap on I would have noticed what kind of a face he was making. My Englishman was a good sportsman, but by and by the thing became a little too hot for him. He had to decide whether he would land on German ground or whether he would fly back to the English lines. Of course he tried the latter, after having endeavoured in vain to escape me by loopings and such tricks. At that time his first bullets were flying around me, for so far neither of us had been able to do any shooting. When he had come down to about 300 ft he tried to escape by flying in a zigzag course, which makes it difficult for an observer on the ground to shoot. That was my most favourable moment. I followed him at an altitude of from 250 feet to 150 feet, firing all the time. The Englishman could not help falling. But the jamming of my gun nearly robbed me of my success. My opponent fell shot through the head 150 feet behind our line.[39] Leutnant Manfred von Richthofen, Jasta 2

The final attack of the Battle of the Somme had taken place in the Ancre sector just five days before on 18 November and in the face of appalling weather Haig finally suspended the offensive. The question of its success or failure has descended into a morass of argument typified by the controversy over the veracity of casualty returns. In essence it can only be judged on whether it achieved the objectives identified when it was conceived. As such, the pressure was taken off Verdun when the German Army was dragged involuntarily into a second morass of attrition. But the German line was unbroken and the wanton process of wearing down the enemy also debilitated the British. During the battle the essential nature of the war in the air was firmly established and the role of the air forces was not only settled but revealed to be of great tactical importance. No competent general doubted the importance of regular detailed photographic reconnaissance of the trenches facing his men; they welcomed the contribution of the observation aircraft in establishing artillery control of the battlefield area; they called for the continuous bombing of the reserve areas; they looked for bombing raids on strategically significant railway junctions at the onset of major attacks; and above all they insisted that the RFC scouts should deny similar opportunities to the Germans. If Trenchard had not met their requirements he would have been dismissed out of hand. There could be no greater tribute to the new status of the RFC than that serious proposals were made by two of Haig's army commanders that the corps squadrons should be removed from the RFC and placed directly under the command of the Royal Artillery. Haig would have none of it – he was satisfied that any difficulties could be smoothed away by closer liaison and not the crude cudgel of dismembering. The RFC could look back on the whole Somme campaign with considerable pride, satisfied that its contribution to the war was now universally regarded as absolutely essential.

CHAPTER SEVEN

Zeppelins

Outside the immediate confines of the Western Front the First World War unleashed a storm of elemental forces that buffeted combatants and non-combatants alike in every direction. Of greatest impact were the temptations and horrors revealed by the new means of dealing death and destruction from the air. Aircraft could now range above the earth, seeking out targets to attack and engaging them either directly with their intrinsic armaments or by dropping lethal projectiles. The first bombs had been dropped in 1911 during the Turko-Italian War in Libya, but only to limited effect. By 1914 the technology had improved slightly and the revised Schlieffen Plan implemented by the Germans included a contingency for the deliberate bombing of Britain from Calais by six squadrons of the German Air Force under Major William Siegert. But when the German advance failed to reach Calais, Siegert was obliged to locate his force instead at Ostend from where they were unable to reach Britain. Consequently high priority was given by the Germans to developing bombing aircraft with a longer range and in time this led to the production of the Grosskampfflugzeug or G-plane, the best known of which was the Gotha G-IV. Frustrated in their plan to attack Britain from the air with aeroplanes, the German authorities turned once again to their fleet of airships. Since 1908, when they had first come to international prominence, they had grown significantly in size and capability. The model ordered from Count von Zeppelin by the German navy in 1913, the L2, had a massive volume of 953,000 cubic feet and was powered by four 165 horsepower Maybach engines. After years of predictive warnings, no doubt remained in the minds of the British public that these behemoths represented a grave threat to their well-being and they were viewed with a mixture of fear and suspicion. The need for concern had been underlined by the failure of the 1907 Hague Conference to prohibit the use of aircraft for purposes of bombing, leaving the dilemma between martial expediency and moral rectitude firmly in the consciences of the belligerent nations with predictable results.

By the outbreak of war the War Office and the Admiralty were fully aware of the need to create and maintain an aerial defence of Britain. Unfortunately neither could agree on how this should be done. Since the first days of military aviation the army had jealously guarded its claim to complete responsibility for defending the nation's skies. Yet with all of the RFC's strength designated for France or to training replacement pilots, the army found itself in the position of a bald man arguing over a comb. It was clearly impossible for them to carry out their task and in effect the country was left defenceless from aerial attack. Fortunately the RNAS, in the time-honoured fashion of the Royal Navy, had to some extent simply ignored the RFC's claims.

The War Office claimed on behalf of the Flying Corps complete and sole responsibility for the aerial defence of Great Britain. But, owing to the difficulties of getting money, they were unable to make any provision for this responsibility, every aircraft they had being earmarked for the Expeditionary Force. Seeing this and finding myself able to procure funds by various shifts and devices, I began in 1912 and 1913 to form under the Royal Naval Air Service flights of aeroplanes as well as seaplanes for the aerial protection of our naval harbours, oil tanks, and vulnerable points, and also for the general strengthening of our exiguous and inadequate aviation.[1]
Winston Churchill, First Lord of the Admiralty

Despite constant protests from the army, the RNAS thus established a series of seaplane bases along the east coast facing the perceived threat emanating from Germany. With anxieties quick to rise over Britain's vulnerability to attack from the air following the declaration of war, the RFC was forced to turn for help to the RNAS. With no maritime equivalent of the BEF to support, the commitments of the RNAS were still relatively light and on 3 September 1914 an agreement was reached whereby the War Office relinquished *de facto* responsibility for the aerial defence of the realm to the Admiralty. The army would merely co-operate with anti-aircraft fire where possible and make available any new aircraft and pilots who were awaiting transfer to the Front. On 5 September, only forty-eight hours after assuming this responsibility, Churchill laid out the basic premises under which he would operate in a prescient memorandum which revealed the extent of his previous consideration of the subject.

There can be no question of defending London by artillery against aerial attack. It is quite impossible to cover so vast an area; and if London, why not every other city. Defence against aircraft by guns is limited absolutely to points of military value . . . Far more important than London are the vulnerable points in the Medway and at Dover and Portsmouth. Oil tanks, power-houses, lock-gates, magazines, airship sheds, all require to have their aerial guns increased in number . . . Aerial searchlights must be provided in connection with every group of guns . . . But after all the great defence against aerial menace is to attack the enemy's aircraft as near as possible to their point of departure . . . The principle is as follows:

(a) A strong overseas force of aeroplanes to deny the French and Belgian coasts to the enemy's aircraft, and to attack all Zeppelins and air bases or temporary air bases which it may be sought to establish and which are within reach.

(b) We must be in constant telegraphic and telephonic communication with the overseas squadrons. We must maintain an intercepting force of aeroplanes and airships at some convenient point within range of a line drawn from Dover to London, and local defence flights at Eastchurch and Calshot.

(c) A squadron of aeroplanes will be established at Hendon, also in telegraphic communication with the other stations, for the purpose of attacking enemy aircraft which may attempt to molest London . . . It is indispensable that the airmen of the Hendon flight should be able to fly by night and their machines must be fitted with the necessary lights and instruments.

Agreeably with the above, instructions must be prepared for the guidance of the Police, Fire Brigade and civil population under aerial bombardment. This will have to be sustained with composure. Arrangements must be concerted with the Home Office and the Office of Works for the extinction of lights upon a well conceived plan.[2]

Winston Churchill, First Lord of the Admiralty

In accordance with this policy the RNAS Eastchurch Squadron under Commander Samson, which in late August 1914 had originally been sent to establish an advance base at Ostend before it fell to the Germans, was ordered to move to Dunkirk to establish a forward anti-Zeppelin base. This policy was clearly explained by the Admiralty in a letter to their counterparts at the French Ministry of Marine: 'The Admiralty desires to reinforce officer commanding aeroplanes with fifty to sixty armed motor-cars and two hundred to three hundred men. This small force will operate in conformity with the wishes of the French military authorities, but we hope it will be afforded free initiative. The immunity of Portsmouth, Chatham, and London is clearly involved.'[3] Samson was extremely short of serviceable aircraft and, in truth, was not unnaturally distracted by the fluctuating military situation on the Western Front. He commenced a series of splendid 'Boys' Own' adventures careering round northern France and Belgium in his improvised armoured cars operating in a purely military sense. Nevertheless aerial attacks were also launched on the Zeppelin sheds at Dusseldorf and Cologne from the forward base established at Antwerp, the most successful of which took place on 8 October when Flight Lieutenant Reginald Marix, flying a Sopwith Tabloid, took off as the advancing Germans were actually entering the outskirts of the city. He flew to Dusseldorf and dropped his bombs from only 600 feet above the Zeppelin shed. The roof was seen to collapse and flames leapt some 500 feet in the air to mark the total destruction of the Zeppelin inside. Less effective was an imaginative scheme to bomb the Nordholz Zeppelin station which was erroneously believed by the Admiralty to be located at the Cuxhaven naval base. After a number of false starts three seaplane carriers accompanied by supporting units moved into the area off the north German coast and launched a seaplane raid on 25 December 1914. The raid was, in truth, a total failure as none of the nine seaplanes located the Zeppelin sheds and the bombs were dropped on naval installations which had no military significance. The 'Cuxhaven Raid' is nevertheless of significance as an indication of the future possibilities offered by combined aerial and naval operations.

Behind these 'forward' defences the resources allocated to the next line, in Great Britain itself, were thin on the ground, a point illustrated by the treatment meted out to the first pilot assigned to the RNAS flight at Hendon which was intended to defend London.

> I met the CO and he said, 'Can you fly a Caudron?' I said, 'No!' He said, 'Well you've got to it's the only one we've got! Do you know the way to Hendon?' I said, 'No!' 'Well at dawn tomorrow you will fly in a Caudron to Hendon!' I went straight to the Admiralty after I landed and the fellow in charge of aeroplanes there said, 'Now, you are the air defence of London – the only one!' I said, 'But I've got no guns or observer or anything, what sort of protection can I give against the Germans?' He said, 'I'll leave that to you!' So I hoped the Zeppelins wouldn't come over![4] Flight Sub-Lieutenant Eric Beauman, Hendon Flight, London Air Defence, RNAS

Landing grounds that were later to develop into full-blown stations were prepared at Hainault Farm and Joyce Green with emergency landing grounds in the major London parks. In addition to the paucity of viable aeroplanes, the provision, disposition and manning of high angle anti-aircraft guns also proved to be a difficult problem. The very heart of London, between Buckingham Palace and Charing Cross, encompassing the Admiralty, War Office and Houses of Parliament, was to be defended by a small, linked system of searchlights and guns, all controlled from a central gun position at Admiralty Arch. As the Royal Navy were unable to supply enough men to man the installations it was decided to return to the army the responsibility for all anti-aircraft gun defences outside of London and the few remaining suitable guns were distributed in penny packets to such obvious military targets as busy dockyards and key munitions factories around the rest of the country. This whole system of defence was to be expanded as quickly as possible once more guns and trained personnel became available.

From the start attempts were made to disguise the capital against detection from the air but they were tempered by the fact that London's size meant that it could never be totally concealed. It was agreed that the best results would be achieved by a general reduction in light sources, coupled with specific measures designed to confuse any Zeppelin pilot as to his exact location above London once he had found it. Thus, in September 1914 easily identifiable roads, such as the Victoria Embankment, were 'disguised' by leaving amorphous gaps in the lighting; while conversely the major parks such as Regent's Park had rows of lights erected across them to avoid equally identifiable tell-tale areas of darkness within the city.

Lighting regulations were very strict in London and the streets were very dark at night. In Princes Gate every other lamp was lighted and in many places only every 3rd or 4th. All illuminated shop-signs were forbidden, also bright head-lights on motor cars etc. Blinds had to be pulled down as soon as the lights were lit and all skylights shaded and the penalties for breaking the rules were pretty severe. People began to make preparations for Zeppelin raids: one big wine dealer was reported to have let several of his cellars, and people we knew had furnished theirs and slept with big coats and handbags for valuables by the bedside. Most people had water or buckets of sand or fire extinguishers on every landing. We rather laughed at this at first but by degrees everyone came round to taking certain precautions.[5] Winifred Tower

Ironically, after all the pre-war Zeppelin scares and fears the first bombing offensive on Britain was launched, albeit in a minor key, by a trio of German seaplane raids on the Dover and Sheerness areas in December 1914. These raids achieved little, but blazed a trail that others could, and would, follow. The much vaunted Zeppelin threat failed to materialise in 1914. Before the war both the German Army and Navy had fostered an interest in the long-term development of airships and by August 1914 the army had six Zeppelins (Z4, Z5, Z6, Z7, Z8 and Z9) and one of the wooden-framed Shutte-Lanz type (SL2). But three of this seemingly promising force were destroyed by ground fire in their first operational flights when undertaking the severely misguided role of close support and reconnaissance to the army during the opening frontier battles. The navy was in an even worse state. Catastrophic accidents to the new L1 and L2 in the autumn of 1913 had not only resulted in the destruction of these ships but also nearly all of their trained personnel. The L3, delivered in May 1914, was kept fully occupied in its reconnaissance role for the High Seas Fleet. The only mitigating factor for the naval air service lay with its new and extremely able commanding officer, Peter Strasser, who remained committed to the expansion and development of the Zeppelin force and its deployment in a strategic bombing role.

By 1915, nine new Zeppelins had been completed, of which five were allocated to the navy and four to the army. With the full backing of Kaiser Wilhem II, who asked only that civilian areas and the royal palaces should be avoided, the commencement of a policy of regular bombing raids brought the crude essence of war a good deal closer than ever before to the British civilian population. The first raid was carried out by the naval Zeppelins L3, L4 and L6 on 19 January 1915. Although L6 had to turn back with engine trouble, L3 and L4 reached the Norfolk coast and dropped their bombs in an apparently indiscriminate fashion on the towns of Yarmouth and King's Lynn, neither of which were in any way defended against aerial attack. In consequence of the resulting civilian outrage which swept the country, the anti-aircraft measures already begun elsewhere were strengthened. A mobile anti-aircraft force of machine-guns, pom-poms and searchlights mounted on lorries was formed, not to 'chase' Zeppelins, but to take advantage of any air-raid warnings received from shipping or the coastal towns and to move the guns into the anticipated path of the airships to intercept them. The RNAS coastal stations were instructed to have aircraft constantly ready for immediate action should a Zeppelin be sighted and a programme of providing fixed anti-aircraft batteries was accelerated as fast as possible. King's Lynn had been a fully illuminated target with no blackout and as a result lighting restrictions were extended to many more towns across the south and the Midlands.

A series of raids by both naval and army Zeppelins followed against a variety of targets until the momentous night when London was attacked for the first time by LZ38 under the command of Hauptmann Erich Linnarz. He arrived unseen over Stoke Newington at 23.20 on 31 May and, passing over east London, dropped grenades and incendiaries on to the houses below. One of the streets hit was Cowper Road.

> I had just got into bed when I heard a terrible rushing of wind and shouts of 'Fire' and 'The Germans are here'. I jumped out of bed and carried my four children into the basement and then went out to the street door and saw the house next door was on fire and people were helping to get the children out. The father was burnt and the daughter, who my daughter used to play with, had met her death . . . We later found the poor little dear had crawled under the bed to get away from the flames.[6]
> Mrs C. Smith

The girl, Elsie Leggett, was only three years old, and fascination at her untimely demise, coupled with that of her sister May who died shortly afterwards from her injuries, was such that thousands of people were reported to have paid a penny each to walk through the remnants of her former home. Their sense of anxiety and fear bore little relation to the material damaged caused, and the fact that only 3,000 lbs of bombs were dropped by a single Zeppelin, with only seven people killed and thirty-five injured, proved of little comfort to the bewildered population. There was little real German pretence that the bombed areas contained significant military installations and the cynical indifference of their Government showed that, as had been feared, major conurbations with their self-defining concentrations of people, factories, industry and commerce were now regarded as legitimate targets in their own right.

During the raid Linnarz flew so high that although LZ38 was heard, it was not seen. The anti-aircraft batteries were helpless and the nine aircraft that took off to intercept the Zeppelin could not find it in the Stygian gloom. The only pilot that sighted LZ38 was promptly brought ignominiously down by engine failure. The anti-Zeppelin pilots throughout the country had an extremely difficult job.

The Zeppelin alarm usually came during the night. It was rather absurd but to please everybody you had to put on a show of going out to chase Zeppelins! You had about as much chance of spotting a black cat in the Albert Hall in the dark.[7] Lieutenant Graham Donald, RNAS

On the ground the army attempted to deploy some of the multitudes of units under training in the south of England. But, as might be expected, it had great difficulty in co-ordinating their efforts and many did not yet understand the serious nature of the Zeppelin threat which often cast a farcical shadow over their activities.

About 4 a.m. a major of the Bucks arrived in a large car. I gathered from his highly excited instructions that a fleet of Zeppelins would shortly arrive. In preparation for their arrival he served us out with ten more rounds of rifle ammunition per man! He then told me to stay where I was till further orders and departed. About 6.30 a.m. I was discussing with the sergeant the important question of breakfast for the men when we saw a farm cart in the distance on the main road accompanied by armed men with fixed bayonets. For one wild moment I hoped it might be breakfast, but just then the horse began to trot, canter and then gallop! The man leading it made a gallant attempt to hang on, but was soon thrown into a hedge; two large boxes fell out, upon which the guard who had been doubling with their rifles at the slope, halted, ordered arms and stood at ease, one on each side of the boxes, with faultless precision. The horse came on at a brisk pace, but just before he came to us he met a bit of a slope and stopped of his own accord, when practically the whole of his harness fell off. I afterwards found that this party had been despatched to bring yet more ammunition.[8] Captain H.C. Meysey-Thompson, 2/4th Battalion, Berkshire Regiment

The raids continued over the following weeks and varied greatly in effect, largely depending on the chance of where the bombs actually fell. On occasions they could cause considerable loss of life, as during Kapitanleutnant Heinrich Mathy's raid in L9 on Hull on 6 June when high-explosive bombs and incendiaries rained down and killed twenty-four people, wounded forty and destroyed much property. The local people were incensed and in some areas, for want of a proper target for their spleen, attacked anyone within their community who could possibly be regarded as of German origin. In London there was also a very real sense of disbelief that the heart of the British Empire was under attack in this way.

I turned out of bed & looking up I saw just above us 2 Zepps. The searchlights were on them & they looked as if they were among the stars. They were up very high & like cigar shaped constellations. They kept getting away from the searchlights only to be found out & caught again. It was lovely & I ran upstairs to the attic from where I had a lovely view when the guns began & the whole place was full of smoke but not much where I was. It all made an infernal row & all the time I felt as in a dream. Can this be London? Jane Ingleby

Partial revenge was extracted by the RNAS forward line of defence at Dunkirk. On 6 June the army Zeppelin LZ38, which had carried out the first attack on London a week before, returned early from an attempted raid due to mechanical problems, only to be caught and destroyed while lying helpless in its shed at Evere in Belgium. Even more dramatically the Zeppelin LZ37 was caught in mid-air by Lieutenant Reginald Warneford of 1 Squadron RNAS. He first sighted the airship over Ostend at 01.05 on 7 June 1915 and immediately began to pursue his gigantic quarry.

I arrived at close quarters a few miles past Bruges at 1.50 am and the Airship opened heavy maxim fire, so I retreated to gain height and the Airship turned and followed me. At 2.15 am he seemed to stop firing and at 2.25 am I came behind, but well above the Zeppelin; height then 11,000 feet, and switched off my engine to descend on top of him. When close above him (at 7,000 feet altitude) I dropped my bombs, and, while releasing the last, there was an explosion which lifted my machine and turned it over. The aircraft was out of control for a short period, but went into a nose dive and the control was regained.[10] Lieutenant Reginald Warneford, 1 Squadron RNAS

The doomed Zeppelin crew fell to their deaths in a morass of flames and eventually crashed on the hapless nuns of the St Elizabeth Convent.

The men in the forward control car were the first to feel the great shudder of the impact and explosion. Above us the vast envelope quivered and began to wrinkle and collapse. The wheel went dead in my hands, and the gondola trembled. All around were shouts and confused orders; we were encompassed by an increasing and terrible heat. I saw dark shapes of men silhouetted against a ruddy glow as their flailing hands tried to protect their faces. Some of them climbed over the sides of the car and flung themselves into space. I could not make myself let go of the wheel. I clung to it like a drowning man until it broke in my hands. I was flung to the floor. The scorching heat increased and increased, and our clothes burst into flames. The gondola began to tilt and rock until, with a terrible sound of breaking wood and metal it tore away from the main structure and plunged towards the ground. I knew no more until I woke up in hospital.[11] Coxswain Alfred Muhler, LZ37

Muhler was rather lucky to survive as he fell through the roof of the convent but right into an empty bed – he was fortunate indeed to escape with burns, bruising and shock. Warneford was immediately awarded the VC but was killed just a few days later in a flying accident.

The first real success for the home-based anti-Zeppelin defences occurred when L12, commanded by Oberleutnant Peterson, was caught in the sights of three-inch anti-aircraft guns as he flew relatively low over Dover on 9 August. One shell hit the airship and, although she managed to escape by rapidly gaining altitude, a gradual loss of gas forced her to ditch in the sea off the Belgian coast. The German Navy towed the ship to Ostend, but their rescue mission was subject to the concerted attention of the RNAS based at Dunkirk and in the process L12 was virtually destroyed by fire. A month later, on 7 September, SL2, under the command of Hauptmann Richard von Wobesser, flew first over the East End before crossing the Thames to drop bombs on south London. The raid resulted in eighteen killed and thirty-eight injured. The inquests and 'post mortems' held into such deaths did much to encourage survivors to speculate as to why they had survived and the less fortunate had not, exaggerating the overall sense of jitteriness already triggered by the apparently random nature of the bombing.

I slept with my sister Dolly aged 6, in a front room of a top floor flat at No. 181 Ilderton Road, Rotherhithe. My mother and father slept in an adjoining room and along a short passage was another bedroom where my other 3 sisters, Minnie, Kittie and Elsie, slept in one big bed. On this particular evening, Minnie had been out until 10 o'clock with my parents, as she had just won a scholarship and wanted a new outfit for her school next day . . . Being so late home, she kept right on the edge of the bed to avoid disturbing her sisters' sleep. During the night, I was awakened by a terrible crash. I pulled Dolly out of bed and pushed her into the arms of my mother and father, who had just opened their door in alarm. As they left their bed a wall collapsed across it. I went dashing across the corridor to call the other girls, followed by my mother. She pulled up in horror when I vanished; where there had been a bedroom, there was nothing and I fell through 3 floors into the ruins of the house. My mother and father and Dolly were carried down from the front window on a fire-escape ladder. The other 3 girls were buried for hours; when they were finally reached, Elsie (the baby) and Minnie (who was 11) were just alive; Kittie (who was 9) was dead. Minnie owes her life to her late night because, being on the edge of the bed, she missed the crushing weight of concrete which killed her sisters. Poor little Elsie, who was always with Kittie in life, joined her in death.[12] Mrs F.W.Smith (then a schoolchild aged eight)

On the following night the next raid, carried out by the increasingly effective Mathy, this time in L13, caused severe damage as the bombs tumbled down across London from Euston station to Liverpool Street station. One bomb scored a direct hit on a bus.

> I boarded the No. 8 bus at Old Ford. When we reached the top of Bethnal Green Road, I heard a loud bang and screams. Looking up at the sky, I saw the searchlights all meet on a Zeppelin. As the bus went on, round Norton Folgate, I was very frightened and started to cry. A woman on a seat opposite came and sat by me and cuddled me up to her. Something seemed to tell me to get off the bus and I broke away, though she made a grab at me to pull me back. There was an explosion and a blinding flash like lightning. The poor woman fell back with a terrible scream.[13] Florence Williams

The passengers were helpless as the blast shredded the bus with a combination of shrapnel and glass.

> We had got as far as the Great Eastern Railway electric light station when a bomb fell on the bonnet of the bus ... I was of course knocked unconscious but have some recollection of being inside a blazing bus and stumbling over someone on the floor.[14] Mr H.W. Player

In all nine passengers and the bus driver were killed, while another ten were injured.

> I felt myself going down and my fall was broken by a man on the bottom step; we got entwined and fell into the roadway ... He lay in the road with my hat in his hand and was later picked up dead. A woman inside the bus screamed, 'My baby! My baby!' I heard afterwards she and her husband and baby were killed. I just got a glimpse of the conductor still standing at his post on the platform. He, poor man, had an eye destroyed but remained there, on duty. It turned out I had been peppered with shrapnel.[15] Florence Williams

The raid resulted in twenty-two deaths, eighty-seven injured and serious damage to property and business premises. Although all the London defences opened up, Mathy soon climbed higher to avoid their fire and escaped unscathed. Behind him he left a stunned city.

The noise of the guns & shells bursting & the bombs bursting was terrific & most awesome. It was a great sight but I hope to be spared seeing it again. Women simply went off their heads & were difficult to control. I locked my lot, wife & all, in the kitchen, but in less than ½ a minute they were out through the window.[16] Mr W.A.Phillips

Some Londoners, embittered perhaps by a sense of helplessness, worked themselves into a frenzy of bile and hatred for the Germans.

To see the blasted bombs being dropped on helpless civilians and peaceable houses made the blood go to fever heat and I felt absolutely MAD. Anyway they did some damage to poor little children and some harmless civilians going home from their daily toil, and the GermHun devils call it WAR. They don't know what WAR means, Mack, and they shew it immediately they get up against the British bayonets, behind which are boys of the Bulldog breed, like yourself, for they immediately begin to cry and whine like whipped curs. Yet when they can injure innocent unarmed people they make a big crow, and shout and wag and wave flags and proclaim it as a great victory and that they have struck terror into the English people in London. Well I can only say this that it has had the effect of making Londoners at any rate, more determined than ever that the GermHun power shall not be only beaten but ABSOLUTELY CRUSHED out of existence. We have full trust in the boys at the Front and know they will not spare a single vile GermHun's life. He is not worth it. He is nothing but a mass of skulking cowardice when it comes to a fair fight man to man . . .

The pity is that I can't do what I should and want to do.
Still you and the other boys are there.[17] Mr J.H. Stapley

Such feelings were widespread and led to an outcry in the press at the
naked vulnerability of the capital. As a result the acclaimed pre-war
naval gunnery expert, Admiral Sir Percy Scott, was appointed to
take command of the London defences. He promptly removed
the almost useless pom-pom guns and drew up proposals for
104 anti-aircraft guns and over fifty accompanying searchlights.
A mobile 75 mm French anti-aircraft gun formed the basis of a
special London mobile anti-aircraft section under the command
of Lieutenant Commander Alfred Rawlinson. At this stage the
question arose whether to continue to use aircraft as a means of
defence after empirical evidence, coupled with an investigation
into the defence of Paris, had thrown considerable doubt over their
efficacy against night Zeppelin raids. Consequently programmes
to expand the number of night-trained pilots, aircraft and landing
grounds were for the time being shelved.

The last great raid of 1915 took place on 13 October. Five
Zeppelins roamed over southern England, often confused about
their exact location, but dropping bombs on seemingly worthwhile
targets. When a confidential warning that they were approaching
was passed to Rawlinson, he and the crew of his mobile anti-aircraft
gun set off for their designated gun site at the Artillery Ground
in Moorgate Street. In doing so they inevitably made public the
news of what was about to happen.

The streets on this occasion were crammed both with
vehicular traffic and pedestrians. Everyone understood
at once, in the light of their experience during the
previous month, the moment they saw us coming, that
an air raid was imminent. They did not, however, know
'where to go' or 'what to do', though none of them
had any doubt at all that the *most pressing* and *most
vital* thing they had to do was TO GET OUT OF OUR
WAY. I feel quite confident that no man who took that
drive will ever forget any part of it, and particularly
Oxford Street, which presented an almost unbelievable
spectacle. I had such an anxious job myself that I had
no time to laugh, but I am sure I 'smiled' all the way.

After passing the Marble Arch the traffic in Oxford Street became much thicker. The noise of our 'sirens' being as 'deafening' as the glare of our 'headlights' was 'dazzling', the omnibuses in every direction were seeking safety on the pavements. I also observed, out of the corner of my eye, several instances of people flattening themselves against the shop windows.[18] Lieutenant Commander Alfred Rawlinson, Mobile Anti-Aircraft Section, RNAS

After their frantic drive they finally reached the Artillery Ground and quickly prepared the gun for action. They were just in time, as L15, under the command of Kapitanleutnant Joachim Breithaupt, approached dropping bombs in Holborn and the Strand.

There was no time whatever to use any altitude finding instruments, or even a range finder, and I therefore had to form a lightning estimate of the enemy's speed, and of what his altitude and range would be, on the course he was then following, by the time our gun was ready to fire. My report shows that I estimated the range would be 5,000 yards and the altitude between 7,000 and 8,000 feet by the time the necessary 'corrections' for speed of target, range and altitude had been 'put on' by the sight setters, the fuses set, the gun loaded, and the telescopic sights focused on the target. As soon as I got the 'Ready, sir,' from the gun-layer, I instantly gave them, 'Fire', and we then all watched anxiously, during the interminable seconds of the 'time of flight' of the shell, to observe the 'burst'. When it finally came it was 'short', but it must have very considerably surprised the enemy who had been informed, with what had been great accuracy a fortnight or so previously, that there were no anti-aircraft *high-explosive* shells in the London defences.[19] Lieutenant Commander Alfred Rawlinson, Mobile Anti-Aircraft Section, RNAS

Rawlinson's satisfaction at the effect of his shells was justified when, after the raid, the Germans reported a great increase in defensive fire. Although none of the airships were hit they were forced to stay high to avoid the bursting shells and were prevented from aiming at specific targets, instead merely unloading their bombs in a random manner. The L15 dropped a string of bombs across London's theatre-land which caused twenty-eight deaths and seventy wounded.

> I was playing in the 'Prodigal Son' at the Aldwych Theatre. Milton Rosser was speaking his lines when we heard a terrible 'Boomee'. A bomb had found its mark in the middle of the road opposite the Lyceum Theatre and the burst gas main became ignited. I was standing at the side of the stage and was scared stiff – frozen still. I took one look at the audience and saw that there was panic. In terror, I hid behind a piece of scenery, but only for a second; then I rushed on to the deserted stage and shouted to the pianist 'Play Tipperary'. He did, and I started to sing it to the fighting, scrambling mass that was the audience. My action had the desired effect, and some people began to applaud. Then Milton Rosser returned and took up his lines with me, although I was not concerned with the lines he was speaking! We carried on until the other actors returned, and the show proceeded.[20] Sydney Hart

No RNAS aircraft were mobilised due to the continued naval scepticism as to their effectiveness against Zeppelins at night-time but five RFC aircraft took to the air and tried to intercept the German intruders. Second Lieutenant (much later Marshal of the Royal Air Force Sir) John Slessor was on anti-Zeppelin stand-by that night at Sutton's Farm airfield. Although keen to get into action, he was unconvinced as to how effective his BE2 C would be if a Zeppelin was encountered given the extraordinary nature of his armament.

> [I had] a small oblong bomb full of petrol, of which three or four were carried in the cockpit. They were pushed by hand through a tube in the floor. In the tube an electrical contact lighted the fuse, whereupon the bomb burst into flames and a bunch of large fish-hooks came out at the top. These, theoretically, would catch in the Zeppelin's envelope and allow the burning bomb to do the rest. It

was a weapon worthy of Heath-Robinson at his best.[21]
Second Lieutenant John Slessor, 23 Squadron RFC

Despite his reservations, once the telephone warning had been
received, Slessor took off and began to climb over London. During
his slow ascent he could see that the attempts to black out the city
were still largely ineffective.

The lights of the capital presented a wonderful spectacle.
They did more. They illuminated quite effectively the
great silver shape of Zeppelin L15. Long before I
had reached my patrol height I saw above me the
impressively vast bulk of the airship – like a cod's-
eye view of the *Queen Mary*.[22] Second Lieutenant John
Slessor, 23 Squadron RFC

Breithaupt, who was fully aware of the incipient threat posed by
aircraft, spotted Slessor and the other pilots as they approached.

The L15 was caught in the beams of a large number of
searchlights, the illumination, especially above the City,
being as bright as day. Unusually violent anti-aircraft
defence fire opened and the airship was soon surrounded by bursting shrapnel. Even more sinister was
the appearance of another danger in addition to the
anti-aircraft guns. Four aeroplanes, at first observed by
the flames from the exhausts and then clearly showing up
in the beams of the searchlights, endeavoured to reach
the airship and shoot her down with incendiary ammunition.[23] Kapitanleutnant Breithaupt, Zeppelin L15

Unaware that Slessor was armed with little more than inflammable
fish-hooks, Breithaupt took immediate action.

When I was still a good thousand feet below him, I saw
streams of sparks as his engines opened up. The great
bulk swung round and then – the most extraordinary
sight – cocked its nose up at an incredible angle and
climbed away from me.[24] Second Lieutenant John Slessor,
23 Squadron RFC

Although L15 avoided the British aircraft, they at least succeeded in curtailing the raid and preventing further damage and loss of life. For the civilians on the ground this was of little immediate consolation. The Germans had still got through and escaped unscathed to return another day. The cumulative pressure of six months of sporadic raids was beginning to show. After returning to base Slessor had to travel through the East End and he noticed incipient signs of demoralisation among the frightened population.

I set off at once in an old Crossley tender and trailer to collect spare parts to mend my poor aeroplane which wasn't at all serviceable and coming back through the East End down the Mile End Road just after dark. People had just recently had a few bombs from Zeppelins – nothing – but they were in such a panic that we had a hell of a job to get through. Eventually we had to stop at Stepney Police Station and collect a Bobby to stand on each side of the Crossley to get us through.[25] Second Lieutenant John Slessor, 23rd Squadron RFC

That same night the Zeppelins struck elsewhere in southern England. L14, under Kapitanleutnant Bocker, appeared over Tunbridge Wells where it achieved little of a concrete nature, but nevertheless terrified a sizeable proportion of the civilians below.

It was coming nearer & nearer, it was unquestionably a big aircraft of some sort. 'Zeppelin!' We said, 'Hark! the great thump, thump of the huge engines' . . . Straining our eyes & looking up into the beautiful starlight night, we said, 'Look, there it is!' A long, black cigar-like shaped object coming very slowly. We knew then what it was for certain. But the awfulness of it was, it seemed right over our field. Then the terrible thing stopped . . . I put my arms around mother. And I can tell you I don't know how we felt, it was awful – horrible! We could see the horrid thing & it was making now different noises with its engines or something, so we knew they were preparing something for us. Then suddenly a report, a flash, then a second, then a terrible explosion, which sounded worse than thunder. Mr & Mrs Huggett, Mother and I had our

arms right round each other & we were crouching in our
own front hedge in front of the sitting-room window.
Mother was praying out loud. Well there were three of
those awful bombs dropped, & it seemed they must come
right on top of us. When the last explosion had gone off,
we breathed a bit (but we really thought our last hour had
come) . . . You can guess our teeth were chattering & we
were white with fright. I discovered after a bit I had no
frock on, only a mac' over my petticoats . . . Everyone
seemed unconscious of appearances – till afterwards –
when it seemed very funny.[26] Christine Smith

In the manner of the man who missed the proverbial barn door
with his shotgun, despite hovering over the town for some minutes
the three bombs dropped by L14 hit only the empty space of a park
situated slapbang in the middle. This fortunate escape did little to
assuage the paralysing sense of panic that had spread like scrub fire.
The reaction of the men and women of Tunbridge Wells was by
no means unique since across the country the general public were
becoming increasingly concerned. They wanted to know what
was going on, who was responsible for the continued German
raids and what effective action was to be taken.

Owing to the 'hide the guilty' censorship, nothing has
appeared in the press in detail, so you see we are all
kept in the dark . . . the people who pay are getting
very furious at this wretched secret way this awful war
is conducted, they wish to know how we stand & it is
not Mr Asquith's war or Mr Lloyd George's – it's the
Nation's war & our men are doing the work. The lack
of news does no good because as a Nation, the Spirit
of the thing is lost, and a feeling of 'don't care' takes
place.[27] Charles De Lacy

During the course of the winter, when the weather forced the
Germans to suspend their raids, a great deal of effort was expended
in improving London's anti-aircraft defences. Rawlinson's mobile
anti-aircraft section was expanded into a complete Mobile Brigade
armed with a variety of guns and searchlights mounted on lorries
and trailers and based at Kenwood House on Hampstead Heath

from where they could be dispatched when intelligence was received of an incoming raid. Fixed batteries were also sited at key points around the capital. Design work was also initiated into the development of high-explosive shells to ensure that they fragmented in such a manner that lethal large pieces were not left to fall on the hapless inhabitants of London.

In the first raid of 1916 the Germans attempted their most ambitious raid yet when, on the night of 31 January, a fleet of nine airships set out in the direction of Liverpool. *En route* navigational confusion overwhelmed the airship commanders and none reached their targets. Instead they dropped their bombs across the Midlands, which hitherto had considered itself safe from attack and had not introduced either black-out precautions or gun batteries. The defence of Britain's industrial heartland was just one RFC aircraft based near Birmingham. Casualties were heavy, with seventy people dead and 113 injured, and, although not rated a success by the Germans, the raid showed what could have been achieved if the Zeppelins had avoided the magnet of London which was the only area of the country to be really well defended. As a result of the raid the area of blackout was extended and arrangements tightened up for the prompt dissemination of air-raid warnings across the country.

The escalating public outcry prompted by the airship raids, which had tailed off during the winter hiatus, now arose again. Some form of visible response was demanded and the most obvious one seemed to be that of revenge. During the opening months of 1916 the calls for reprisals grew steadily. In spring the *Daily Mail* began one of its inimitably xenophobic campaigns under the banner 'Hit Back! Don't Wait and See!' and the same theme was adopted by Noël Pemberton Billing, a long-standing supporter of aeronautics and a former pilot in the RNAS, when he stood in two by-elections. At the second by-election in March he was successfully elected as the self-styled 'First Air Member' and immediately began to advocate in Parliament one of his key campaign themes – a ruthless policy of hitting back directly at German civilians. To achieve this he suggested the creation of an independent air force specifically to bomb Germany. In the vigorous pursuit of a 'forward defence' policy, he promoted offensive action as the best means of protecting Britain. Despite the limited damage caused to date by the raids, as opposed to the moral effect and injury to British pride, Pemberton Billing resurrected the possibility of a devastating attack on Britain by a large force of enemy bombers which could paralyse the country. His concerns were echoed by other 'air minded' MPs, including Winston Churchill who was no longer able to encourage the RNAS to carry out its ambitious programme of pre-emptive bombing against German military targets having been removed from his position of First Lord of the Admiralty as a result of the Gallipoli scandal in May 1915, and William Joynson-Hicks, another long-standing promoter of aviation who was appointed Chairman of the new all-party Parliamentary Air Committee created to promote the idea of raids against Germany.

From early 1916 the idea also began to take root of an independent Air Minister, either to sit at the head of a new Air Ministry and be responsible for initiating reprisal raids against Germany independently of the tactical needs of the BEF, or more simply to provide a degree of co-ordination between the competing and at times opposing interests of the RFC and RNAS and to remove the obvious waste that this caused. The establishment of a new ministry would be a difficult undertaking in wartime, but the appointment of a figure to liaise between the two services appeared to be more straightforward. In an attempt to avoid the more difficult choices resulting from a major reorganisation of the air services but with pressure mounting on them to take some form of action in response to the raids, in February Asquith's Government followed the lines of this argument and announced the formation of the Joint War Air Committee under the Chairmanship of Lord Derby, which led to it being more commonly known as the Derby Committee, with Lord Montagu of Beaulieu, a long-standing advocate of air power, as his Deputy. But, reluctant to move things too far too fast, the Prime Minister decided to base the new body on the pre-war Air Committee. Consequently it was given no executive powers and was charged only with the investigation of the limited matter of the supply of planes to the military and naval authorities, focusing on the types that were being developed and their means of production. Except to highlight the depth of rivalry that had grown up between the two air services since their emergence as distinct bodies with different aims and policies and the complete lack of co-operation which existed between them, the Derby Committee soon found itself unable to achieve anything and on 10 April both

Derby and Montagu resigned. Derby informed Asquith that he believed only the complete amalgamation of the RFC and RNAS would provide any effective solution but this would probably be too disruptive at that time. The only alternative was a re-formed committee with greater executive authority but even this would encounter problems in making headway given the obduracy of the positions held by the War Office and the Admiralty.

In line with this general advice the Air Board was formed on 11 May under the Presidency of the Lord Privy Seal, Lord Curzon, a former Viceroy of India. It was given much wider terms of reference than the Derby Committee and, in addition to the co-ordination of supply and co-operation between the services, was ordered to deliberate on wider matters of air policy such as the possibility of the introduction of a long range bombing offensive against Germany. It was also given stronger powers and was able to recommend appropriate courses of action to the War Office and the Admiralty which, if they refused to accept them, could then be referred back to the War Cabinet for arbitration. But it was still not able to force changes on them directly. Despite its more powerful position, the Air Board also eventually failed, principally as a result of Curzon's partisan sympathy with the RFC. Like them, he believed in using air power principally to support the army on the Western Front and he was sharply critical of the way the RNAS was using part of its strength in France to carry out independent 'strategic' bombing raids from Luxeuil near Belfort during the later stage of the crucial Somme offensive in 1916.

The Admiralty involvement in long range bombing operations carried out by the Third Wing, RNAS between October 1916 and April 1917 with the object of bombing the German industrial conglomeration of the Saar, was the cause of considerable controversy. Quite apart from the element of revenge, proponents of this kind of bombing also believed that hitting German industrial targets would seriously damage their war effort; ironically the same argument that had initially persuaded the Kaiser to sanction attacks on Great Britain. The results of the long-distance bombing raids were not inconsiderable mainly due to the disruptive effects they had on shift production through air-raid alarms, real or false, an experience which matched that felt by the British during the German raids on England. German concern was serious enough for the President of the Dusseldorf Steelworks to make a direct plea to the military authorities pointing out that, 'The perpetually increasing curtailment of night work due to these raids not only results in an average decrease of thirty per cent of the steel works' output, but it is feared that night work may soon have to be entirely suspended. Since, in order to carry out the vast programme, we are instructed to increase production at these very works on the Western Front, we consider that better protection is absolutely necessary'.[28] Pressure from this and other key figures in the German industrial network was hard to resist and the same kind of co-ordinated defence programme of anti-aircraft guns, searchlights and scout aircraft as had been introduced by Britain was put into place.

From his perspective in command of the RFC in France, General Trenchard feared that becoming drawn into an escalating pattern of bombing, defence, reprisal and more bombing would begin to redirect valuable resources away from the RFC's front-line strength both to carry out the raids and to defend Britain against the inevitable strikes that would be made against it. Since the initial raids would be of no direct assistance to the prosecution of the military campaign in France, he categorically rejected the concept of strategic raids and it is one of the supreme ironies of the war that when Chief of the Air Staff in the 1920s he became one of the leading advocates of strategic bombing in order to justify the independence of the RAF. However, in 1916 and 1917 he unequivocally believed in the need to concentrate all the efforts of the flying services in support of the army's operations in the main theatre of war and to prevent the diversion of any part of them into independent operations solely on political grounds. On balance, given the difficulties he encountered in attaining and keeping control of the air over the crucial battlefields during the Somme offensive, Trenchard was probably correct in his adjudication between the relative value of the slightly nebulous claims made about likely disruption to the German war effort as against the concrete results that were being attained on the Western Front.

Curzon fully endorsed Trenchard's viewpoint and, given his hugely egotistical nature, it was inevitable that he would become embroiled in a series of increasingly bitter clashes over this issue as well as the whole question of air procurement with the new First Lord of the Admiralty, Sir Arthur Balfour. Balfour's position was partly disingenuous for the stance of the Admiralty over procurement and the control of 'strategic' bombing was in essence a reflex response by an established and traditional body fiercely proud of its independence from 'outside' interference. The clash of personalities significantly contributed to the inability of the Air Board to achieve its desired goal and in frustration Curzon resigned in December 1916. The demise of the Air Board both contributed to and coincided with the fall of Asquith's administration and when he was replaced as Prime Minister by David Lloyd George, the Air Board was re-formed, acquiring for the first time specific powers to allocate resources to the two service ministries and to resolve directly any disputes that arose between them.

The War Office had never really accepted the dominant role in the provision of Home Defence allocated by necessity to the RNAS in 1914 and as the RFC grew in numbers and strength they began negotiations to regain their former position as the sole defender of the homeland. After protracted negotiations, complicated by vacillation on all sides, a decision was finally made and approved at the Cabinet meeting of 10 February 1916, which vastly simplified the situation. Henceforth the navy and RNAS were to deal with all aircraft attempting to reach Britain. The army and RFC would deal with all those that succeeded.

On resuming its former responsibilities, the army did not change the direction of anti-Zeppelin defences with the exception of a greater enthusiasm than the Admiralty for the potential of aircraft, assisted by rings of searchlights, in protecting key targets. A fairly comprehensive plan was drawn up for the whole country including all the major industrial centres. More and more anti-aircraft guns were needed and although previous manufacturing orders were nearing completion, the pressure to find resources was such that ninety eighteen-pounder guns were specially adapted for anti-aircraft fire to fill the gaps. The increasingly efficient Mobile Anti-Aircraft Brigade was transferred lock, stock and barrel to the army for the duration of hostilities. The 'early warning' system was also overhauled with a particular view to eliminating false alarms which had not unnaturally proliferated after the shock of the raid on the Midlands in January. Such Zeppelin scares severely impeded war production as huge areas were blacked out and factories closed down the length and breadth of the country. The consequent loss of production achieved more for the German war effort than any bomb could directly and had to be avoided as far as possible. As a result a system of observers was set up, not only on the coast, but right across Britain. The observation posts were connected to Warning Controllers who passed on information by telephone to the various sub-districts in his area over which it looked likely that the Zeppelins might pass. Each of these sub-districts maintained a 'warning list' of authorities that needed to take precautionary action, such as industrial firms, churches and places of 'amusement', so that they could be telephoned in the event of attack.

Since the start of 1915 the RFC had deployed 'specially trained' night flying pilots on readiness for anti-Zeppelin duties while they were waiting to go overseas. Training in night flying was still in its infancy and Arthur Harris, who was to have no little connection with aerial bombing later in his career, received scant instruction before being nominated as the 'anti-Zeppelin' pilot at Northolt.

When I reported to the adjutant who said, 'Can you fly in the dark?' I said, 'Well I can't fly in the daylight – maybe it's easier in the dark!' He said, 'Well you're the anti-Zeppelin pilot here.' So I said, 'What does that mean?' He told me, 'Well the station supplies a pilot every "odd" night and you are the permanent Zeppelin pilot every "other" "odd" night. There are two machines up in the end hangar which you have to look after – they are your machines – go to it!' That very night in thick drizzly weather the station commander who was the duty pilot that night went up and killed himself before he'd got 100 yards beyond the end flare. That was my introduction. The next night it was my turn! I was told to see if I could find an army airship which was going to fly around pretending it was a Zeppelin. Well by the most astonishing bit of good fortune, both for the airship and myself, I found it by very nearly running into it. It had put its lights on in a panic when it saw me coming and I suppose that was regarded as a bit of skilful scouting navigation on my part whereas as a matter of fact all I had done is to fly blindly into the night and hope for the best.[29] Lieutenant Arthur Harris, RFC

Despite the pressing demands of the Western Front it was decided that special Home Defence Squadrons were absolutely essential and as a result a new Home Defence Wing was formed with squadrons disposed at key locations across the country and with 39 Squadron responsible for the defence of London. One key factor had changed in the battle between the pygmy aircraft and the giant Zeppelins – the invention of effective incendiary and explosive bullets. Previously a drum or two of Lewis gun bullets would just pass through the Zeppelin hydrogen gas bags and cause leaks which might busy those members of the crew responsible for patching it up, but would not usually cause enough gas to be lost to do more than inconvenience the Zeppelin. Once the Lewis gun drums were filled with a combination of Buckingham, Brock and Pomeroy bullets the Zeppelin became incredibly vulnerable.

As the Zeppelin raids continued in the spring and summer of 1916, notwithstanding the occasional failure, it was clear that the improved anti-aircraft batteries were not only having a deterrent effect, by forcing the Zeppelins ever higher, but were now capable of scoring damaging hits. The L15 had the worst experience when, after evading an aircraft, it was hit by the Purfleet anti-aircraft battery and then subsequently attacked by an aircraft carrying explosive darts. Crippled, it came down in the sea on the morning of 1 April. The Zeppelins had several times been intercepted by aircraft, but somehow they always managed to escape. Their luck changed during the raid launched against London by sixteen Zeppelins on the night of 2/3 September. In one of the most important psychological moments of the war the technological initiative passed finally and irrevocably to the aircraft.

At 2.30 I was awakened by a terrific explosion & was at the window in one bound when another deafening one shook the house. Nearly above us sailed a cigar of bright silver in the full glare of about 20 magnificent searchlights. A few lights roamed around trying to pick up his companions. Our guns made a deafening roar & shells burst all around her. For some extraordinary reason she was dropping no bombs. The night was absolutely still with a few splendid stars. It was a magnificent sight &

the whole of London was looking on holding its breath.[30]
Muriel Dayrell-Browning

Into this natural theatre flew Lieutenant William Leefe Robinson
on anti–Zeppelin patrol. He had taken off at 23.08 in his BE2 C
from 39 Squadron's headquarters at Sutton's Farm airfield and
climbed slowly to his patrol height. After pursuing his prey for
nearly three hours it finally came into his sights.

At about 2.05 am a Zeppelin was picked up by the
searchlights over NNE London (as far as I could judge).
Remembering my last failure I sacrificed height (I was
still 12,900 feet) for speed and made nose down in the
direction of the Zeppelin. I saw shells bursting and night
tracer shells flying round it. When I drew closer I noticed
that the anti-aircraft aim was too high or low; also a good
many some 800 feet behind – a few tracers went right
over. I could hear the bursts when about 3,000 feet from
the Zeppelin. I flew about 800 feet below it from bow
to stern and distributed one drum along it (alternate
New Brock and Pomeroy). It seemed to have no effect;
I therefore moved to one side and gave it another drum
distributed along its side – without apparent effect. I then
got behind it (by this time I was very close – 500 feet
or less below) and concentrated one drum on one part
(underneath rear). I was then at a height of 11,500 feet
when attacking Zeppelin. I hardly finished the drum
before I saw the part fired at glow. In a few seconds
the whole rear part was blazing. When the third drum
was fired there was no searchlights on the Zeppelin and
no anti-aircraft was firing. I quickly got out of the way of
the falling blazing Zeppelin and being very excited fired
off a few red Very lights and dropped a parachute flare.[31]
Lieutenant William Leefe Robinson, 39 Squadron RFC

The airship was not in fact a Zeppelin but a Schutte-Lanz, the
SL11, constructed round a wooden frame and containing highly
inflammable hydrogen. Once alight the blaze quickly became a
conflagration which could be seen both at close quarters by Leefe

Robinson and in the distance by the teeming thousands standing in the streets of London:

> When the colossal thing actually burst into flames of course it was a *glorious* sight – wonderful! It literally lit up all the sky all around and me as well of course – I saw my machine as in the fire light – and sat still half dazed staring at the wonderful sight before me, not realising to the least degree the wonderful thing that had happened! My feelings? *Can* I describe my feelings. I hardly know how I felt. As I watched the huge mass gradually turn on end, and – as it seemed to me – slowly sink, one glowing, blazing mass – I gradually realised what I had done and grew wild with excitement. When I had cooled down a bit, I did what I don't think many people would think I would do, and that is I thanked God with all my heart. You know darling old mother and father I'm not what is popularly known as a religious person, but on an occasion such as that one must realise a little how one does trust in providence. I felt an overpowering feeling of thankfulness, so it was strange that I should pause and think for a moment after a first 'blast' of excitement, as it were, was over and thank from the bottom of my heart, that supreme power that rules and guides our destinies.[32]
> Lieutenant William Leefe Robinson, 39 Squadron RFC

For his tenacity and courage Leefe Robinson was awarded the Victoria Cross, the first to be given for an action fought with the enemy over or on British soil. From the ground the dramatic fall from the heavens of SL11 was quite extraordinary.

> From the direction of Barnet & very high a brilliant red light appeared (we thought it was an English fire balloon for a minute!). Then we saw it was the Zep diving head first. *That* was a sight. She dived slowly at first as only the foremost ballonet was on fire. Then the second burst & the flames tore up into the sky & then the third & cheers thundered all around us from every direction. The glare lit up all of London & was rose red. Those deaths must have

been the most dramatic in the world's history. They fell –
a cone of blazing wreckage thousands of feet – watched
by 8 million of their enemies. It was magnificent, the most
thrilling scene imaginable.[33] Muriel Dayrell-Browning

Crashing helplessly from the night sky, SL11 eventually fell to earth
near Cuffley in Hertfordshire, directly in front of the house where
Patrick Blundstone, a fifteen-year-old schoolboy, was staying on
holiday.

There right above us was the Zepp! It had broken in half
and was in flames, roaring and crackling. It went slightly
to the right, and crashed down into a field!! It was about
100 yds away from the house and directly opposite us!!!
It nearly burnt itself out, when it was finished by the
Cheshunt Fire Brigade. I would rather not describe the
condition of the crew – of course they were dead, burnt
to death. They were roasted, there is absolutely no other
word for it. They were brown, like the outside of roast
beef. One had his legs off at the knees and you could
see the joint![34] Patrick Blundstone

As if this first success over London had broken the spell, over the
following month three more airships were brought down. On the
next raid, on 23 September, L33 was destroyed by a combination
of anti-aircraft fire and an attack by Lieutenant Alfred Brandon,
while Lieutenant Frederick Sowrey shot down L32 over Great
Burstead. A week later, on 1 October, this chapter was symbolically
closed when Mathy himself, commanding L31, was shot down by
Second Lieutenant W.J. Tempest over Potters Bar. His end was
dramatic indeed.

All at once, it appeared to me that the Zeppelin must
have sighted me, for she dropped all her bombs in one
volley, swung round, tilted up her nose and proceeded
to race away northwards climbing rapidly as she went.
At the time of dropping her bombs I judged her to be
at an altitude of about 11,500 feet. I made after her at all
speed at about 15,000 feet altitude, gradually overhauling
her. At this period the A.A. fire was intense, and I, being

about five miles behind the Zeppelin had an extremely uncomfortable time. At this point misfortune overtook me, for my mechanical pressure-pump went wrong and I had to use my hand-pump to keep up the pressure in my petrol tank. This exercise at so high an altitude was very exhausting, besides occupying an arm, thus giving me 'one hand less' to operate with when I commenced to fire. As I drew up with the Zeppelin, to my relief I found that I was free from A.A. fire, for the nearest shells were bursting quite three miles away. The Zeppelin was now nearly 15,000 feet high and mounting rapidly. I therefore decided to dive at her, for although I held a slight advantage in speed, she was climbing like a rocket and leaving me standing. I accordingly gave a tremendous pump at my petrol tank, and dived straight at her, firing a burst straight into her as I came. I let her have another burst as I passed under her and then banking my machine over, sat under her tail, and flying along underneath her, pumped lead into her for all I was worth. I could see tracer bullets flying from her in all directions, but I was too close under her for her to concentrate on me. As I was firing, I noticed her begin to go red inside like an enormous Chinese lantern and then a flame shot out of the front part of her and I realised she was on fire. She then shot up 200 feet, paused, and came roaring down straight on to me before I had time to get out of the way. I nose dived for all I was worth, with the Zepp tearing after me, and expected every minute to be engulfed in the flames. I put my machine into a spin and just managed to corkscrew out of the way as she shot past me, roaring like a furnace. I righted my machine and watched her hit the ground with a shower of sparks. I then proceeded to fire off dozens of green Very lights in the exuberance of my feelings.[35] Second Lieutenant W.J. Tempest, 39 Squadron RFC

This series of triumphs marked a turning–point in the Zeppelin menace and most of London celebrated wildly. Finally the beleaguered civilians felt that they had hit back and had shown the Germans that they could not come and go as they pleased. They had cast aside their ignominious sense of impotence and regained their pride.

They say it was wonderful to hear all London cheering – people who have heard thousands of huge crowds cheering before say they have heard nothing like it. When Sowrey and Tempest brought down their Zepps I had an opportunity of hearing something like it, although they say it wasn't so grand as mine, which could be heard twenty and even thirty miles outside London. It swelled and sank, first one quarter of London, then another. Thousands, one might say *millions*, of throats giving vent to thousands of feelings. I would have given anything for you dear people to have heard it. A moment before dead silence (for the guns had ceased to fire at it) then this outburst – the relief, the thanks, the gratitude of millions of people. All the sirens, hooters and whistles of steam engines, boats on the river, and munitions and other works all joined in and literally filled the air – and the cause of it all – little me sitting in my little aeroplane above 13,000 feet of darkness! It's wonderful![36] Lieutenant William Leefe Robinson VC, 39 Squadron RFC

Some, however, could not forget the pain of the burning Germans as the Zeppelins fell to earth.

I was staying with some friends in Harrow when the whistles and the shouts went off. Of course the Zeppelin made a big noise – I suppose its engines were pretty powerful. We went out on to this little balcony and we saw this awful sight. It was like a big cigar and all of the bag part had caught fire. It was roaring flames – blue, red, purple . . . It seemed to come floating slowly down instead of falling down with a bang. We'd always been told that there was a crew of about 60 people and they were being roasted to death. Of course you weren't supposed to feel any pity for your enemies – nevertheless I was appalled to see the kind, good hearted British people dancing round in the streets at the sight of 60 people being burnt alive, clapping, singing and cheering. My own friends

were delighted. When I said I was appalled that anyone could be pleased to see such a terrible sight they said, 'But they're Germans, they're the enemies!' Not human beings – and it was like a flash to me that this is what war did. It created this utter inhumanity in perfectly decent, nice, gentle kindly people. I couldn't go on with it – I just turned my back on it then, but I'd everything to learn after that. You don't know the answers just instinctively. But I suddenly thought, 'This is not right, it is wrong and I can't have any further part in it!' So it was rather like Paul on the road to Damascus. I can't explain it better than that and I've never looked back – I still think it![37]
Sybil Morrison

Generally, the feeling was one of relief and a widespread sense that the dreaded Zeppelins were no longer undefeatable. The next raid did not occur until 27 November 1916 when ten Zeppelins returned to the Midlands and the north of England. But they found that there were no longer easy pickings to be had as the defences throughout the country had gained in strength and the defenders had learnt from the experiences of their compatriots in London. The German misfortunes continued and L34 was shot down by Second Lieutenant I.V. Pyott, falling into the sea off Middlesbrough. To the south, as L21 began its journey back, it was detected by several aircraft.

We were warned that the Zeppelin had dropped bombs in the Midlands and was making its way to the coast and I, with two other pilots, immediately got into the air to wait for it. I saw the Zeppelin approaching the coast and immediately chased after it. It was flying at about 5,000 feet when I first saw it and it immediately climbed to 8,000 feet and I went after it. I approached from the stern about 300 feet below and fired four drums of explosive ammunition into its stern which immediately started to light. At the same time one of the other pilots was flying over the top of the Zeppelin and to his horror he saw a man in the machine-gun pit run to the side and leap overboard. Having seen the Zeppelin circle down to the sea in a blazing mass – a most horrible sight –

I went back to Yarmouth and landed. I could not say I felt very elated or pleased at this, somehow I was overawed at the spectacle of this Zeppelin and all the people aboard going down into the sea. But it shows how events strike people differently, one of the other two pilots was most enthusiastic and terribly pleased with the results. Somehow I didn't feel any satisfaction about it at all and didn't want to discuss the matter at all.[38]
Lieutenant Egbert Cadbury, Yarmouth Station, RNAS

The string of British successes in autumn 1916 showed that the Zeppelin threat had been overcome. When an aeroplane armed with the new incendiary and explosive ammunition got an airship in its sights, then it was inevitably doomed. The attacking plane did not even need to be a new, high-performance machine. The much castigated BE2 C, which although still prevalent on the Western Front was already regarded there as a fatal encumbrance, enjoyed a triumphant Indian summer in Britain and was ultimately responsible for destroying nine of twenty-one airships downed by aeroplanes. The pre-war fear, which had appeared to come true in 1915, that the German crews would be able to range with impunity above Britain had literally been exploded and, though airship raids continued until August 1918, by the end of the second year even the Germans could see that the hour of the airship had passed. The steady improvements made to the British defences once their inherent weaknesses had been identified, meant that the risks encountered by airships soon outweighed the benefits. The impact of airship raids had not matched up to exaggerated expectation and this point would be dramatically made when a new generation of aeroplane raiders appeared in British skies during the early summer of 1917.

CHAPTER EIGHT

Naval Aviation

During the first three years of its existence, under the patronage of Winston Churchill, the Royal Naval Air Service pursued an innovative and experimental course. In both its technical developments and the policies it espoused, it showed a more imaginative understanding of the wider application of aviation in wartime and as such it was at the forefront of developments in home defence and strategic bombing. Unfortunately, in the process, it failed to carve out for itself a sufficiently unique naval identity in the way the RFC had forged a clearly-defined role within the BEF. As a result when the war started the RNAS was not in a position to meet the naval demands that were the reason for its original formation. The main aerial requirement of the navy was for long range reconnaissance, working either directly with the Grand Fleet or by patrolling the great expanses of the ocean to make sure that they remained clear of German surface ships and submarines. If elements of the German High Seas Fleet emerged from their lair at Wilhelmshaven, they would have to be located and tracked. Forearmed with this information, the Grand Fleet Commander-in-Chief, Admiral Sir John Jellicoe, would be able to bring his enemies to battle in a situation of his own choosing to gain the maximum tactical advantage.

The simplest method of reaching beyond the horizon to extend the vision of the fleet was through the use of balloons. These could either be tethered to or towed by ships. The first British kite balloons were ordered in early 1915 when the former tramp steamer, *SS Manica*, was hurriedly fitted with a Silicol hydrogen gas generator, compressor, winching gear and kite balloon and sent for war trials as part of the Eastern Mediterranean Squadron during its assault against the Turks at the Dardanelles. On arrival *Manica* successfully spotted the fall of shot for the Fleet's gunfire during the military landings in April 1915 and her work was so highly-regarded that a series of balloon ships were prepared, all performing useful services, mainly in spotting during shore bombardments. Unfortunately such vessels did not address the main problem of providing greater awareness for the Grand Fleet since they were incapable of keeping up with its larger, more powerful ships once under way and the value of balloon ships thus declined until the Grand Fleet Aircraft Committee eventually decided to phase them out in 1917. By that date the problems of attaching kite balloons to the battleships themselves had been resolved and the necessity for separate ships disappeared.

Airships, with their long-range capacity, had an obvious application to naval operations. Unfortunately the British airship programme had been dogged by indecision and disaster since its earliest days. In March 1909, in line with the recommendations of the Aerial Navigation Sub-committee, Vickers, Son & Maxim, who had played an important role in the development of submarines, were contracted to begin work on the navy's first fully-rigid dirigible at Barrow-in-Furness. Known officially as No.1 Rigid Naval Airship it was more commonly referred to as the *Mayfly*. Powered by two 180 horsepower Wolseley engines, at 512 feet in length, forty-eight feet in diameter and with an overall volume of 700,000 cubic feet, it was much larger than any ship that had been produced by the army at its Balloon Factory. Unfortunately this very factor precipitated its downfall. When, on 24 September 1911, it was brought out into the open for only the second time, the heavy superstructure broke and the whole ship was wrecked. The inaptly named *Mayfly* did not. In the ensuing investigations the whole policy of naval airships was re-examined and suspended by the Admiralty until 1913 when it was agreed with the War Office that the RFC's dirigibles would be handed over to the navy. Consequently, by the start of the war the RNAS had only six working airships.

The first task that fell to the RNAS was the vital duty of covering the BEF at its most vulnerable point when the troops were conveyed across the English Channel to take up their position alongside the French in mid–August 1914. Airships such as the *Astra-Torres* could hover aloft on patrols for up to twelve hours, in contrast to the maximum of three hours which the seaplanes could offer. The BEF crossed in safety but the extent of the submarine menace was sharply revealed by the sinking of three British heavy cruisers, the *Aboukir, Hogue* and *Cressy*, by a single submarine on 22 September. The subsequent German declaration of submarine warfare on merchant shipping early in 1915 thus threw the whole shortage of RNAS aerial patrols into high relief. As a direct result in February, the First Sea Lord, Admiral of the Fleet Lord Fisher, called for the immediate development and production of a new fleet of airships capable of carrying 160 pounds of bombs on eight-hour anti-submarine patrols. As with any project undertaken by Fisher he went for it '*totus porcus*'.

I went up to the Admiralty with Holt-Thomas to meet the Director of Contracts there, Sir John Black. We were negotiating about how to get these airships made quickly and the door literally burst open and Jackie Fisher burst in with a face like a turkey cock. He said, 'I believe you two are talking about getting some of these airships done?' We told him, 'Yes!' 'For the love of Mike get a move on, because any airship might shorten this war by one day and that's a lot of money and a lot of lives!' That was his way of looking at it. Oh, I can remember his face like a turkey cock – blue eyes staring.[1] Hugh Burroughes, Director, Aircraft Manufacturing Company, Hendon

The solution that was arrived at was to use a mass–produced aircraft fuselage hanging beneath a gas bag envelope. The resulting 'Submarine Scout' or SS Airship was hardly elegant but it was practical and the prototype was aloft in a mere three weeks.

Commander Cave Brown Cave called James, another engineer and myself, with two coxswains, to a little conference where he told us what he wanted us to do. We were to construct a BE2 C fuselage underneath a Willows envelope. In the fuselage was a Renault engine which we overhauled in the meantime. The difficulty was

to get the fuselage in a correct position with the envelope which had a much large diameter in the front and then it tails off. You had to get that suitably balanced with the fuel and everything else aboard and attached to the envelope. This wasn't too easy because every time we wanted an alteration the patches on the envelope had to be taken off. These were pieces that the cables could be attached to – fabric doubled back on itself with a sort of iron loop strip in it to which the steel cables down to the fuselage could be attached. Every time there was an alteration these had to come off and the new positions prepared and stuck on again. Of course you couldn't attach any weight on them until they'd really, properly dried which took about 24 hours. Relatively speaking you did an extraordinarily small amount of work over a long period due to rearrangement of the equilibrium of the fuselage. Eventually we got that to the satisfaction of Commander Cave Brown Cave. I should say we were about three weeks on that – maybe a month. We couldn't do it any faster as there was no previous experience. It had to be flexible, yet rigid, as all the controls came down to the fuselage and if they weren't quite in the right tension then of course they wouldn't work. When we'd finished it was taken out of our hands and everything in detail was put in on paper and the rest of the SSs were made from it.[2]
Chief Petty Officer Engineer J. S. Middleton, Kingsnorth Station, RNAS

Once this basic machine had been conceived the next problem was to find a source of adventurous young men willing to undergo a crash course of training. It was decided that young midshipmen or sub-lieutenants in the Royal Navy, chaffing at the bit in enforced inactivity at Scapa Flow, would be ideal material.

A signal came round to all the battleships and battle cruisers in the Grand Fleet saying that each captain was to recommend one young officer of about 18, 19 or 20 for special service and they would have to report to the Admiralty in 48 hours time. There were certain qualifications to the telegram to the effect that they'd got to be able to navigate and take charge themselves. At any rate I was sent for by my captain, he showed me the telegram and said, 'I picked you and you will go and report to the Admiralty!' The rumour was, and we all thought, that we were picked to command motor boats on the canals in Flanders assisting the British Army. When we got to the Admiralty we were escorted into the room of the First Sea Lord, Lord Fisher, whose opening remarks were, 'You young gentlemen are going to fly, you'll probably be dead within a year or you may get the VC! But you've been selected to start a new airship service which will be the counter to the U-Boat menace which looks to be the biggest menace we have in this war. If you don't want to fly, or your parents don't want you to fly you can come and tell me in 48 hours time.' Then he offered us some bait of ten shillings a day extra pay from that day – my pay was only one and sixpence of which I only saw sixpence – and six weeks training in London. After being abroad two years and up at Scapa for the last six months it was a bait that none of us shut our eyes to.[3] Midshipman Thomas Elmhurst, HMS *Indomitable*

Once selected the pupils' learning process started with flights in manned balloons launched from the Hurlingham Club in London. First, they had to learn to inflate and prepare the balloons for flight.

The balloon consisted of the fabric bag itself covered with a net to which the basket is attached. The first procedure is to lay out the gas bag in a flat circle on the ground, fasten the gas valve into the centre of the circle and cover the balloon with a net. Gas is then put into the balloon through what eventually becomes the bottom neck of the balloon which is connected to the gas main. As the balloon rises sandbags are hung round the net and gradually moved lower down the net until the balloon is fully inflated. Then a ring is attached to the bottom of the net and to this ring the ropes leading to the basket are attached. The neck of the balloon is then tied up with a loose slip knot until the balloon is ready to ascend. If it was a solo trip the pupil would get into the basket and the Squadron Commander would give two orders, one of which sounded rather frightening, 'Break your neck' and 'Try your valve'. The order to 'Break your neck' did not in fact refer to the pupil but to the neck of the balloon which had been tied up with a slip knot. This had to be released before the balloon ascended to allow for the gas in the balloon to expand as it rose in the air. The balloon was then released and the pupil sent away on his trip.[4] Frederick Verry, RNAS

The first balloon flight was a strange, slightly unsettling, but nevertheless exhilarating experience for the young pilots.

They simply took their hands off and let go of the guys and you drifted up in the air. You then had the experience of being airborne – seeing not yourself rising but the ground sinking away from you. That's what distinguishes balloon flying from other things, you don't feel the acceleration of ascent you just notice the ground is receding.[5] Victor Goddard, RNAS

Once aloft the balloon would go more or less where the wind dictated and they had only very simple methods of controlling the altitude at which the balloon carried them.

The handling of the balloon is very simple. You allow it to rise until you reach the height which you decide, or the balloon stops expanding. As the balloon goes up the gas expands and is forced out through the neck of the balloon and it gradually loses its lifting power. The tendency then may be for it to start to fall and this fall is checked by the use of a certain amount of ballast. Normally only a little sand need be thrown out in order to check the descent.[6] Frederick Verry, RNAS

As they gained experience it was not a hard life and indeed it seems to have been much safer than contemporaneous flying training for aircraft pilots. However, landings could be bumpy if the approach was ill-judged, and Goddard certainly picked the wrong spot when he gate-crashed a tempting-looking garden party.

We used to do our navigation in such a way that we would come down, only ostensibly by accident, in some splendid park where we were pretty sure that we should be provided with an excellent tea. And I must say one day we did land at Theobalds where we disturbed a tennis party, wrecked a conservatory and landed finally in their duck pond behind a batch of trees. We thoroughly disorganised the tennis party, but thoroughly enjoyed the strawberries and cream which were prepared for the tennis players. Then we motored back to London. I didn't discover till just before we were leaving that that house was the property of the Admiral commanding at Portsmouth and Lady Mays said, 'What a shame the Admiral wasn't there!' I thought what a very good thing it was that he wasn't there![7] Victor Goddard, RNAS

Having survived such mishaps the 'balloonatics' had to learn the art of flying the actual SS Airships themselves.

The car of my airship was nothing other than a BE2 C fuselage with two seats in tandem, one behind the other. In my seat, which was the back one I had an instrument board just the same as an aeroplane instruments board except the instruments were different; I had an altimeter; a pilot tube to measure your forward speed, a statoscope which measured the pressure of the atmosphere; a pressure gauge to show the pressure of the gas inside the gas bag which was kept at what it should be by a pump, pumping in air or letting out air. Then you had your physical controls. A foot bar connected to wires which went to your rudder and you steered by putting your foot over. To steer to the right we would push our left foot right over as though it was a tiller whereas in an aeroplane it goes the other way. For going up and down you would depress or raise your elevator flaps by a wheel which was in the vertical plane in front of you, either wind the wheel up or down. It was rather a nuisance because it got in the way of the little chart board holding one's map. I rigged my own up so that you could keep your chart in front of you and do your navigating with the aid of the usual instruments. An essential control was the 'crabpots' as we called them. They were sleeves of fabric inside a major fabric sleeve to allow the air which went up through the duct pipe behind the propeller, which drove the air into either the forward or after balloonet. You operated them with cords which were hooked into the fuselage. Then you had two valves: a gas valve which was the automatic safety valve which blew off when the thing came up to pressure that you could also open by hand and one on top of the ship which also had a string. The other strings were the controls for the water ballast.[8] Victor Goddard, RNAS

On approaching the land the ropes were thrown out for the ground crew to catch so that the airship could be slowly guided in without damage. In doing their duty they ran a not inconsiderable risk of serious injury.

It was a rule that no man was to touch the trail rope until it had first of all earthed itself and snaked along the ground a bit. If the airship came over with its trail rope not touching the ground but just within hand height a man could easily get more or less electrocuted with the static charge that would go down through his body to the ground. But it was quite a usual thing for the enthusiast to forget this rule and a chap could take a very nasty shock – enough to make him fall over backwards. Then they had to be stalwarts. Once they grabbed the trail rope – which might be snaking through the grass at as much as 10, 15, perhaps 20 miles an hour – they would suddenly find themselves dragged across the ground at very high speeds. Two or three other stalwarts flung themselves at the rope as well and it became rougher than a rugby scrum. A whole bunch of men grabbing on to a rope and determined not to let go – once you'd got it you didn't let go until the ship's speed was arrested. When your landing party was grabbing on to the rope and was vertically below you, you could find that you were coming down faster than you liked and looked like hitting the ground. In which case you would let go a lot of water ballast that would immediately swamp the ground crew – a sort of shower bath of spray![9] Victor Goddard, RNAS

It was not very long before the airships acquired a nickname which, then and now, was peculiarly appropriate. Not many realised the actual origin of the term 'blimp' but Goddard was present when the term was inadvertently coined.

My station commander was A.D. Cunningham and on Sunday mornings he carried out the usual naval routine of inspecting the whole of his station. Any airships that weren't on patrol had their crews with them at attention and smartly dressed. He would see that they were properly cleaned, properly maintained and asked questions of the Captain. He walked by my ship and to see that I'd got it properly up to pressure he flipped the envelope and it made a sound which he imitated by saying, 'Blimp!' I told this story at lunchtimes and thereafter my airship became called 'Blimp!' That name became the generic name for all the SS type of airship and has ever since been applied to most airships.[10] Victor Goddard, RNAS

The design work may have been rushed but the SS Airships were a resounding success and were followed by a series of bigger and better variants on the theme. The SS Zero and the Coastal Airships increased performance exponentially until finally the North Sea Airship, which appeared late in the war, could stay aloft for up to three days with much improved crew accommodation. It was even possible to 'stunt' an airship as was demonstrated when an SS Zero was flown at low level along the river Thames with the traditional not too enthusiastic passenger.

I remember having to jump over bridges all the time trying to keep close to the water. I'd reach a bridge and I'd flick over the top of the bridge. It was a lovely test of the Zero because they seemed to hop over like a horse. I looked at Tower Bridge and thought now shall I go in between the two bridges? No – it's taking too much of a chance. So I went over the top bridge. Eventually I got out to sea and turned round at the mouth of the Thames to ask if what I'd done was satisfactory – hadn't had a word from my passenger the whole time. So I turned round in my seat and looked round and there was nobody there. I slowed down my engine and turned into the wind, called to my wireless operator and said, 'Where's the passenger?' He leaned over and said, 'I can't see him!' I got up and there he was lying on the floor. Absolutely green, shocking sight![11] Thomas Williams, RNAS

Throughout the war the airships patrolled the seas surrounding Britain looking for submarines. Although the hours were long the patrols could still be reasonably enjoyable.

To fly a ship on a nice day was a really delightful experience. One felt that the air was entirely one's own, you could go where you liked within the ship's range, fly at what height you like, what speed you like, you could stop and examine something down below or you could go along at quite a respectable speed. One of the things I used to enjoy after a rather boring day on patrol was to come home more or less like a motor boat with the guys of the ship just tipping the waves – then one really appreciated the speed of the ship.[12] Frederick Verry, RNAS

On patrol the airships could carry a bomb load but little time had been wasted by the designers and manufacturers on sophisticated technicalities such as bomb racks, a release gear or bomb-sights.

We could keep up long hours but our bomb capacity wasn't very great at all. We had quite small bombs which were more or less lying loose, rolling about on the floor. Eventually we hung them over the side on bits of string and carried sheath knives to cut the bit of string to drop the bomb. We had no bomb sights; simply knocked a

couple of nails in as a rough indication of the trajectory.[13]
Thomas Williams, RNAS

The long hours aloft meant that nature had to have its way in a manner not usually experienced by aircraft pilots.

> There were several methods. Some people carried cans and some carried bottles. I found this after long patrols rather unpleasant so I evolved my own system which I believe became standard in the end. It was to bore a hole in the floor and attach some rubber hosing to it. At the other end – the business end – a petrol funnel. I had a brass cup hook in the side of the fuselage and just hooked it on. I found that was a distinct home comfort.[14]
> Thomas Williams, RNAS

The airships may have lacked the 'teeth' to destroy any sighted German submarines but their patrols provided a flow of information. When they sighted a submarine they made an immediate report of the precise location as determined through reference to the Royal Navy wireless direction-finding stations which allowed the nearest destroyer or sloop to be directed to that area.

As the war progressed the necessity of providing air reconnaissance and cover for the Grand Fleet became ever more paramount. The solution lay in providing aircraft to accompany the Grand Fleet at sea but aircraft endurance ranges were so limited that it was impossible to use land-based aeroplanes. Consequently, some kind of aircraft carrier was required to carry either seaplanes or, in the longer term, conventional aircraft. Any such carrier had to have the speed to maintain station at sea, which meant at the very least twenty-one knots for the Grand Fleet, and twenty-four knots for the Battlecruiser Fleet.

Early pre-war experiments had resulted in some success and aircraft entered the naval firmament when Charles Samson flew a Short Pusher Biplane off a sloping track which descended from the forward twelve-inch turret to the prow of HMS *Africa* on 10 January 1912. Experiments continued apace and eventually culminated in the first parent ship for seaplanes, HMS *Hermes*, which was briefly commissioned in 1913 and carried out tests that year in launching seaplanes using a two tracked take-off platform. They took off via bogies or wheels recessed into their floats and then landed on the sea prior to being winched back on board using a long aircraft handling boom. The Short Folder Seaplane had the advantage, as its name artfully suggests, of folding wings which reduced the wing span from fifty-six feet to a mere twelve feet. The potential of the seaplanes was demonstrated during the 1913 naval manoeuvres when *Hermes* was attached to the 'Red' Fleet and her Short Folder No. 81, fitted with a wireless transmitter, took an active part in the exercises.

On the outbreak of war three cross-Channel steamers were swiftly converted into seaplane carriers by the installation of handling booms and seaplane shelters to accommodate three aircraft per vessel. The seaplanes were intended to be winched off the ship and to take off from the sea under their own power. The conversion of the *Empress*, *Engadine* and *Riviera* was completed in September 1914 and, although originally designed to fulfil a reconnaissance role for the Grand Fleet, they were eventually assigned to the Harwich Force to bomb the German bases in Belgium.

The ship would lie to as we call it – come up head to wind, then get broadside on the wind and lower the planes over on the leeside of the ship. The ship was 600 feet long and they'd take off on the sheltered side of the ship and be airborne. If it was very rough and you sent a plane off then you'd never get her back again the same because coming down on the water she'd hit the first big rollers and swipe her floats off. So if a plane was coming in we'd lower a motor boat over the side – they were good sea boats and they'd go and stand by. The plane would come down as near to the ship as he could and try to make a landing but they came in at least 40 miles an hour and although the floats were wire braced the sea's pretty solid stuff to hit at that speed you know and it could swipe the floats off. Then the plane would go straight on her belly. It was only fabric and wood frame and all we had to do was save the pilot and observer and, if possible, save the engine. A rope would be passed round the engine and the boat would tow it back to the ship's side where it could be hoisted in – the plane itself would be destroyed. We only did that when we were forced to do it. If it was possible for a plane to get back to sheltered water at Scapa Flow then the plane could land there with much more safety.[15] Air Mechanic George Stubbington, HMS *Campania*, RNAS

Unfortunately it was soon discovered that the early under-powered seaplanes, loaded with bombs, were extremely fastidious about the sea conditions required for a successful take-off. If there was any sort of a sea running they could not take off and, perversely, if the sea was dead calm, then they would not 'unstick'. Clearly this placed severe limitations on their operational effectiveness and there were many disappointments for both the pilots and their admirals. One such example, illustrating the mutual incomprehension of the two cultures, occurred during a series of efforts to launch a pre-emptive raid on the Zeppelin sheds on the north German coast from the *Engadine* and other seaplane carriers during summer 1915.

We were just beginning to hoist the Schneider Cup Sopwiths out when somebody put up an alarm, 'Submarine sighted!' So the Admiral immediately ordered his destroyers to circle the flotilla – he'd got to protect his ships against submarine attack. About a dozen powerful destroyers began to circle making a circle of perhaps two miles in diameter, looking marvellous and going like the hammers. They were making a cross swell which no seaplane had the hope of a celluloid cat in hell of taking off. However we did our best and one chap actually bounced off the top of a wave and made it – got off and managed to score a hit on one of the sheds. Every other aeroplane we put out including my own simply turned arse over tip owing to the impossible artificial sea conditions. If it hadn't been for this appalling swell put up by the destroyers the sea conditions were perfect. I saw at least seven or eight fins and rudders sticking up out of the water with 'Sopwith Aviation Company, Kingston upon Thames, written on them – that was all that was visible of the Sopwith Schneiders![16] Lieutenant Graham Donald, HMS *Engadine*, RNAS

The most famous chance to use the extended horizon offered by the seaplanes occurred during the Battle of Jutland which commenced in the North Sea on 31 May 1916. The *Engadine* was with Vice Admiral Sir David Beatty's Battlecruiser Fleet, in advance of the Grand Fleet itself, when they became aware of the near presence of the German High Seas Fleet. The *Engadine* was carrying two Short and two 'Baby' Sopwith Seaplanes. At 14.40 Beatty ordered a seaplane reconnaissance to investigate the area to the north-north-east where smoke had been reported. Flight Lieutenant F.J. Rutland took off at 15.07. He left behind an aggrieved Lieutenant Graham Donald.

Word came through, 'Investigate with aircraft!' There was some activity just on the horizon in the direction of Schleswig Holstein. I was on the aft deck with my old Short Seaplane 8359 all ready to go, clad in flying gear, sitting in the cockpit waiting for instructions, engine warming up, chain hooked on ready to hoist – I'd have been in the water and away in about a minute and a half. Unfortunately just as I got my engine nicely warmed up our senior flying officer Flight Lieutenant Rutland appeared, waved me down with my observer and told me that he'd got the Captain's sanction – he was to go! So my Short Seaplane 8359 went – but without me![17] Lieutenant Graham Donald, HMS *Engadine*, RNAS

By such chances are a man's role in history defined. Rutland flew off and made aerial contact with the cruiser screen of the German High Seas Fleet but his luck ran out when his petrol pipe fractured in mid-flight and he was forced down on to the sea. Although he repaired the problem, he was recalled to the *Engadine* and so ended the only flight during the Battle of Jutland. None of Rutland's wireless messages had reached Beatty and in essence the flight achieved nothing. Yet the very failure of aerial reconnaissance merely highlighted how desirable it would be if it could be done properly. Jellicoe in the flagship of the Grand Fleet was forced to make all his decisions in a vacuum of ignorance as to the whereabouts, not only of the German Fleet but also elements of his own force. Meanwhile, the German commander Vice Admiral Reinhard von Scheer, had the benefit of Zeppelin reconnaissance reports to confirm the safety of his proposed escape route back past Horns Reef to port. Despite some of the reports proving to be inaccurate, largely due to the prevailing poor visibility, they helped him to execute the withdrawal of his ships from the ring of steel which, by mere guesswork, Jellicoe had attempted to throw around him.

The RNAS seaplanes and the larger flying boats also flew on anti-submarine patrols from bases on the British coast and at Dunkirk. As the war continued the menace of submarine warfare did not abate, although the Germans suspended it for a while after the furore generated by the sinking of the *Lusitania*. On the resumption of unrestricted submarine warfare without warning in February 1917, the urgency of the situation was greatly exacerbated and new technologies were brought into the battle. It was discovered that the Royal Navy's wireless direction stations could identify the position of German submarines by getting a 'fix' on their wireless transmissions. These were carefully logged and soon it became apparent that many of the smaller submarines operating close to the British Isles were in the habit of passing in the vicinity of the North Hinder light vessel where, in order to conserve the electrical batteries which powered their engines, they were almost always on the surface. Using this information a carefully constructed 'spider's web' of patrolling flying boats from Felixstowe was planned which centred on the light vessel and traversed the whole area on a regular basis. The system was initiated in April 1917 and soon began to pay dividends. The first U-boat to be sunk by bombing action from the air was the ill-fated UC 36 which was hit by two bombs while on the surface on 20 May 1917. Gradually, as the patrolling system became more sophisticated with patrols criss-crossing the seas all around the British Isles, the twin threats of submarines and Zeppelins were sought out and where possible destroyed. All told, the risks of long-range patrols were fairly high but the patrolling airmen understood that they played an important deterrent role in the war against commerce raiders. They craved the sight of a submarine.

Looking for a periscope in a rough sea was almost an impossibility. On one occasion south of the Isle of Wight we were told a submarine was on the surface. We thought that was a particularly marvellous opportunity. It was a

188

very, very misty day, one of those low sea mists that you used to get very often in the Channel. When we were about 30 miles south of the Needles my observer shouted to me, 'Look, Bill, there's a submarine – there – can you see it through the mist?' I looked down and I could see a grey hulk on the sea. We turned round quickly and we dropped four 100 lb bombs on it – to see a submarine fully awash was something out of this world – marvellous! We circled a bit and I was wondering what would happen and whether or not I could see any survivors swimming about but it didn't change except in the fact that it changed slightly in its colour from a dull grey to kind of a dirty cream. So we came down lower in the mist to see what it was – and of course you know what it was don't you, it was a whale! That was a bit of an anti-climax![18] F. Silwood, RNAS

The seaplanes and flying boats had several successes against the submarines often in the most unpropitious circumstances.

It was one of those days where it wasn't fit for dogs to walk about in. It was pelting down – raining and blowing – a terrible day. In consequence I never though that we'd have to go out on any sort of flights – it wasn't fit to walk in never mind fly in – but Samson had other ideas. He'd got information that there was a U-boat sculling around somewhere beyond the Yarmouth Roads. Since it was such a bad day he expected it to be on the surface because the U-boat commander wouldn't suspect that we'd be daft enough to fly in that weather. Anyway out we went. We were equipped with two, maybe four, 500 lb bombs in the shape of depth charges – they went off after they reached a certain depth. True enough there was a submarine on the surface. We dived down and I think the second pilot dropped the bombs. The U-boat stood up in the air with her stern down, her nose up and went down. There were patches of oil. I was fighting the foremost guns and was in the position to see most of the action. When we got back Samson sent for me – he'd got gimlet blue eyes which bored right into you – you couldn't tell a lie of any kind! He cross-examined me very carefully on what had happened and from that point we claimed a submarine.[19] Thomas Thomson, RNAS

Silwood also finally got the chance to sink a real submarine rather than a whale.

We were on patrol somewhere in mid-Channel and my observer shouted out to me, 'There's a periscope!' And there sure enough was a periscope. It was travelling towards a lone cargo ship coming up Channel. We managed to drop four 100 lb bombs on it and advised Portland what had happened. They sent out an armed yacht and between us the submarine was totally destroyed. After we'd dropped our bombs I flew low over this cargo boat and there was the Captain on the bridge, obviously with something in a glass, toasting us as we flew by with a violent waving of arms![20] F. Silwood, RNAS

Inevitably there were many occasions when the seaplanes and flying boats were forced by engine failure to ditch in the sea. Although the North Sea may not seem terribly large on a map, when viewed at sea-level in often very rough weather it seemed a dismal prospect to a ditched crew. Pigeons were often the only means of communication left open to them since wirelesses did not respond well to immersion in large quantities of seawater. However, even the pigeons could be recalcitrant.

My engine conked out and we were lucky to get on the sea to start with. We made a sort of pancake landing against a big wave and we got down. We released our pigeons. The trouble was it was blowing so hard the pigeons wouldn't leave the aeroplane. So we threw everything we had almost at them – I threw my last half crown at them! They eventually got back to the loft and a half crown was never better spent because 16 hours afterwards we were picked up. We were in a pretty sorry state by then I can assure you![21] F. Silwood, RNAS

*   *   *

Although aircraft ranges were getting longer all the time as engine power and efficiency improved they were still not adequate for land-based aircraft to provide the kind of continuous cover required by the Grand Fleet during its sweeps of the North Sea. The difficulties that had become apparent when taking off in a seaplane directly from the surface of the sea had directed attention and experimentation back towards the original idea of launching seaplanes from the more stable deck of a ship without having to lower them into the sea. Thus a launching platform of some 165 feet was installed on the converted carrier HMS *Campania*.

To fly a seaplane off the deck you had to have temporary wheels. We fitted the Schneider Seaplanes with axles and two wheels under the floats and the ship would be going straight into the wind. The seaplane would be fastened down to the boat, she'd rev her engine up and at a given signal we'd release the plane and before she got to the end of the flight deck she would have flying speed and she'd lift off. Once she was off she could release the axle and wheels, drop them into the sea and a motor boat would pick them up – we didn't want to lose them every time. When she left the flight deck she'd be at least 40 feet from the water so that was a 40 foot drop even then for the wheels and sometimes that would damage them. If she was slow in releasing them they would be ruined entirely. The plane would have to go back to Scapa Flow to land or if it was a quiet day of course she could come down on to the water to be picked up.[22] Air Mechanic George Stubbington, HMS *Campania*, RNAS

Although the seaplanes improved, the manifestly superior performance of land-based aircraft, which of course did not have to carry the large and heavy unaerodynamic floats, meant that by 1917 it was imperative that trials be carried out into the possibility of launching and landing aircraft from ships to counter the Zeppelins. Victor Goddard witnessed one such set of experiments launched from ramps on the turrets of HMS *Indomitable*.

We had two 12″ turrets one on either side of the ship. On the starboard forward turret was a fighter, a Camel and on the after port turret was a two-seater reconnaissance aircraft – the Sopwith 1½ Strutter. The aircraft were permanently secured to the rear end of the turrets and when one was required to fly off a platform was quickly rigged up with the planks on the turret right out to the end of the guns. With the guns at a certain degree of elevation the total slope of the platform was slightly downward. That gave a run for the aircraft of about 75 or 80 feet at the very most. That meant to say that the aircraft became airborne after a run of only that length of platform – there was a further resource in the pilot's hands, which didn't amount to very much – and that was the height of the platform above the level of the water. That was not more than 40 feet at the most. When the ship was about to fly off one of these aircraft the ship would be turned into the wind, go to full speed and the turret would be turned slightly outboard so that the effective wind speed was right down the barrels of the guns. Then with the engines of the aircraft running full out the pilot would be slipped and he'd charge down the runway into the wind, come off the end still without flying speed and swoop down like a swallow to gain final flying speed. Then just before he hit the water he would pull up and would climb away. It was a great risk that the pilot would not get flying speed and would stall and fall into the water. But he would only miss the crest of the waves by not more than a couple of feet if he'd judged the thing properly. It was an extremely hazardous operation and I used to watch these pilots with enchantment – with great admiration for their courage and skill.[23] Victor Goddard, RNAS

In March 1917 it was decided that the eighteen-inch light battlecruisers ordered by Fisher early on in the war were no longer required in that form and that HMS *Furious* should be radically reworked by removing the forward eighteen-inch gun and replacing it with a 228 foot take-off deck. It was the task of a group of heroic individuals to master the techniques of actually landing on this forward deck while the ship was at sea. The first deck-landing experiments were made by Squadron Commander

E.H. Dunning in a light and manoeuvrable Sopwith Pup on 2 August 1917.

> The first thing we had to do was to learn to fly on and off the foredeck. That wasn't as simple as it sounds really. I remember the Captain said, 'You may as well take a revolver and blow your brains out!' The plane came over and hovered and you have to synchronise the speed of the ship with the speed of the plane which is quite difficult although we were a fast oil-fuelled ship that could do 30 knots full out a plane went 60 miles an hour or more. We got the pilot to hover over the ship and then we grabbed on to the undercarriage – jumped up and grabbed it! We had to crouch a bit with the wind and the running propeller you had to keep clear of. Squadron Commander Dunning took off and he tried to land. He wasn't happy about the landing, took off again, crashed into the sea and it killed him.[24] Armourer William Hawkins, RNAS

Further expensive conversions to *Furious* were made during the winter of 1917 when she lost her other eighteen-inch gun for an aft landing-deck. Experiments using various types of skids instead of wheels with primitive arrester gear and cables across the landing-deck were plagued by the wind eddies caused by the original centre line superstructure and as a result the landing experiments were suspended.

A successful mission, however, was launched from HMS *Furious* screened by the 1st Light Cruiser Squadron on the Zeppelin sheds at Tondern on 19 July 1918. Each of the seven Sopwith Camels which comprised the bombing force carried two 50–pound bombs. They took off at 03.14 from a position some eighty miles from the coast and as they approached they found the Germans utterly unprepared.

> Captain Jackson dived right on to the northernmost shed and dropped two bombs, one a direct hit on the middle and the other slightly to the side of the shed. I then dropped my one remaining bomb, and Williams two more. Hits were observed. The shed then

burst into flames and an enormous conflagration took place rising to at least 1,000 feet, the whole of the shed being completely engulfed.[25] Captain William Dickson, HMS *Furious*

Immediately after, the second wave of Camels roared in over the stricken sheds.

I discovered the sheds, two larger and one smaller, one of the larger having the roof partially destroyed and emitting large volumes of dense black smoke. When in position I gave the signal and dived on the remaining large shed, releasing my bombs at 800 to 1,000 feet. The first fell short, but the second hit the centre of the shed, sending up a quantity of smoke or dust. Whether this burst into flames later I am unable to state, as the whole surroundings were thick with mechanics or soldiers armed with rifles and machine-guns, which gave so disconcerting a fire that I dived with a full engine to 50 feet and skimmed over the ground in a zigzag course to avoid it.[26] Captain Bernard Smart, HMS *Furious*

The first shed had contained the Zeppelins L54 and L60, which were totally destroyed in the fire, but the second shed survived. Yet the Camels were in a precarious situation in a sky full of clouds with a gathering wind and petrol sufficient for only three to three and a half hours' flying. In the absence of a deck–landing facility even if they located the *Furious* and her attendant cruisers they would have to ditch in the sea.

We arrived at the rendezvous at about 4.35 and could find no sign of Captain Dickson. The clouds were about 2,000 feet. As anti-aircraft guns were still firing I waited in the clouds constantly diving out to see if I could see Captain Dickson. At 4.55 my engine spluttered and stopped and I could only get it to go again by turning over to gravity.* I then made off steering 330 degrees, engine well throttled down and trying to climb as much as possible. Lieutenant

* The gravity tank – an extra petrol tank.

Williams was following. We lost sight of the ground very quickly. When about 8,000 feet up I had to go through a cloud and lost Lieutenant Williams. I reached 10,000 feet still being unable to see the ground. At 5.25 knowing that the gravity tank could not last much longer I shut off the engine and glided down through the clouds. When at 1,500 feet I found that I was over land and unable to recognise my position. The coast was not in sight and the visibility was very poor. I then started to the NW to try and reach the coast. I made several efforts to try my pressure tank again but the engine would only give one spurt and then stop. I was inclined to think that it was dirt in the tank. At 5.35 about my engine stopped altogether and I was obliged to land with the coast just in sight. I hit a fence and turned completely over. The country was full of farm houses so I at once started to set fire to my machine.[27] Captain W.D. Jackson, HMS *Furious*

In the end four of the pilots had to land in Denmark where they were interned. Dickson and Smart were picked up by British ships.

I sighted Lyndvig Lighthouse and one of our destroyers at the same time, the time then being about 05.45. I steered for the furthermost destroyer and after circling round landed in the water about 300 yards ahead of her. I climbed on to the tail after closing the Air Bag Tap and took hold of the wire which is connected to the slings. To this I bent on a heaving line which was thrown to me from the destroyer and passed same up to them, then hoisted aboard.[28] Captain William Dickson, HMS *Furious*

Although the raid had not been a complete success and was expensive both in terms of personnel and aircraft, it had demonstrated that the power of the air strike had increased enormously since the fiasco of the Cuxhaven raid in 1914. The experience gained during operations with HMS *Furious* was of great value in facilitating her eventual emergence as a through–flightdeck aircraft carrier with the classic off-centre superstructure in a further post-war series of reconstructions.

A fully operational carrier which would allow aircraft both to take off and land in safety was still some years away from development. But as the ranges of land-based aircraft continued to expand and their bombing capacity increase, so the formerly inviolate dreadnoughts began to receive timely intimations of their future mortality should they come under direct threat from the air. One clear illustration of the future shape of naval war was given in the eastern Mediterranean where the *Goeben*, bottled up in the Dardanelles since the end of the Gallipoli campaign in January 1916, was watched constantly by the RN and RNAS. On 20 January 1918 the *Goeben* and *Breslau* moved out of the Dardanelles Straits with the intention of attacking the vulnerable British monitors in the Imbros area. It was the opportunity for which the British had been waiting for two years but not all of the RNAS pilots were at the peak of their readiness that morning. Indeed, Captain Graham Donald for one was lucky not to have a hangover!

We had a very successful party which lasted until one or two am. To everybody's horror we were wakened up in the very early hours of the morning by the shouts of, 'The *Goeben*'s out! The *Goeben*'s out!' They had slipped out well before dawn, slipping through our minefields quite successfully. The dawn patrol reported the Straits clear not knowing that the *Goeben* and *Breslau* were actually behind them – were out in the Aegean. Why they didn't attack Mudros and Lemnos and blow the Headquarters to pieces, I don't know. They may have thought the *Lord Nelson* was there but she was in dock in Malta. So there weren't any heavy ships to stop them. But they didn't – they turned back and that was where we came into the picture. There I was about 25 stricken miles away from where the *Goeben* was and no new aeroplane – my old 'plane was unserviceable. The bombers were ready to attack and got under way, so it was just a case of all available aeroplanes and everybody for himself. I got a Camel, got the tank filled up and got going mainly to escort the bombers against attack from any German

196

fighters from the mainland. We were hitting both ships with quite small bombs from a low height. In truth the bombs were not very heavy and they couldn't have done armoured ships much harm but the crews definitely lost their nerve and instead of proceeding in a straight line for the mouth of the Dardanelles they started to zigzag – and in a minefield that is fatal.[29] Captain Graham Donald, RNAS

Even for aircraft without bombs there was an atavistic joy in shooting at these symbols of German naval might still preposterously sailing under their Turkish flags and the frenetic nature of the air attack provided a potent distraction from the task in hand.

With no German fighters appearing, just for the hell of it we attacked with machine-guns pelting everything we could at them. Merely as a gesture but it was quite funny to see machine-gun bullets bouncing off conning towers. It couldn't do much harm unless you could shoot somebody through a slit. Anything you could do to rattle them – raking the decks with tracer. The *Breslau* hit several mines and began to sink most convincingly. So we concentrated on the *Goeben* and she hit at least two. Being a heavier armoured ship she didn't show such signs of distress but she slowed down and began to settle a bit lower in the water. By the time they reached the mouth of the Dardanelles the *Goeben* was going slowly and the *Breslau* had sunk. It wasn't our bombs that had sunk her but we'd bombed her on to the minefield so we claimed it as a RNAS victory.[30] Captain Graham Donald, RNAS

The forts, mobile howitzers and minefields which had defended the Straits so successfully against the best efforts of the British Fleet earlier in the war held no terrors for the British pilots of the RNAS who flew effortlessly thousands of feet above them.

We followed the *Goeben* up the Straits. Machines were going back and forwards from Mudros and Lemnos, loading up with every bomb they could get, coming back over and pelting away. The *Goeben* was going slower and slower and by the time she was halfway up from Cape Helles to Chanak we thought she was just on the verge of sinking. The only thing they could do, and they did it brilliantly, was beach her as fast as they could at Nagara Point which is just at the Hellespont on a very suitable sloping beach which allowed her to sit there without sinking, absolutely stuck solid. They had picked a very good place to beach her at Nagara Point – it was the German Seaplane Station and had the finest battery of anti-aircraft guns in the Middle East. It was just the most gosh-awful place to fly at normal times let alone with the *Goeben* there. Believe me the sky was full of the stuff. They brought up their fighter squadrons and the air was stiff with German fighters. They were attacking our bombers – we got several shot down. The Camels' job was to hang around the bombers and keep the fighters off and I think we got quite a few of them down. A small Halberstadt Fighter climbed up to attack Ralph Sorley and Smithy in their DH4 at an unbelievably steep angle. He was right below me so I put my old Camel into a vertical dive and practically fell on top of him with both Vickers going. He went down in a queer sort of tumbling spin – but nobody saw him crash. It was one long, confused *mêlée* of a dogfight above the Dardanelles – just one hell of a crowd of aircraft and anti-aircraft shells.[31] Captain Graham Donald, RNAS

Despite their persistent attacks, the British found the problem was that the aerial bombs available, although full of potential for the future, had relatively little high-explosive inside them.

We were bombing her from all heights and getting quite a lot of hits. We had every available thing we could get hold of to keep bombing her. The bombs weren't terrifically heavy – actual physical serious damage was just not on, the bombs were not powerful enough, they weren't armour piercing – but we weren't doing her any good. We were hoping to delay the repair long enough till she got stuck in the mud and she couldn't get off. But it just so happened they did – by going full speed astern when they'd got her patched, their luck was in, they slid off and she got away in the night.[32] Captain Graham Donald, RNAS

Beyond the exuberant joy of releasing years of pent-up frustration, the predicament of the *Goeben* highlighted the vulnerability of even the most powerful ships to aerial attack. Although the fully-fledged concept of the 'fleet aircraft carrier' had not been fully realised during the First World War enough had been done to uncover the Achilles' heel of the battleship as the primary unit of naval warfare. Without protection from the air and under the sea they would be little more than death-traps by the start of the Second World War.

CHAPTER NINE

1917

Despite widespread disappointment that the hard-fought battles of 1916 had resulted in such limited gains, the Allies began the new year on an optimistic note. Verdun and the Somme were believed to have hit the Germans hard and they underlined the grim determination of both the French and the British to pursue the thorny path of victory to its painful end, however far off that might yet be. In the closing months of 1916 a series of well-executed but limited attacks at Verdun had clawed back the final remnants of the initial Germans gains and thus restored the shattered bedrock of French pride. The key figure in these successes was General Robert Nivelle and as a result he was projected into a position of such prominence that on 12 December he replaced General Joffre as Commander-in-Chief of the French forces. Nivelle was convinced that the methods he had employed at Verdun could be repeated on a much grander scale and that if every available man and gun was concentrated for an attack along the Chemin des Dames near the river Aisne during April he would be able to achieve the much-hoped-for 'knock-out blow' that had eluded all other generals. Charismatically expressed, his supreme confidence appealed in particular to the politicians who had to explain the consequences of each failed offensive to their bewildered constituents and by the end of January 1917 his plan had been adopted as the main Allied thrust for the coming spring.

To support the French initiative it was agreed that the BEF would first take over a further sector of the French line to release the troops needed to carry out Nivelle's offensive, before launching a series of diversionary operations intended to squeeze out the German salient which had been left exposed between the Scarpe and the Ancre rivers by the advances made during the Battle of the Somme. A plan was drawn up for the British Third Army to attack from the Scarpe once its northern flank had been secured by the capture of the German strongholds on Vimy Ridge and in front of Arras. If all this went according to plan, then the Fifth Army was to continue the momentum by launching an assault further south of the Ancre. However, the recently promoted Field Marshal Haig introduced a *quid pro quo* for his agreement to Nivelle's proposals. If the offensive failed, the French were to support him in equal measure later in the year when he put into practice a long-cherished desire to burst out of the infamous salient at Ypres and swing round in a giant right hook to seize the Channel ports of Bruges, Ostend and Zeebrugge which were being used by the Germans as submarine bases. The Admiralty had made it abundantly clear that Britain's ability to prosecute the war was under serious threat if the German submarine campaign against Allied merchant shipping was allowed to continue unchecked.

In the event neither Nivelle's nor Haig's plans unfolded as they were originally conceived, primarily because the Germans lamentably failed to co-operate by remaining in a position of tactical weakness. In late February they began an ordered withdrawal from the precarious salient between the Scarpe and the Ancre to the new, heavily-fortified Hindenburg Line, endowing the British attack at Arras with much greater significance as a distraction from the looming Nivelle offensive. Once the French attack finally began, even though the individual battles were partially successful, the great results that Nivelle had promised did not materialise and the venture was considered to be a failure. The French armies rapidly became demoralised and in May Nivelle was summarily removed from his command to be replaced by one of his subordinates at Verdun, General Philippe Pétain. Over the summer a series of mutinies threw the French Army into disarray and Haig was left to carry out his Flanders offensive unsupported.

The exponential growth of the RFC had continued unchecked during the winter and by the start of the spring offensives it consisted of no less than five brigades, each of two wings usually comprised of four squadrons. In addition there were five aircraft parks and five balloon wings. Last, but by no means least, was the Ninth Wing of seven squadrons under the direct control of RFC Headquarters. The RFC was buoyed up by all it had achieved in 1916, but understandably anxious over the immediate future. The proven superiority of the German Albatross D I, and the even better D IIs that were beginning to appear on the scene, was of great concern while the reorganisation of the German Air Service had also resulted in the establishment of no less than twenty-five Jastas. In contrast the RFC had only eight single-seater scout squadrons among its service strength of thirty-eight squadrons. Of these eight, only two were armed with machines that could equal the Albatross on a head to head basis. The corps squadrons were for the most part still soldiering on in the hopelessly outclassed BE2 Cs. Action to replace them could not be put off any longer and on 12 December 1916 the Army Council responded to Trenchard's and Haig's urgent requests for a substantial increase in the size of the RFC. They agreed that it could be enlarged to 106 service squadrons underpinned by ninety-five reserve squadrons.

New classes of aircraft had already been designed in response to Trenchard's increasingly desperate demands. Unfortunately, the persistent difficulties in securing trouble-free production meant that sufficient numbers of machines to equip whole squadrons for continuous active service were rarely available. As a result there was considerable delay from the time an aircraft was designed and approved until it was actually ready for service. The first of the new single-seater scouts to come on-stream was the low-powered but agile Sopwith Pup flown initially by 8 Squadron RNAS and then by 54 Squadron RFC which arrived in France on 25 December 1916. The Sopwith Triplane was also delivered to several of the RNAS squadrons that had been attached to the RFC and it made a considerable impression when it arrived in France in February 1917. The new all-purpose corps machine, the RE8, which should have entered the fray in late 1916, was unfortunately plagued with problems and its introduction was seriously delayed, forcing the hopelessly obsolescent BE2 Cs and BE2 Es to trundle on into 1917. The new aircraft that did arrive were, in a sense, an interim generation of aircraft, linking the old machines with the new even more powerful SE5 and Sopwith Camel single-seater scouts, the two-seater Bristol Fighter and the DH4 which were already in production but would not arrive on the Western Front until the late spring and summer of 1917.

In addition to the new hardware, there was also another round of innovations, consolidations and general improvements to the working methods employed by the corps squadrons which sought to capitalise on the lessons learned during the protracted Somme campaign. Rail junctions and key areas of the lines were to be photographed as a matter of routine and the results were considered sufficiently valuable to justify taking heavy risks to get good photographs.

In later days no reconnaissance machine ever crossed the lines without a camera. Now in a good photo, taken from a reasonable height, 6 to 8,000 ft, and enlarged from a quarter-plate to a half-plate, it is wonderful what you can see. You can count railway trucks and engines in sidings; from their positions you can frequently tell whether they are empty or full. You can distinguish between main lines, temporary light railways, roads, cart tracks and footpaths; and if you march half a dozen men across a field in single file, their tracks can be picked up with a magnifying glass. The gunners spend half their lives trying to hide their guns or camouflage their battery positions and it frequently deceives the casual glance of an observer; but if you once get a photo of the field that they are in, you will even in all probability see the muzzle of their guns, to say nothing of the limber tracks along the hedges. If you make a trench and enforced it with barbed wire, you will not only be able to see if it is a deep trench by the shadows or if it has water in it, but you will be able to see how many rows of barbed wire entanglement it has in front of it and which way the field was last ploughed.[1] Captain Robin Rowell, 12 Squadron RFC

Advances in the technology of wireless sets had also continued and by 1917 it was possible to put aloft an artillery observation aircraft equipped with a wireless set on a ratio of one for every 1,000 yards of front line without running the risk of the signals jamming each other. Wireless messages between batteries and observation aircraft were monitored by central wireless stations so that failures of communication could be swiftly detected and corrected. At the squadrons more and more wireless operators were trained and deployed to maintain a continuous and efficient service. All these measures were intended to meet the almost insatiable demand of the artillery for ever more observation aircraft.

The increasingly aggressive stance of the German Air Service meant that they pushed back the axis of aerial fighting from their rear areas to the front lines. It was soon noticed that formations of up to eight Albatross were engaged in regular patrols of the line in an effort to sweep the skies of the relatively defenceless army co-operation machines. As a result there was an inevitable demand for closer escort by British scouts. This was a difficult conundrum, for if defensive aircraft were supplied as requested then they would not be available for offensive operations, and with the consequent easing off of the pressure the initiative would pass ever further to the Germans. Eventually a compromise was adopted and close escorts of two scouts per artillery observation aircraft were provided but only in sectors where consistent and excessive losses had been incurred. These dedicated escorts were backed up by general line patrols of up to seven aircraft, while offensive patrols sought to intercept and destroy the German predators before they got anywhere near their prey. Overall, it was now apparent that scout aircraft had to act in formations, flying under the control of a patrol leader who maintained a strict cohesion in the air at all times. Not only was this vital when the British were flying aircraft inferior to the German scouts, but it greatly added to the impact of an attack when the enemy were surprised and brought into action in circumstances that were unfavourable to them.

Formation flying could be a tricky business for novice pilots as Lieutenant William Bishop found when he joined 60 Squadron in early March 1917. They were still equipped with the Nieuport 17 Scout which, although relatively under-powered, was sufficiently manoeuvrable to demand respect from the Albatross.

I was to bring up the rear of a flight of six machines, and I assure you it was *some* task bringing up the rear of that formation. I had my hands full from the very start. It seemed to me that my machine was slower than the rest, and as I wasn't any too well acquainted with it, I had a great time trying to keep my proper place, and to keep the others from losing me. I was so busy at the task of keeping up that my impressions of outside things were rather vague. Every time the formation turned or did anything unexpected, it took me two or three minutes to get back in my proper place. But I got back every time as fast as I could. I felt safe when I was in the formation and scared when I was out of it, for I had been warned many times that it is a fatal mistake to get detached and become a straggler . . . The way I clung to my companions that day reminded me of some little child hanging to its mother's skirts while crossing a crowded street.[2] Lieutenant William Bishop, 60 Squadron RFC

Bishop's first patrols were largely confined to monitoring the progress of the staged German retreat to the Hindenburg Line. On 25 March he had his first real dogfight which also demonstrated the sort of subterfuge necessary to bring faster aircraft to close grips.

From the corner of my eye I spied what I believed to be three enemy machines. They were some distance to the east of us, and evidently were on patrol duty to prevent any of our pilots or observers getting too near the rapidly changing German positions. The three strange machines approached us, but our leader continued to fly straight ahead without altering his course in the slightest degree. Soon there was no longer any doubt as to the identity of the three aircraft – they were Huns, with the big, distinguishing black iron crosses on their planes. They evidently were trying to surprise us, and we allowed them to approach, trying all the time to appear as if we had not seen them. Like nearly all other pilots who come face to face with a Hun in the air for the first time, I could hardly realise that these were real, live, hostile machines . . . Finally, the three enemy machines got behind us, and we slowed down so that they would overtake us all the sooner. When they had approached to about 400 yards, we opened out our engines and turned. One of the other pilots, as well as myself, had never been in a fight before, and we were naturally slower to act than the other two. My first real impression of the engagement was that one of the enemy machines dived down, then suddenly came up again and began to shoot at one of our people from the rear. I had a quick impulse and followed it. I flew straight at the attacking machine from a position where he could not see me and opened fire. My 'tracer' bullets – bullets that show a spark and a thin little trail of smoke as they speed through the air – began at once to hit the enemy machine. A moment later the Hun turned over on his back and seemed to fall out of control.[3] Lieutenant William Bishop, 60 Squadron RFC

To ensure his victory Bishop followed the Albatross down and was satisfied only when he had seen it smashed to pieces on the ground. In his enthusiasm he allowed his engine to choke during the dive and was extremely lucky to skate down to land just 150 yards behind the British front line.

Preparations for the Arras offensive were now well under way and on 31 March Bishop and two other pilots were ordered to provide escort cover for a formation of FE2 Bs from 11 Squadron engaged in a vital photographic reconnaissance. Although he scored a personal success, his conduct during the action underlined the reason why there was sometimes a little friction between the corps aircraft and their escorting scouts.

We were assigned to escort and protect six other machines that were going over to get photographs of some German positions about ten miles behind front-line trenches. I had my patrol flying about a thousand feet above the photography machines when I saw six enemy single-seater scouts climbing to swoop down upon our photography machines. At the same time there were two other enemy machines coming from above to engage us. Diving towards the photography machines, I managed to frighten off two of the Boches; then, looking back, I saw one of my pilots being attacked by one of the two higher Germans who had made for us. This boy, who is now a prisoner of war, had been a school-mate of mine before the war. Forgetting everything else, I turned back to his assistance. The Hun who was after him did not see me coming. I did not fire until I had approached within 100 yards. Then I let go. The Hun was evidently surprised.

He turned and saw me, but it was too late now. I was on his tail – just above and a little behind him – and at fifty yards I fired a second burst of twenty rounds. This time I saw the bullets going home . . . I rejoined the photography machines, which unfortunately in the meantime had lost one of their number.[4] **Lieutenant William Bishop, 60 Squadron RFC**

Bishop was lucky that his dereliction of duty did not have more serious consequences as the five surviving FE2 Bs returned safely with the photographs required. Over the next few months Bishop claimed many more victims and was an extremely effective exponent of the kind of lone patrols that Albert Ball had practised.

The concerted British air offensive designed to sweep the Arras skies of German aircraft to allow total freedom of operation for the corps artillery and reconnaissance machines during the battle was launched on 4 April. It began with an attempt to pluck out the prying eyes of the German observers swinging in the baskets beneath their kite balloons.

I tackled my first balloon yesterday, and consider it even more difficult than going for a Hun; at least, I think one gets a hotter time. We had received orders a week ago that all balloons *had* to be driven down or destroyed, as they were worrying our infantry and gunners during the advance. We had been practising firing the Le Prieur rockets for some time – a most weird performance. One dives at a target on the ground, and when within about fifty yards of it presses a button on the instrument board. Immediately there is a most awful hissing noise, which can be heard above the roar of the engine, and six huge rockets shoot forward from the struts each side towards the target. We did not think these were much of a success, owing to the difficulty of hitting anything, so decided to use tracer and Buckingham bullets instead. These are filled with a compound of phosphorus and leave a long trail of smoke behind them. On the morning we were detailed to attack the balloons the weather was so 'dud' that none of them were up, although we went across twice to have a look. We got a pretty hot time from Archie, as we had to fly below the clouds, which were about 2,000 feet, and dodge about all over the shop. Next day the weather cleared and we decided to carry out our strafe. We all went off individually to the various balloons which had been allotted us ... I personally crossed the trenches at about 10,000 feet, dropping all the time towards my sausage, which was five or six miles away. It was floating in company with another at about 3,000 feet, and reminded me of that little song, 'Two little Sausages.' I started a straight dive towards them, and then the fun began. Archie got quite annoyed, following me down to about 5,000 feet, where I was met by two or three strings of flaming onions, luckily too far off to do any damage. Then came thousands of machine-gun bullets from the ground – evidently I was not going to get them without some trouble. I zigzagged about a bit, still heading for the balloons, and when within two hundred yards opened fire. The old Huns in the basket got wind up and jumped out in their parachutes. Not bothering about them, I kept my sight on one of the balloons and saw the tracer going right into it and causing it to smoke. As our armament consists of a Lewis gun, I had to now change drums. This is a pretty ticklish job when you have about ten machine-guns loosing off at you, not to mention all the other small trifles! However, I managed to do it without getting more than half a dozen or so bullet-holes in my grid. By this time the second balloon was almost on the floor. I gave it a burst, which I don't think did any damage. The first sausage was in flames, so I buzzed off home without meeting any Huns. On the way back a good shot from Archie exploded very near my tail, and carried away part of the elevator. Don't you think this is the limit for anyone who wants excitement?[5] Captain W.E. Molesworth, 60 Squadron RFC

The ground offensive began at 05.30 on 9 April and, although Vimy Ridge was swiftly captured by the Canadians, the fighting soon settled down into the familiar pattern of 'bite and hold' operations designed to move the line forward in stages. A week later, on 16 April, Nivelle's much vaunted offensive was launched along the Aisne but floundered almost at once, necessitating a continuation of the effort at Arras to deflect as much German attention as possible from the French attack. In the skies above Arras the British had raised the stakes from a position of real weakness and as the battle raged on throughout April the RFC suffered dreadful losses. The cycle of aerial superiority was now fixed firmly in the Germans' favour, leaving the British hopelessly outclassed by the new range of enemy machines. But the exigencies of the infantry locked below them in a life-or-death struggle of equal measure meant that there was no alternative but to continue stoically. Trenchard's philosophy of the offensive now faced its sternest test. Certain tasks *had* to be successfully accomplished and if one attempt failed then another effort would have to be launched immediately regardless of the inevitable casualties. The strange mixture of despair, humour and determination needed to carry on regardless in the face of continuous casualties was epitomised by one long-range reconnaissance patrol flown over Lille by the Sopwith 1½ Strutters of 45 Squadron RFC on 6 April. In a bid to escape the black hand of fate Second Lieutenant F.G. Truscott devised a cunning plan.

Truscott was Mess President of 'B' Flight and kept the Mess Funds in assorted bunches of French currency. One morning a reconnaissance was announced which promised to be sticky (it was) and Truscott was going as observer with Marshall. As we got ready, Truscott made a big show of putting a fat envelope of paper francs into the pocket of his flying coat and informed us: 'This is my special system of self-preservation. You see, when you observe my machine being attacked you will all say, "Look, there go our Mess Funds" and you will all rally round to protect me.' I suppose, at the age we were then, the idea of being shot down was always somewhat academic, so nobody took any more notice. During the show, Campbell was shot down first. Marshall, with Truscott, was flying a little high to the left and slightly behind me, and another machine was between us. Six or eight Huns were coming up, apparently too far behind to start shooting. We never knew what actually happened, but possibly a long-range fluke shot from the Huns hit Marshall's rigging, for I saw his right wing fold up and, as he twisted round, he crashed into the next machine. Both wrecks, with bits flying in all directions, missed my tail by a few feet and, of course, there was no hope for the four fellows inside. With the inevitable lack of any sense of proportion which goes with such affairs, I thought, 'Goodbye, Truscott, but what about our Mess money?' And then another dogfight started and there was no time to think of anything else. When Austin, my observer, and I finally walked into the Mess hut, a corporal came up to me, with a fat envelope: 'Mr Truscott told me to give you this if he didn't come back this evening.'[6] Second Lieutenant Frank Courtney, 45 Squadron RFC

Even the experienced 60 Squadron flying the still respected Nieuport Scouts found that under the stress of continuous, desperate action the unit was falling apart because the replacement pilots and machines initially failed to reach the standard of their predecessors.

In three days, ten out of eighteen pilots were lost, and had to be replaced from England by officers who had never flown this particular type of machine, because there were none in England. Our new machines were collected from Paris, and the chance of a trip to fly one back was eagerly looked forward to by every pilot. Some of these new machines were not well built, and began – to add to our troubles – to break up in the air.[7] Major Jack Scott, 60 Squadron RFC

The RFC did have a new machine available in the form of the Bristol Fighter F2 A which was a two-seater aircraft armed with a fixed forward firing synchronised Vickers machine-gun while the rear observer/gunner had a Lewis gun. Its great advantage, which distinguished it from other machines such as the Sopwith 1½ Strutter, lay in its overall performance. It was powered by the new Rolls-Royce Falcon engine which allowed a top speed of just over 110 miles per hour at 10,000 feet and a fast rate of climb. Trenchard had decided to hold back its introduction through the new 48 Squadron RFC until the moment when he believed it would have maximum impact and great hopes were pinned on the new design. It was therefore doubly unfortunate that the first offensive patrol flown by the new fighters on 5 April ended in outright disaster. Led by Captain Leefe Robinson VC, the Bristols ran straight into a formation of the latest Albatross D IIIs commanded by Manfred von Richthofen. In the ensuing dogfight four of the Bristol Fighters were shot down, including the hapless Leefe Robinson, and the other two were lucky to escape. It was a bitterly disappointing end to Leefe Robinson's service. He was imprisoned in Germany and, although released after the Armistice, with his health undermined by the strains of captivity he died of influenza on 28 December 1918. With no previous experience of air fighting on the Western Front he had been given command of his flight purely on the basis of his Zeppelin shooting exploit and as an *ingénu* he was completely out of his depth in the bitter, vicious fighting that prevailed in April 1917. For a short while after its introduction the potential of the Bristol Fighter was undermined through being handled too timidly as a result of unfounded rumours about lurking structural weaknesses. Fortunately, before long, it was realised that it had to be flown and thrown about in the sky in just the same way as a single-seater scout, using the Vickers as the primary weapon and leaving the rear gunner to cover the tail. Once used in this fashion the Bristol became a formidable weapon indeed.

Another new aircraft which Trenchard held back to increase the impact of its introduction during the Arras air offensive was the DH4. It was the first two-seater aircraft specifically designed as a day bomber, being able to carry a substantial bomb load, and was powered by the Rolls-Royce 200 horsepower Eagle engine. The end result was a fast and powerful aircraft that was easy to fly and able to take considerable punishment. The first DH4 unit to reach the Western Front was 55 Squadron on 5 March 1917 and immediately it began a series of bombing raids.

The last aircraft to be held back by the British was the SE5, which proved to be one of the finest aircraft of the war and a great all-round scout. It was introduced to the Western Front through the arrival of 56 Squadron on 7 April. A strongly built biplane, it was primarily armed with a Vickers machine-gun fitted with a Constantinesco interrupter gear but it also carried a Lewis gun mounted on the top wing. Its Hispano–Suiza engine generated 114 miles per hour at 10,000 feet and gave an effective ceiling of 17,000 feet. Nevertheless, the SE5 at first appeared to be a considerable disappointment when a multitude of teething problems rendered it almost useless. After a spell of home service Captain Albert Ball returned to the fray for another tour of duty as a flight commander with 56 Squadron. He was not impressed with the new scout.

> Albert Ball finally decided that the SE5 was such a bad aeroplane that it would be quite unsafe to fly it over the lines. He got General Trenchard to let him have a 110 Le Rhône Nieuport again. He and I sat for many hours at night trying to work out how to make the SE5 work. He was a very unusual combination of a fighter pilot with a real interest in aeroplanes. The majority of them didn't have aeroplane knowledge but he definitely had. Between the two of us we finally cooked up the SE5 so that it really worked. General Trenchard approved finally and all our other aeroplanes were altered to the same design that we'd evolved and improved on Albert Ball's machine.[8]
> Engineering Officer H.N. Charles, 56 Squadron RFC

As a result of this hard graft a myriad of changes were made. Some were trivial, others crucial, but all gradually raised the performance of the machine to a more acceptable level.

An élite formation of scout pilots, the members of 56 Squadron were specially selected by their Commanding Officer, the redoubtable Major Blomfield, because of their proven fighting qualities or great promise. They began well, despite being plagued by a series of gun jams that were caused for the most part by the mechanics' lack of familiarity with the intricacies of the new Constantinesco interrupter gear. Their maiden patrol was made on 22 April and Ball scored the squadron's first victories, one in the Nieuport and one in an SE5, during his solo patrols on 23 April. Gradually, as its teething problems were overcome, Ball recognised the strengths of the SE5 and after his brief flirtation with his beloved Nieuport, he acclimatised to the more powerful aircraft. He took a regular part in the increasingly important formation patrols, as was expected of a flight commander, but, as was his wont, he also spent considerable additional time in the air as a lone wolf.

He preferred to patrol alone rather than to lead his flight on patrol . . . He wanted always to be in the air. During flying weather he was up and out by five o'clock in the morning and – completely exhausted by his efforts – he would be in bed and asleep by six o'clock in the evening.[9] Recording Officer T.B. Marson, 56 Squadron RFC

In applying himself so relentlessly to the task at hand, Ball himself must have been aware of the risks he was taking and of the probable consequences. He had a particularly close escape on 5 May and was severely shaken when he was almost rammed in a head–on clash with a German pilot.

On his return to the aerodrome, his engine was found to have been shot through, and there were several bullets through the back of the pilot's seat. Flushed in the face, his eyes brilliant, his hair blown and dishevelled, he came to the squadron office to make his report, but for a long time was in so over-wrought a state that dictation was an impossibility to him. 'God is very good to me.' 'God must have me in His keeping.' 'I was certain that he meant to ram me.' The possibility that his opponent, finding himself mortally hit, had determined to have a life for a life occurred to him. In that event his nerve failed him at the last – Ball did not flinch. But in nervous exhaustion he paid the price.[10] Recording Officer T.B. Marson, 56 Squadron RFC

Ball's good fortune could not possibly last, particularly in the face of the increasingly sophisticated tactics adopted by the German scouts. Combining their patrols to collect as many as twenty aircraft, they would sweep along the front line with the intention of overwhelming and totally destroying the much smaller British formations that they encountered. This new approach demanded a response and on 7 May a strong offensive patrol from 56 Squadron was ordered to sweep across the area of the German airfield at Douai. The formation became split up in the cloudy conditions and after severe fighting Ball crashed to the ground at Annoeulin in somewhat mysterious circumstances. Although his death may have been due to a flying accident, exacerbated by the strain of combat both upon him and his aircraft during that last hectic flight, it nevertheless showed that Ball's simple, aggressive tactics were no match for the swarms of Albatross which appeared across the sky in the spring of 1917. His death caused consternation in the RFC to which he had become an inspirational figure not just for his successes – he was credited with some forty-one victories – but for the sheer *élan* with which he achieved them. A month after his death he was gazetted with a VC.

As one star of the new firmament expired so another pilot, who eventually was to surpass him, was taking his first tentative steps towards mastering the arcane arts of successful air combat. On 6 April, Second Lieutenant Edward Mannock was posted to 40 Squadron RFC which was equipped with Nieuport 17 Scouts. He flew on his first patrol on 13 April but took some time to get his bearings. Mannock, aged twenty-eight in 1917, was a complex character whose maturity formed a sharp contrast to the near schoolboys who made up the complement of many of the scout squadrons. He was also fairly unusual in that he combined a fervent socialist outlook with a virulent hatred of the Germans. As an imaginative and intelligent man he initially found some difficulty in ignoring the risks pilots took every time they flew over the German lines and encountered considerable problems in controlling his natural trepidation in action.

> Now I can understand what a tremendous strain to the nervous system active service flying is. However cool a man may be there must always be more or less of a tension on the nerves under such trying conditions. When it is considered that seven out of ten forced landings are practically 'write offs', and 50% are cases where the pilot is injured, one can quite understand the strain of the whole business.[11] Second Lieutenant Edward Mannock, 40 Squadron RFC

Determined to contain his fear, and also to shoot down his detested enemies, Mannock tried hard but was dogged by a run of bad luck during the first few weeks of his career.

> 'C' Flight escorted 4 Sopwiths on a photography stunt to Douai Aerodrome. Captain Keen, the new commander,

leading. We were attacked from above, over Douai. I tried my gun before going over the German lines, only to find that it was jammed, so I went over with a revolver only. A Hun in a beautiful yellow and green 'bus' attacked me from behind. I could hear his M.G. cracking away. I wheeled round on him and howled like a dervish (although of course he couldn't hear me) whereat he made off towards old Parry & attacked him, with me following, for the moral effect! Another one (a brown speckled one) attacked a Sopwith, and Keen blew the pilot to pieces & the Hun went spinning down from 12,000 feet to earth. Unfortunately the Sopwith had been hit, and went down too, and there was I, a passenger, absolutely helpless not having a gun, an easy prey to any of them, and they hadn't the grit to close. Eventually they broke away, and then their Archie gunners got on the job & we had a hell of a time. At times, I wondered if I had a tail-plane or not they were so near. We came back over Arras with the three remaining Sopwiths, and excellent photos, and two vacant chairs at the Sopwith squadron mess! What is the good of it all?[12] Second Lieutenant Edward Mannock, 40 Squadron RFC

Although he was promoted to lieutenant, at times Mannock came very close to a nervous breakdown which, had it come about, would have resulted in his being returned in disgrace for home service.

We engaged a Hun over Henin Lietard and chased him over towards Courcelles. I turned east & Keen turned west. I was inevitably attacked by 3 Huns. My gun jammed – Keen was almost out of sight. 'Aldis' sight oiled up, and the engine failed at the crucial moment. I thought all was up. We were 16,000 feet up at the time. I turned almost vertically on my tail – nose dived and spun down towards our own lines, zigzagging for all I was worth with machine-guns cracking away behind me like mad. The engine picked up when I was about 3,000 feet over Arras & the Huns for some reason or other had left me. I immediately ran into another Hun (after I had climbed up to 12,000 feet again) but hadn't the pluck to face him. I turned away and landed here with my knees shaking and my nerves all torn to bits. I feel a bit better now, but all my courage seems to have gone after that experience this morning. The CO was very good and didn't put me on any more line jobs for the rest of the day.[13] Lieutenant Edward Mannock, 40 Squadron RFC

The senior officers of 40 Squadron, possibly recognising the tenacity of his determination to succeed, handled Mannock with considerable understanding.

Feeling nervy and ill during the past week. Afraid I am breaking up . . . Captain Keen very decent. Let me off flying for today. I think I'll take a book and wander into the woods this afternoon – although it rather threatens rain. O! for a fortnight in the country at home![14] Lieutenant Edward Mannock, 40 Squadron RFC

His junior contemporaries were less reserved in their treatment of him and publicly expressed their not unfounded doubts about his temperament. In an effort to improve his performance Mannock made a careful study of single-seater tactics and, whether it was that, his constant practice on the target range to enhance his marksmanship, or just a change in his luck, by early June 1917 he had begun to shoot down Germans with a vengeance. Clearly, by then, he had grasped the essence of the truism that the closer a pilot got to his intended victim the more likely he was to score multiple and damaging hits.

We escorted F.E.s over Lille on bomb dropping business – & we met Huns. My man gave me an easy mark. I was only 10 yards away from him – on top so I couldn't miss! A beautiful coloured insect he was – red blue green & yellow. I let him have 60 rounds at that range so there wasn't much left of him. I saw him going spinning & slipping down from 14,000. Rough luck, but it's war, & they're Huns.[15] Lieutenant Edward Mannock, 40 Squadron RFC

Despite such attempts in his personal diary to adopt a callous sang-froid, he was not always so successful in the face of the gruesome effects of his handiwork.

> Had the good fortune to bring a Hun two-seater down in our lines a few days ago. Luckily, my first few shots killed the pilot & wounded the observer (a Captain) besides breaking his gun. The bus crashed south of Avion. I hurried out at the first opportunity & found the observer being tended by the local M.O. and I gathered a few souvenirs, altho the infantry had the first pick. The machine was completely smashed and rather interestingly also was the little black & tan terrier – dead – in the observer's seat. I felt exactly like a murderer. The journey to the trenches was rather nauseating – dead men's legs sticking through the sides with putties and boots still on – bits of bones & skulls with the hair peeling off, and tons of equipment & clothing lying about. This sort of thing, together with the strong graveyard stench & the dead & mangled body of the pilot (an NCO) combined to upset me for a few days.[16]
> Lieutenant Edward Mannock, 40 Squadron RFC

Over the summer Mannock perfected his personal tactics and became a match for most German pilots in single-handed combat.

> Had a splendid fight with a single-seater Albatross scout last week on our side of the lines and got him down. This proved to be Lieutenant von Bertrab,* Iron Cross, who had been flying for 18 months. He came over for one of our balloons – near Neuville St Vaast – and I cut him off going back. He didn't get the balloon either. The scrap took place at 2,000 ft up, well within view of the whole front. And the cheers! It took me 5 minutes to get him to go down, & I had to shoot him before he would land. I was very pleased that I did not kill him. Right arm broken by a bullet, left arm, left leg deep flesh wounds. His machine – a beauty, just issued (June 1/17)

---

* Coincidentally, Bertrab had shot down Truscott, who had unsuccessfully tried to use the 'mess funds' as a protective ruse during the Arras offensive.

with a 220 HP Mercedes engine, all black with crosses marked out in white lines – turned over on landing and was damaged. Two machine-guns with 1,000 rounds of ammunition against my single Lewis & 300 rounds! I went up to the trenches to salve the 'bus' later, and had a great ovation from everyone. Even Generals congratulated me. He didn't hit me once.[17] Lieutenant Edward Mannock, 40 Squadron RFC

Unlike Ball and Bishop who were 'naturals' and to whom success appeared to have come easily, Mannock was forced to work hard to overcome several impediments which might have defeated a less determined character. As a result he appreciated more clearly the need for precise training and, in contrast to many others who seem to have jealously guarded them, once he had acquired skills himself he sought to teach others the secrets he had so painstakingly learnt. In August he was promoted to flight commander and he began to work hard at propagating effective formation tactics with a particular emphasis on methods of safely 'blooding' new pilots. It was in this area that he was to achieve greatness rather than in merely amassing a huge personal 'score'. One of the most remarkable things about Mannock was the breadth of his character, which ranged from virulent hatred to poetic sensitivity. Occasionally, in calm moments as at least one member of his flight observed, he would seize upon the landscape of the sky to express this usually hidden side of his nature.

We emerged from the bitterly cold cloud into a world of glittering white iciness. The sun was shining brilliantly and a glistening expanse of white hills of powdered snow appeared before us as a newly created world. The reflected light from the clouds was blinding, and as the 'hummocks' and slopes were clearly defined, the silhouettes of our machines showed up with almost perfect definition, each one surrounded by a circular halo of rainbow colours. On every side of us the clouds stretched right to the horizon, the intense whiteness of those furthest away bearing testimony to the crystal purity of the atmosphere. It was indeed an entrancing world in which our SEs were suspended, and very soon the rest of us realised that it had cast a spell over [Mannock]. There were no other machines in sight, the world was ours, and [Mannock] 'wagged' his wings once, asking us to take up our wing-tip-to-wing-tip formation, and, without the second 'waggle' that would have signified the presence of the enemy, dived slowly towards the clouds. He flattened out just above them, and began contour chasing among the steep feathery mountains and valleys, round one peak, down the slopes into a hollow, zooming up to avoid the next mountain, occasionally dashing into an overhanging precipice of freezing cold, billowing cloud, all the time with the silent rainbow spectres following us or preceding us across the arctic expanse. In the thrilling excitement of flying in such exceptionally magnificent circumstances, and following a leader with such an appreciation of the beautiful and glorious scenery, we all entered into the spirit of the chase, forgetting the war in our enjoyment.[18] Second Lieutenant William MacLanachan, 40 Squadron RFC

*   *   *

As the fighting began to die down around Arras, British attention switched north to Flanders which, after Nivelle's failure, was the scene of the main Allied offensive in the second half of 1917. The first stage was marked by the explosion of nineteen huge mines deep beneath the German lines at Messines Ridge on 7 June. This ridge, although not of any great height itself, overlooked the whole Ypres area and hence provided a vantage point from which the Germans could observe the British preparations for the main offensive from the Salient itself. The supporting role of the RFC was now established as an integral part of any major attack and inevitably it provoked a strong German aerial response. As a result there was a great deal of hard fighting in the air above this key sector of the line and with the new generation of British scouts still only present in limited numbers many British aircraft were still markedly outclassed by the latest Albatross D III. One ominous development in the aerial war was the formalisation of the attack groupings of German scouts, when the 4, 6, 10 and 11 Jastas were combined under the command of Richthofen into Jagdgeschwader No. 1. Following Richthofen's lead, as in so many other things, the German pilots personalised their machines with garish colour schemes and soon Jagdgeschwader 1 was sardonically nicknamed 'The Flying Circus' by the RFC.

The Battle of Messines erupted at 03.10 on 7 June when the combination of the mines and a pulverising artillery bombardment fired by the British from a concentration of 2,233 guns – one gun for every four and a half yards of the British Front – wrought devastation along the German front-line trenches. The dazed and confused German defenders could offer little serious resistance to the British troops as they swept forwards with the village and ridge of Messines being quickly captured and, more importantly, held. This success meant that the way was now clear in Flanders for what was to be officially termed the Third Battle of Ypres, but known more evocatively as Passchendaele. The offensive's aim was an initial 'snatch' to capture the Passchendaele Ridge and then, by pushing deeper into German territory, to threaten the rear of their lines between Ypres and the coast. In conjunction with an amphibious landing further along the Belgian coast, a final thrust would be launched in the Nieuport sector, with the intention being to clear the whole Belgian coastline right up to the Dutch border.

In view of the importance of the operation Trenchard remained greatly concerned about the shortage of replacement aircraft and pilots which had been exacerbated by the heavy casualties of the spring and early summer. On 10 June, in a memorandum to his brigade commanders, he requested that they achieve the impossible.

> I would ask that as far as possible you do your best to point out to your Armies that it is of the utmost importance that the Flying Corps should avoid wastage in both pilots and machines for some little time. My reserve at present is dangerously low, in fact, in some cases it barely exists at all, and the supply from home is not coming forward sufficiently freely to enable us to continue fighting an offensive in the air continuously . . . It is of the utmost importance, however, that the offensive spirit is maintained in the Flying Corps.[19] Major General Hugh Trenchard, RFC Headquarters

This tricky situation was made worse at the beginning of July when Trenchard was ordered to send two of his best scout units,

66 and 56 Squadrons RFC, to bolster the defences of London against the emerging threat of the Gotha daylight raids. Both squadrons returned to the Western Front later in the month but, even so, many in the RFC felt bitter at what they perceived as an unnecessary distraction to their real work.

There seems to be an awful panic about the big daylight raid and No. 56 Squadron, the only squadron of SE5s we have had up our way in France, have been recalled to defend London. It appears not to matter in the least that the unfortunate pilots and observers who have to do all their work in factory machines over the German lines are left without adequate protection so long as London can feel she is having the best of everything.[20] Recording Officer Lieutenant Thomas Hughes, 53 Squadron RFC

It was perhaps fortunate that at this time another of the new generation of British scouts made its appearance on the Western Front and established itself as the most enduring popular symbol of the war in the air. The Sopwith Camel was an idiosyncratic aircraft which, in a sense, made a virtue out of its main defect. Armed with two synchronised Vickers machine-guns housed in the distinctive hump which inspired its name, it was powered in the early production models by the 130 horsepower Le Clerget or 110 horsepower Le Rhône engines. Inherently unstable, with all its weight packed into the first seven feet of the fuselage, it was a real pilot-killer if not handled sympathetically, but when controlled by an adept pilot it was manoeuvrable in the extreme and could achieve around 112 miles per hour at 15,000 feet with a ceiling of over 20,000 feet. The SE5 and the upgraded SE5 A were fast and strong, excelling in zooming on to their prey, but the Camel offered different advantages for a pilot in action.

The Sopwith Camel was so quick to control. Quick to turn, good performance, wonderful manoeuvrability. For a dogfight the perfect machine: twin machine-guns; Sopwith-Kauper interrupter gear with the guns firing through the propeller; all the weights concentrated very close together – engine, guns, pilot, tank – everything very close; and very small tail fin and rudder which didn't slow down your movement. She wasn't a machine that you wanted to be ham-handed with but in my opinion she was and still is the finest fighter ever designed by the hand of man![21] Captain Graham Donald, RNAS

The instability of the Camel was the source of one of its greatest assets, allowing the aircraft consistently to out-turn any German aircraft during a dogfight.

The Camel was a very tricky aeroplane to fly because of the right-hand torque with the fairly small wing span and this very powerful engine. If you put your right wing down in a right-hand turn if you weren't very careful you spun down on the torque. It was so light that you were over and spinning before you knew where you were! Conversely turning to the left was fairly heavy.[22] Lieutenant Archibald Yuille, RFC

Objectively considered, the SE5 appeared to be the better machine for securing an ideal position from which to shoot down a German aircraft in an initial strike, whereas the Camel excelled if such a strike failed or other aircraft intervened and a general dogfight developed, when its superior agility and minimal turning circle were invaluable.

The Third Battle of Ypres, which opened on 31 July, was a tremendous clash both on the ground and in the air. The role of the corps squadrons was absolutely crucial to the effective conduct of operations and, in anticipation of the coming infantry assault, the air offensive began three weeks earlier on 8 July. Its aim was twofold, both to sweep the skies to allow the British aircraft to operate without hostile interference and also to deprive the Germans of their own 'eyes in the sky'. Above all, every detail of the German defences had to be photographed. This was a dangerous job since the new reconnaissance machines, such as the RE8, remained absolute sitting ducks and were almost completely unable to defend themselves from roaming predators.

The RE8 was not really defensible. It was such a delicate operation. They had to go up and down, up and down without diverting to get a mosaic of photographs. The pilot had a Vickers gun which synchronised through the propeller. But nine times out of ten it didn't – it hit the propeller. They were wooden propellers and the result was a tremendous vibration because of the imbalance. You never used your gun – you relied on the observer who had a Lewis gun.[23] Sergeant George Eddington, 6 Squadron RFC

Above the corps machines were meant to be the defending close escorts but they were often almost as vulnerable as the hapless RE8s. Lieutenant Frederick Winterbotham was on an escort patrol in a near obsolescent Nieuport 17 Scout.

I'd been out on dawn patrol. We hadn't had a scrap but everything was obviously hotting up. I came back and thought, 'Well, I've got the day to rest!' and I went and sat down to breakfast. In came my commanding officer, de Crespigny, who was an absolute fire-eater – he was a splendid fellow. He said, 'You've got to go up again!' I said, 'Look, my engine wasn't going very well and I put it in to have it overhauled ready for this evening.' He said, 'That doesn't matter, borrow an aeroplane and take your flight up because you've got to escort some photographic machines, the Army wants it!' So I went and found somebody who'd got a machine but those little machines were very personal things. You got your seat just at the right height, you got your rudder bar at the right place, you got your gun sight so it was just opposite your eye. If your flying machine was somebody's who was a foot or so shorter than you then everything was wrong and they couldn't alter all this in time. I was also minus my silk garter which always went round my compass which was a great help to me. Off I went with my flight to escort these machines. The instructions were: 'Fly over at 8,000 feet. As soon as you see the photographic machines going down', they had to go down to about 2,000 feet to take their pictures, 'dive after them, escort them and look after their tails.' Well the time came and I was watching out for the machines to go down when suddenly there was an enormous barrage of anti-aircraft fire between us and the photographic machines, this was a new trick by the Germans. I couldn't see what the machines below were doing – and at that moment when our whole attention was on these aircraft we were attacked out of the sun by about a dozen German fighters. I'd only got my flight of five. We had a hell of a scrap. In the first three minutes my gun jammed – it wasn't my gun, I hadn't looked at the cartridges – but there I was without a gun! One was supposed to haul your gun down off the top plane on its hinges, steering your aeroplane in the middle of a dogfight with your knees, put your gun right and put it back up again so you could fire again. That was supposed to be the drill – of course quite impossible! It was during the time that I was trying to clear the stoppage that somebody got on my tail, I don't know how he did it. I didn't even feel or hear anything except that my engine just went 'phutt'. I was then left in the middle of a dogfight with no gun and no engine. We were so far over the German lines that it was absolutely hopeless to try and get back again and in any case I had started to go down. I looked round and seeing that I was being left alone for a minute I turned my nose towards home – hopefully. But somebody very soon came and shot at me so I had to go down. I was tremendously lucky because I was feeling rather cold about the legs and when I looked down I found that my boots had been shot off my legs, hadn't hit me, but the bullets that had stopped my engine had missed my petrol tank by about an inch. My left winger had been shot down in flames a minute before, so I was in rather a bad way really. One had been taught to fly professionally, you concentrated entirely on flying and I went into a 'falling leaf' so they couldn't really shoot at me. It was fortunate that it was so far behind the German lines because if you came down in the German front line they shot you out of hand. I noticed a bit that was shell hole but there was some grass about – there didn't seem to be any trenches there – so I sort of floated down on to this, side-slipping. Eventually I went nose into a shell hole and the aeroplane turned upside-down. The only thing wrong with me was that

I'd got my head jammed between the top wing and my nose was broken. I pulled myself out, I was terrified of fire and crawled out from underneath this shattered aeroplane to find myself surrounded by German soldiers all pointing their rifles at me. Fortunately there was a very nice German anti-aircraft officer who pulled me up, my nose was bleeding rather badly. He took me back to his battery, got a doctor and fed me with coffee and things until such time as they came and picked me up.[24]
Lieutenant Frederick Winterbotham, 29 Squadron RFC

Winterbotham survived both imprisonment and the war to rise to prominence in the Ultra code-breaking organisation responsible for many Allied triumphs in the Second World War – so it could be said that he got his revenge!

By 1917 artillery had become absolutely fundamental to the success of any battle and consequently they had a paramount call on the services of the RFC. As each new battery moved into the battle zone the routine registration of known targets and key positions was the first vital step in preparing them for the coming offensive. Messages sent by wireless from the artillery observation aircraft were received at the batteries by specialist RFC wireless operators. The means of conveying corrections had changed little since 1915 but after two years of continuous use the system had become extremely effective.

The short wave tuner enabled you to receive with headphones messages which were being sent in Morse from the air by pilots and observers. You could record that on your message pad and transmit it to your battery commander. You opened up your station when the machine came up from the squadron and called you at the battery. You had your own specific call signs which you recognised immediately. It gave the squadron sign and the battery sign. From then on the observer would ask you to stand by. He had already been told the target on which he'd got to range. The shoot would commence by your signalling to the observer by means of an American white strip about two feet wide, weighted at each end and put out in the forms of letters such as 'K' or 'L' or 'N' or 'D' as the case may be in accordance with a code. When you were ready to engage a target he should have been flying from the battery position to the target. As he was approaching the target he would give you what was called a 'G' signal which meant 'Fire!' You would pass that signal immediately to your battery commander who would then give the order for one of his guns to fire. Your observer was still proceeding towards the target hoping to arrive at practically the same time as the shell which was due to burst on or near the target. He would then turn and come back towards the battery having worked out the correction. As he came back he would signal that correction to you and you would again report that to your battery commander. He was able to correct where that shell had fallen by means of a device called the 'clock code'. It comprised of a circular disc of transparent material which had twelve radial lines coming out from the centre of a pin and eight concentric circles. The observer would fix that device on to his map on his dashboard in the cockpit. He would register where that round had fallen by giving the correction on direction based on one or other of those twelve lines corresponding from one to twelve on a clock. Then the rings would be varying distances from the target and they were lettered 'Y' 'Z' 'A' 'B' 'C' 'D' 'E' 'F', with the inner ring being ten yards from the target, the next one twenty-five, the next one which would be 'A', 50 yards, 'B' 100 yards and so on. If you got a correction coming back 'A9' it would mean that the round had fallen within 50 yards of the target at nine o'clock on the clock. The battery commander was in a position to correct his gun or guns for subsequent rounds so that eventually with any luck at all he would be able to register an 'OK' on his particular target. When a point was reached that the observer felt that he could not get any more accuracy he would come back to you in the air and give you a signal which meant, 'Go on firing' or 'Gunfire'. You would pass it on to your battery commander and he would then know that he could let fly because he was registered on his target and he could do as much damage

as possible. After the gunfire signal the observer would carry on for quite a little while longer registering general corrections. He might for instance get four bursts at a time if the whole battery was firing to spot. Then he would send what would be called a 'most correction'. Mostly 'A9' or mostly 'Y5' or mostly 'OK'. Then he would really have completed his job and he would give you a signal called 'CI' which meant 'Coming in!' – he'd finished his shoot, he was going back to the squadron. You could report to your battery commander that the shoot was finished.[25]
Wireless Operator Leslie Briggs, RFC

The infantry went over the top on the morning of the last day of July. From the start the offensive was riven by misfortune. In particular it coincided with a period of low cloud and heavy rain which quickly saturated the low-lying, shell-pocked battlefield, impeding the British troops as they tried to move forward. In the air these conditions also severely disrupted the flying programme. However, the contact patrols still had to fly and as during the Somme, by using klaxons to get the infantry to light coloured flares they attempted to follow the progress on the ground. Not unnaturally, the infantry were often reluctant to co-operate with this procedure when in close proximity to the enemy. For Lieutenant Jack Walthew flying an RE8 this was only one of many problems he experienced that day.

Zero hour was fixed for 3.50 am so at 3.15 am we were all called to stand by our machines. I managed to get a couple of boiled eggs and some tea. The weather was most hopelessly dud. The clouds were at 800, so we had to fly at 700. This was almost suicidal as a machine is a very big and easy target. However as we were the contact patrol flight we had to go up and try to do something . . . I left the aerodrome at 5.30 am and scraped over houses and trees etc. until I got to our guns. Here the fun started as there was, so experts tell me, the worst Barrage that has ever been known, and I had to fly through it. I could hear, and occasionally see, the shells and every minute I was expecting to see one of my wings vanish. However, nothing hit us until we got over the line (which had been pushed forward considerably) and here in 8 minutes we got 30 holes through the machine from machine-guns. Ten of them passed within a few inches of Woodstock; the wireless transmitter valued at £200 disappeared; three spars on the wing were broken; and lastly a bullet went through the Petrol tank. I smelt a smell of Petrol and in a few minutes it all came rushing over my feet and legs. How we got back I don't know, it seemed the longest journey I have ever made; but eventually we landed safely. I had to write out a report on the flight and then had a shave, and was just going in to have some breakfast when I got orders to take up another machine to try and find the 30th Division who had got lost. So off I went again and tootled over our lines for an hour. The first thing that happened was that the wireless transmitter again disappeared, leaving only a big hole in the fuselage. After this we weren't hit quite so much as before. Meanwhile we called to the infantry to light flares for us; but as they wouldn't do this, we had to draw the fire of the Huns into ourselves so as to discover where the enemy line was, and deduct ours from it. We managed to do this fairly successfully and came back unhurt. Immediately we were put into a car and taken to Corps Headquarters where we were interviewed by several old Generals and Brass Hats. So altogether we had a pretty busy morning.[26] Lieutenant Jack Walthew, 4 Squadron RFC

The bad weather persisted and indeed was severe enough to force the temporary suspension of the ground operations as the battlefield became a morass of liquid mud. When the offensive resumed on 16 August the initially promising situation soon degenerated into possibly the most awful of the 'soldiers' battles' that litter the history of the First World War. For the next three months the infantry crawled in appalling conditions and abject misery towards the objective of the Passchendaele Ridge which they had been supposed to reach on the first day. Secure in a network of concrete pill-boxes the Germans doggedly resisted, forcing the British troops to fight hard for every yard of primeval ooze. Only accurate shelling could reach the innermost recesses of the German defences and this had to be directed from the air. The Germans were fully aware of the power symbolised and expressed by the corps aircraft and sought to dash them from the sky.

We were going on a shoot and I had with me Lieutenant Dormer who hadn't been with the squadron very long. He'd been up with me twice before and seemed to get on with it very well. We took off and reached the target – it was quite a clear day and we were at 6,000 feet. He did all the sending using the clock code while my job was to get as close to the target as possible. There was nobody about at all which is sometimes a bad sign so I said, 'You'll have to keep your eyes skinned!' After a while he said, 'Can you go further over, I can't see the target properly!' I said, 'You've got to be careful because there's a bunch of Huns on the right.' He said, 'They're not Huns, they're British Nieuports!' I said, 'Well, I'd watch them if I were you!' I thought, 'I suppose he'll think I've got cold feet.' So I went further over but I made up my mind to keep an eye on them myself! It was quite an interesting shoot – to watch the shell bursts as they corrected their range to as near as they could to the centre. I could see where the shells were falling. All of a sudden, without any warning, I heard a burst of gunfire. Eight Albatross had crept up on me – they saw easy prey with nobody about. Their usual method of attack was to dive down from the back and pop off the gunner first – once they've got the gunner they've got the aircraft to themselves because you can't do anything. I looked round and there was Mr Dormer lying flat out on the floor, they'd got him with the first burst – I thought, 'That's it!' There I was with eight of them round me and I had to depend on my own initiative. I tried to avoid combat by making a series of wide flat circles which deprived the enemy of any chance of getting a straight line on me. If you crawl round it is like a slow moving car in a stream of fast traffic – their fighters were much faster than me. All the time I was losing height because I knew that in the end they'd get me. This went on for a little while then I glanced round to see an aircraft diving down, out to make a proper job of it. I had to do something pretty quickly. We had had strict instructions that we were never to stunt or loop an RE8 because it would break up on you but I was left with no option – I decided to do an Immelmann Turn! Nobody had ever heard of anyone doing that in a RE8 but it was the only way out . . . I stood her up on her tail – pulled the stick right back, kicked the left rudder just as she was coming up and she started spinning – and spinning is the quickest way down as long as you can get out of the spin! I was quite cool and even at that stage one doesn't think of death. Down she went and the firing stopped. They could see me spinning down and I suspect they were just waiting to see the shower of sparks. The supposed way of getting out of a spin was to centralise everything – rudder, joystick, the lot . . . I centralised everything and just as I was coming out of the dive into the straight I heard two sharp bangs. I knew it wasn't gunfire. Both the wing extensions had broken off short up against the struts and been carried right away. That left me with no lateral control at all. I didn't know where I was or which side of the lines and I was going down straight and quite fast and there was nothing I could do about it. I looked round and shouted to Dormer, 'We're going to crash!' but of course he was still out. As soon as I found I was out of control I switched off the engine because they always caught fire. I waited until we got to about 30 foot of the ground and then very heavy on the controls I pulled back with both hands on the stick into my stomach. It pulled her back a bit but she dived into the ground with one colossal bang. I remembered no more – I'd landed in Sanctury Wood and an artillery officer dragged me out – they'd already got the observer out.[27] Sergeant George Eddington, 6 Squadron RFC

The RE8s had gained a reputation equal to that of the BE2 Cs as a stable aircraft that would almost fly itself. This was demonstrated by a bizarre incident when an RE8 continued to fly, and indeed landed, despite the death in action of its crew, Lieutenant J.L.M. Sandy and Sergeant H.F. Hughes.

Sandy and Hughes; Garret and his observer; and myself and my observer all went up about the same time to do a job. The last I saw the aircraft was apparently flying normally on its job. That being so we didn't take any further notice of it. There was no particular air activity at the time – that doesn't say there wasn't any, but nothing exceptional. Sandy and Hughes didn't come back at the normal time and inquiries were started all round the RFC as to whether anybody could report an aircraft missing or a forced landing anywhere. No aircraft had forced landed that anybody could tell us of. But then later on word came in that an aircraft had apparently crashed or forced landed at a certain spot. We sent out people to investigate it. What had happened was that Sandy and Hughes were apparently killed by the same bullet. He had his controls set for normal level flying – you set the tail plane. The tail plane is pivoted and you have cables from it coming back into your cockpit where you have a trimming wheel which winds forward or backwards. In normal sort of still air conditions it would fly level unless something disturbed that – a change of wind or up current – and the aircraft just went on and on until it ran out of fuel. The engine of course ceased to function and it glided down and landed, comparatively unharmed, of its own accord.[28] Lieutenant H.N. Wrigley, 3 Squadron, Australian Flying Corps

Long-distance bombing raids were launched throughout the battle to render key German installations unfit for effective use during the critical period. Sergeant Charles Burne was an air gunner and observer in a DH4 of 5 Squadron RNAS during a bombing raid on Engel airfield when they were intercepted by German scouts.

It was one of those mornings when there was a very, very early sun which was very high and bright. We were approaching the target and to drop the bombs one had to get down on one knee. You had a stop watch strapped to your knee and a bomb-sight on the side of the machines. It took a fair amount of concentration – you had to start your stop watch and take a sight from the two pegs to your objective. Then take a sight from the peg a little bit further back on the objective which gave you a stop-watch reading of so many seconds. Then you had a movable scale on the bomb-sight which you set to your air speed as known, and the stopwatch indication. When you'd set that you took a sight through these two new pegs on to your objective. That took some time down on one knee. Well one never knows quite why a thing is done but at the last minute instead of concentrating on dropping my bomb I stood up and looked round. Just at that time all I could see was two lines in the sun and the holes appearing in the machine. I felt a blow on my leg and this chap was just coming down – he was so close that he had to loop to avoid hitting us. During that couple of moments I got my guns on him and shot him down. He went into his loop, hung at the top for what seemed a long time, smoke pouring out and then he went down. I got down and dropped my bombs – two 65-lb and twenty 16-lb bombs. I had a direct hit on the target and stood up, dragged the leg on top of the other so I could stand. There's no feeling of hurt just a numbness as if you'd been kicked very heavy. We'd carried out our job and I'd shot the machine down that got me. There were 120 bullet holes in the machine when they counted them up to patch them and all I'd got was four![29] Sergeant Charles Burne, 5 Squadron RNAS

The primacy of the land battle can be judged by the fact that after successful experiments during the Battle of Messines a new role was devised for the fast and agile scout aircraft of low–level ground strafing to provide direct assistance to the infantry.

Our task was to fly into that tunnel below the flight of the field-gun shells, look for any target we could see – any Germans in trenches, enemy machine-gun posts – anything at all – shoot it up, fly through the 'tunnel' and

come out at the other end. We were warned that we must not try to fly out sideways, if we did we would almost certainly meet our own shells in flight and be brought down by them. Once we entered the 'tunnel' there was nothing for it but to carry on and go through to the very end. We flew in pairs. I led, being flight commander. I and my companion flew to the south of the tunnel, turned left and entered it. Instantly we were in an inferno. The air was boiling with the turmoil of the shells flying through it. We were thrown about in the aircraft, rocking from side to side, being thrown up and down. Below was mud, filth, smashed trenches, broken wire, limbers, rubbish, wreckage of aeroplanes, bits of men – and then in the midst of it all when we were flying at 400 feet I spotted a German machine-gun post and went down. My companion came behind me and as we dived we fired four machine-guns straight into the post. We saw the Germans throw themselves on the ground. We dived at them and sprayed them – whether we hit them we didn't know there was no time to see – only time to dive and fire, climb and zoom on to the next target. We saw a number of the grey-green German troops lying in holes, battered trenches that had been trenches and were now shell holes. We dived on them, fired and again we were firing at a target which we could not assess. We were being thrown about. A third time we dived on another target and then our ammunition was finished. We flew on rocking out of that inferno, out of the 'tunnel' and escaped. I felt that never at any time had I passed through such an extraordinary experience when we ourselves were shut in by a cloud of shells above real damnation on the ground.[30]
Lieutenant Norman Macmillan, 45 Squadron RFC

The scouts were also often required to carry four twenty-five-pound Cooper bombs attached to simple racks with which they were to hit any targets that they should find – anything to harry and torment the Germans and to distract them from their real enemies, the British infantry and artillery.

The changes in the pattern of air fighting which had begun earlier in 1917 continued as the two sides strove to attain mastery of the skies above the blood-drenched Salient. The British responded to the increasing size of German formations, not in kind, but with a degree of tactical flexibility which was peculiarly effective when it worked. Essentially, they continued to fly in flights, but at different levels. When contact was made with large German formations the various flights from different squadrons would join in the battle as required combining, separating and recombining as the situation developed. Of course this unstructured approach could easily break down, but tactics were becoming ever more sophisticated. The faster pace of the dogfights meant that more opportunities were there to be taken by those who had the knack or ability to shoot down their opponents, projecting new 'aces' quickly to the fore in the turbulent skies. James McCudden, by now a Captain, joined 56 Squadron in mid-August and in the early evening of 23 September led his B Flight over the lines. The sky seemed full of aircraft and McCudden led his men to the rescue of an SE5 of 60 Squadron which was being attacked by a Fokker Triplane. And so began a classic dogfight.

> Down we dived at a colossal speed. I went to the right, Rhys Davids to the left, and we got behind the triplane together. The German pilot saw us and turned in the most disconcertingly quick manner, not a climbing nor Immelmann turn, but a sort of flat half-spin. By now the German triplane was in the middle of our formation, and its handling was wonderful to behold. The pilot seemed to be firing at all of us simultaneously, and although I got behind him a second time, I could hardly stay there for a second. His movements were so quick and uncertain that none of us could hold him in sight at all for any decisive time. I now got a good opportunity as he was coming towards me nose-on, and slightly underneath, and had apparently not seen me. I dropped my nose, got him well in my sight, and pressed both triggers. As soon as I fired up came his nose at me, and I heard clack-clack-clack-clack, as his bullets passed close to me and through my wings. I distinctly noticed the red-yellow flashes from his parallel Spandau guns. As he flashed by me I caught a glimpse of a black head in the triplane.[31] Captain James McCudden, 56 Squadron RFC

The pilot was Leutnant Werner Voss who, having shot down forty-nine aircraft since his first success in November 1916, was second only to Richthofen in the German pantheon. While the SE5s struggled to get a bead on the jagging triplane an Albatross joined the fight as a formation of British Spads held off another threatening group of German scouts. Voss showed remarkable courage throughout this epic fight.

> At one time I noted the triplane in the apex of a cone of tracer bullets from at least five machines simultaneously, and each machine had two guns. By now the fighting was very low, and the red-nosed Albatross had gone down and out, but the triplane still remained. I had temporarily lost sight of the triplane while changing a drum of my Lewis gun, and when I next saw him he was very low.[32] Captain James McCudden, 56 Squadron RFC

Through his actions Voss was not just defending himself, but with his accurate fire he forced two of McCudden's pilots to retire with badly damaged aircraft. Indeed several of his opponents that day felt that he could have used the superior climbing characteristics of the triplane to escape suggesting that, for whatever reason, Voss chose to fight on, until at last Rhys Davids managed to latch on to the triplane's tail.

> Eventually I got east and slightly above the triplane and made for it, getting in a whole Lewis drum and a corresponding number of Vickers into him. He made no attempt to turn, until I was so close to him I was certain we would collide. He passed my right-hand wing by inches and went down. I zoomed. I saw him next with his engine apparently off, gliding west. I dived again and got one shot out of my Vickers; however, I reloaded and kept in the dive. I got in another good burst and the triplane did a slight right-hand turn, still going down. I had now overshot him (this was at 1,000 feet), zoomed, but never saw him again.[33] Second Lieutenant Arthur Rhys Davids, 56 Squadron RFC

McCudden, however, did see the crunching end of Voss.

I noticed that the triplane's movements were very erratic, and then I saw him go into a fairly steep dive and so I continued to watch, and then saw the triplane hit the ground and disappear into a thousand fragments, for it seemed to me that it literally went to a powder.[34] Captain James McCudden, 56 Squadron RFC

Rhys Davids himself was killed in combat just a month later on 27 October and so the strange, tragic game of aerial musical chairs continued. Below them the Ypres offensive, which had triggered the heightened aerial fighting, finally ground to a halt on 10 November in a welter of blood and mud forcing the British authorities to recognise that the Belgian coast would not be liberated in 1917.

The enormous pressures of the Ypres offensive had forced the Germans to weaken other sections of their line to concentrate resources at the point of greatest danger. Realising this, Haig sought to launch a gigantic 'raid' in the Cambrai area just ten days after the suspension of the Flanders offensive with the intention of making the Germans think twice before thinning the line. Although Haig himself was short of reserves a new form of offensive was planned to make the most of his minimal resources. The Tank Corps were to be given the opportunity which they had craved since the first tanks rumbled forward in isolation on the Somme in September 1916. A mass tank-attack across relatively unspoilt country backed up by a sudden bombardment crashing out dead on zero-hour and without preliminary registration was intended to secure total surprise. The tanks were to crash through the German barbed wire, closely followed by the infantry. The usual programme of aerial photography had been undertaken in a discreet fashion while special preparations were made for the rapid notification by corps aircraft of all identifiable German artillery positions and concentrations of infantry capable of launching counter-attacks once the battle began. The ground attack duties of the RFC were again expanded as an integral part of the overall plan. The primary objective was a clean breakthrough of all the German defences with the possibility of an exploitative attack by cavalry on German communications. In the dream scenario there would also be a subsequent rolling up of a section of the German line stretching to the south. However, this was never really a possibility given the complete lack of reserves for a further 'proper' offensive and the main intention remained to give the Germans a bloody nose and balance the disappointment of Ypres by a final success at the end of the year.

The innovative British plans worked splendidly and the tanks and their accompanying infantry burst through the much vaunted Hindenburg Line on 20 November. The weather was not really suitable for aerial operations but the low altitude ground-strafing pilots had no choice and at dawn they took off.

We passed over the deep wide trenches of the dreaded Hindenburg Line, with its vast belts of barbed wire, through which the first waves of tanks had crushed hundreds of lanes. From then on the mist was made denser by the smoke screens laid in front of the advancing tanks from zero-hour onwards, which still hung around. We passed over the rear waves of the advance, reserve and supply tanks, field artillery, support troops and so on, then quickly caught up with the first wave. Everything flashes by like a dream, and as we rush forward at over ninety miles an hour, twenty feet up, I get split-second glimpses that remain vividly in the memory. I see the ragged line of grey diamond-shaped monsters, thirty to fifty yards apart, stretching into the mist on either flank, rolling unevenly forwards, their tracks churning round, their exhausts throwing out blue-green smoke. I see, behind each tank, a trudging group of infantry, casually smoking, looking up at us. Other knots of infantry stroll along a little in the rear, between the tanks. To a flank, I see a disabled tank, flames leaping up, the troops standing helplessly around. A chance enemy shell bursts between two tanks, knocks down a small bunch of soldiery like ninepins. The ground slopes upwards, trapping us under the clouds, so that our wheels almost touch the grass. I have to rise to clear a tank ahead, skim over it, dip down in front.[35] Lieutenant Arthur Lee, 46 Squadron RFC

Lee's target was a group of 5.9-inch artillery batteries located in Lateau Wood immediately behind the Hindenburg Line.

The 5.9s below are firing, producing more smoke, Charles and Hanafy have vanished, engulfed in cloud and smoke, and so there we are, the three of us, whirling blindly around at 50–100 feet, all but colliding, being shot at from below ... in this blind confusion there wasn't a hope of picking and choosing. The main thing was to get rid of the darned bombs before a bullet hit them. In a sharp turn I saw a bunch of guns right in line for attack, so dived at 45 degrees and released all four bombs. As I swung aside I saw them burst, a group of white-grey puffs centred with red flames. One fell between two guns, the rest a few yards away. Splinters suddenly splash in my face – a bullet through a centre-section strut. This makes me go hot, and I dive at another group of guns, giving them 100 rounds, see a machine-gun blazing at me, swing on to that, one short burst and he stops firing. As I climb up, a Camel whizzes past me out of the mist, missing me by a yard. It makes me sweat with fright. This is too dangerous, and I lift into the cloud to 300 feet.[36] Lieutenant Arthur Lee, 46 Squadron RFC

Ground-strafing operations of this type conducted in bad weather meant that casualties were inevitable and scout squadrons were soon minced in a manner that made it clear they could only be used in this role when it really mattered.

Although the initial attack was a great success the inevitable hold-ups arose, particularly around the village of Flesquières, which was not captured until early on 21 November. The chimera of a total breakthrough fluttered away and it was decided to concentrate efforts on seizing control of Bourlon Ridge in readiness for the inevitable counter-attack. The Germans used extreme care in moving up their reserves to avoid aerial observation and were considerably assisted by the misty weather. On 30 November they launched a devastating and unexpected strike and in effect premiered their own tactical developments in response to the British innovations. They attacked on a narrow front, with only a brief, if concentrated, preliminary bombardment, supported by swarms of low-flying aircraft which raked the bemused and terrified infantry in the British trenches. The line broke and the British fell back, after not a few desperate moments of heroic defence, to the

Flesquières Ridge where a final position was consolidated on 7 December.

The worst year of the war was over. The far-reaching movement through open fields towards the coast remained as out of reach as ever; 1917 had been a hard slog – a year of failed promise. Punctuated by fleeting moments of success, it had been predominantly characterised by frustration and disappointment and its dark malevolent atmosphere hung as heavily over the RFC as any other branch of the British Army. The great hopes of the Allied military commanders and their nervous politicians had been dashed with few tangible gains to show for the vast daily casualty lists which marred the morning newspapers. Yet vital lessons had been learnt as increasingly sophisticated methods of deploying artillery, tanks, infantry and aircraft in varying combinations had begun to emerge. The war had grown beyond all expectations since the start of trench warfare just three years before and during that time, as the aerial perspective of war grew ever wider, the RFC had moved from the periphery into the eye of the storm.

CHAPTER TEN

Dawn Patrol

Throughout the war reconnaissance and artillery co-operation remained the core work of military aviation. Without the uninterrupted execution of these missions there was little point to the army maintaining an air service. Yet through an iniquitous and disparaging quirk of fate, since 1918 these vital activities have been cast into undeserved obscurity by the more glamorous experiences of the scout pilots who were, after all, only there to enable these functions to be carried out. It is easy to see how this came about. During the war itself the achievements of men such as Albert Ball, William Bishop, James McCudden and Edward Mannock created enduring legends that captivated the minds of a war-weary public. The intense, kaleidoscopic nature of aerial combat, particularly as individual confrontations grew into the massive dogfights of the later years, was dramatic and visually exciting. Men pitted their wits against other men face-to-face, like the chivalrous knights of old. It was a captivating image, ideally made to be repeated time and again once the war was over in books and, even more effectively, in films. Soon it alone appeared to be the very purpose of the war in the air. However, as might be expected, for the men who lived this life the reality was very different. There was little time for the notions of nobility and romance. Survival, both in mind and in body, was paramount and what faint whiff of chivalry did hang about them was usually linked to a protective self-delusion intended to distance them from the human pain and suffering that were the ultimate goals of their job.

There was undoubtedly a sense of chivalry in the air. We did not feel that we were shooting at men. We did not want to kill men; we were really trying to shoot down the machines. Our enemies were not the men in the machines, our enemies were the machines themselves. It was a case of our machine is better than yours and let's down yours. Almost like a game of ninepins. A game of skill, a game in which we pitted ourselves against them and they pitted themselves against us – each to prove the better man.[1] Lieutenant Norman Macmillan, 45 Squadron RFC

The overall purpose of an offensive patrol was exquisitely simple, but inordinately difficult to achieve.

Our job is to see that the Boche does not get a chance to do any work in the air at all – I mean useful work like bombing and observation. What advantage do we gain? We just gain the supremacy of the air, bless you, that's all: we'll 'ave a notice board put up to the effect.

> AERIAL PARK.
> PRIVATE.
> HUN TRESPASSERS WILL BE
> PROSECUTED.

And we keep our own machines safe.[2] Second Lieutenant Arthur Rhys Davids, 56 Squadron RFC

In the air the responsibility for everything that happened lay solely with the individual scout pilot himself. Those who survived gained experience exponentially and after several years of combat they knew that the difference between success and failure depended on the thoroughness of their preparations. A hard-headed, if unglamorous, attention to detail on the ground was crucial to long-term success in the air.

I am a stickler for detail in every respect, for in aerial fighting I am sure it is the detail that counts for more than the actual main fighting points. It is more easy to find a Hun and attack him from a good position than it is to do the actual accurate shooting. It may sound absurd, but such a thing as having dirty goggles makes all the difference between getting or not getting a Hun.[3] Captain James McCudden, 56 Squadron RFC

Many of the aces either had, or developed, considerable mechanical abilities which allowed them to make minor improvements to their aircraft in order to extract every last bit of performance. Through careful observation of the way his aircraft handled in the air, combined with an effective relationship with his ground crew, a pilot could use even the most marginal improvement to carry him another rung up the ladder of success.

One basic area in which every pilot bore personal responsibility for his own safety was in the maintenance and loading of his machine-guns. The complications of the Constantinesco gear meant that the Vickers gun was extremely prone to 'jamming' with possible fatal consequences when in combat. Pilots complained ceaselessly about the number of German aircraft that escaped thanks to machine-gun malfunctions and utmost care was needed to reduce 'jamming' to a minimum.

> The Vickers gun had a disintegrating belt made of little aluminium links and the bullets themselves were the pins between the links that held the whole thing together. In 56 we weren't allowed to have the armourers do any of the preparation of ammunition belts for fighting – we did it ourselves. We spent two or three hours every morning loading and making the belts that we should use on the afternoon patrol. By taking care with the way the belts were put together we got them so that they wouldn't jam in the breech.[4] Lieutenant Cecil Lewis, 56 Squadron RFC

The guns had to be aligned exactly with the sights. Keen pilots would spend their spare time at the butts where the aircraft was trued-up as if in flying position aiming at the target. By closely observing the firing pattern the pilot could shift the gun mountings to get his sights exactly synchronised on the gun burst at a particular range. The machine-guns were the scalpel with which the pilot sought to excise his enemies from the sky. As such, possession of a blunt instrument could easily be the difference between success and humiliating or fatal failure. Even pilots commonly regarded as 'thrusters' soon became aware that inaccuracy negated any other skills in the air and led to a continuous cycle of missed opportunities and subsequent self-recrimination.

> I should have destroyed this Hun, but poor shooting had enabled him to escape. Going home, I spent an hour that day practising at a square target on the ground. Thereafter I gave as much time as possible to shooting practice, and to the accuracy I acquired in this way I feel I owe most of my successes.[5] Lieutenant William Bishop, 60 Squadron RFC

The confidence that such care and marksmanship engendered meant that if one of the 'aces' such as McCudden, Mannock or Bishop were successful in getting into one of their favourite attack positions they could almost guarantee success in shooting down a hapless victim in just a few rounds.

Each scout squadron flew several patrols a day depending on the operational requirements. But the first, and often the most strenuous, was carried out shortly after daybreak. Before each take-off the air mechanics went through a precisely observed routine to start up the aircraft.

> The officer would get into the aircraft cockpit and you would see that the chocks were put in front of the wheels. Then you would go to the propeller and you would say to him, 'Petrol On. Switch off. Suck in.' Then you would turn the propeller a few times so as to get a sufficient charge into the cylinders of the engine. When you thought you'd got it ready to fire, you would say, 'Contact, Sir!' He would answer, 'Contact', and he would switch into contact. Then you would be very careful how you approached the propeller. You'd hold it with two hands and give a tremendous swing – and if you were lucky it would fire. But if it didn't fire you had to say, 'Switch off, Sir', and he would reply, 'Switch off'. Then when you'd got it in the right position for another swing you would say, 'Contact' and you'd give it another pull

– and if it fired that was all right. It would start to run and you'd get clear to stand by the chocks. When he waved his hand you would pull the chocks away and you knew he was ready for take-off. That was the prescribed procedure – you couldn't say anything else – only those particular words which were repeated by the officer so there could be no mistake. On a bright summer day it would go on about the second or third swing but in winter when it was frosty and foggy you might swing for twenty minutes. The thing was to swing the propeller and stand quite near – as near as you dared. If you swung it and tried to jump back you might slip into it. It was always a very ticklish job – you had to be very careful.[6]
Air Mechanic Cecil King, 3 Squadron RFC

Once aloft the machines flew in formation, a practice that after initial difficulties became second-nature to the pilots.

It more or less comes naturally. It's like driving a motor car. You'd think that going at 130 miles an hour it would be a job to keep formation but it wasn't. You were stationary in relation to each other and you didn't realise that you were going at all that speed five or six feet apart. It never used to worry us.[7] Lieutenant Ernest Tomkins, RNAS

The supreme tactical advantage in aerial warfare that every patrol leader sought was height which not only granted speed and surprise in attack, but also the opportunity to escape if things went wrong. The gradual climb would be done while the patrol was still on the Allied side of the lines and having gained the requisite altitude the patrol would approach the trench lines and fly into German territory. At this point they would meet the first expression of their enemies' displeasure as German anti-aircraft batteries opened up on them. As the patrol moved further into German territory constant vigilance was absolutely essential if the patrol was not to be ambushed with fatal consequences.

We were continually on the alert against the enemy whom we had to fight. We had to look in front of us, above us, around us, behind us and below us. We had to develop an entirely new sense of sight, of vision, the enemy might be anywhere. On the ground the enemy was ahead, in the air he might be anywhere. We had to live a life within a sphere instead of a life that was horizontal on the ground.[8] Lieutenant Norman Macmillan, 45 Squadron RFC

Aloft in another world among the clouds there was plenty to distract a pilot but the experienced pilot never relaxed his concentration.

Our eyes were continually focusing, looking; craning our heads round, moving all the time looking for those black specks which would mean enemy aircraft at a great distance. Between clouds we would not be able to see the ground or only parts of it which would sort of slide into view like a magic lantern screen, far, far beneath. Clinging close together about 20 or 30 yards between each machine, swaying, looking at our neighbours, setting ourselves just right so that we were all in position. Sooner or later we would spot the enemy.[9] Lieutenant Cecil Lewis, 56 Squadron RFC

A patrol leader had to be aware that inexperienced pilots would often be completely oblivious to the presence of the enemy and he therefore had to adjust his tactics accordingly to protect them from more alert predators.

It was an extraordinary thing that a fellow coming out couldn't see half the things that were going on. Their eyes didn't register into the far distance. We had to see things – just a twinkle of the sun on a bit of metal – that's all we would need to make us conscious that there was something in the sky way in the distance. From that we might manoeuvre our position. But we would get into dogfights even and they hardly knew what was going on. They were shot down pretty freely. I didn't like this so any fellow coming out new to my flight as soon as he was ready to go over the lines flew next to me and outside him was an experienced man. So I never lost one of these boys who was new to the game. I kept my own eye on them and other people did too. As soon as they became better acquainted to what was going on then they were on their own then.[10] Lieutenant Gwilym Lewis, 40 Squadron RFC

Confirmation of this complete lack of awareness can be seen in the bafflement of Second Lieutenant R.J. Brownell at the antics of his fellow pilots during his first patrol over the lines with Lieutenant Norman Macmillan of 45 Squadron.

The Flight Commander more or less took me under his wing and the remainder of the formation – all experienced – kept an eye on me ... Off we went and apart from dodging a bit of 'Archie', we flew along tranquilly enough until at about 12,000 feet. I noticed the leader firing his guns, so I did the same – thinking this was just to warm the gun, and then there was a lot of dodging about and I thought this was a try-out for me at keeping with the formation. On several occasions during our patrol, similar manoeuvres took place, and, as instructed, I fired a few bursts at odd intervals to ensure no freezing up took place. However, no matter how hard the leader tried to lose me, I kept my eye glued on him and retained my place at his left in the formation – which I noted had become somewhat disintegrated by this time. Finally we turned for home and landed, and I secretly felt quite pleased with myself for having kept formation – with all the dodging about that I imagined had been done to test me out. When we got out of our buses and commenced to thaw out, Macmillan came across to me and said, 'Damn good show, Brownell, I saw you shooting at that Hun though I don't think you got him.' I looked at him in amazement and said, 'What Hun? I didn't see any!' Mac said, 'But I saw you close beside me shooting right into one of the enemy buses.' 'I must have just been keeping my guns warm', I said, 'as I never saw any hostile aircraft at all!!' I was the joke of the place after that and felt a complete ass ... Anyway, I suppose it was good experience for me – specially the ticking off the Flight Commander gave me for not keeping my

blinking eyes open.[11] Second Lieutenant R.J. Brownell,
45 Squadron RFC

The first sight of the enemy and the decision on how to respond
was crucial. The flight commander had to draw on all his experience
to decide exactly what he and the men placed in his charge should
do, whether to seek action immediately, manoeuvre to improve
the tactical position, or to withdraw with all possible speed. If the
odds appeared reasonable, and especially if the German aircraft
were below, then attack was the usual option given the offensive
tradition already inculcated into the RFC and RNAS. As they
dived into action they were irrevocably committed to facing the
ultimate test of their combat skills. But they also had to fight their
own internal battles in the narrow confines of their cockpits.

On the ground we had the comradeship of the men
around us, we had the intimate society of being thrown
together all the time, both in the line and out of it. In
the line one had the constant support of the men who
were beside one. One knew that they were there, they
would back one up and one would back them up. We
had a feeling of community, a feeling that we were all
together in the same thing, each helping the other, each
one the intimate and immediate companion of all the
men about him. Almost like a pyramid of strength. In
the air when we were flying there was no question of
any contact with the ground. Once we left the ground
we were individual and alone. Even when we flew in
formation we had no means of communication, one
with the other, except by rocking the wings, making
some particular motion of the aircraft, firing a Very
light or by waving a hand. The sensation was entirely
different – spiritually and emotionally we were shut in
– we were self-contained individuals. We did not have
the feeling of the community spirit that we had known on
the ground. Everything had to be the thought and action
on the part of the one individual; he was entirely and
inseparably alone. Even when he looked outside and saw
the machines beside him, even then he still felt himself
shut in responsible almost entirely for himself and every

action. In combat it was the individual in the machine who had to make the decisions – not the man outside. It might be that the leader led others into action but once action was joined every man had to fend for himself.[12]
Lieutenant Norman Macmillan, 45 Squadron RFC

If a kill was not achieved in the first dive out of the sun then a dogfight would begin as the two formations sought to achieve mastery. One principle was paramount.

The great thing is never to let the enemy's machine get behind you or 'on your tail'. Once he reaches there it is very hard to get him off, as every turn and every move you make, he makes with you. By the same token it is exactly the position into which you wish to get, and once there you must constantly strive for a shot as well as look out for attacks from other machines that may be near. It is well if you are against odds never to stay long after one machine. If you concentrate on him for more than a fraction of a second, some other Hun has a chance to get a steady shot at you, without taking any risks himself.[13]
Captain William Bishop, 60 Squadron RFC

Once in the thick of the action engine performance was of less importance than agility in the air, since the more highly-powered aircraft had wider turning circles and found it difficult to turn sharply enough to get their guns sighted on slow but manoeuvrable aircraft such as the Sopwith Pup. Often dogfights involving large numbers of aircraft were indeterminate because as the swirling aircraft twisted and dodged, getting in each other's way, they were unable to take little more than snapshots at fleetingly glimpsed opponents before having to take violent evasive action which rendered accurate aiming impossible. A fully-fledged dogfight was a kaleidoscopic experience.

It's not really possible to describe the action of a fight like that. Having no communication with each other we simply had to go in and take our man and chance our arm – keep our eyes in the backs of our heads to see if anybody was trying to get us as we went down. But there was always the point where you had to go down anyway whether there was anybody on your tail or not. The fight would begin – engage and disengage with burst of 30 or 40 rounds three in one tracer so there was always some idea of where you were firing because your sights were really no good in these dogfights – there wasn't time to focus – it was just snap shooting. The whole squadron would enter the fight in good formation but within half a minute the whole formation had gone to hell. Just chaps wheeling and zooming and diving. On each others' tails – perhaps four in a row even – a German going down, one of our chaps on his tail, another German on his tail, another Hun behind that – extraordinary glimpses. People approaching head-on firing at each other as they came and then just at the last moment turning and slipping away. The fight would last perhaps altogether ten minutes or quarter of an hour and would come down from 15,000 feet right down almost to ground level. By that time probably ammunition exhausted or guns jammed and then there would be nothing left but to come back home again. That was how it went.[14] Lieutenant Cecil Lewis, 56 Squadron RFC

The mental strain of these dogfights was incredible for any one of a multitude of instantaneous decisions could lead immediately to fatal consequences or glorious success.

In combat we were swirling round without regard for horizon or any other aspect of flight. We had been trained to fly with our noses on the horizon so that we could keep our aircraft level, so that we could turn right and left, roll our machines in accordance with the horizon that we could see. But in combat there was no horizon, there was only a sphere. We flew like goldfish in a bowl swimming around the sky in all directions – sometimes standing on our tails, sometimes with our heads right down, sometimes over on our backs, sometimes at right-angles to the ground – any attitude. The only attitude which enables the nose of the aircraft to point where we wanted it to point – in the direction of the enemy so that the guns could register hits. It was a fantastic type of flying and our machines could turn in such tiny circles that we simply swerved round in an amazingly small space of air, missing each other sometimes by inches. Missing enemy aircraft, missing our own aircraft, dodging in and out amongst the others in the sky, weaving the most fantastic patterns.[15] Lieutenant Norman Macmillan, 45 Squadron

In such a desperate situation when a gun jammed at some crucial moment, pilots were often reduced to tears of frustration, rage and terror.

The real preoccupation that a pilot had on going into combat was whether his guns would continue to fire or not. The SE5 had two guns – Lewis gun on the top plane with 100 rounds of ammunition in it on drums and we carried spare drums in the cockpit and a Vickers gun which fired through the propeller by the Constantinesco gear. Those guns could, and very often did, jam, and when they jammed in the middle of the fight the pilot was in a very precarious position. The un-jamming of a gun when you're flying at 100 miles an hour plus, with icy hands, at 15,000 feet was a very difficulty thing. You had to put your hand out round the windscreen into the wind, get hold of the handle on the gun and jerk it over in order to clear the collapsible belt which used to get jammed in the breech. Or if you'd had a good go at a Hun and got rid of all your Lewis gun ammunition then you'd have to change drums. This was a terrific job because the gun was up on the top plane and there was a sort of brass quadrant down which it slid when you caught hold of the back of it and released the catch – the gun came down into your hand pointing vertically upwards. The drum was quite a heavy thing and with the wind blowing past it at a hundred miles an hour as soon as you unclipped it, it flew back and you had an awful job to get it down into the cockpit. Then you had to get the full drum up, again out into the wind and push it on to the gun, then push the whole gun up on to the top plane and lock it into position. This was quite a thing to do with your right hand, flying with your left hand, Huns about and coming down on you in the middle of it. I was caught in such a situation more than once and it was really frightening.[16] Lieutenant Cecil Lewis, 56 Squadron RFC

Many of the novice pilots had not the slightest clue of how they would respond when they actually met the German scouts. Split-second 'fighter' tactics were not as obvious in the heat of battle as they might appear in hindsight. Second Lieutenant MacLanachan for one knew in theory exactly what he should do but lamentably failed to do it.

I heard a sudden tat-tat-tat of a machine-gun and saw trails of smoke passing my machine between me and the right wing-tip. Glancing round hastily, I caught sight of a pointed-nosed machine diving straight past my tail plane. No sooner had it disappeared than the tat-tatting was repeated and another storm of smoke streamers flew by. I turned right round this time, to see another one pulling up out of a dive . . . [Later] on examining my machine they found several bullet holes in the right wing, and while the other pilots were filling in their combat reports, Walder took me aside and asked me if I hadn't seen the Germans . . . 'Why on earth didn't you dive as I told you to?' he asked. 'I forgot, and I was too interested in seeing what a German machine looked like anyway,' I replied. He then gave me another bit of information, 'Whenever you hear a machine-gun, you may bet there's someone firing at you.' This first official patrol 'up the line' amply demonstrated to me that my education was just beginning. In fact, almost every flight for several months revealed some new feature of aerial warfare to me. It was like going to school for the first time. The principal points about my first baptism of machine-gun fire were: that I did not see the German till after his bullets had missed me, and that, observing that someone was shooting at me, I made no attempt to get out of his line of fire.[17] Second Lieutenant William MacLenachan, 40 Squadron RFC

Novice pilots lacked the experience and instinctive reactions that could extricate them from positions of danger which meant that patrol leaders had to take a personal responsibility for any new pilots in their flight, even if this entailed some risk to themselves.

I was in a flight of five Camels led by Roy Brown, I was the last one. We attacked a German two-seater machine towards Ostend. Then down out of the sun came four Albatross fighter scouts diving at us. Roy Brown's guns had jammed and he pulled away into climbing turns. From inexperience, and because I was the last man, I was lagging behind and before I could join them I was hit. The bullets came through my cockpit and grazed my back. The engine stopped and petrol squirted all over my leather coat and sheepskin boots. Immediately Roy Brown came down and although his guns were jammed he did a lot of stall turns and manoeuvres above the four Germans who just left me alone. Then the sky cleared – they'd disappeared – gone away! I was left to do the long glide back more or less in peace.[18] Flight Sub-Lieutenant Ronald Sykes, 9 Squadron RNAS

A fast learning curve was essential in such circumstances. Many of the aircraft shot down on both sides were the result of a harsh juxtaposition of raw novices and experienced 'aces' who made fewer mistakes and exploited every opportunity offered through the mistakes of others with consummate skill. Each time a pilot survived a dogfight, it gave him more experience and confidence. He became more valuable to the patrol and eventually was able to assist the patrol leader in the actual fight. Thus, a novice like Sykes eventually became a useful member of his squadron rather than a lame duck who needed special attention.

A Fokker D VII came out of the formation on our right and flew straight underneath us fairly asking for a fight. Kinkead pointed to me and I dived down. As soon as I got on top of him close to him he just went into sharp turns. I realised he was confident of keeping out of my line of sight. I'd got a bit of speed left from the dive so I pulled up to do an Immelmann turn – pulled up to do a half roll and then pulled back hard on the stick and then came down on him. But as I went up Kinkead streaked down past me straight on to the German's tail and there he stuck. They were twisting, turning, half rolling, vertical banks – this way and that all over the sky. The other three Camels stayed up high and there seemed to be enemy fighters all over the sky. I made a few attacks but he was able to deal with them quite easily so I thought my best duty was to guard the leader's tail all the time. We went on for a time then I discovered that the sky had cleared and we were down to ground level. They were in vertical banks but Kinkead gave an extra hard pull on his stick – just managed to get his sight on the German's rudder and hit it, putting it out of action. The German levelled up and landed and found he was among Australian troops to his disgust – he thought he was on his side of the lines. He was quite a famous German pilot and he'd got a squadron of trainees with him. His idea was that he would show them how to break up a British formation and start a real dogfight. Fortunately for us it didn't come off that way.[19] Flight Sub-Lieutenant Ronald Sykes, 9 Squadron RNAS

Although the formation would split up in the hurly-burly of a dogfight, each member of the team had to be on the qui vive to protect any of his companions who had got themselves into a dangerous situation.

We were in a formation of four led by a man called Courtney. We were flying at about 10,000 feet. We encountered a German formation of Albatross DV of the same strength flying about 1,000 feet above us and coming straight at us. Their leader immediately dived on our leader. I dived on him and I got so close to him that he filled the whole of the lens of my Aldis sight. I shot him, then he slumped over his controls and went into a vertical dive with his engine full on. After falling for about 1,000 feet his right-hand lower wing broke off and floated down separately and that of course was the end of him – no parachutes in those days. But immediately afterwards one of the other Germans was firing at me from behind! So I circled as quickly as I could in as small a radius as possible to evade his fire and one of the other members of the formation attacked him and drove him off.[20] Lieutenant George Jones, 4 Squadron, Australian Flying Corps

The much sought-after 'kill' brought forth a swathe of conflicting emotions in the victor. Triumph mingled with pity and often a strange fellow-feeling for the 'enemy' pilot. This was particularly the case when an aircraft went down in flames.

A burning machine is a glorious and yet a most revolting sight to the victor; but there is no question as to the completeness of the victory. To watch a machine burst into flames after its petrol tanks have been pierced by incendiary bullets is a ghastly, hypnotising sight. At first a tiny flame peeps out of the tank as if almost ashamed of what it is about to do; then it gets bigger and bigger as it licks its way along the length and breadth of the machine; and finally, all that can be seen is a large ball of fire enveloping in a terrifying embrace what was a few minutes before a beautiful bird of wood and metal flown by a probably virtuous youth who loved flying and life.[21] Lieutenant Ira Jones, 74 Squadron RAF

The scout pilot was surrounded by petrol and once the aircraft was alight he had almost no hope but to endure the most awful of deaths.

Suddenly there was a blaze in the sky nearby. I looked. It was Begbie's S.E. A sudden feeling of sickness, of vomiting, overcame me. Poor old Begbie, I thought. How terrible! The kak-kak-kak of a machine-gun a few yards behind me warned me of my own danger. Poor Begbie had to leave us without a farewell wave. I had another peep at him as I flew near. A Hun was still at him, pouring more bullets into his machine. He was making sure of him, the dirty dog. While he pursued his victim, an S.E. – it was Giles – dived on his tail. There was a kak-kak-kak! and the Hun dived away, not to be seen again. I hope he was killed, too. One by one, the Huns left the fight. Giles and I flew towards Begbie's machine, which was floating enveloped in flames. It was a terrible sight. I hope he followed Mannock's advice and blew his brains out as soon as he realised he was on fire. Perhaps the Hun saved him the trouble.[22] Lieutenant Ira Jones, 74 Squadron RAF

The terrible inevitability of the first flicker of flame, the sudden silence of an engine failure, the rending and flapping of collapsing wings have led many to suggest that parachutes should have been issued to airmen to offer them at least a sporting chance of escaping a crippled aircraft. Trenchard refused to countenance the issue of parachutes because he felt that it might tempt flying crew to abandon aircraft which would have survived. This was an unintentional insult to many of the brave men who served under him but there were other practical reasons which made the question less clear-cut than it seems in hindsight.

The answer's a very simple one. The development of parachutes was in its infancy and the only available parachutes were so cumbersome and big that there simply wasn't room for them in the cockpit. The harness would have affected the efficiency and mobility of the personnel in the aircraft – they'd have been jammed into their seats. It simply wasn't practical to have them.[23] Major Archibald James, 6 Squadron RFC

During a patrol a flight could meet several opponents and often, having lost formation, had to return home separately. When outnumbered, out of ammunition, or in a damaged aircraft, breaking out of a dogfight could lead to a hair-raising few minutes. It was then that a lack of engine power made it extremely difficult to throw off opponents who could climb and dive much faster.

First you must turn, bank ninety degrees and keep turning. They can't keep their sights on you. Watch the sun for direction. Now there's one on your right – shoot at him.

Don't try to hit him – just spray him – for if you try to
hold your sight on him you'll have to fly straight and
give the others a crack at you. But you put the wind up
him anyway and he turns. Quick, turn in the opposite
direction. He's out of it for a moment. Now there's another
one near you. Try it on him – it works! Turn again, you are
between them and the lines. Now go for it, engine full on,
nose down! Two of them are still after you – tracer getting
near again. Pull up, zoom and sideslip and, if necessary,
turn and spray them again. Now make another dive for
home and repeat when necessary. If your wings don't fall
off and you are gaining on them, pull up a little. Ah, there's
Archie, that means they are behind you – woof – that one
was close – you now have another grey hair – they've
been watching you – better zigzag a bit. You can laugh
at Archie, he's a joke compared to machine-guns. You
dodge him carefully and roll in derision as you cross the
lines and hasten home for tea.[24] Lieutenant John Grider,
85 Squadron RFC

Easy! Sometimes with a severely damaged aircraft there was just
no option other than to lurch desperately back across the front line
to safety. Lieutenant Sardar Malik was caught by a large formation
of Germans during a patrol with his flight commander Captain
William Barker.

I was very soon hit by a German pilot who dived on me
and shot me through the right leg. On the Camel you sat on
the main petrol tank, it was under your seat. These bullets
that hit me came through the tank itself. Fortunately not
through the empty part of the tank but through the liquid
and that's why it didn't catch fire. Otherwise if it had
come through the vapour it would have caught fire. I
was disabled because my petrol leaked, my tank was
finished and I had nothing except the gravity tank and
with the gravity you couldn't climb – and if you couldn't
climb you couldn't fight. So I was completely at the mercy
of the German pilots. Well the man that shot me I shot
him down because he, instead of turning back, he dived
straight in front of me and I was able to shoot him down.

An RE8 pilot photographed by his observer (*above*) with the complementary view (*below*) of the observer taken by his pilot.

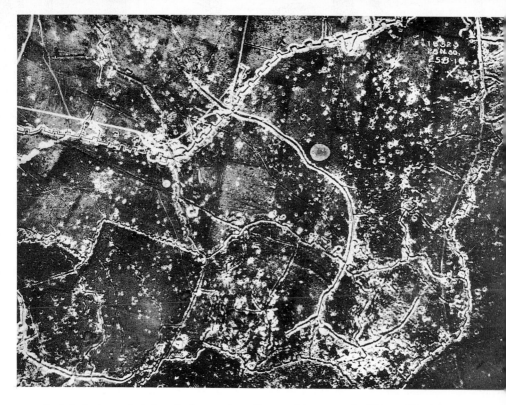

Aerial photograph (*above*) of a section of ground between the Ypres-Comines Canal and the La Bassee Canal taken in 1915, with (*below*) a diagrammatic key showing its distinctive features.

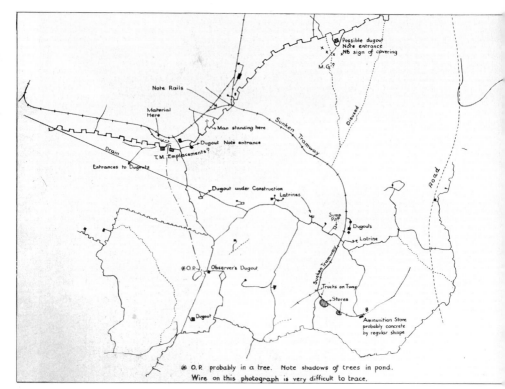

A BE2 C fitted with a camera for aerial photography.

A 'mosaic' map being assembled from aerial photographs.

An observer demonstrating the use of the CFS bombsight.

The groundcrew of 149 Squadron, RAF loading a 230 lb bomb on to an FE2 B at Dunkirk, 1 June 1918.

A non-rigid Submarine Scout (SS) airship, or 'blimp', clearly showing its BE2 fuselage suspended from the cylindrical balloon, used by the RNAS to counter the submarine threat in the middle years of the war.

Sopwith Camels on the deck of HMS *Furious* in 1918.

(*Right*)
Devastated homes in
Chambers Street, east
London following an
airship raid on the night
of 13/14 October 1915.

(*Below*)
A bomb damaged
London bus brought into
Willesden garage after
being hit near Liverpool
Street.

(Left)
William Leefe Robinson VC, the first pilot to shoot down an enemy airship over Great Britain in September 1916.

(Below)
Naval Zeppelin L70, one of the later generation of German airships, which was destroyed by Egbert Cadbury and Robert Leckie off the coast of Norfolk on 5 August 1918.

Gotha bombers lined up at their aerodrome near Ostend from where they launched their bombing campaign against Great Britain in the Spring of 1917.

A letter of sympathy to the parents of a girl wounded in the bombing of Upper North Street School, east London in June 1917.

London County Council.

Education Offices,

Victoria Embankment, W.C. 2.

20th June, 1917.

Dear Mr. Brewis,

As Chairman of the Education Committee for London I feel that I must write you a few lines of heartfelt sympathy. The injury to your little girl Catherine through the sudden and terrifying disaster of last Wednesday, 13th June, must have been a very severe blow to you. It may, however, be some comfort to you to know that so many people are thinking of you in your trouble. In the days to come your little girl will be remembered as one who suffered for her country just as much as if she had been a soldier wounded while fighting at the front. My sincere sympathy is with you.

The Minister for Education, Mr. Herbert Fisher, asks me to convey to you his warmest sympathy.

Yours very sincerely,

Chairman of the Education Committee.

Mr. J. G. Brewis,
    54, Gough Street,
      E.14.

Then three German fighters followed me because all I could do was get as low as possible and get back home, but home was 40 miles away as we were on the wrong side of the lines. All I could hope to do was somehow or other to get back. So I flew very low, what they call treetop flying. I was shot at from the ground and these three German fighters chased me and shot all they had at me point-blank coming as close as possible. At the beginning I thought that I would definitely be shot down or killed but after a bit when they seemed to be unable to hit me again I somehow lost the fear and had the feeling I'd be all right, I didn't feel panicked at all. I simply kept flying. In due course they left me because they must have shot a lot of ammunition but I was still shot at from the ground until I got to the lines. I remember seeing the big landmark which was the Zillebeke Lake and as soon as I saw it I looked for ground where I could come down. But there was no flat ground anywhere at all because the whole of that part of the line had been shot up for so many years that there was nothing but shell holes full of water. Finally I got down and the next thing I remember was being in a stretcher and being taken to the casualty clearing station. Later on when my plane was recovered by my squadron and examined they found over 400 bullet marks on the plane but not a single one after the first hit me or any vital part of the plane – the greatest luck![25]
Lieutenant Sardar Malik, 28 Squadron RFC

After such experiences it is not surprising that many pilots suffered severe nervous and physical reactions on reaching safety. One such was Lieutenant Verschoyle Cronyn who had been badly shot up by a burst of machine-gun fire from Leutnant Werner Voss during his last epic confrontation with 56 Squadron. Cronyn made an erratic return, with his controls almost completely shot through, and only just managed to avoid crashing on landing.

I got out of the machine, and the relief of being on the ground was so great that I practically collapsed. For a minute or two everything went black. It seemed pitch dark, and I could hear somebody asking where I had been hit. Then the Major arrived, and someone took me by the arm and sat me down on a bench. I seemed to have no strength in my knees. My head was buzzing, and everything seemed disconnected and out of reach. I wanted to laugh because I had managed to get down without crashing, but instead of laughing I started to cry. This does me little credit, but nerves play uncontrollable tricks. Why, I don't know, but when I managed to pull myself together I felt a thousand times better: as though a very tight steel belt had been released from about my chest, the singing left my head, and my sight became reasonably clear. The Major was sitting on the bench beside me, unbuttoning my flying coat and pulling off my cap. He offered me a cigarette but I first took a good drink of brandy . . . I went down to the Mess, and consumed large quantities of nerve producer, so by dinner time I was feeling quite OK. But my speech was affected in the same manner as in the summer of '14 when I had that nervous breakdown. However, that might be only temporary, as my hands are quite steady. After Mess I went up to the hangar to have a look at my machine. It was a 'write off' and no mistake . . . I went to bed as soon as I had a good look over the machine, but could hardly sleep a wink. I just lay in bed perspiring, although it was quite a cold night.[26] Lieutenant Verschoyle Cronyn, 56 Squadron RFC

Having once been exposed to this sort of mental trauma it could take a little while to regain any semblance of normal composure.

But my nerve was badly shaken up – being chased without any ability to retaliate. Every time I thought of it I could hardly hold a knife and fork if I was having a meal – they'd almost fall out of my hands. After they repaired my aeroplane I took it up and brought it into land at what they said was 120 miles an hour whereas I should have brought it in at 65. I ran right across the aerodrome, turned over again, upside-down and in the mud. I stood there on my head until they lifted the fuselage off me. My nerves were terribly shaken up –

that was what caused me to make such a tremendous error of judgement. It took a lot of hard thinking to get myself into a condition of stability to keep on flying but I did manage to overcome it.[27] Lieutenant George Jones, 4 Squadron, Australian Flying Corps

In just twelve years aircraft had been transformed from the Wright brothers' Biplane to single-seater 'scouts' or 'fighters'. In the process new forms of combat had been added to warfare. Although as murderous in intent as its terrestrial cousins, aviation still offered a sense of glamour and excitement through its position on the cutting edge of modern technology.

There was a joy, a thrill, an exhilaration – call it what you will – that had fox-hunting, boat sailing, football and skiing beaten into small and uninteresting pieces.[28] Second Lieutenant Duncan Grinnell-Milne, 16 Squadron RFC

But there was always another patrol, another dawn until even the best could stand no more. For the truism that in a single-seater fighter there was only one seat was never more apparent than when on patrol over German lines, with a prevailing wind to contend with. 'Gradually it sort of dawned on one as perhaps the tension and tiredness grew, how utterly alone you were, how independent. Once you left the ground no power on earth could bring you down again except yourself.'[29]

CHAPTER ELEVEN

Gothas

By spring 1917 pressure on the Government for some kind of visible response to the pattern of German air raids against Britain had started to fade. Despite continued calls from MPs including William Joynson-Hicks and Noël Pemberton Billing in the Commons and Lord Montagu of Beaulieu in the Lords for retaliatory strikes against military targets in Germany, the apparently successful defeat of the Zeppelins in the previous autumn, when six of them had been destroyed, and the natural reduction in the number of raids over the winter, meant that public concern had noticeably waned. This growing self-confidence was also reflected by a slight scaling down of the anti-Zeppelin measures which had been introduced during the height of the crisis in 1916. Facing spiralling casualties on the Western Front the RFC in the Field was desperately short of experienced reinforcements and the lull in air raids provided an opportunity for a reduction in the establishment of Home Defence squadrons to enable many of their trained night-flying pilots to be posted overseas. The resurgence of the German campaign of unrestricted submarine warfare coupled with the sinking of a number of British merchant ships caused great alarm at the Admiralty and, believing that the threat from the air had decreased, a number of the guns originally intended for anti-aircraft purposes were diverted to arm merchantmen. In consequence, the number of men needed to operate the anti-aircraft guns was reduced and, with the exception of coastal batteries, those that remained in operation were told to ignore incursions inland by German aircraft or seaplanes.

Politically, the hoary question of what to do about aviation also seemed to have been solved. Although on the whole Lord Curzon had been able to achieve little during his tenure as President of the Air Board, by the time of his resignation he had succeeded in establishing the foundations of control over the supply of aircraft and, perhaps more importantly, also introduced at least the principle of direct political control over the air services, even if he had not gained it himself. His fortunate successor as President, the industrialist Lord Cowdray, thus found himself in a better position at the start of his administration in January 1917. By April the most serious issue that had faced Curzon, the quarrel between the RFC and the RNAS over the conduct of strategic bombing raids in Germany, was also resolved when the navy finally ended its controversial campaign in France and agreed that all land-based operations should be carried out by the RFC, leaving the RNAS to concentrate on the development of a more specific naval role, a matter that had become more urgent following the escalation of the submarine threat. Released from this irritating diversion which had sapped so much of Curzon's energy, Cowdray was able to concentrate on the additional responsibilities that had been given to his re-formed Board, namely to oversee the procurement of new aircraft and liaise with the Ministry of Munitions over the production of engines and airframes which, in a significant political move, had been placed within its jurisdiction. Through Sir William Weir, the newly appointed Controller of Aeronautical Supplies, the Ministry of Munitions became a key player in the conduct of air policy.

When Weir, like Cowdray, a successful industrialist, took over the means of production in 1917, he found them to be in a grossly inefficient state. The previous two and a half years of unplanned growth and competition between the RFC and RNAS had left the aircraft industry in need of extensive reorganisation. Most urgently reform was needed in the area of the manufacture rate of aero-engines and in the first six months of 1917 Weir successfully increased their production by 74 per cent, from 600 to over 1,000 per month, a significant achievement by any measure. In January 1917, the new administration of David Lloyd George had agreed to the Army Council's request to expand the RFC to a strength of 106 squadrons and to achieve this Weir estimated that 2,000 engines would have to be manufactured each month. In May

1917, believing that the improvements effected by Weir could be maintained if sufficient resources were allocated to it, the Air Board reported to the War Cabinet that the rate of engine production would reach 1,500 per month by August, 2,000 by October and that by the end of the year it would have climbed to 2,500. In fact, although continued improvements were made, for several reasons these sanguine levels of productions were not attained. But the figures were accepted and vital decisions were taken on the strength of them.

Having allowed themselves to drift back into a position of complacency about attack from the air, the British authorities were completely unprepared for the dramatic reversal of fortunes caused by the commencement of aeroplane bombing raids in May 1917. The Germans had always intended to use aeroplanes to bomb Britain and only a combination of the lack of suitable long-range aircraft, the relative distance of their home bases and the distraction of the fighting along the Front had restricted their operations to infrequent, small-scale 'tip and run' raids which by the end of 1916 had killed twenty-five people. Now, in the Gotha GIV they had finally developed a machine that matched the means with the avowed intent.

The large, purpose-built bombers were known as Grosskampf-flugzeug, and the largest, the GIV, became infamously known as the Gotha after the name of its factory, the Gothaer Waggonfabrik. The length of the Gotha's fuselage was more than forty feet with a wing span of almost seventy-eight feet and it was armed with three machine-guns. Powered by two 260 horsepower Mercedes engines it flew at between seventy and eighty miles per hour. The weight of bombs it could carry varied according to flying height. In daylight, it needed to fly at 18,000 feet and so was able to carry only around 700 pounds. But at night, when it was able to fly lower at 10,000 feet, the bomb load could be increased to 1,100 pounds. The first Gothas were delivered in March 1917 to Kampfgeschwader 1, the bombing unit that had succeeded the original Ostend force. Many of the personnel from the 1914 unit were still serving in it and this close relationship between the two highlights the link between the original German intention to bomb Great Britain and the eventual advent of aeroplane raids in 1917. After training on the new machines at the original base in Ostend, Kampfgeschwader 1 was ready to begin operational flying by the middle of May.

The first Gotha air raid occurred in the early evening of 25 May 1917 when twenty-one aircraft arrived over Britain and, having been deflected from London by foggy conditions, bombed Shorncliffe Camp and Folkestone. In all casualties totalled ninety-five killed and 195 injured. Although many RNAS and RFC pilots attempted to intercept the raiders the lack of any co-ordinated plan of defence became evident as individual pilots tried to attack the high flying German formation which deployed massed machine-guns. This raid caused a return to tighter anti-aircraft precautions and the restrictions on the gun batteries were promptly removed. After a second attack was diverted to Sheerness on 5 June, a week later the German bombers found their real target. During the afternoon of 13 June 1917 a formation of fourteen Gothas sprayed bombs liberally across east London and the City. At first the bewildered population did not really grasp the significance of the threat that the bombers posed. One, an experienced RFC pilot, should certainly have known better.

I was up in town on a day's leave and you did not go in uniform, you always went in civvies. I was wandering as an ordinary 'civilian' down Cheapside and into King Street which leads into the Guildhall when a raid started. Raids hadn't become a very serious thing and everybody crowded out into the street to watch. They didn't take cover or dodge. A bomb went off right over the Guildhall and it seemed to me, having had quite a bit of experience of dropping bombs myself, that it was very disappointing for the chap who had thrown it at the Guildhall and it had gone off two or three hundred feet overhead. I couldn't help saying, 'Oh, bad luck!' This got me into disfavour with the people standing around and I saw that I had said quite the wrong thing and had to make off![1] Lieutenant Charles Chabot, 39 Squadron RFC

In contrast to the earlier Zeppelin raids which were mostly carried out at night, the Gothas attacked during daylight, and 162 people died and 432 were injured, many having been caught standing exposed in the streets gaping upwards. The most horrible tragedy occurred when a bomb scored a direct hit on the Upper North Street School in Poplar.

Our teachers had been warned of an approaching air raid and were endeavouring to keep us all calm by getting us all to sing together. Soon, however, the noise of the anti-aircraft guns and the detonation of the enemy bombs became audible above even our shrill voices.[2] Miss I.A. Major

The bomb crashed through the school penetrating three floors before exploding in the infants' class on the ground floor.

I was having a singing lesson at the time. I recall the tremendous bang and of course everybody was panic-stricken. A big fat girl called Kitty Chalmers fell on top of me . . . but I picked myself up. The teachers were marvellous. They were saying 'Don't panic' and 'File down quietly' . . . I distinctly remember one of the teachers carrying a girl – I think her name was Pittard – whose leg was severed. What really frightened me so much was seeing all those little children being carried out. They were all black and their hair ginger from the TNT.[3] Esther Levy

The chaos in the school was appalling as the pupils, teachers, parents and rescue services tried to establish who was alive, dead or needed urgent medical treatment.

Thinking only of my little sister aged five, I rushed down the stairs with another pupil. I forced my way along the corridor which was filled with men and women frantically searching for their children and all were screaming and shouting. I could not find my sister anywhere and it was two hours later when my father found her dead in the mortuary.[4] Mrs T. Myers

No less than ninety-two aircraft took off in an attempt to intercept the raiders but were again stymied by lack of organisation and their inability to gain the necessary altitude. Among those who desperately chased after the intruders was James McCudden, still on home service as an instructor prior to joining 56 Squadron on the Western Front.

I caught up to them at the expense of some height, and by the time I had got under the rear machine I was 1,000 ft below. I now found that there were over twenty machines, all with two 'pusher' engines. To my dismay I found that I could not lessen the range to any appreciable extent. By the time I had got to 500 ft under the rear machine we were twenty miles east of the Essex coast, and visions of a very long swim entered my mind, so I decided to fire all my ammunition and then depart. I fired my first drum, of which the Hun did not take the slightest notice . . . How insolent these damn Boches did look, absolutely lording the sky over England! I replaced my first drum and had another try after which the Hun swerved ever so slightly, and then that welcome sound of machine-guns smote my ears and I caught the smell of the Hun's incendiary bullets as they passed me. I now put on my third and last single Lewis drum (each drum held 47 shots), and fired again and, to my intense chagrin, the last Hun did not take the slightest notice . . . On my way back I was absolutely furious to think that the Huns should come over and bomb London and have it practically all their own way. I simply hated the Hun more than ever.[5] Captain James McCudden, Home Establishment, RFC

The horror of this raid, and its 'slaughter of the innocents', was seized upon most ghoulishly by the press. Once again the need to satisfy popular demand by being seen to be hitting back became a prime political concern. Under military law it was permissible for an aggrieved nation to carry out a reprisal raid if the consequences of its attack were less severe than those perpetrated on its own population. The possibility of reprisals was also intended to deter the original attack. Nevertheless, within Britain there remained strong moral resistance, particularly among the clergy, to entering into this new murky area of warfare and many felt that by sinking to the depraved depths of the enemy the nation risked becoming equally as repugnant. On 2 May 1917, the Archbishop of Canterbury had spoken out strongly in the House of Lords against any kind of raids against Germany. But the Gotha raids significantly reduced support for this point of view and instead it was replaced by widespread calls for reprisal raids on Germany.

With pressure increasing again on the Government, their scope for action was severely limited by the refusal of Major General Trenchard and the military commanders in France to allow their resources to be diverted. It was evident that the size of the British air forces would have to be enlarged and on 2 July the War Cabinet ordered another significant expansion of the RFC to 200 squadrons. Despite already having failed to raise the rate of engine and airframe production to the levels he had predicted for the end of June, Weir produced another optimistic report in July which laid out his projected figures for the next twelve months. By spring 1918 he claimed that 2,400 new engines would be completed each month, a figure which was in excess of even the newly increased military and naval demand. In addition to this domestic production it was hoped that the recent American entry into the war would place the vast industrial might of the USA at the disposal of the Allies and that new resources, particularly engines, would soon be forthcoming from that source to supplement the Allies' own stretched industries. Yet in the end, despite high hopes and confidence, in the twelve months following the American declaration of war they only managed to produce fifteen planes.

In the short term Trenchard's grudging offer of the temporary loan of two experienced RFC squadrons from the Western Front for temporary fighting patrols on either side of the Channel was accepted. On 20 June 56 Squadron was sent back to England, while 66 Squadron was based in Calais. The loss of these scout squadrons caused painful consequences on the Western Front during their absence, but the anxiety and panic at home were such that something concrete had to be done to satisfy the general public. However, this political exigency was unable to overrule the determination of the military hierarchy to bring both units back into the fold. Within a month they were returned to front-line duties, ironically a day before the next Gotha raid on London on 7 July. Once again the bombs tumbled down over the East End and City, causing fifty-four more deaths and 190 injuries. This time ninety-five aircraft took off to counter the raid but the unfocused attacks on the German bombers were as futile as before, despite the presence of several of the latest scout aircraft.

Once again McCudden's response was typical as he took off in his Sopwith Pup.

> He obviously wanted to go up and tackle these blighters. He went almost mad rushing about. I believe his Vickers gun was not loaded but he had a Lewis gun on the top plane. He was dashing round grabbing magazines of ammunition – all he could get from various mechanics – he stuck these in the wire round his cockpit and away he went.[6] Second Lieutenant J.C.F. Hopkins, RFC

Having gained sufficient height, McCudden launched a lone attack on the formation.

> I could now discern a lot of big machines in good formation flying east. I had plenty of time to determine what to do, and also a lot of height to spare. As soon as all the formation had passed by, I dived on the rearmost machine and fired a whole drum at close range. In diving I came rather too near the top plane of the Gotha and had to level out so violently to avoid running into him that the downward pressure of my weight as I pulled the joy-stick back was so great that my seat bearers broke, and I was glad it wasn't my wings. I remained above again and now thought of a different way to attack the rearmost Gotha. I put on a new drum and dived from the Hun's right rear to within 300 ft, when I suddenly swerved, and changing over to his left rear, closed to within 50 yards and finished my drum before the enemy gunner could swing his gun from the side at which I first dived. I zoomed away but the Hun still appeared to be OK. Then I put on my third and last drum and made up my mind that I should have a good go at getting him. I repeated the manoeuvre of changing from one side to the other and had the satisfaction of seeing my tracer bullets strike all about his fuselage and wings, but beyond causing the Gotha to push his nose down a little, it had not the desired effect. I was very disappointed, as I had used up all my ammunition and the Huns were only just over Southend. It was very silly of me only to carry

three single drums of ammunition when I could easily have carried a dozen without affecting the climb and speed of my machine, for I now had nothing else to do except fly alongside the Huns and make faces at them.[7] Captain James McCudden, Home Establishment, RFC

Public outcry increased exponentially at this second demonstration of impotence in the face of the Gotha threat and an emergency meeting of the War Cabinet on 8 July ordered two experienced scout squadrons to be sent back to join the Home Defence establishment, this time permanently, and also instructed that preparations be set in hand for reprisal raids on German towns such as Mannheim which lay within range of British bombers. Haig, who was preoccupied with the preparations for his mammoth offensive at Ypres, protested vigorously, if tactfully, at this decision.

Two good fighting squadrons will proceed to England to-morrow as ordered. Request following facts may be laid before War Cabinet at once in connection with this decision. Fight for air supremacy preparatory to forthcoming operations was definitely commenced by us this morning. Both enemy and ourselves have concentrated fighting machines for this struggle in the air which will undoubtedly be the most severe we have yet had. Success in this struggle is essential to success of our operations. Withdrawal of these two squadrons will certainly delay favourable decision in the air and render our victory more difficult and more costly in aeroplanes and pilots. If raid on Mannheim is undertaken in addition our plans will have to be reconsidered entirely and the operations may have to be abandoned.[8] Field Marshal Sir Douglas Haig, Commander-in-Chief, BEF

This scarcely veiled threat was successful and the reconvened War Cabinet reduced their demand to one squadron and postponed the planned raid on Mannheim. But the attention of the very highest authorities had been drawn to the seriousness of the air situation as a whole. This was to have long-term effects and indeed result in the formation of the RAF. Even the Chief of Imperial General Staff, General Sir William Robertson, who supported the primacy of the Western Front, saw that there was a very real problem to be dealt with.

> Of course it is necessary that these raids should be put an end to, or at any rate severely punished. We saw Saturday's raid from the War Office windows. Our anti-aircraft artillery was apparently of no use, and our airmen arrived in driblets and were powerless, but succeeding in getting one machine down. The fact is we have not got enough machines to meet our requirements . . . I doubt if any real progress will be made until a different organisation is established. The Army and Navy now say what they want, the Air Board consider their wants, and then Addison [Minister of Munitions] makes the machines. I am inclined to think that we need a separate air service, but that would be a big business.[9] General Sir William Robertson, Chief of the Imperial General Staff

In accordance with a fine British tradition the hard-pressed Government established a committee under Lieutenant General Jan Christian Smuts to consider firstly the state of the Home Defences and secondly the whole question of the organisation of the war in the air. Smuts was a South African politician sent to London in March 1917 as his country's delegate to an imperial conference. He had quickly gained the confidence of many leading British figures and at the beginning of June he was invited to attend meetings of the War Cabinet, soon after joining the élite members of the War Policy Committee. It was in this capacity that the Prime Minister asked him to join the new committee and, as they were to be the only two permanent members, it became in effect Smuts's own personal investigation. His two reports, in effect only long memoranda of a few thousand words each, were based on his own observations of the recent raids on London, public opinion, as reflected by the press, and the personal views of leading politicians such as Lloyd George and senior officers including Major General Henderson, the Director-General of Military Aeronautics. Their conclusions were not strikingly original and incorporated many ideas that had been current since the beginning of the previous year, but the reports appeared at a time when solutions were eagerly being sought and succeeded in galvanising the Government into action.

The first report into the state of the Home Defences appeared quickly on 19 July. In it Smuts depicted London as the centre of the imperial war effort and believed that strong measures were required to protect its unique position. Since he believed increasingly heavy raids were to be expected he recommended consolidating control of all London's defences, including fighter planes, intelligence of imminent raids, searchlights and anti-aircraft artillery, under one central body. Subsequently this became known as the London Air Defence Area under the command of Brigadier General Ashmore. But Smuts stressed that this must be done without prejudicing the operations of the front-line air services in France. The report also recommended a concentration of resources to meet the threat posed by large Gotha formations that were not as vulnerable to the single aircraft or anti-aircraft guns as the inflammable Zeppelins. All the guns that could be spared from areas not considered under immediate threat were concentrated in a barrage line east of London and the raising of three new scout squadrons with relatively modern aircraft was immediately undertaken. The idea was first to project a mass of exploding shells into the sky to break up the bombers' formation. Once scattered by such a 'wall of steel' the Gothas would lose the advantage of their combined defensive machine-gun fire and would themselves come under concentrated attack by formations of defending aircraft.

Air-raid warnings were also given to the civilian population as a whole rather than just to those in significant public utilities and factories. Warnings had long been a point of controversy with the authorities forced to balance public safety against the disruption to production and normal routine that such warnings would cause. The numbers of casualties from the general public resulting from the daylight raids in June and July 1917, however, finally forced the authorities to reconsider the situation and a warning system of explosive rockets, called maroons, coupled with police activity using whistles and placards to clear the streets, was reluctantly introduced in late July. Sirens, the seemingly obvious solution, were at that time both scarce and insufficiently powered to be heard above the hustle and bustle of London street traffic.

Policemen went through the streets carrying a placard with the words 'Take Cover' on, and at the same time blowing their whistles. When this happened I would report to Blackheath Road Police Station and at the 'All Clear' I would accompany a policeman and blow the 'All Clear' on my bugle . . . On one occasion after a raid I was sent out with a special constable who had a motor-cycle and sidecar. I sat in the sidecar and away we went. When I put the bugle to my mouth and tried to blow, it acted like a wind tunnel and the air blew back nearly choking me. We stopped and I had to lie on my stomach facing over the back of the sidecar in order to blow the bugle.[10] Boy Scout A.T. Wilkinson

The second report prepared by Smuts (often referred to as *the* Smuts Report), which dealt with the general question of the use of air power and the organisation of the air forces, was presented to the War Cabinet in its final form on 17 August. In particular it examined the concept of the strategic bombing of enemy cities and the possibility of setting up a force to carry out these independent operations against Germany. Smuts made it clear that a number of key factors had influenced his final conclusions and overall recommendations. Most important of all was his belief that aviation was rapidly becoming a powerful means of waging war, which made it essential that Britain should strive towards the goal of air supremacy in the same way that it had enjoyed supremacy of the seas.

As far as can at present be foreseen, there is absolutely no limit to the scale of its future independent war use, and the day may not be far off when aerial operations with their devastation of enemy lands and destruction of industrial and populous centres on a vast scale may become the principal operations of war, to which the older forms of military and naval operations may become secondary and subordinate.[11] Lieutenant General Jan Christian Smuts, War Cabinet

Smuts had little hard evidence to support this statement but, in terms of morale and the psychological impact of air raids on the nation's population, they had already become key factors in the war strategy. The unquestioning acceptance of this point by the Government is perhaps explained by their belief that the raids witnessed so far were merely a sign of greater devastation to come and their desire to find a means of justifying visible strikes at the enemy in order to retain public confidence.

Smuts was fully aware that as things stood in 1917, if widespread strategic bombing was to be undertaken as part of a concerted effort to gain supremacy of the air, it would not be possible to combine this with the tactical requirements of the RFC on the Western Front. However, during the course of his investigations he received a memorandum from Cowdray which referred to the latest figures for aircraft production worked out by Weir. Cowdray explained that from the end of 1917 a 'Surplus Aircraft Fleet' would be available beyond the immediate tactical requirements of the two air services. Smuts felt that if the political will existed this surplus could be used as the basis for an independent air force capable of taking the air war direct to Germany, striking at targets far behind the front lines and in the process strengthening Britain's own forward defences. The 'Surplus Aircraft Fleet' would enable strategic operations against Germany and German military targets to be undertaken without jeopardising the tactical support that was essential to both the army and navy. Its availability would also allow a clearer distinction to be made between the battlefield use of aviation and the more politically orientated role of carrying out independent strikes at strategic targets in the enemy's homeland and industrial heartland.

If maximum use was to be made of the 'Surplus Aircraft Fleet' it could not be done using the current dissipated control of the air service. To be most effective Smuts felt that the co-ordination of these operations would best be served by a central minister at the head of a separate staff. Such a figure would also be well placed finally to overcome the divided control of the two established air services that had resulted in such waste over the previous three years. In a memorandum submitted on 19 July, Henderson, still nominally head of the military air service although now completely isolated from those who commanded it on the Western Front, reminded Smuts that the RFC had originally been intended on its formation in 1912 to be a joint corps, incorporating both naval and military wings. The unilateral establishment of the RNAS as a separate body by the outbreak of war coupled with the refusal of the two services to work closely together, particularly in the area of procurement and development, had frustrated both the Derby Committee and Curzon's Air Board. Only the radical merger of the two services into one under the control of a single minister with a permanent staff now appeared capable of solving this fundamental problem. Yet it was recognised that effecting this in the middle of a war, with the amalgamation of two distinct services, each with its traditions, uniforms, rank structures and chains of command, would be extremely difficult and to arrive successfully at this ultimate goal it would be necessary to proceed cautiously.

As an overall conclusion to his report Smuts recommended that a separate Air Ministry should be established as soon as practicable and, through an Air Board and Air Staff, it should be given independent control of a unified air service. The new service's strategic role would not supersede the current tactical one undertaken by the RFC and RNAS but complement it. The support of military and naval operations by the new air force would still be its primary function but once this had been satisfied it would then be able to carry out independent operations in pursuit of a new goal – the strategic bombing of Germany. In recognition of the difficulties involved Smuts suggested that the Ministry and Staff be formed first so that they could then work out how the amalgamation was to be effected over the course of the winter.

Despite lingering service objections, the War Cabinet accepted the recommendations of Smuts's second report on 24 August and to oversee their implementation he was immediately appointed to chair a new Air Organisation Committee made up of representatives from the War Office, Admiralty, Treasury and Air Board, with Henderson as his assistant. But it was agreed that no public announcement of the decision was to be made until this second committee had reported back, at which point the final conclusions would be presented to Parliament. Perhaps in an indication of the immense problems that it faced, as well as the easing of political pressure on the Government as public concern gradually rescinded until reignited by the intensity of the night raids at the end of September, the deliberations of the Air Organisation Committee took considerable time to come to fruition. In France Haig and Trenchard, although absorbed by the Third Battle of Ypres, fiercely resisted the proposed changes. Yet in London both Robertson and Field Marshal Sir John French gave them their support. The proposal also received cautious backing from the latest First Lord of the Admiralty, Sir Eric Geddes. Following a public statement by Smuts that the Government had with reluctance decided on a policy of reprisal, on 16 October the Chancellor of the Exchequer, Sir Andrew Bonar Law, on behalf of the Prime Minister, announced to the House of Commons that a bill would shortly be presented to create a unified air force. The Air Force (Constitution) Bill was given Cabinet approval on 16 November and received Royal assent on 29 November. It stated that the Air Council was to be formed on 3 January 1918. Subsequently, on 7 March, the new service was given the title of the Royal Air Force and its formal date of establishment set for 1 April.

The Smuts Report probably attributed an unmerited degree of menace to the German raids on Britain, which had never been intended to bomb the nation into submission, and in many ways now appears to have been an over radical response. By summer 1917 many of the organisational problems that had dogged the air services during the previous two years had already effectively been resolved. The respective areas of responsibility of the RFC and RNAS had been clarified and made much more distinct, Cowdray's Air Board had gained a degree of political control and was able to co-ordinate relations between the two services and the Ministry of Munitions had started to produce and develop new planes with greater efficiency. Only the direction of an independent bombing force required the establishment of a new service. But the operating capacity of this was ultimately undermined by the failure to produce, as promised, the resources needed to fulfil the extant tactical demands of the army and the navy while simultaneously propagating the strategic bombing role.

Although London was not attacked again in daylight, a series of raids was made on coastal towns in July and August. But the combined effectiveness of the anti-aircraft guns and the increased efficiency of the modern scout aircraft caused growing casualties among the Gothas and a policy of moonlit night raids was introduced in early September which allowed them to extend their scope back to the capital. By then the Gothas were supplemented by the even larger, aptly-named Giant bombers. The moonlight raids were a sore trial for the people of London. Many of them faced the bombs from their own homes, taking shelter in cellars and any other 'safe places'.

They came first at about 6.30 last night, we heard the whistles blow & the policeman shouting 'Take cover', however there was only a very distant bombardment and then 'All Clear' went by 7.30. Nevertheless by 8.30 back they came again! Poor dear Mary is dreadfully nervous so we took her downstairs and esconced her in the first floor passage in a very safe place, then Phyllis and I stole away to the top window which looks East to watch. I have never seen such a sight, the sky seemed full of shells, first North – then South – then right across, the noise was deafening but even above the roar you could hear the scream of the Archies as they rushed past. Then there was a dead pause – very terrifying after all the noise, – then coming from the East we heard the hum of the machines. We nearly killed ourselves trying to spot them, but we could see nothing in the fog. In the meanwhile they had arrived overhead, so we thought it was time to go downstairs. We were just saying nonchalantly to Mary that we had come down because there was nothing to see, when the most hideous noise started, and personally, I thought we should have a bomb on us at any moment. As a matter of fact it was the shells bursting directly overhead that made the row, but – Heavens – there was a noise. The place was covered in shrapnel.[12] Celia Croft

Others took shelter in well-constructed public buildings which offered at least an illusion of being bomb proof. Lady Morrison-Bell, with her daughter Shelagh, arrived by train at King's Cross station in the middle of a raid to be met by her chauffeur, her child nurse and what seemed to be a large part of London's population.

The station was a sight to see. Crowds & crowds of poor people from the slums all around King's Cross had assembled & brought their beds & furniture & babies, & had encamped there under this concrete railway arch. A policeman told me they come every night and stay there *all* night. Of course Shelagh wanted to 'sit down' in the middle of the bombardment so I took her out & sat her down in the middle of the crowd on the pavement! But nothing seemed to matter that night, & it was pitch dark too as all the station lights were extinguished – & only bursts of shrapnel lit up the scene. The chauffeur was cheering, as he kept on saying that the concrete roof would keep off shrapnel but a bomb would come through it like matchwood. One could hear the dull thud of bombs falling, so different from the roar of the guns. They do make a *desperate* noise. Every few minutes there was silence, which was more nervy than the roar of the bombardment – & then the guns would begin again, as the raiders tried to attack again from a new position. In one of these silences a poor woman in the crowd flung her arms round my shoulders & buried her face in my coat, & another woman near me gave a wild shriek & fainted, & it was rather horrible hearing her fall heavily in that dense crowd. And when she came to, the guns were just at their loudest & she must have wished she had stayed unconscious I expect! . . . I took Shelagh & held her up to see the 'fireworks' – as there was a big open aperture to the sky, in the wall of our archway, & at one moment brilliantly clear against the moon I saw 5 or 6 enemy aeroplanes in the sky & bright jets of fire bursting all around & underneath them. I climbed up on a pile of luggage to see better, & it was a thrilling sight . . . The shrapnel pattering down was the most frightening thing I think. A very tall officer in a kilt and a Scotch bonnet came up & talked to me & kept by us through it all . . . He was rather nervous of the guns & turned rather white, so I talked away to divert his attention. He was such a nice boy, it was so curious when one thinks it over after, how close a common danger brings one to a perfect stranger. We talked that night as if we had known each other for years, & he told me all he felt about dying . . . It was an interesting experience, but I would rather be in the house during another night raid! But when one thinks that that night of horror is what the people at the front go through *hourly*, it makes one feel ashamed to make any fuss . . . It really was rather awful, though I never felt the least frightened, only very excited & interested, but I was afraid all the time for the effects on *her*, & then too one felt so sorry for all the poor people around who were in *terror*. It is rubbish to say that London isn't in a panic, but I suppose by the end of this winter they will no longer be, as we shall all be so used to it![13] Lady Morrison-Bell

Another obvious source of shelter was the underground railway network. Thousands of Londoners congregated in the tube stations and spent the night on the platforms. Lady Burford-Hancock was a Red Cross volunteer at the Earl's Court station and as such had to deal with a variety of minor medical ailments and varying degrees of hysteria. One case in particular, involving a soldier who had been shot through the head at the Front, illustrated how the war reached out to encompass even those who might legitimately have considered that they had earned the peace and quiet of their 'Blighty' wound.

He had the most terrible fits of breathlessness & struggled violently thinking each time he was dying. At times he became unconscious & on coming to each time he thought he was on the Battlefields & kept saying 'Middlesex Men don't hang back', 'All right I'll carry on', 'I'm hit' & so on. We had some difficulty removing a very stiff collar & we got him on to the floor of the Dressing Station, put wet towels on his head & fanned him & once when he came to he felt the water dripping & put his hand up quickly & said 'Blood'. A nurse who was with us thought so seriously of the case that she advised us to send for a doctor, which we did, but the shrapnel was falling so fast it was some time before he arrived.[14] Lady Burford-Hancock

The night raids once again harshly exposed the scarcity of pilots trained in night flying, particularly among the new scout squadrons, and a crash programme of training was instituted. Unfortunately the very instability which made high-performance aircraft, such as the Sopwith Camel, so effective as scout aircraft was not conducive to easy night flying. In addition it was extremely difficult for the pilots, as well as the gunners and searchlight crews, to see the relatively small targets offered by aircraft in contrast to the huge girth of the Zeppelins. Further problems arose through the danger of guns, unable to distinguish between British and German aircraft, opening up on RFC machines. After Smuts carried out further investigations into the state of the defences against night bombers, another round of measures was introduced which included moving all the anti-aircraft guns out of the area patrolled by defending scouts into a clearly defined zone ten miles from the centre of London, and forbidding British aircraft to enter this area so as to prevent any confusion. Lines of tethered balloons raised to 9,500 feet, linked by horizontal wires from which were suspended wire streamers, created a physical barrier that forced the Gothas to fly higher and so reduced their bombing accuracy. Finally, there was a resurgence of interest in promoting a forward defence policy by attacking the German bombers on the ground in their airfields and in the whole question of reprisal raids. To his annoyance Trenchard was ordered to give high priority to bombing German cities.

The task of the British defenders was further complicated when the Zeppelins returned, modified and with new tactics, to join the Gothas over London. To avoid the unsustainable casualties which they had been suffering the German airship fleet was drastically altered.

> Everything was so perfectly contrived to save weight, while the ship itself was even bigger, even though it had grown lighter and so rose higher. The cars were smaller, it is true; we were more crowded; our rest quarters had been suppressed; machine-guns had gone so as to reduce all weight. Height and speed, we were told, would be our true defence. Six thousand metres would be easily attained and no English gun or aeroplane, it was stated by our officers, could touch us at that height. Alas! our hopes were not to be fulfilled so literally as that.[15] Anon., Helmsman, L45

Height did indeed grant the Zeppelins some protection from the more obsolescent types of defending aircraft but only at a commensurate loss of bombing accuracy and increasingly difficult operational conditions for the hapless crews, as the new extreme altitudes turned raids into a physical and mental torment which undermined the health and morale of many of them.

What brought consternation to some of us was the effect of the height; and not only the actual height but also the rate of ascent. It was soon found during the actual height trials of the new ships that the strain exerted by their terrific ascending power was greater than many of us could stand. Height-sickness, nausea, giddiness, we nearly all suffered from them, in some form or other . . . Then there was another trial – the cold! That was far worse than the height in its effects. The engine ratings were not so badly off; they at any rate could feel the warmth of the engine while we, poor devils, in the forward car, with at first no means of heating ourselves, suffered terribly. It was all very well for the short trips, that lasted only two, or three, or even six hours at a high altitude. That was play compared to the long flights that now fell to our lot.[16] Anon., Helmsman, L45

One of the last notable raids occurred on 19 October. As the attacking Zeppelins approached the British coast they climbed to between 16,000 and 20,000 feet in an effort to avoid the probing searchlights, guns and aircraft. Unfortunately, unusual meteorological conditions that night meant that while it was calm at ground level, there were gale-force winds at much higher altitudes. The experiences of those on board L45, commanded by Kapitanleutnant Waldeemar Kolle, starkly encapsulate the difficulties faced by the Zeppelin crews.

We started in our naval base Tondern and we had fixed our course to Sheffield. But the terrific tempest from the north made us lose our way. We came to the British coast but we had no precise orientation from the ground. Suddenly we saw some lights, afterwards darkness. We tried wireless bearings from Germany but we couldn't obtain them. We started again to the west.[17] Leutnant Karl Schutz, Second in Command, L45

As the hours passed the cold literally numbed the senses of the crew.

> For nearly two hours we struggled to keep our westward course but the wind blew ever stronger and I could tell that our navigation was getting more and more uncertain. We dropped a few bombs at some faint lights but providence alone knows where they went. I scarcely believe that Leutnant Schutz, our second in command, even troubled to set the bombing sight. By this time it was bitterly cold. Hashagen once read the thermometer aloud and gave over 30 degrees of frost . . . Hahndorf, an engineer, now came in to report to Kolle that the men were feeling the cold. The sailmaker in particular, who was attending to the valves of the gas bags, complained of his feet. Well he might do so, for he could not wear his felt boots when climbing about the ship. He said he could not go on much longer. Two engineers, so Hahndorf said, were sleepy; while the petrol rating was grumbling and fumbling over his work.[18] Anon., Helmsman, L45

Eventually Kolle gave the order to turn back but, by sheer chance, they found themselves over London.

> At about 11.30 we began to see lights below and as the lights continued so it dawned upon us that it could only be the city of London that we were crossing in the air. Even Kolle looked amazed at the dim lights as Schutz suddenly shouted 'London!' . . . Kolle clearly had but one thought – that was higher. So he released more ballast and the bombs – first two sighting shots and then the rest. Over London! We had achieved what no other German airship had done since Mathy had bombed that proud city over a year ago! And his last trip across the city had proved his undoing. Fortunately for us we were unseen; not a searchlight was unmasked; not a shot was fired; not an aeroplane was seen. If the gale had driven us out of our course, it had also defeated the flying defences of the city! It was misty or so it seemed, for we were above a thin veil of cloud. The Thames we just dimly saw from the outline

of the lights; two great railway stations, I thought I saw, but the speed of the ship running almost before the gale was such that we could not distinguish much. We were half frozen, too, and the excitement was great. It was all over in a flash. The last big bomb was gone and we were once more over darkness and rushing onwards.[19] Anon., Helmsman, L45, German Navy

They now faced the challenge of finding their way back to Germany intact if their success was not to be Pyrrhic indeed.

Running before the wind with a full speed we dropped the large bombs, they were 600 pounders and I heard later on one great bomb fell on the Piccadilly Circus. But we had no time to look, we must give our course to Germany which we hoped to reach over France or Belgium. Now our misfortunes began. Three engines stopped working and a machinist was intoxicated by the gas of the exhaust pipe which had a leak. I tried to help him back to life with cold water. After he was better, I ordered him to go in the ship to his hammock. Alas he never came in the ship – he stumbled on the ladder and fell down 18,000 feet.[20] Leutnant Karl Schutz, Second in Command, L45

With engines failing, short of fuel and buffeted by the relentless winds L45 eventually crashed in Switzerland and the crew was interned for the rest of the war.

On the ground the anti-aircraft guns were helpless and, as the sound of the distant airship engines was muffled or blown away in the high-altitude winds, it became aptly dubbed the 'Silent Raid'. The defending RFC pilots desperately tried to get to grips with the Zeppelin.

I was out on this night in a BE2 E and the only possible way of picking up any idea of what was going on was watching around the sky for Archie bursts and searchlight beams and I located not only a Zepp but two Zepps up around Hertford. I trekked up there to see what I could do. I was flying in the normal pilot's seat and I had the front seat cowled in with a gun of my own special contrivance. I made a clip on to the cowling just in front of the pilot into which I clipped the pistol grip of the Lewis gun and had some wire bracing which took the nose of the Lewis gun to an angle which just cleared the top of the prop something like 20 or 30 degrees up from the line of flight. I was right on the top of my climb, say 12,000, you were jolly lucky if you got 12,000 and the Zepps were 2–3,000 above working together. I'd got some ammunition and I might as well have a bang so I pushed off two or three drums in their direction – the best you can do is shoot in that direction. Then in pulling the machine up in order to get the gun on to one, I was in a semi-stalling position in any case and I fully stalled the darned thing. The nose went down with a crack and I spun for several thousand feet before I got out of it and that was the end of the contest so far as I was concerned. But it is interesting that one of these Zepps was flying very, very low over France the following day and it's just possible, I can't claim anything, that one of my shots might have gone into the bags and punctured the balloons. That might have been the reason for her getting caught over France.[21] Lieutenant Charles Chabot, 39 Squadron RFC

Chabot ended up by being reprimanded for not keeping his valves clean and told that he should have been able to reach the Zeppelins at 15,000 feet – which was of course well nigh impossible in a BE2 E. Although most of the British defences were helpless against the high flying Zeppelins, the weather was so extreme that four of the Zeppelins were lost. These losses were crucial in discouraging the Germans from attempting further airship raids. Had they done so they might otherwise have exposed the weaknesses in the British aerial defences against attacks from such extreme heights. The defenders of London had been severely rattled and knew all too well how lucky they had been.

The most outstanding feature of the raid was the conclusive proof afforded that, on that occasion at any rate, the defences were powerless to offer any effective resistance to the attack, which successfully achieved its main objective. That is to say, the enemy were able to place their fleet in a commanding position over London, in spite of every effort on the part of the defence to prevent their doing so. Here, indeed, is a matter for serious thought and considerable apprehension. It is futile to assume that, because the 'act of God' in the matter of the 'freshening wind' saved the town and brought the subsequent destruction of the enemy's fleet, the defence, as then conducted, was in any way responsible for that merciful result; the actual fact being that the defence was powerless to offer any resistance at all to an attack delivered in silence from so high an altitude.[22] Lieutenant Colonel Alfred Rawlinson, West Sub-Command, Royal Garrison Artillery

In the end the Zeppelins never did return to London but the Gotha raids continued into 1918. Gradually the new measures introduced to tighten the country's defences began to take effect, making each new incursion more costly. The efficiency of the anti-aircraft defence personnel gradually improved as the effectiveness of the three component elements of guns, aircraft and searchlights was maximised. The last aeroplane raid occurred on the night of 19 May 1918 when no less than forty-three bombers set off to raid London. The response they encountered marked a sea-change similar to that which had disarmed the Zeppelin threat in September 1916. Everything about the defences seemed to click as the guns not only shot down three bombers but deterred many of the others from even approaching London. Meanwhile, the patrolling aircraft, now all modern fast scouts flown by experienced night pilots, were successful in shooting down a further four bombers. The writing was now writ large on the wall and, coupled with the increasing demands for bombers emanating from the hard-pressed German Army on the Western Front, the whole Gotha campaign against England was ignominiously abandoned. It was left to the increasingly marginalised Zeppelins to have the last word by launching one final assault on 5 August, when five Zeppelins, with the German airship service commander Peter Strasser aboard the new L70, set out with the intention of bombing the Midlands. Well before they reached the coast they were spotted from a lightship and Major Egbert Cadbury, accompanied by his observer Captain Robert Leckie, was ready for them as they approached.

> When my observer and I climbed into our DH4 at Great Yarmouth we just saw for a moment three Zeppelins above the clouds steering for England. Having climbed through the clouds I saw three Zeppelins high above us silhouetted against the northern lights. I reckoned that their height was about 17,550 feet. I climbed up towards them until I got the position where I was dead ahead. I then came along underneath the leading Zeppelin and my observer fired his two Lewis guns straight into the bottom of the airship. It was a most fascinating sight – awe-inspiring – to see this enormous Zeppelin blotting out the whole of the sky above one. As we went along the length of the ship so she started catching fire until within seconds almost she burst into a mass of flames and dived headlong into the clouds below us. It was one of the most terrifying sights I have ever seen to see this huge machine hurtling down with all those crew on board. We both felt very elated both my observer and myself because it really was some achievement in those days to have brought this gigantic machine down.[23] Major Egbert Cadbury, Great Yarmouth Station, RAF

They had destroyed L70 and all on board perished, including Strasser who had remained the leading proponent of airships in Germany. With his death the Zeppelin menace was finally extinguished.

The British statistics identify fifty-one Zeppelin raids unleashing 5,806 bombs which killed 557 and injured 1,358. In the fifty-two aeroplane attacks 2,772 bombs were dropped killing 857 and wounding a further 2,508. Although these figures pall into insignificance when compared to the horror of the losses suffered in the major offensives on the Western Front, the casualties were mainly British civilians who for centuries had been almost inviolate from the direct consequences of enemy action in times of war. As such, the widespread sense of shock within the civilian community at the first ever concerted air offensive was amplified exponentially until it, in itself, became a strategically significant factor.

The material effects of the raids were mainly indirect. Often overlooked is the vast disruption to wartime production that they caused. The bombs may not actually have hit many of the great munitions factories or indeed killed significant numbers of the work-force but they had a huge impact nevertheless. Production was lost every time a factory blacked out when a raid was threatened. In cases such as the iron and steel industry there was a serious danger of explosion or lasting damage to plant equipment from the suspension of normal working procedures because of the enforced blackout. Transport systems, particularly the railways, were vulnerable to almost total disruption which made a large proportion of the work-force late for work on the morning after a raid. The efficiency of the workers was further affected by the impact of disrupted sleep from the panic of night raids and absenteeism rose dramatically. All these consequences were amplified by the equally dramatic effects of false alarms. There was also the direct effect of the air raid precautions introduced by the British to counter the raids. Thousands of men manned the anti-aircraft guns and searchlights, observers dotted the countryside and trained RFC squadrons had to be allocated to Home Defence duties. As an example, at the height of the Gotha panic, in response to a raid on 22 August 1917, no less than 137 aircraft left the ground to intercept the interlopers. This diverted vital resources that might otherwise have been deployed on the all important Western Front. The Zeppelins and Gothas may not have achieved any of the wilder dreams of destroying London but they certainly made a substantial impact and were a harbinger of greater things to come.

CHAPTER TWELVE

On the Ground

The airman's life differed in almost every respect from that of the ordinary infantryman in the trenches save one: the prospect of an early grave was common to both. The infantry looked on the airmen with a strange mixture of jealousy and admiration, while many pilots were only too aware that they were regarded as lucky as they flew over the gashed and mangled strips of ground that separated and encompassed the front lines.

> When we were flying at about 17,000 feet it gave you a wonderful feeling of exhilaration. You were sort of, 'I'm the King of the Castle!' You were up there and you were right out of the war. I'd been in the infantry and we were always lousy, filthy dirty and very often hungry, whereas in the Flying Corps it was a gentleman's life. You slept in a bed, put on pyjamas every night. You had a decent mess to come back to. You had about two and a half hours patrol in the morning and two and a half in the afternoon and that was the job. So altogether it was much more pleasant.[1]
> Lieutenant Percy Douglas, 11 Squadron RFC

Many pilots found it difficult to reconcile these sharply conflicting states of mind and body. Moving from extremes of terror, frozen stiff in the biting cold of high–altitude flying, to the relative security of the squadron base in a matter of minutes was a difficult discipline to sustain throughout the six months of an average active service posting.

286

You were 15 to 20 miles behind the lines, you had a comfortable bed, you had sheets – even an electric light. We were either in deadly danger or no danger at all. This conflict between something like being at home and being in really a quite tight position had a great effect on us all and produced a certain strain probably because of the change. People were being killed every day. My best friend was there one evening and he wasn't there next day at lunch. This was going on all the time. People reacted to that. You couldn't live that sort of a life and be entirely indifferent. You may have been cold blooded in the air because you had to fight as if there was nothing but you and your guns. You had nobody at your side. Nobody who was cheering with you, nobody to look after you if you were hit. You were alone. You fought alone and died alone.[2] Second Lieutenant Cecil Lewis, 56 Squadron RFC

In such a highly-stressed environment, with most of the officers barely out of their teens, the role and influence of the commanding officer was paramount in determining the nature of each squadron. His efficiency was of primary importance and set the tone for the whole unit.

When I first joined 5 Squadron there was a very efficient Squadron Commander there called Major Hearson. He was a regular engineer officer and he wasn't a good pilot but he could fly an aeroplane. He was very efficient indeed – very particular about the way we entered up our log books and report sheets when we came back from every flight. He saw to it that the morale of the men was good, that the maintenance of the aircraft and engines was well looked after. He was a very good squadron commander and was eventually promoted and became a Wing Commander when he left us. Then we had another man who wasn't nearly so good. He was an ex-gunner and more fond of the drink – rather more lackadaisical and slipshod, leaving things to his flight commanders rather than seeing to it himself. He was not nearly so particular about the way that pilots and observers wrote up their reports when they came back from operations. All personnel had to make a report whether they had anything to say or not, even negative reports were better than nothing. Some of them would write a few lines and not expand at all about what had happened during the flight. The squadron commander should have seen to it that they made better reports. These reports were sent up to a higher authority from which they gained all the information they could and it was all reported in daily orders of the wing. Pilots and observers weren't so punctual to their machines when it was time to take off and there were delays. It might be a question of bad weather coming up and getting the job done before the weather deteriorated so it was very important that a squadron commander should see that his men were punctual. Another way was how people dressed themselves – whether they went about looking sloppy, whether their hair was long or they'd taken the trouble to dress properly for the different meals or if we had visitors. These are little things but they all add up and they all point to whether you've got an efficient and enthusiastic squadron commander or not. This had an effect on the slackness of all the personnel in the squadron – right the way from the pilots and observer, down to the airmen themselves. I think it most important that the squadron commander should be a hundred per cent efficient.[3] Captain Alan Jackson, 5 Squadron RFC

A really bad commanding officer could be disastrous to squadron morale.

The CO asked me the reason for the state of nerves of so many of the officers and I could not give him the only answer, 'A fish rots first at the head.' The Squadron has got demoralised and jumpy simply because officers, in addition to the great strain of work in the air, have been so hunted and insulted by Ross Hume on the ground that they don't know where they are at all. And yet Ross Hume would never realise what he is doing or think otherwise than that he was a most efficient

Squadron Commander and not the subject for ridicule and contempt throughout the whole Corps. Another Squadron Commander remarked to me the other day, 'Oh, that fellow (he didn't say fellow) is so incompetent that he is certain to be made a Wing Commander soon.'[4] Captain Harold Wyllie, 23 Squadron RFC

Pilots and observers were often desperately tired, largely as a result of the cumulative stress of their flying duties. Many prayed quite unashamedly for bad weather when flying was quite impossible. In the jargon of the time this was known as a 'dud day'.

The greatest joy I know is to be wakened after an all-too-short sleep by: 'It's six o'clock, sir, but I don't think there'll be any flying.' When a pilot starts his day thus, he manages to murmur: 'Is Captain Dash up?' The batman goes to ascertain, and returns with: 'No, sir, the patrol's a wash-out.' A still-tired head falls back on to a pillow, and a pleased airman mutters something about '9.30' and 'waking' . . . Everyone is late for breakfast and arrives in some futurist garb which consists usually of brilliant pyjamas, bright scarf, flying boots and a grease-ruined tunic.[5] Lieutenant Stauton Waltho, RFC

Many would use these mornings for writing letters to family, friends and girlfriends. Their correspondence would often display a kind of sardonic, self-deprecatory humour which, while funny, could not completely disguise the strain from which it originated.

This bad weather has just come at a very opportune moment as we have been having a very hard time lately, and needed a rest very badly. Just at present I am fostering an aggressive spirit by chasing and killing the numerous ear-wigs which have their being in my tent. So even when we are prevented from flying my love of War prompts me to acts of slaughter.[6] Lieutenant Jack Walthew, 4 Squadron RFC

The multifarious pursuits of the pilots reflected their equally diverse personalities. McCudden, for instance, demonstrated that his competitive spirit was not simply confined to the burning desire to shoot down German aircraft.

> After breakfast I played Maybery for the ping-pong championship of 56 Squadron, and after a long tussle Maybery won. I believe there was keener competition in the Squadron to be ping-pong champion than to be the star turn Hun-strafer.[7] Captain James McCudden, 56 Squadron RFC

The strain of combat and the constant risk of death meant that the pilots often defied the strict conventions of acceptable behaviour and took enormous risks for a little boisterous fun which in a less forgiving time might equally be considered as rank hooliganism.

> We came upon two steam-rollers, their funnels smoking gently while the drivers had their tea. In a brace of shakes two officers had climbed aboard, and away went the steam-rollers down the hill, of all things. What a sight! One finished on its side in a ditch, minus its funnel. The other one hit a tree. No one was hurt.[8] Lieutenant William Johns, 55 Squadron IAF

At times there could be a real cultural divide as some of the more highly-educated pilots were disappointed by the lack of any real intellectual stimulus in the mess.

> There are only one or two people in the squadron I have the faintest hope of making a real pal of, and it is next to impossible that I can do even that. They are all just the 'ordinary good fellows' with nothing remarkable about them; none of them have any real intellectual ambitions.[9] Second Lieutenant Arthur Rhys Davids, 56 Squadron RFC

From this inauspicious start Rhys Davids eventually acclimatised to life in the mess where his considerable personal charm, and perhaps more importantly, his reputation as a 'thrusting' scout pilot, made him a popular but still slightly eccentric figure.

He always used to have classical works in his pocket and he said that when he went into action he shouted out Greek warriors' cries from the siege of Troy which raised him right up above himself.[10] Engineer Officer H.N.Charles, 56 Squadron RFC

His idea of a relaxing day would have driven most of his fellows back into the air no matter what the weather.

The dear old CO very sportingly said I could take a day in bed, which I did, and finished off the little pamphlet on the Poetic View of the World, which is good reading. But then as Blake said in a curious moment 'to generalise is to be an idiot' – almost as bad as the Irishman who said it was very unlucky to be superstitious. I think one can't *distinguish* philosophical, religious and poetic world views, though each have their points, but it was absorbing reading and taught me a lot. Then I read some 400 lines of Euripides and wrote 3 or 4 letters, altogether very delightful.[11] Second Lieutenant Arthur Rhys Davids, 56 Squadron RFC

For those who sought the simpler pleasures of the flesh, rather than the mind, this usually required a visit to the nearest town to sample the delights of civilisation.

On 'dud' nights, we'd go into Toul or Nancy, have a good feed and then go round to see the girls. They were always pleased to welcome 'les Anglais Aviators, plenty money'. Old Madame Lefroy would pull the slide along to see who was there, her fat, greasy old face would beam, and with the request of 'une minute', she would dash off and clear out the 'locals', making us, in consequence, mighty unpopular with some of them. Number nine, with the red lamp, was a dingy-looking hole, the meeting room, as we called it, reeking of cheap scents and powders. The floor was bare for dancing and over in the corner was an antiquated piano, minus a few ivory-tipped keys, the rest having a nasty habit of continually sticking down. Crofty used to produce some nasty dischords on it. The walls revelled in a display of tall, short, fat and lean nude females, and underneath each, scrappy quotations written in many hands. Madame would see us all with a drink, clap her hands and in would stream the mademoiselles. This parade always amused us, especially the piece of tulle draped diagonally across, plus shoes and stockings. Why the attempt to hide? They might just as well have been the pictures on the wall. Dix, who had been a shop-walker before joining up, insisted on the parade being carried out properly and wanted them in one at a time, the same as mannequins. The piano stool was placed in the centre of the room and each female mounted in turn and posed as Venus, one of us revolving the stool in order to allow the audience to pass comments, favourable or otherwise. There was Marguerite, the little tubby one, who looked great. Fifi, the tall, dark one, also the favourite; another with a very flat nose like a boxer and whom we nicknamed 'Pug', and then a very big girl with fat legs. Johnny used to call her 'Tiny'. They were some girls with a happy knack of making you buy cheap champagne at a big price which helped to swell their commission. They enjoyed our visits and we were out to have a good time. Fun ran high and we spent a lot of money, which was all that mattered to them.[12] Lieutenant Reg Kingsford, 100 Squadron IAF

The officers' mess was normally the centre of squadron life where the commissioned pilots and observers would gather to unwind. In the evening after dinner a fairly languid air would prevail, slightly redolent of a gentlemen's club in London.

The old hands of the RFC sit around over coffee and discuss old members in familiar terms – referring to Generals by pet names and talking of machines of which the newer members of the squadron have never heard. A card game or two commences – the Canadian element usually forming a 'poker school', and the ground officers, having, by length of years and experience, learnt the folly of the game, start bridge.[13] Lieutenant Stanton Waltho, RFC

Not everyone fitted into the mess which invariably reflected the rigid class structure of the time. Two Americans, Lieutenants Elliot Springs and John Grider of 85 Squadron, RAF, noticed that some prejudices were expressed about even the greatest of pilots simply because he happened to have been promoted from the ranks.

> The General came over and had tea with us and asked us who we wanted for CO. He wanted to send us McCudden but we don't want him. He gets Huns himself but he doesn't give anybody else a chance at them. The rest of the squadron objected because he was once a Tommy and his father was a sergeant-major in the old army. I couldn't see that that was anything against him but the English have great ideas of caste.[14] Lieutenant John Grider, 85 Squadron RAF

Music played an essential part in the process of relaxation. But, given the rudimentary conditions which existed in many messes, raising basic noise to the heights of harmonious melody could often pose a challenge. There was always someone willing to give it a go.

> There was an old upright piano in the mess with keys so yellow they looked as if the keyboard had been smoking for about 50 years. There were two or three notes missing and it was out of tune – it was a terrible piano but it didn't matter. We had one chap who played and he'd sit down in the evening and he'd play the tunes of the time, the reviews on in town, things we knew by heart and we used to sing in chorus. Occasionally a bit of Chopin on the nights when we felt that that sort of thing was appropriate.[15] Second Lieutenant Cecil Lewis, 56 Squadron RFC

A wide range of parodies were written which encapsulated the fatalistic humour of men who lived under the shadow of death. One of the most famous was sung piteously to the mournful tune of 'The Dying Lancer'. This is an expurgated version of a lyric which could be as vulgarly and anomatically explicit as the singers felt appropriate to the mood of the moment.

THE DYING AVIATOR

A handsome young airman lay dying.
Lay dying. (Chorus)
And as on the aerodrome he lay.
He lay
To the mechanics who round him came sighing.
Came sighing.
These last dying words he did say.
He did say.
'Take the cylinder out of my kidneys.
Of his kidneys.
The connecting rod out of my brain.
Of his brain.
The cam box from under the backbone.
His backbone.
And assemble the engine again.'
Again.[16]

For obvious reasons, whenever available, gramophones were also popular and every officer lucky enough to go on leave was required to bring back records featuring the 'hits' of the big shows in London.

> The gramophone worked overtime: Violet Loraine and George Robey singing, 'If you were the only girl in the world,' Elsie Janis singing 'Give me the moonlight,' and Jose Collins singing 'Love will find a way,' were the records which had to stand up to the greatest strain. Mannock had a passion for Irish airs, in particular 'The Londonderry Air'. Often he would play this record before going on the dawn patrol, much to the annoyance of the other members of his flight who were feeling like anything other than listening to a gramophone.[17] Lieutenant Ira Jones, 74 Squadron RAF

For more formal occasions, some squadrons even had their own band, the most notable of which belonged to 56 Squadron. When the squadron was being formed its commanding officer, Major Blomfield, sought out not only the best pilots, but also accomplished musicians to form the ground crew until he was able to field a veritable orchestra. Trenchard's aide Maurice Baring dined with them on 19 July 1917.

> Ian Henderson, Blomfield, Maybery, Bowman, Max-well, Coote, Marson and Rhys Davids were there. The Squadron band played during dinner. The Sergeant who conducted was before the war an important factor in the Palace Orchestra. The oboe belonged to the Coliseum in happier days. They played Mendelssohn's 'Spring Song'. One of the pilots said it was being played too slowly; and the conductor thought he said it was not being played slowly enough, and said, 'Mendelssohn was played sprightly.'[18] Lieutenant Colonel Maurice Baring, RFC Headquarters

Lieutenant Duncan Grinnell-Milne was equally astonished when he joined the squadron in 1918. By then, it seems, the prevailing musical tastes had coarsened slightly with the pressures of war service.

> A band? I was amazed as I watched six members of the orchestra file in by a side door past the small bar and pantry. A piano stood in a corner of the room; drums, violins, a double-bass gathered round it – men of the Squadron, led by a broad-shouldered, moustachioed Sergeant. 'Strike up!' ordered Gilly. 'And start off with the Squadron tune.' To some it might make pleasant reading were I able to record that, with the Squadron-commander and his gallant officers standing stiffly to attention, the orchestra played a selection from 'Pomp and Circumstance', beginning with a noble and full-throated chorus of 'Land of Hope and Glory' . . . The melody chosen by the Squadron to which I now had the honour to belong could only, I am afraid, be regarded as frivolous. It was called 'The Darktown Strutters' Ball', and the first line of its refrain informed some unnamed lady that: 'I'll be there to get you in a taxi, honey.' But nobody objected to the words and the rhythm was invigorating. It was a damn good tune! And the orchestra played wonderfully well, superbly I

thought. We shouted the chorus over the third and fourth round of drinks.[19] Lieutenant Duncan Grinnell-Milne, 56 Squadron RAF

The question of the amount of drinking that took place in the officers' mess has been blurred in the popular imagination by a failure to recognise that each mess was different and that the quantity drunk therefore varied greatly. As a generalisation it is perhaps true to say that alcohol played an important role in almost every mess and that certain standards had to be maintained if there was not to be an uproar. Alcohol is a mild depressant and its relaxant qualities offered some relief when taken in moderate quantities by young men stretched to the very limits of their endurance.

The centre of the Squadron seemed to be in the bar. When you think of the tensions they lived through day to day – they would come in in the evening and ask about their best friend, 'Where's old George?' 'Oh, he bought it this afternoon!' 'Oh, heavens!' The gloom would come, the morale would die and the reaction was immediate, 'Well, come on, chaps, what are you going to have?' That was the sort of spirit that kept you going and although people are against alcohol I think that it played a magnificent part in keeping up morale.[20] Major F.J. Powell, 41 Squadron RFC

Several squadrons developed individual games of forfeit to jolly along newcomers and make them feel part of the mess, while conveniently relieving them of the burden of an over-filled wallet.

In 40 Squadron it was forbidden to mention the word 'Archie' in the mess. If you did you had to pay a forfeit – that was pay for drinks all round and when you have 30 people to treat it's no mean thing. It was something that had grown up in the squadron. When a new pilot used to come into the mess they would say, 'You've been on patrol then today have you?' and all sorts of questions, 'Well did you see anything, any movement?' and the great thing was to get him to say, 'Oh, there was lots of Archie about!' Then a cheer would go up and he'd have drinks to pay all round. I think that was a Mannock custom.[21] Lieutenant Laurie Field, 40 Squadron RAF

Mess games were often of a violent nature as indeed were traditional guest nights throughout the British Army.

When we got tired of singing we played *high-cock-alorum* and other rough games, ending up the party with a rugger scrum – the coloured troops versus the rest (the 'coloured troops' being the nickname which Grid gives to all Colonials). In this case the coloured troops were much too rough for the delicate British Islanders, and many were the scars of battle after the 'rough house'. It was a glorious evening.[22] Lieutenant Ira Jones, 74 Squadron RAF

When an officer scored his first 'victory', was decorated, promoted or left for home service it was a legitimate excuse for a substantial 'binge' when many officers would really let rip and guests from other units would be invited to a mess–night dinner. Occasionally things would get a little over–boisterous.

I dined at A Flight where Hodges was giving a farewell dinner. It was a great success. Kinnear and other 42vians came over with their suite in the shape of 2 mess orderlies with soup tureens, eggs and bottles with which they established themselves at the end of the table and proceeded to make 'Leopard's Egg' and things got brighter and brighter. Then someone from 42 brought round one of their tenders which was soon filled with excited if foolhardy aviators. We whirled round and round the aerodrome firing Very lights to the annoyance and alarm of Major C. Stamford Wynne Eyton who at first suspected it of being one of his tenders.[23] Recording Officer Lieutenant Thomas Hughes, 53 Squadron RFC

On other nights it would just get right out of hand!

Had a great banquet last night. Everyone who counted in the RFC was there and it was *some* show with a full orchestra (the Cheshire Regt's Band lent specially for the occasion). Some of our guests – rather tight and in a carefree mood – prior to leaving the Mess, set fire to our Mess Hut and Quarters, and I was very busy for a time rushing round pulling chaps out who had gone to bed, as the Quarters were well alight. *Not* a very clever joke! Our guests' line of argument was that as the night was nearly over, we wouldn't need our Mess or sleeping quarters any more![24] Second Lieutenant R.J. Brownell, 45 Squadron RFC

Some squadrons were renowned for regular or persistent 'hard' drinking and one of the most notorious was 85 Squadron during the brief period it was commanded by Major William Bishop, a *bon viveur par excellence*.

We live well. We went down to Boulogne and got an ice-cream freezer and we are the only outfit at the front that has ice-cream for dinner every night. 'In the midst of life we are in death.' And in the midst of death we manage to have a hell of a lot of fun. Bronx cocktails, chicken livers *en brochette*, champagne, strawberry ice-cream, and Napoleon brandy.[25] Lieutenant John Grider, 85 Squadron RAF

Bishop had selected a number of kindred spirits and once in France they sought out like-minded individuals from other squadrons.

We invited the C.O. and the flight commanders of 211 over for dinner to return their hospitality and a colonel from the A.S.C. who was a friend of MacDonald's in Salonika. Everybody calls the C.O. Bobby. He is a great drinker and has the reputation of being able to drink the rest of the world under the table. We certainly gave him a good opportunity to exhibit his jewels. Springs and I were detailed as pacemakers and we mixed up a big bowl of punch and we all had a bottoms-up contest that was a classic. We had speeches from everyone after dinner and the colonel tried to get on the table to make his reply but it wasn't strong enough to hold him. Then we had a football game in front of the mess. Cal and Bish collided head on in the dark at full speed and were both knocked cold. Bobby lived up to his reputation and won the contest easily. We had to carry the colonel out and put him in his car feet first. He came back to-day and wanted to know what was in the punch. When we told him what was in that innocent drink he nearly fainted.[26] Lieutenant John Grider, 85 Squadron RAF

It appears that many stories of high living and perpetual drunkenness among pilots originated in this period of 85 Squadron's history, before a more focused disciplinary approach was introduced by Bishop's replacement, Major Edward Mannock. But under closer study this behaviour emerges as the exception rather than the rule. The monumental hangovers which inevitably resulted from such binges had a serious effect on the participants' ability to fight and at this point alcohol ceased to be an amusing diversion and became instead a threat to their long-term physical and mental health. With the exception of the occasional 'binge', most pilots realised that such indulgence was not conducive to survival in hostile skies where quick reactions and clear thinking were essential.

As a squadron we were not a drinking squadron. There were some squadrons who were drinking squadrons but we were not ever. I was careful myself holding a theory that I needed all the wits I'd got and bullets travelled faster than my wits so I'd better be careful![27] Lieutenant Gwilym Lewis, 40 Squadron RAF

Right from the start of his command Trenchard had established a policy of 'No empty chairs at breakfast' whereby replacement pilots were immediately posted to a unit to minimise the sense of grief and anger in the face of casualties. Nevertheless, the loss of those who had died was sharply felt by their friends and in one mess they actually preserved the images of the squadron past and present on the walls in the most eerie manner.

They had one very strange custom but after a pilot or observer had been there for a day or two he was sent down to the photographic office. There he went inside and the photographers took a silhouette of his head. They cut it out in black paper and they went on to a white frieze in the mess. They were rather extraordinarily good – I mean you could pick fellows out as to who they were. This may sound rather macabre but it wasn't really. One looked up there and when I was there it was over halfway round. Some fellows were still with the squadron, some observers had gone home to become pilots, some pilots had gone home for a rest and some had gone for an eternal rest. The thing that was strange in a way was that they would refer to fellows whose silhouette was on the wall by name. Tell you all his faults, all his goodness and exactly what sort of pilot he was as though he still lived. They'd tell you, 'Oh he was shot down at such and such a place' or 'He was extraordinarily good!' all in a very friendly sort of way and in a way that they missed him intensely. It was extraordinary – as though they were still there in spirit. I had mine up there.[28] Lieutenant T.E. Rogers, 6 Squadron RFC

When a pilot or observer was shot down the squadron commander and often the padre would write to his family. This was an exceptionally difficult task given that in many cases it was often impossible to determine exactly what had happened. Second Lieutenant Jack Walthew was killed when his RE8 was shot down during a photographic reconnaissance in the Ypres area on 19 September 1917. The padre wrote to his mother and struck a delicate balance between raising and removing hope.

You have no doubt heard from the C.O. of the squadron about your son 2nd Lieutenant J.S. Walthew, who was reported 'missing' on the 19th. I knew your son well, & thought possibly you might care to hear from me. There is little information as to where he went down or in what way. Two or three machines of the same type as he was flying were seen to go down on that day, & from what I can gather all were badly broken. If he was not hit in the air, it is quite possible that he has escaped with his life, though I am afraid he must be badly hurt by the crash. There does not really seem to be much hope, though one can never tell, as officers do sometimes have wonderful escapes after bad crashes. I think I have put the position fairly, as I should like to have done to me. You would not have me raise false hopes I am sure. I only pray that he may somehow have escaped with his life. You will be glad to know that your son frequently made his Communion at the services I have held, & was always a regular attendant at the other services. Everyone in the squadron liked him immensely, and all are very sad that he is missing. He was carrying out his duty bravely at the time, & whatever has happened you may well be proud to have had such a son. May the Holy Spirit comfort you in your time of anxiety.[29] Reverend P.H. Wilson, 22nd Wing RFC

The writing of such letters forced a premature maturity on many of the senior squadron officers who had often risen with great rapidity to these positions of responsibility.

The most difficult duty of a squadron commander was that on many occasions one had to write to the next of kin to advise them of the death or capture of their sons – that was a horrifying thing for a boy of 21 to have to do.[30] Major F.J. Powell, 41 Squadron RFC

Although most of the pilots, air gunners and observers were originally officers, as the war dragged on the number of NCOs recruited to fulfil these roles grew. Denied the full status of commissioned rank, these men often found themselves in a rather anomalous position.

It was simply a question of class, but if an NCO was lucky enough to get his wings and he was the pilot then he was absolutely in charge and would not take any instructions from the officer, however senior he was. If the officer wanted to see a certain thing he requested the pilot to let him see it – he didn't order him. For instance, if he told you to land in a certain field and you didn't think it was safe, you just told him out straight, 'No, I'm not landing there, I'll land you in that field over there'. Of course it didn't always do to assert yourself too much because as soon as the aircraft landed and you stepped on the ground you were very much back in your proper position. The passenger got his own back if he liked![31] Sergeant S.S. Saunders, 1 Squadron RFC

It was not an ideal working arrangement as the essence of teamwork between a pilot and his observer, both of whom depended on the other for their mutual continued existence, was of close friendship and trust. Differences in rank acted as an unnatural barrier to the development of a successful partnership.

We were all professional soldiers. I always said, 'Sir' and they always said, 'Sergeant' to me. We had our job to do and we did our job. I knew what time I was going up but I didn't even know what job I was on until the observer came out – always an officer in my case. I said, 'Good morning, Sir' and we got on with our job. When we came down he got out and went to make his report. He did all the reporting – what he'd found, what he'd seen, what he'd photographed. I went to the sergeants' mess and I had no further contact.[32] Sergeant George Eddington, 6 Squadron RFC

On the ground the NCOs had a separate mess but the fliers were isolated even among their peers.

I couldn't make friends. I had nothing in common – I didn't have access to the officers' mess, I didn't know what they thought. In the Sergeants' mess they were all fitters and riggers – I wasn't in their world any more than they were in mine. Dreadfully lonely.[33] Sergeant George Eddington, 6 Squadron RFC

It is sometimes presumed that a squadron consisted only of the flying crew. But they were actually just part of the personnel. While the officers were in the mess the ground crew swung into action. When an aircraft had been in combat the damage had to be assessed and immediately repaired for the next flight. Sometimes the aircraft were in a truly dreadful state and needed a major overhaul or even scrapping. After his close escape in the final dogfight with Voss, Cronyn examined what was left of his aircraft.

After Mess I went up to the hangar to have a look at my machine. It was a 'write off' and no mistake. The right lower longeron had a bullet hole through it, while the left lower was nearly cut in two, either by Archie or bullets, but there was only about a quarter of an inch thickness left in one place, while about eighteen inches further along three bullets had cut right through. The right lower plane had been ripped by Archie cutting a couple of the incidence or internal cross-bracing wires. One stagger wire cut, and one aileron control cable cut, which put both out of action. A sliver from Archie had ripped the right upper wing. Two main spars were shot through, and one of the ribs of the tailplane was fractured, by the only bullet he had got into me when on or nearly on my tail. There were also several other bullet holes in wings and fuselage. Besides these few details the machine was all OK![34] Lieutenant Verschoyle Cronyn, 56 Squadron RFC

Whenever an aircraft had been over the Front, every inch had to be checked to ensure that damage from a stray bullet or fragment of flying shrapnel did not pass unnoticed. The engine fitter had an especially difficult and responsible job as some of the engines were temperamental in the extreme, a fact which was greatly exacerbated by the treatment meted out to them by the pilots as part and parcel of combat flying.

McFall, my mechanic, was continually struggling to keep engine performance up to the demands of the patrols. Ballraces went; cylinders; pistons; tappet rods fell out. On one patrol a cylinder began to miss, making the engine vibrate so violently that I could not keep up with the flight ... I myself may have been partially the cause of these engine incidents ... there could be no compromise with the feelings of my long-suffering little engine. It was frequently screamed up to an appalling rate of revolutions and mercilessly stressed on full throttle climbs.[35] Lieutenant Gordon Taylor, 66 Squadron RFC

In such circumstances the engine fitter had to have a sense of dedication.

> We looked on our aircraft like the cavalryman looked on his horse: see that the fuel was all right, everything in working order, everything properly adjusted. When I thought an engine had done sufficiently long running I'd just say to the pilot, 'I'll change this engine when you come down'. Immediately the flight was over I would take the engine out. The ésprit de corps was so great that anybody else who didn't happen to be doing anything would come and work together to take it out. There were two spare engines at the back of the hangar and we took one from there to put back in the aircraft. As soon as that was installed properly we'd pull the old engine to pieces, check it up, examine it. Any part that we thought wanted renewing, we'd renew it.[36] Sergeant S.S. Saunders, 1 Squadron RFC

In charge of the ground crew was the flight sergeant and his level of competence could make a great deal of difference to the overall efficiency of a flight.

> Each flight sergeant had to do the disciplinary and technical work in his flight in order that his flight could work independently. He was expected to look after his men, see to their leave, see to their clothing, look after their discipline and take them over in parades. There was very little paper work, very little indeed – just the rostas and the rolls of names, ranks and addresses of the men. The flight sergeant had to do everything – whatever cropped up – he was responsible in every way in every aspect of service life. There was no one where he could run to someone above and say, 'What shall I do about this?'[37] Air Mechanic Cecil King, 5 Squadron RFC

Success or failure in the air often depended on very small margins. Although superior in rank and position, most pilots knew that they owed a huge debt to the skills of their ground crew whose devoted attentions could mean the difference between life or death in the air.

I noticed them looking at me strangely. I stopped, wondering what was up. Then I realised. Both the elevator and the rudder controls were shot away. The wires trailed behind in the grass, just lying on the ground. For a moment I couldn't believe it. How could I possibly have got back? I saw bullet holes; in the fin, the rudder, the tailplane, and more up the fuselage. None as far forward as the pilot's seat . . . Obviously some Hun had got a terrific burst into the tail, cutting the control wires. Yet I was still alive. Corporal Ellins, my rigger, was there with McFall, my fitter. 'How could I have got back, Ellins, with these wires gone? How could the controls still have been working?' For a moment he said nothing: just looked at me with steady eyes. Then he spoke. 'Well, sir, you came back the other day with some bullet holes in the tailplane. I thought, maybe, one day, they'd get your control wires. So I spliced up some new wires and duplicated the controls.' He just stood there in his brown overalls. No drama. No great emotional scene. What could I say that could be any kind of answer to the thoughtfulness that had saved my life? In the end I said, 'Thank you, Ellins.'[38] Lieutenant Gordon Taylor, 66 Squadron RFC

CHAPTER THIRTEEN

1918

January 1918 found the British forces on the Western Front in an unusual position. Not since the late spring of 1915 during the Second Battle of Ypres had they faced a determined German attempt to break through their line. But since the end of 1917 it had been clear that the German Commander-in-Chief, General Erich von Ludendorf, was gathering his resources for a major offensive at the first possible opportunity in the new year. The collapse of Russia had released vast numbers of fresh German troops who had been uninvolved in the titanic clashes of the previous twelve months and like a dripping tap filling a bath these men had been moved westwards unit by unit to take their place in the line on the Western Front. Ludendorf himself had won some of his greatest victories in the east and he was now determined to repeat his successes in the west by destroying the British and the French as he had the Russians. In contrast the Allies were tired and frustrated. Their grand plans for 1917 had yielded little and now, after a year of hard graft, they were forced on to the back foot to try and maintain their positions until the vast resources of the United States, who had joined the war in 1917, could enter the contest at their side. The British in particular were unaccustomed to adopting such a defensive posture, having taken the war to the enemy incessantly since the commencement of hostilities. A new approach would be needed to counter the innovative tactics unveiled in the German counter-attack at Cambrai, where a fierce, crushing bombardment had immediately preceded an infantry assault spearheaded by 'stormtroopers' whose job was to push on as fast as they could, bypassing pockets of resistance which were to be mopped up by the following conventional troops. The challenge of introducing the kind of elastic defence structure needed to withstand such an attack was exacerbated by the overall weakness of the British line which was extended in February 1918 south of the Somme as far as the river Oise to bring a further twenty-eight miles of front line within the jurisdiction of the BEF. Field Marshal Haig also found himself further hamstrung by the determination of David Lloyd George to withhold troops from what he considered to be the maw of the Western Front, a dangerous political gamble which left the BEF desperately short of manpower. Poorly supported by artillery, the Fifth Army which had taken over the new sector was weakest of all and hard-pressed to establish itself in the former French positions. Through a combination of intuition and accurate intelligence assessment, Ludendorf identified this very section of line as the fulcrum of his offensive which he hoped would finally tear apart the junction of the two Allies.

For British aviation the future was also wreathed in uncertainty. The imminent formation of the Royal Air Force through the unification of the RFC and RNAS was a radical step to take in the middle of a war. If mishandled it could result in a disastrous fall in morale and efficiency. Central to the successful completion of this difficult transition would be the appointment of the leading professional and political figures to see it through. General Henderson appeared to be one possible candidate for the key position of Chief of the Air Staff at the newly formed Air Ministry in London. Yet his advocacy of strategic bombing in his submission to General Smuts had finally isolated him from many of the more influential members of the RFC. Despite the objections of Haig, who wished to retain him at the Front, Trenchard was recalled to take up the post. He was in an unrivalled position both within the RFC and the popular imagination as the public face of military aviation and his appointment was almost inevitable. Lord Cowdray, as President of the Air Board, expected to be appointed Secretary of State for Air but a rift had developed between him and Lloyd George over allegations, published in one of Cowdray's newspapers, that the Prime Minister's personal fear of air raids had driven him out of London during the Gotha raids. Furthermore, to secure widespread political support for his own position, Lloyd George was determined to appoint a figure with close links to the popular press. Consequently he offered the post to Lord Northcliffe. Only when Northcliffe ostentatiously rejected the position in *The Times*, did Cowdray realise he was not to be selected and not unnaturally immediately resigned as President of the Air Board. In pursuit of his aims, Lloyd George then offered the post to Northcliffe's brother, Lord Rothermere, a newspaper magnate in his own right, who accepted.

Unfortunately the relationship between Rothermere and Trenchard proved to be disastrous, racked with mistrust and rancour on both sides. In particular the two men disagreed over the central idea of how best to use aviation strategically; while Trenchard also took great exception to what he saw as political intrigues against Haig, his former Commander-in-Chief. With both Rothermere and Trenchard accustomed to operating autocratically, they soon found it impossible to work together. On 19 March 1918 Trenchard resigned, a fortnight before the Royal Air Force officially came into being on 1 April. Aware of the political consequences of the loss of such a prominent figure, Rothermere persuaded him to carry on, especially after the launch of the long feared German offensive three days later and the desperate position which soon developed in France. Trenchard's resignation was thus suspended, but not withdrawn, and it was finally accepted on 13 April. When it became public knowledge the apparent loss at such a moment of the unchallenged leader of Britain's air force, under whatever title, resulted in an outcry not against Trenchard, but Rothermere who was forced to resign only a fortnight later. His position was taken by Sir William Weir, who was quickly elevated to the peerage, and Trenchard's by his old rival from the first year of the war, the now Major General Sir Frederick Sykes. A team had now been put in control of the new service which was united in its belief in the underlying value of strategic bombing. Unable to let Trenchard go completely due to his popularity, Weir forced him to return at the beginning of June to take command of the Independent Air Force (IAF) which was intended to implement the policy of bombing Germany.

While these games of 'musical chairs' were being played in London, the military authorities were dancing to a much more serious tune. In February, Trenchard had been replaced in command of the RFC in the Field by one of his acolytes, the relatively junior Major General John Salmond, and consequently the essential areas of policy remained the same. While preparations were put in hand for the great union, endless routine work kept the service fully occupied on any days when the weather allowed flying. Reconnaissance had never been more important than at this time when signs were being eagerly sought of the impending German assault. The RFC played a vital role in keeping GHQ supplied with accurate intelligence and, although the Germans prepared several possible sites for their offensives, it was soon correctly deduced from the ominous stream of reports detailing new ammunition and supply dumps, airfields and unusually large troop movements, that the blow would fall against the fronts held by the Third and Fifth Armies which stretched from the Oise to the Scarpe around the linchpin of St Quentin.

While the reconnaissance aircraft continuously plied back and forth garnering this information, the RFC also had to defend the British line against the incursion of a new generation of high-performance German reconnaissance aircraft. Flying at extreme altitudes to evade the British patrols these machines were intent on bringing back the raw data needed by the German High Command to formulate their plans. This led to a strange resurgence of the 'lone wolf' tactic as one man in particular devoted his considerable energies to bringing down as many as possible of these high flyers. Captain James McCudden turned his socially unpardonable background as a former ground-crew engine fitter to great advantage in tuning his SE5 to peak performance.

I used to go up day after day waiting at 17,000 up to 20,000 feet for the German two-seaters, who were always over our lines during the clear visibility. I expect some of those Huns got a shock when they came over at 18,000 feet and were dived on by an S.E. from above, for in the winter it was an exception to the rule to see an S.E. above 17,000 feet, which was the ceiling of the average 200 h.p. S.E. with its war load. My machine had so many little things done to it that I could always go up to 20,000 feet whenever I liked, and it was mainly the interest which I took in my machine which enabled me to get up so high. By getting high I had many more fights over our lines than most people, because they could not get up to the Rumplers' height, and so could

not engage them successfully.[1] Captain James McCudden,
56 Squadron RFC

McCudden was the consummate professional, a 'player' rather than
a 'gentleman', who eschewed romantic notions of air fighting and
sought only to achieve his ends with minimal risk.

> My system was always to attack the Hun at his disadvant-
> age if possible, and if I was attacked at my disadvantage
> I usually broke off the combat, for in my opinion the
> Hun in the air must be beaten at his own game, which
> is cunning. I think that the correct way to wage war is
> to down as many as possible of the enemy at the least
> risk, expense and casualties to one's own side.[2] Captain
> James McCudden, 56 Squadron RFC

He reached his peak over the Christmas period of 1917 when he
sent a veritable and verifiable cascade of German aircraft literally
crashing down from the heavens.

> I got up to 17,000 feet in half an hour, and very soon
> saw a Rumpler coming towards me, slightly lower, from
> the direction of Bourlon Wood. We were very close, and,
> getting into position quickly, I fired a short burst from both
> guns, and the Rumpler went into a right-hand spiral dive.
> Then his right-hand wings fell off at about 16,000 feet,
> and the wreckage fell on our lines north of Velu Wood.
> I watched the wreckage fluttering down like so much
> waste paper, and saw the fuselage and engine going
> down at a terrific speed, leaving a trail of blue smoke
> behind it. After a look round, I soon saw another Rumpler
> west of me towards Bapaume, slightly below me. I went
> over to him and, having got into position, fired a burst
> from both guns. Flames at once issued from his fuselage,
> and he went into a spin at 17,000 feet and took about two
> minutes to reach the ground, on which he crashed near
> Flers, which, at that time, was about twenty miles west
> of the lines. I saw the poor devil strike the ground in a
> smother of flame. Then I had a look round and at once
> saw a German being shelled by British A.A. guns over

Havrincourt Wood. I flew all out, and soon overhauled the L.V.G., which at 16,000 feet was much slower than my machine . . . As soon as I got within range and opened fire the Hun at once dived for his lines. By the time he had got down to 9,000 feet, diving at 200 miles per hour, I opened fire for a second time into him, whereupon he burst into flames, after which the whole machine fell to pieces owing to the speed at which it was going, for I had most likely shot some of his main flying wire, too. This L.V.G. went down in a shower of flaming pieces, and the wreckage finally fell in our lines at Havrincourt village. I now started climbing again, and having got up to 18,000 feet, again saw an L.V.G. coming south over Lagnicourt. I dived down, but he saw me and ran for it. However, I was much faster, and having got into position, fired a burst from my Lewis, as the Vickers at once stopped. A small flicker of flame came from the L.V.G., but it went out immediately. By this time I was well over the Hun lines, so I had to return . . . I felt very disappointed at having missed the last Hun, for if my Vickers had not stopped at the crucial moment, I think I should have dispatched him with much celerity.[3] Captain James McCudden, 56 Squadron RFC

This kind of performance attracted a good deal of attention and admiration within the RFC.

The expert out here now is one McCudden. On the day in question there were eight Huns lying our side of the Lines alone, of which he had three this side. In about three days he brought down eight Huns, seven of which I believe fell this side. An unparalleled success.[4] Lieutenant Gwilym Lewis, 40 Squadron

Lewis himself was no novice having flown a tour of duty with the DH2s of 32 Squadron over the Somme in 1917. But when he came out to 40 Squadron in December 1917 he found he still had a lot to learn. An intelligent man who was aware of his own faults he catalogued an awesome list of sins in one account of an attempt to shoot down a German two-seater. It is perhaps instructive to compare his confession with the almost chilling, mechanical efficiency of McCudden's equally candid account.

I got up to 16,500 feet when a beastly two-seater Hun insisted on coming in my direction. I simply had to see him, much as I was dying not to. Of course I made a mess of things as usual. I had to wait to see his markings before I fired, and by that time his nose had started to go down. I made a mighty lunge round and pushed at everything I could in a wild frenzy of excitement. Unfortunately I left my engine full on during my headlong flight, and it soon ceased to function in an orderly manner. By that time I had blazed off a drum from my Lewis gun, but to my great annoyance my Vickers refused to '*marche*'. This was later accounted for owing to my not having loaded it! (Don't you dare to tell anyone else!) Anyway the Hun would not stop one of my bullets and went home.[5] Second Lieutenant Gwilym Lewis, 40 Squadron RFC

The continual upgrading of aircraft design and engines meant that no one could rest on their laurels for long and McCudden soon discovered that the German Rumplers had ascended to levels of even higher altitude, leaving him lagging behind once more.

I resolved that I should catch them somehow, and I very soon procured a set of high-compression pistons, such as are used in the newer sorts of engines. At this time my new high-compression engine was nearly ready, and I was very keen to get it going, and then go up and see the Rumpler pilot's hair stand on end as I climbed past them like a helicopter ... On January 28th my machine was ready, having been fitted with my special high-compression pistons, and as the engine gave many more revolutions on the test bench than did the standard 200 hp Hispano, my hopes of surpassing the Maybach-Rumpler looked like materialising. The morning was pleasant and I left the ground at 9.30 am. As soon as I opened the throttle I could feel the increase in power as the fuselage at my back pressed me forward hard in its endeavour to go ahead quickly. After I had left the ground, the increase in my machine's climb was very apparent, and although I will not mention exact figures, I was up to 10,000 feet in a little more in minutes than there are days in the week . . . I knew that my machine was now a good deal superior to anything the enemy had in the air, and I was very pleased that my experiment, of which I had entirely taken the responsibility, had proved an absolute success.[6] Captain James McCudden, 56 Squadron RFC

McCudden's chosen method of fighting meant that he spent countless hours at extreme altitudes, half, if not completely, frozen and suffering from severe oxygen deprivation. When he landed he was often in a terrible state.

I felt very ill indeed. This was not because of the height or rapidity of my descent, but simply because of the intense cold which I experienced up high. The result was that when I got down to a lower altitude, and could breathe more oxygen, my heart beat more strongly and tried to force my sluggish and cold blood round my veins too quickly. The effect of this was to give me a feeling of faintness and exhaustion that can only be appreciated by those who have experienced it. My word, I did feel ill, and when I got on the ground and the blood returned to my veins, I can only describe the feeling as agony.[7] Captain James McCudden, 56 Squadron RFC

By this time McCudden's unique skills and experience could undoubtedly have been put to better use in developing new aircraft or in theoretical tactical work. He was beginning to show distinct signs of stress which he probably recorded unknowingly in his memoirs. He had started to adopt a noticeably more callous attitude to the fate of his victims, as was demonstrated in his remarks over an aircraft that he shot down on 24 January 1918.

I shot down a D.F.W. that was doing artillery work over Vitry at 12,000 feet. This D.F.W. crew deserved to die, because they had no notion whatever of how to defend themselves, which showed that during their training they must have been slack, and lazy, and probably liked going to Berlin too often instead of sticking to their training and learning as much as they could while they had the opportunity. I had no sympathy for those fellows.[8] Captain James McCudden, 56 Squadron RFC

The unceasing strain slowly took hold as increasingly he began to exhibit a dangerous self-confidence in the air, which was perhaps not unnatural, but which presaged the abandonment of his own tactical philosophy – the reason for his success and relative longevity.

I had no guns working, but I felt awfully brave, and as the remaining Pfalz and Albatross were very dud, I started chasing them about with no gun, and once very nearly ran into the tail of the Pfalz at whose pilot I could have thrown a bad egg if I could possibly have got one at that moment.[9] Captain James McCudden, 56 Squadron RFC

This new devil-may-care attitude was perhaps best illustrated in his rash approach in shooting down the Hanover which became his final victim on 26 February.

I now made an instant resolve. I had attacked many Hanovers before and had sent several down damaged, but I had never destroyed one, so I said to myself: 'I am going to shoot down that Hanover or be shot down in the attempt.' I secured my firing position, and placing my sight on the Hanover's fuselage, I fired both guns until the two-seater fell to pieces. The wreckage fell down slowly, a fluttering monument to my 57th victory and my last over the enemy for a time.[10] Captain James McCudden, 56 Squadron RFC

By spring 1918, since first joining the Royal Engineers as a Boy Bugler eight years previously, McCudden had risen through the ranks to become the leading 'ace' of the RFC. Finally, on 2 March, he was ordered home for a well-deserved leave. But the mental state of such a naturally cool individual was clearly shown by his intemperate reaction.

In bed that night I thought over it all and more than ever regretted that I had to leave a life that was all and everything to me, and I confess I cried.[11] Captain James McCudden, 56 Squadron RFC

A month after he returned to Britain it was announced that he had been awarded the VC, the culmination of a long string of gallantry awards he had earned since receiving his commission. Rarely among aviation VCs he was able to receive the thanks of the King in person at an investiture at Buckingham Palace on 6 April. After a four-month rest McCudden was posted back to the Front as a Major to take command of his own squadron. Tragically he was killed *en route* in a simple flying accident when his engine failed on take-off on 9 July. The veteran was just twenty-three years old. James McCudden VC, DSO and Bar, MC and Bar, MM was one of the greatest air fighters that the RFC ever possessed – a true all-rounder who excelled at flying, marksmanship, the hurly-burly of the dogfight and above all the patient stalking of his kills.

After weeks of rising tension and fearful anticipation the great German offensive finally burst through a blanket of misty conditions at 04.45 on 21 March 1918. The sheer force of the bombardment destroyed many of the British front-line positions and furthermore cut much of the communication with the rear. The German troops surged over the forward positions, swirling round isolated pockets of resistance and in some cases reaching the artillery line before the gunners knew what was happening. The greatest advances were made on the Front of the Fifth Army and considerable inroads were made towards Amiens. The German Air Service fully appreciated the shock-value of close air support and as soon as the fog lifted they zoomed into action. As ever with such low-level work casualties were high since they not only had to contend with fire from the ground but also fell easy prey to any British scouts they encountered.

We were originally ordered to accompany the infantry at low altitude and support the actions by machine-gun fire from the aircraft. But dense fog on the morning of the 21st March prevented this action. When the fog lifted later on in the afternoon I was ordered to destroy

a bridge which was in front of the moving line. It was
a fairly hopeless order because we had to fly without
any fighter protection. I was 'caught by five Spads – very
good single-seaters! It was a very brisk encounter and I
was really a dead duck because my machine was much
less manoeuvrable and my observer was soon put out
of action by a shot through his chest. I could never use
my two machine-guns because when I tried to turn the
very manoeuvrable single-seaters flew rings round me.
It was my first really sharp encounter in the air but I
wasn't really scared. It was really this feeling of almost
detachment. I believe that when one is near to death the
second ego steps out and observes one – I had a feeling
that I observed myself – and I was quite satisfied that
I took the whole situation so calmly. I imagined that I
had been wounded several times because I saw bullet
holes appearing in my dashboard and I was surprised
that it didn't hurt. Then I was wounded in the leg and it
was like a sledge-hammer blow. Then I did something
that was totally against the book of rules. I went into
a straight sharp nose dive. But it saved me because
I dived into the layer of cloud which made visibility
in the oblique direction. So with tremendous speed I
approached the ground. My engineering instincts told
me that if I pulled up the machine too sharply then
the wings would go so I pulled up very, very slowly
and the machine recovered. Then I was at very low
altitude over the trenches. The apathy came now which
is a characteristic of the shock after being wounded. My
first instinct was to land – to be out of it. I had my packet
and I wanted to be out of it. There I saw in front of me
a mound completely covered with barbed wire – I was
gliding straight towards it and I didn't care a damn – I
wanted to be out. Then suddenly somebody knocked
me on the head and yelled, 'Gas!' so I opened the throttle
again and I carried on. Then my calm decision returned
and of course it struck me as ridiculous to crash into
barbed wire and the right decision was of course to fly
straight on until a town appeared on the horizon and to
land on the field in order to get into a hospital as quickly

as possible as we both were very severely wounded. That I did.[12] Leutnant Gustav Lachman, German Air Service

The British threw every aircraft they could into the breach. The Bristol Fighters roamed low over the battlefield looking to strafe any likely target while above them the Camels and SE5s sought to neutralise the swarms of German artillery, reconnaissance and scout aircraft. Before returning to base the British machines habitually emptied what remained of their ammunition in low-level attacks.

We began attacking troops and transport. All the roads were very busy and time and again we dived on motor-transport and on columns of men and saw them scatter wildly. We also dropped our remaining bombs. It was difficult to see what happened to these as we were so low. Unless we turned immediately after releasing a bomb our vision of the burst would be obstructed by our own machine. Each machine only carried four 25-lb bombs on a rack mounted under the fuselage. Bristols were not designed for bombing purposes and carried no special sights for this work. The pilot simply sighted over the right wheel and when the objective was in line with the rim he pulled the release cable. A Vickers gun normally fires about 600 rounds per minute but ours were fitted with special recoil springs which increased the rate to 1,000 per minute. When a road thickly covered with troops was sprayed with bullets at this rate the damage done must have been considerable. All this time we were being subjected to a good deal of rifle fire from below and were frequently shot at by Archie batteries.[13] Lieutenant Vivian Voss, 48 Squadron RFC

The German anti-aircraft guns had great difficulty in dealing with aircraft flying at nearly ground level in a landscape littered with their own troops. Leutnant Fritz Nagel was in command of a 77 mm light anti-aircraft gun mounted on a truck when he was caught up in the congested Albert road.

Royal Flying Corps planes seemed to be everywhere and tried to stop the advance. Most of the time they were too low for us, zooming down with machine-guns going full blast, and never high enough to become safe targets. We could not fire on a plane operating over the heads of our own men. The chances of hitting such fast-moving targets were practically nil, while the danger of hitting our soldiers and showering them with splinters was great. Ordinarily, good anti-aircraft fire forced the enemy to fly high, but this was a life-or-death struggle and these RFC flyers continued to dive in regardless of the risk. Only a direct hit could stop them.[14] Leutnant Fritz Nagel, Kraftwagen Flak 82

It is difficult to judge the exact nature of the RFC's achievement in disrupting and holding up the German advance but at the time it was certainly regarded as crucial. During the retreat from Mons in 1914 the few available RFC machines had been able to do little more than observe the progress of the German columns beneath them. But by 1918, in less than four years, they had acquired considerable killing power which, although still limited, was increasing all the time as bomb-carrying capacity increased and new technology brought ever more powerful weapons into the equation. These could only be effectively exercised by men willing to risk their lives in squadrons which sometimes suffered up to 30 per cent casualties each day. Statistically this meant the turnover of a squadron's personnel in just four days. At night the bombers sought to disrupt the constant flow of German troops into the battle area.

The principal target for attack was the Bapaume–Albert road on which the Germans were advancing rapidly. The weather was very fine – bright moonlit nights. The road showed up almost white in the moonlight. You'd see an obvious column of troops marching, a long black blob along the road. Then you'd see vehicles, you could pick out individual vehicles from about 1,500 feet. We dropped as many bombs as we could. Most of the bombs were anti-personnel bombs. We had very little retaliation from the enemy because they were obviously holding their fire in order not to give away their concentration. Well that was all very nice; it was just jam for us! We just went out, dropped bombs, came back, loaded up, went out and dropped more bombs. We did a great deal of damage and stopped these columns from going along the road.[15] Lieutenant J.C.F. Hopkins, 83 Squadron RFC

To determine the nature and exact direction of the threat as it approached what remained of the British defensive lines new night reconnaissance methods were employed.

Reconnaissance work was accomplished by flying at around 4,000 feet over a particular area and then dropping what were known as parachute flares. These were magnesium flares suspended on a parachute. They were rather like a bomb launched through a tube – as they went through an electrical contact fired the magnesium compound. It dropped a certain distance – say, 500 feet – and the parachute opened and at the same time the flare caught alight. We would fly along, drop these flares in a line and then turn round and come back over the top of the flares to observe anything we could see. This was not a pleasant business because it was quite obvious to the Germans that having dropped the flares we were going to come back and they were waiting for us. At the height we flew we were within machine-gun range and they had these things called 'flaming onions' which were great balls of fire on wires. These things were shot into the air and they looked like enormous roman candles – quite terrifying but as far as I know they never did any damage at all except put the wind up you.[16] Lieutenant J.C.F. Hopkins, 83 Squadron RFC

Moving inexorably forward, the Germans reached Albert and, in so doing, regained all the ground so painstakingly won during the British Somme offensive of 1916. But as they attempted to move on towards Amiens their advance began to run out of steam and the British managed to re-establish a tentative defensive line.

Against the background of these cataclysmic events the unification of the RNAS and RFC took place as planned on 1 April. But, as can be imagined, in the circumstances the actual change-over was barely noticed. The overall reaction was one of resignation as the two previously distinct services attempted to work in harmony.

> I think none of us in the RNAS wanted to be amalgamated, nor I expect, did the RFC wish to be amalgamated. We were accustomed to our own traditions as customs we'd grown up with for the last couple of years. I think we were all rather sorry. But we saw the point for by that time we'd learnt that the air had a definite function of its own to perform apart from just supporting the Navy or Army and that the obvious thing was to get together and make a do of it – make a service of it. So we very soon got over our little regrets. That's why we got together so easily because we had then created our own traditions and, as it were, inherited each other's traditions – it all became air force traditions instead of either RNAS or RFC.[17] Lieutenant Aubrey Ellwood, RNAS

Just over a week later, on 9 April, the Germans launched the second phase of their offensive around the river Lys near Hazebrouck to the south of Ypres. The pace of the air war was accelerating out of control and the sky was full of aircraft, with both sides seeking control of the battlefield zones. The strain on the combatants was incredible, with one life-or-death situation succeeding another in a kaleidoscopic maelstrom. Battle fatigue was inevitable but the very success of the 'aces' meant that there was intense pressure to keep them flying as long as possible.

This was particularly marked in the case of Germany's leading airman, Manfred von Richthofen, who had received a severe head-wound from which he never fully recovered when he was shot down by the crew of an FE2 D on 6 July 1917. Nevertheless, he had returned to the head of his 'circus' by 16 August 1917 and seemed at least on the surface to have lost none of his deadly skills as he attained the unparalleled 'score' of eighty victories. However, on 21 April 1918 he made a series of errors of judgement which led to his death in action. A free-wheeling dogfight over the Somme valley had resulted in an inexperienced pilot, Lieutenant Wilfred May, making an attempt to break away when the guns of his Sopwith Camel jammed. Richthofen followed him as he had followed so many others.

The first thing I knew I was being fired on from the rear
... I noticed it was a red triplane, but if I had realised
it was Richthofen, I would have probably have passed
out on the spot. I kept on dodging and spinning, I
imagine from about 12,000 feet until I ran out of sky
and had to hedge hop over the ground. Richthofen was
firing at me continually.[18] Lieutenant Wilfred May, 209
Squadron RAF

Richthofen followed May lower and lower, crossing the Front over
to the British side. His actions from this point were completely
atypical.

I looked over at Herr Rittmeister and saw that he was
at extremely low altitude over the Somme near Corbie,
right behind an Englishman. I shook my head instinctively
and wondered why Herr Rittmeister was following an
opponent so far on the other side.[19] Leutnant Joachim
Wolff, German Air Service

Unknown to Richthofen another aircraft had left the dogfight.
Captain Roy Brown saw that a Camel was in trouble and dived
to attempt a rescue.

Went back again and dived on pure red triplane which
was firing on Lieut. May. I got a long burst into him
and he went down vertical and was observed to crash.[20]
Captain Roy Brown, 209 Squadron RAF

The laconic words of Brown's combat report marked the death
of Germany's greatest 'ace', although it is considered by some
that Richtofen was actually shot down by ground fire. However,
as he had managed to get himself in a situation where he was
flying at an extremely low level behind enemy lines, under
considerable machine–gun fire from the ground and with an
unseen opponent with considerable experience immediately on
his tail, he was effectively doomed by an accumulation of his own
mistakes. The precise origin of the fatal bullet is irrelevant and
over-fevered speculation merely reflects a gratuitous morbidity.
The main point was that Richthofen was dead and would kill no
more British pilots and observers as they plied their trade behind

the German lines. Some felt a feeling of regret at the passing of such a worthy opponent.

> A feeling of happiness as regards the fact that the circus was broken but it wasn't a feeling of hate. It was a feeling that a very good man had gone. That was true – he was a good fighter, a clever fighter. He used every move that he was taught and more. He was instinctive. To be a good pilot you have got to become part of the aeroplane that you're flying.[21] Lieutenant Jack Treacy, 3 Squadron, Australian Flying Corps

Others expressed their views more prosaically. Major Edward Mannock simply said, 'I hope he roasted the whole way down!'[22]

In the intensity of the air combat of 1918 Mannock himself had gone from strength to strength. Men who once reviled him as a suspected coward now looked on him with something closely akin to hero worship. They recognised that their own lives were dependent on his superb tactical skills and ongoing informal programme of education. Lieutenant Gwilym Lewis briefly came under his wing while serving with 40 Squadron and in just a couple of weeks was greatly influenced by his approach. From such young protégés Mannock attracted a variety of friendly nicknames of which the most enduring was 'Mick' in reference to his Irish family origins.

> Mick Mannock was the hero of the squadron at that time. He left the squadron with 21 victories and his victories were good, he came on to form having been older than most of us and a more mature man. He had given great, deep thought to the fighting game and had reorientated his mental attitudes which was necessary for a top fighter pilot. He had got his confidence and he had thought out the way he was going to tackle things. He became a very good friend of mine and I owed a lot to him that he was so friendly. I was unnecessarily reserved and he liked to give people nicknames and he called me 'Noisy'! He was a lot of fun. He had very good humour, quite a lot of

fun and absolutely popular in the squadron.[23] Second
Lieutenant Gwilym Lewis, 40 Squadron RFC

Mannock's first tour of duty was completed in January 1918 but
he returned to France with the SE5s of 74 Squadron in late
March 1918.

The Commanding Officer detailed Mannock to give us
lectures on air fighting. And what delicious dishes of the
offensive spirit they were! He was a forceful, eloquent
speaker, with the gift of compelling attention. After
listening to him for a few minutes, the poorest, most
inoffensive pilot was convinced he could knock hell
out of Richthofen or any other Hun. Since Mannock's
experience of air fighting was extensive, his talks were
most valuable. His first lecture on single-seater fighting
began and ended with the axiom to which he rigidly
adhered: 'Gentlemen, remember. Always above, seldom
on the same level, never underneath.'[24] Lieutenant Ira
Jones, 74 Squadron RAF

He offered his pilots a mass of trenchant advice which encapsulated
the wisdom of his hard–won experience.

He explained how to effect surprise by approaching the
enemy from the east (the side he least expected) and how
to utilise the sun's glare and clouds to achieve this end.
Pilots must keep physically fit by exercise and by the
moderate use of stimulants. Pilots must sight their own
guns and practise as much as possible, as targets are
usually fleeting. Pilots must practise spotting machines
in the air and recognising them at long range, and every
aeroplane must be treated as an enemy until it is certain
it is not. Pilots must learn where the enemy's blind spots
are – that is, the parts of their machine which obstruct
the pilot's view. Scouts must be attacked from above
and two-seaters from beneath their tails. Pilots must
practise quick turns, as this manoeuvre is more used
than any other in a fight; practising stunting is a waste
of time. Formation flying at twenty-five yards apart must

be practised. Pilots must practise judging distances in the air, as they are very deceptive, just as objects across water are. Decoys must be guarded against – a single enemy is often a decoy – therefore the air above should be searched before attacking. If the day is sunny, machines should be turned with as little bank as possible, otherwise the sun glistening on the wings will give away their presence at a long range. Signal lights should not be fired except when absolutely necessary, as they attract attention. Pilots must keep turning in a dogfight and never fly straight except when firing. Pilots must *never*, under any circumstance, dive away from an enemy, as he gives his opponent a non-deflection shot – bullets are faster than aeroplanes. Pilots must keep their eye on their watches during patrols, and on the direction and strength of the wind.[25] Lieutenant Ira Jones, 74 Squadron RAF

Mannock's excellence as a patrol leader was undoubted. Always governed by an exemplary caution, to avoid unnecessary risks he would painstakingly manoeuvre to secure the best possible position from which an attack could be launched in strength.

During patrols, he not only mystified and surprised the enemy, but also the formations he led. Once over the lines, he would commence flying in a never-ending series of zigzags, never straight for more than a few seconds. Was it not by flying straight for long periods that formation leaders were caught napping? As he tilted his machine from side to side, he scanned the sky above and below with the eye of an eagle. Suddenly his machine would rock violently, a signal that he was about to attack – but where were the enemy? His companions could not see them, although he was pointing in their direction. Another signal, and his S.E. would dive to the attack, the red streamer attached to his rudder fluttering faster than the heart-beats of those who followed it with taut nerves. A quick half-roll, and there beneath him would be the enemy formation flying serenely along; the enemy leader with his eyes no doubt glued to the west – the result a complete surprise attack. Mannock would take the leader if possible in order to give his pilots coming down behind him a better chance of an easy shot at someone before the enemy formation split up, and the dogfight began. Having commenced the fight with the tactical advantage of height in his favour, Mannock would adopt dive-and-zoom tactics in order to retain the initiative. Woe betide a pilot who lost the initiative and got himself into such a mess that his comrades had to forgo their tactical advantage in order to extricate him from his perilous position! Whilst the fight was in progress, Mannock, in spite of being in the thick of it, would be summing up the situation the whole time . . . When the enemy had been demoralised and defeated, Mannock would give the signal to re-form, and would not leave the battle ground until he was satisfied that all the machines had seen his signal.[26] Lieutenant Ira Jones, 74 Squadron RAF

Mannock was a stickler for formation discipline, but once a dogfight had commenced his pilots flew as individuals within the basic framework of his overall tactical approach until the clash was over. As soon as they were safely back on the ground he would collect his flight together and go through each combat explaining what had happened, what he had been trying to achieve and looking in a positive manner at any aspect of an individual's performance that raised concern. His approach to his pilots was demonstrated by the advice he proffered to Lieutenant Jones when he was depressed at his inability to shoot down a German aircraft despite having had a number of promising opportunities. Mannock drew on his own difficult introduction to air fighting to make suggestions that were practical and relevant to the failing that both he and Jones had identified as the root cause of the problem.

I've had a long talk with Mick about it. He thinks I am allowing too much for deflection. That is, I'm aiming too much in front of the enemy. He has advised me to do a slight traverse; to sight about 5 yards in front of the engine, then to fire and, while firing, to bring the sight back as far as the pilot, and then to push it forward again. If I do this, he says, I can't help but hit the machine somewhere. I must say it sounds reasonable enough. This is what he says he did at first. With experience, he says, I'll get accustomed to making the correct allowance for the enemy's speed and direction instinctively.[27] Lieutenant Ira Jones, 74 Squadron RAF

Jones took excellent advantage of this advice and finished the war as one of the leading RAF 'aces' credited with forty-one 'victories'. Mannock had a reputation for sharing his own 'kills' with inexperienced members of his flight, with the laudable intention of improving their self-confidence and overcoming the difficulty of shooting down the first German aircraft – another example of his determination to prevent others having to undergo the problems he had suffered in his early days as a scout pilot.

Although he continued to be successful both in combat and as a tutor, Mannock's never steady nerves were soon in a parlous state. His fellow pilots noted with concern the obvious signs of impending breakdown and in particular his obsession with the fear of being shot down in flames.

Whenever he sends one down in flames he comes dancing into the mess, whooping and hallooing: 'Flamerinoes, boys! Sizzle, sizzle, wonk!' Then, at great length, he tries to describe the feelings of the poor old Hun by going into the minutest details. Having finished in a frenzy of fiendish glee, he will turn to one of us and say, laughing: 'That's what will happen to you on the next patrol, my lad.' And we all roar with laughter.[28] Lieutenant Ira Jones, 74 Squadron RAF

In retrospect it is obvious that, like McCudden, Mannock should have been taken off active service for a prolonged period of rest and given a quieter role in training new scout pilots. Instead on 5 July he took over from Major William Bishop as commander of 85 Squadron. Bishop had continued to ply his trade as a lone wolf to remarkable effect. But his squadron was essentially a disparate group of individuals taken out on patrol by the flight commanders while Bishop flew alone, making his kills unencumbered by witnesses. Although Bishop was ever present leading the drinking in the mess, the squadron desperately needed a commanding officer who could instil a sense of discipline, to unify them and lead them in the air. This deficiency did not go unnoticed and after making his last flight on 19 June, Bishop was withdrawn from the Front to work towards the establishment of a Canadian Air Force. He thus survived the war, an enigmatic figure, accredited with seventy-two 'victories'.

Mannock's arrival had an immediate impact on morale and effectiveness. Daily he led patrols into a frantic killing spree which was spurred to even greater heights by news of the death of his friend McCudden. Even in the depths of his personal torment, Mannock never ceased in his efforts to pass on all he had learnt to others. Yet, like so many other masters of air fighting, towards the end he gradually stopped obeying his own precepts.

Mick Mannock came over to my farewell dinner with 40 Squadron in July 1918 and brought with him two of his flight commanders from 85 Squadron which was a nice compliment to me and our friendship. I remember him telling McElroy then, 'Don't throw yourself away, don't go down to the deck – I hear you're going down to the deck – don't do that. You'll get shot down from the ground!' And ultimately that's what happened to him and indeed to Mick Mannock too. Mannock in my opinion had been kept out on the battlefront too long. He'd suffered in losing his judgement as was likely to happen.[29] Second Lieutenant Gwilym Lewis, 40 Squadron RAF

The inevitable end came as he sought to get a first 'kill' for a young and hitherto unsuccessful pilot, Lieutenant Donald Inglis, on 26 July 1918.

While following Major Mannock in search of two-seater E.A.s [Enemy Aircraft] we observed an E.A. two-seater coming towards the line and turned away to get height, and dived to get east of E.A. [The] E.A. saw us just too soon and turned east, Major Mannock turned and got in a good burst when he pulled away. I got in a good burst at very close range, after which E.A. went into a slow

left-hand spiral with flames coming out of his right side.
I watched him go straight into the ground and go up in
a large cloud of black smoke and flame. I then turned
and followed Major Mannock back at about 200 feet.[30]
Lieutenant Donald Inglis, 85 Squadron RAF

It appears that Mannock had killed the observer in his first pass
and left the two-seater helpless for the novice to shoot down.
They then committed the cardinal error of following the victim
down. Edward Naulls was serving in the front line between
Robecq and the Bois de Pacaut when he saw the tragedy unfold
above him.

I watch fascinated as tracer bullets from a German
machine-gun post in the support line enter Mannock's
engine just behind the cowling; there is a swift tongue of
flame followed by belching black smoke and Mannock's
machine falls away helplessly to hit the ground not far
from his victim. Inglis's engine stalls and he lands just
behind the front line in the trenches occupied by a
company of the Suffolks, on the left of our position.
The end comes with incredible swiftness. Never again
will he wave to us as he skims the tops of the poplar
trees that line the La Bassee Canal bank. I was on that
sector for five months and Major Mannock's plane and
his tactics were well known.[31] Private Edward Naulls,
2nd Battalion, Essex Regiment

Mannock was eventually credited with seventy-three 'victories'
and was thus rated the highest scoring British 'ace', but these figures
are almost meaningless as statistics. Like Ball and McCudden he
received many decorations including the DSO and two Bars, and
the MC and Bar. But, in a curious omission, the VC which he
so richly deserved, as a man who had known fear and overcome
it, was not gazetted until almost a year after his death. Edward
Mannock was a virtually unparalleled combination of scout pilot
and patrol leader. Yet, in the end, like Richthofen, he died because
he broke his own rules and paid the inevitable price. Following
his death Trenchard's policy of 'No empty chairs at breakfast' was
particularly difficult to sustain but 'tradition' demanded a 'binge'

to send Mannock metaphorically on his way. Sympathisers and friends gathered from neighbouring squadrons, including his old comrades from 74 Squadron.

> It was a difficult business. The thought of Mick's charred body not many miles away haunted us and damped our spirits. There was more drinking than usual on these occasions; the Decca worked overtime; we tried to sing, but it was painfully obvious that it was forced, as there was a noticeable discord. We tried to prove that we could take a licking without squealing. It was damned hard. Caldwell said in his little speech after dinner that Mick would not wish us to mope. We never do it in No. 74, so let's liven up. And liven up we did – up to a point.[32] Lieutenant James Van Ira, 74 Squadron RAF

The sense of loss among his many acolytes was grievous, but they believed that he had left an enduring legacy.

> We have lost our Squadron Commander. Went down in flames after getting over 70 Huns, and so the Royal Air Force has lost the best leader of patrols, and the best Hun getter it has had. In another month he would have had over 100. However, unlike other stars, he left behind all the knowledge he had, so it is up to the fellows he taught, to carry on.[33] Lieutenant Malcolm McGregor, 85 Squadron RAF

The sheer number of British and French aircraft in the summer of 1918 meant that the German Air Service was increasingly hard pressed. German pilots were continually frustrated by the situation, as even their best efforts seemed to be futile.

> What is the use of shooting down five out of fifty machines! The other forty-five will photograph and bomb as much as they want. The enemy's material superiority was making itself more and more felt, and so dooming us to failure. The impossibility of achieving anything substantial in spite of all our honest efforts was the most demoralising thing we experienced in

the whole war.[34] Leutnant Rudolf Stark, German Air Service

By the end of June the Germans had clearly not achieved the runaway breakthrough that had been the goal of their offensive. Despite massive success which had resulted in the most radical realignment of the Western Front since the autumn of 1914, they had not broken the line or split the British apart from their French allies. They had thrown everything into the attempt and failed. Now in an exhausted state, with their lines of communication severely stretched, they were vulnerable to the inevitable Allied counter-strokes that would be made once the tired but triumphant defenders had first reorganised and then assimilated the newly arriving American troops. The fight back began on 8 August 1918 with the Battle of Amiens, which would prove to be the beginning of the end for the Germans. The much vaunted Hindenburg Line was fatally breached and for the next hundred days the attacks continued unabated until the pressure of the Allied advance precipitated the end of the war on both land and in the air.

During this time tactical bombing, which had developed in effectiveness as bomb loads increased, was carried out continuously against targets such as key railway junctions. The FE2 B, although obsolescent for daytime operations, was still in use with several squadrons as a night bomber where it provided good service. A typical operation began with a posting of orders on the squadron noticeboard usually an hour before sundown. The pilots would then be briefed by the mapping officer.

We had a mapping officer – he was a good chap. He used to go out with the machines at night, fly over sections that we operated in and come back with a whole picture of it in his mind. He used to get big sheets of the old blue sugar bag paper and he used that as a background to paint in the various landmarks: roads, railways, lakes, woods – that kind of thing. When we were given a particular objective in any area he'd bring out his sugar bag paper, put it up on the wall and paint in the actual spot we were supposed to attack. As far as possible he would make it lifelike as to what the thing really looked like at night. We found this a great help because it was surprising how realistic these pictures were when we actually got over the spot.[35] Lieutenant J.C.F. Hopkins, 83 Squadron RAF

The next stage would be to plot a course from the airfield to the target.

We would get our maps, look out the objective indicated in the orders, read the orders as to what we were supposed to do – whether we were to bomb, make observation, machine-gun troops – make quite clear what we were going to do. Then we would go to the mapping room, take our map with us and this little course and distance indicator. There we would get the telegrams from the Meteorological Office giving us wind direction and speed at different heights. With this information we would plot the course allowing for drift due to winds and decide which was the best altitude to fly at.[36] Lieutenant J.C.F. Hopkins, 83 Squadron RAF

To defend the more obvious targets the Germans increased the level of their anti–aircraft precautions to include both gun batteries and machine–guns assisted by searchlights to illuminate the attacking bombers.

We were going to bomb some objective, going along quite cheerfully at about the usual height of 2,000 feet. Suddenly and unexpectedly three searchlights opened up and caught me – all three together – and we were surrounded with red tracer machine-gun fire coming up all round the place. Well the FE2 B was a machine with a big lattice-work tail, it had no body except for a little thing in front. If you canted the machine, banked it so that you were looking horizontally along the wings it was difficult to see. So one of the moves if you were caught in a searchlight was to side-slip down the beam – which I did and I got out of the beams. No sooner had I done that than another one picked me up. I yelled at my observer, 'Joe, for God's sake use your gun!' One way to put a searchlight out was to fire at it! I don't know whether he was terrified, petrified or what but he didn't and I couldn't get a straight enough run because of the machine-guns to drop a bomb. So I did another side slip – well we only started at about 2,000 feet and by this side-slipping we lost an awful lot of height. Next thing I saw Joe get up and he just waved his arms up in the air for me to go up. I looked over the side and found we were skimming over the roofs of a whole lot of buildings. It looked like a factory. So I yanked the machine up giving it a terrific zoom and we got out of the searchlight for a few seconds. As soon as I got high enough – to drop a bomb you've got to be over 500 feet or else the safety mechanism won't have unwound and they won't explode – I let him have four bombs. Well that put them all out for a little while. I rapidly climbed away and got up to about 2,000 feet again, still circling round this place which I thought must be of some importance. I'd still got the big bomb on hand and I circled round waiting for them to open up but they delayed for a long time until the machine-guns opened up aiming at the sound of the machine. Well that was enough for me because with red tracer you could see where it was coming from so I let them have the 112 pounder. I saw it explode, somewhere near the machine-guns anyway and it was enough to silence them.[37] Lieutenant J.C.F. Hopkins, 83 Squadron RAF

The extension of tactical bombing was not a one-way process. After curtailing their raids on Britain the German Gotha and Giant bombers were used against Allied targets far behind the British lines and the British scout pilots were obliged to protect rail junctions, ammunition dumps and other key military installations.

It's very funny night flying. You get a very good horizon to fly against and you can see water very clearly underneath you, but of course you can't pick out roads or railways or anything like that. The main thing is to keep your eye on the horizon and not find yourself getting into a dive when you don't mean to. You had to have

cat's eyes – you had no aids: there was no radar or radio telephone. You were just there up by yourself, in the dark for two hours on a patrol. One of the things one did was sing, quite unconsciously, and you'd come down absolutely hoarse! Well it's lonely, two hours up there seeing absolutely nothing. The bomber pilot had a crew but you were by yourself. It's an extraordinary effect and not anybody has the mentality to do that.[38]
Lieutenant Archibald Yuille, 151 Squadron RAF

Even when located the Gotha and Giant bombers were by no means defenceless so Yuille developed a cautious but effective method of approach.

We knew that they would be flying at 8,000 feet – they were always at 8,000 feet so we always flew at about 7,500 so that we could see him against the sky which was always light whereas you could never see him beneath you against the ground which was always dark. We could only tell that there were raiders there by what I call the 'mess' – the searchlights and the flak. So we used to fly into that area and switch on our light underneath the aircraft that was to stop the Archie shooting while the searchlights went on hunting for the Hun. If we were lucky – and that wasn't very often – we would see the Hun up above us. A black streak going in front of you and you went to try and get behind him. It wasn't very easy but we were faster than he was which let us catch up. This was the whole art of night flying. The aeroplane throws out a slip-stream from the propellers and we used to come up behind feeling the slip-stream on our top wing which just shook the Camel a little bit. Then you knew you were just underneath the slip-stream coming up straight behind him and he couldn't shoot you because he had no gun actually in his tail. That gave you a narrow angle which got narrower as you got in where you were immune from being hit. If you could control yourself enough to get up little bit by little bit by little bit he couldn't hit you and probably didn't know you were there because he couldn't see you either. Then you opened fire from about 25 yards range if you had the nerve to get in as near as that. If you shot from further away you would probably miss. We had tracer bullets, armour piercing bullets with two machine-guns firing through the propeller at 600 rounds a minute each. A pretty good volume of fire which would go on for about two minutes. If you shot straight you only needed one or two short bursts, you could see where the bullets were going because the tracers would tell you. If you were too much to the right or left you adjusted the aeroplane so that you were on target. That really was the whole secret of the thing – to have the patience to get in close after you had been lucky enough to find your Hun – but that was easier said than done.[39] Lieutenant Archibald Yuille, 151 Squadron RAF

By such means Yuille was successful on 25 July in shooting a Gotha over Ypres and just a month later brought down a Giant near Amiens.

Ground-attack operations by the RFC were now as integral a part of military planning as photographic reconnaissance and artillery observation. In a strange echo of 1914, aircraft once again became multi-purpose machines with reconnaissance aircraft carrying bombs and machine-gunning German troops, while scouts dropped bombs and fulfilled their original eponymous role of scouting ahead of the advancing Allied armies.

I went over early in the morning at about 1,000 feet over the Hindenburg Line which was south-west from Cambrai. At that instant a shell burst below me and within a second the whole of the ground seemed to be turning over, boiling up in brown earth that had been thrown up and smoke from the bursting shells. I thought, 'Well nobody can live down there and I don't think I'm going to live long if I stay over the top of it!' So I went straight to the clear air over the German support areas. There I found the sunken roads were full of German troops – within seconds they all vanished into the grass verges so I strafed the verges. I got rid of three of my four little bombs. Then four Fokkers came down from above and attacked me. I saw them coming and

I'd had quite a lot of practice at taking evasive action so I went down to ground level round the trees and zigzagged back keeping out of their way. We'd been told to attack troops and not go in for aerial combat as other squadrons were up above to do that. As I got back into the battle smoke they broke away to the east and left me. I went back to the German infantry and got rid of my last bomb. Then the smoke over the battle area was clearing and I could see the trenches. I spotted one advance trench with some Germans. I dived on it, fired, pulled up and did what I call a cartwheel over the far end and down again. I didn't shoot because they were running and seemed to have their hands up as I got close to them – I pulled up again. Some British troops were just arriving and the Germans started to climb over the parapet going off west as prisoners. Then I went back to our advance landing ground to rearm and refuel.[40] Lieutenant Ronald Sykes, 201 Squadron RAF

One new problem that the Allies encountered as their advance gathered momentum was the sending forward of sufficient supplies. Lines of communication quickly became stretched and almost overwhelmed by the long-forgotten strains of open warfare. To help overcome this problem aircraft were given a new supporting role and instead of dropping bombs began to bombard their own troops with provisions.

Our squadron was given the job to drop food for them into their advanced positions. We were given a map reference of where they were and told to go and drop bags of bully beef. The observer had three sandbags filled with about 50 tins of bully beef to one sandbag. When we came to the destination I saw the Belgian soldiers in their blue uniforms who seemed to expect me. I came down to about 100 feet and did a series of figure of eights. When we were over the troops my observer dropped the sandbags – the ground was all muddy so he just lifted them out and dropped them – there was no parachute attached to them.[41] Lieutenant Frank Burslem, 218 Squadron RAF

The hard-pressed German Air Service tried its best to intervene and had at their disposal a fine new scout aircraft in the Fokker DVII. However, although it had a slightly superior performance to the British fighters, it was essentially of the same generation and did not represent a sufficient leap forward to overcome the numerical superiority of the British.

We encountered a bunch of Fokkers just as we were finishing a patrol. We chased them back to the east but they just flew straight back as if they were trying to get away from us. After we got well inside their territory they simply turned round and easily climbed above us. They must have had much bigger engines that the normal Fokkers. We looked for cover and went under a cloud but they came down through the cloud and started a dogfight. Recognition was difficult in the misty air under the cloud but I did fire at several black crosses in front. Then I saw a Camel just on my right – immediately there was loud machine-gun fire just behind me. I did a sharp turn to my left and as I looked back I could see a machine starting to go down in flames through the misty air. I did a quick dive just below to try and identify it but all I could see was a column of black smoke. I zoomed up again and saw some dim shapes ahead. I joined them and found I'd joined three Fokkers – I was near enough to see the black crosses. I had a pot at the nearest one then pulled up into the cloud, changed direction and dived down into clear air. I saw the three Camels going off to the west but I was afraid that there were a lot of Fokkers still above me in the streams of mist. So I did a lot of evasive action and flew off and joined the other three Camels. We found out that Lieutenant Mills had been shot down.[42] Lieutenant Ronald Sykes, 201 Squadron RAF

Despite the growing imbalance in strength the German Air Service remained a dangerous foe and continued to impede the manifold functions of the RAF in every possible way. Lieutenant Ralph Silk of 6 Squadron was flying an RE8 over Le Cateau when he was 'bounced'.

I was flying above the crossroads at Le Cateau with four bombs on – my duties were to bomb, strafe, take photographs and make a general reconnaissance of the moving troops. We were flying at about 2,500 feet, the sky was clear with the exception of some cumulus clouds which rather worried me because they were always a hiding place for the Huns. I was waiting for the signal from our leading machine to dive in, drop my bombs, make our reconnaissance and get what information we could. The roads below were absolutely chock-a-block. The Germans were retreating left, right and centre. I waited in vain for the signal – something had gone wrong. But then out of the clouds dived a Fokker machine. He was on my tail before I almost realised it. The frontal area of a Fokker machine is so small and he came in out of the sun. He fired a burst at me and I almost felt the bullets whizzing past my head. I replied by giving him two short bursts but he seemed to be encased in a cast-iron shirt – I know my shots were good but still they didn't have any effect. With his speed he passed me and as he passed I saw the red flash and then I realised I was scrapping with one of the German aces. A moment after another machine was on my tail. Again I opened fire and again I heard the tat-tat-tat-tat passing me and I felt my machine lurch. I turned my head over my shoulder and I saw that my pilot had slumped on the controls. Then there was a gasping sound – and an awesome silence – the machine had stopped. There was I suspended in the air with a dead pilot – Huns, bullets, wings all around me. I looked up to the Heavens and I said, 'Oh, God, help me!' The next thing I remember was having a sledge-hammer blow to my head. I put my hand to my helmet and I found it all jagged and torn with a certain amount of blood. Then I had a blackout. I fell through the air like a falling leaf and I think it was the upward rush of the air that brought me to my senses. By the grace of God I had the presence of mind to pull on the joystick to break the fall and the machine staggered, stalled and fell on some trees. I just remember, very faintly, the Germans letting me down by

rope then I lost consciousness again.[43] Lieutenant Ralph
Silk, 6 Squadron RAF

As the endless ground-strafing raids continued, pilots gradually
learned new tactics which maximised the effects of their fire and
gave them the best chance of survival.

If you could shoot up transport and block the road that
was a fine thing – you stopped the whole lot. I used
to try and attack them from the front, that is to say
from the direction to which they were proceeding. If
you could manage to shoot up a couple of transport
wagons the whole road was blocked for some time –
then they were just cold meat – you just went along with
the twenty-pound Cooper bombs.[44] Lieutenant James
Gascoyne, 92 Squadron RAF

Gascoyne was slightly wounded when he made what he considered
to be an elementary mistake in this new type of fighting.

I came across a village where the German troops were
retreating. A whole line of transport in a very straight
street and at the bottom of the street was a church tower.
I was so intent in having a go at this transport I was
not flying at more than about two hundred feet and I
foolishly went absolutely straight down this village street.
Suddenly there was a burst of machine-gun fire right into
my machine. One bullet came through the windscreen,
hit my helmet, made a little hole, a mark on my head – it
felt just like being hit with a brick. I put my hand up and
found there was blood. I stuck my head over the side
and I regained consciousness very quickly. I discovered
where the firing was coming from – the church tower
at around the height I was flying, straight into him![45]
Lieutenant James Gascoyne, 92 Squadron RAF

The ever-increasing scale of the fighting meant that squadrons
began to fly together in sweeps. Operations were planned on
a massive scale, as exemplified on 16 August by operations of
Eightieth Wing under the overall command of the 1914 veteran,
Lieutenant Colonel Louis Strange.

We decided to tickle our opposite numbers up by a raid on Habourdain Aerodrome in which the whole wing was to take part . . . We started off in squadrons independently, but formed up as follows over our rendezvous . . . 4th Squadron, AFC with Snipes from 7,000 feet to 8,000 feet; 88 Squadron with Bristol Fighters at 6,000 feet; 46 Squadron with Camels at 4,000 feet; 2nd Squadron, AFC with SE5s at 3,000 feet and 103 Squadron with DH9s at 2,000 feet . . . I made it clear that no time was to be wasted and that all our energies were to be concentrated solely on the objectives of the raid, for I know how tempting some targets look to a squadron that is flying low down . . . My chief impressions of the show were a perfect mass of Archie's bursts, which took no effect at all, as none of their gunners seemed to get the range of our height, a certain number of German aircraft tearing back from the lines ahead of us, and a few of their scouts above and around us that dared not interfere. Then came the Very light signal, fired by Captain Cobby in the van of No. 4, AFC, and the inspiring spectacle of that squadron diving down to their mark – right down till they seemed mere specks that spat streams of tracer bullets and left bursts of their bombs here, there, and everywhere about the hangars. Then would come a burst of black smoke from first one hangar and then another, as the petrol inside their machines ignited. A Fokker biplane was caught in the air under this Squadron, as luck would have it, and flew straight into a tree. Then down went the SE5s of No. 2 A.F.C.[46] Lieutenant Colonel Louis Strange, Eightieth Wing RAF

As the SE5s screamed at low level across the airfield they were using the latest phosphorus bombs.

We went straight in and as far as the SE5s were concerned our fellows carried six 25 pounder phosphor bombs and six 25 pounder Cooper high-explosive bombs. The phosphor bombs were horrible damn things when they burst, if you got any of that on you then you burnt. The Huns got all their aircraft in the air if they could but they didn't have

much to come home to afterwards![47] Lieutenant Frank
Roberts, 2nd Squadron Australian Flying Corps

The impressive results of this massed raid are symbolic of the fact
that the German Air Force no longer had the resources to match
the brute force and numbers that the British could deploy with a
little forward planning.

In June 1918 the Independent Air Force began its much heralded
operations against Germany. Envisaged by Smuts as a powerful
force dedicated to undertaking a devastating series of strategic
strikes, the IAF was in essence a fraud, having been based on
an RFC formation established the previous October. In direct
response to the series of heavy Gotha raids on London the War
Cabinet ordered one naval and two army bombing squadrons to
move to Ochy near Nancy to carry out raids against industrial
and domestic targets in Germany. Placed under the command of
Lieutenant Colonel Cyril Newall, who had previously commanded
the Ninth Wing under the direct control of RFC Headquarters, the
new Forty-first Wing launched its first attack on 17 October 1917
when eleven planes raided Saarbrucken. In December, Trenchard,
still then head of the RFC, called for increased resources for the
unit and after being allocated two more squadrons in the spring it
was renamed the VIII Brigade. But its campaign lacked intensity,
principally as a result of Newall not being given specific targets to
bomb. His close association with Trenchard led him continually
to choose installations such as railway junctions and aerodromes
which had a tactical value to the army but were of minimal strategic
significance. When the great German offensive broke on 21 March
1918 the VIII Brigade lost any vestige of a strategic role and it did
not regain this until the middle of May, when it was redesignated the
Independent Air Force. When Trenchard was placed in command
of the IAF in June it still consisted of only four day and five night
bombing squadrons.

The day bombing raids over Germany were carried out by the
DH4s of 55 Squadron, IAF. Relying on speed, altitude and a tight
formation to keep themselves out of trouble they probed deep
into Germany. Among the pilots was Second Lieutenant William
Johns who subsequently became better-known to aficionados of the
adventures of his fictional character 'Biggles' as Captain W.E. Johns.

On 16 September, his DH4 was forced to drop out of formation over Hagenau when his petrol tanks were holed by 'Archie'. Once alone he was at the mercy of the German interceptor scouts and his observer was soon hit.

> Sick with fright and fury, I looked around for help, but from horizon to horizon stretched the unbroken blue of a summer sky. Bullets were striking the machine all the time like whip-lashes, so I put her in a steep bank and held her there while I considered the position . . . My ammunition was running low and I was still over forty miles from home . . . Things looked bad. To try to make forty miles against ten or a dozen enemy machines (several others were joining in the fun) was going to be difficult. In fact I strongly suspected that my time had come.[48] Lieutenant William Johns, 55 Squadron IAF

The progenitor of 'Biggles' was lucky for he survived the ensuing crash-landing to be taken prisoner. His observer was killed.

The old FE2 B war-horses of 100 Squadron IAF were finally replaced with Handley Pages to conduct their night raids deep into Germany. These powerful two-engined aircraft had a range of eight hours, flew at just over eighty miles per hour at 10,000 feet and had a bomb load of up to 2,000 pounds.

> We would read our orders – find out our target, the bombs we were going to carry, meteorological reports and then we should work out the course during the afternoon. We would then get into our flying clothes which constituted of a pair of flying boots made of sheepskin, a Sidcot flying suit with fur collar, a helmet and fur-lined gloves. Underneath my gloves I used to wear a pair of silk gloves. As it got towards dusk we would go aboard and get into our aircraft. The pilot would sit on the right-hand side and I should sit on the left of him. The mechanics would wave us away and we should taxi out to the far side of the aerodrome, turn into the wind and then take off. We had no wheel brakes so once we were getting very nearly airborne there was no stopping. We'd fly for about three-quarters of an hour circling round the aerodrome

gaining a little height. When we'd got to about 1,000 or 1,500 feet we'd cross over the front-lines towards our targets. We would arrive in due course. Sometimes we got to a height of 10,000 feet but usually our bombing was from around 3,000–4,000. It was rather cold because we had open cockpits with very small windshields. We would get a block of ice on our chest after two or three hours flying and of course it was very windy. We never thought anything of that. My job was to find the way, set the course, adjusting for any variation of wind. We were flying at about 60 miles an hour air speed so that if we had a 30 mile an hour wind we only had a 30 mile ground speed. If the wind moved at all we would adjust our course. We would carry on for an hour, two hours, perhaps three hours on that course. Then as we approached our target I would crawl through a hatch into the front cockpit where we had two machine-guns firing on one trigger; our bombsights and bomb release controls. To the rear of us we also carried a rear gunner who had two guns firing on the port and starboard. If we were attacked from underneath there was a hole in the body of the machine with another gun firing from there. So he poor chap was running up and down if we ran into any sort of trouble. I would direct the pilot on to the target – right, or left, or straight ahead by signs with my hands. At the same time I would have my right hand on the bomb-release control and as we got on to our target away would go our bombs. We didn't always drop all our bombs in one go. We would observe results and go round and do the same thing again. Then of course we tried to get home as quickly as we could. Unfortunately we had a prevailing wind against us, generally from the south-west, so it took us much longer to come home than going out.[49] Lieutenant Roy Shillinglaw, 100 Squadron IAF

During the raids lingering concerns over the moral rectitude of bombing areas inhabited by civilians were largely dismissed by the bombers' aircrew who appeared to believe that their precautions were successful in minimising unnecessary casualties.

I don't think anybody deliberately bombed civilian houses or people. So far as my colleagues and myself were concerned we were very, very keen to be on our target. There is no doubt that our raids on German towns – railway stations and factories in those towns – must have been demoralising to some of the civilian inhabitants. In our night bombing it was difficult to see our results – we would see a fire burning or the explosion in a works. But next day the day bombers would be over at dawn and as they passed over our targets they photographed them and within 24 hours we would see pictures of our targets and where perhaps we'd hit, or whether we'd just missed and so forth. So that we were very keen to be on target because our errors were shown up on those photographs – there was no kidding the authorities. I think we were pretty accurate on the whole.[50] Lieutenant Roy Shillinglaw, 100 Squadron IAF

Yet, as had been the case in London, from the perspective of the civilians sheltering from the bombs in towns such as Frankfurt, the experience was terrifying.

Then came the dreadful thing of the air raids because nobody knew what such a thing meant. They occurred mainly on cloudless nights – and these nights were horrible. Everybody waited for the raid to start, everybody waited for the siren to go. We had no electric light in our flat so all dresses were put so that one could dress in the dark as soon as possible. Everybody went to the cellar – the whole house reassembled in the cellar. Everybody talked about the dangers and is afraid of a hit. The air raids are now considered harmless but at the time we didn't think them harmless at all and sometimes we had to get up two and three times a night and in the morning everybody's tired and asked what happened during the night.[51] Herbe Haase

When undertaking these long range raids, the British had to pass through a heavy network of German fighters which scored regular and disturbing successes against the relatively slow-moving bombers. It soon became clear that without a reasonable degree of supremacy in the air, which could only be achieved by the unlikely scenario of the wholesale destruction of the German Air Service, effective strategic bombing did not justify the massive drain on resources which it entailed. Throughout the summer of 1918, as the fortunes of the battlefield fluctuated, strong pressure continued to be brought on Trenchard by the Allied High Command to use the IAF against specific tactical targets rather than the more distant industrial complexes in Germany, a view that of course reflected his own priorities which had not changed one whit. Despite objections from Weir and Sykes in London, as casualties mounted Trenchard allocated an increasing proportion of his strength to attacking German airfields in a policy of forward defence. Had the 'surplus fleet' of planes confidently predicted by Weir himself become available in spring 1918 it would have been possible for both parties to be satisfied. But the failure of the Ministry of Munitions to increase its rate of engine production as fast as anticipated and the sudden rise in aeroplane losses in March and April meant that the surplus failed to materialise and despite the enthusiastic championing of the Air Ministry, the IAF was only able to grow at a very slow rate. By November 1918, the IAF possessed only ten squadrons out of a total RAF strength of ninety-nine squadrons.

Between June, when its operations began, and November, the IAF carried out 650 raids, striking regularly at military targets in occupied France and Belgium as well as Germany itself. By the time of the Armistice plans were in hand for a raid against the heart of civilian Germany, Berlin. Yet Britain's first strategic air war ended on a characteristic note of failed promise. Examined retrospectively it is now generally accepted that it did little to help the Allied cause to eventual victory and post-war investigations clearly revealed that the limited operations which were carried out against targets in Germany were of negligible effect. The air services of the First World War have traditionally evaluated themselves in terms of their tactical support to the forces on the ground. The non-materialisation of the 'Surplus Aircraft Fleet' meant that the visionary plans of Smuts and the other proponents of large scale bombing could never be realised. The final word on the achievements of the British strategic bombing campaign is best left to Trenchard who during the war did so much to thwart it, but who within a short space of time would embrace it as the central purpose of the Royal Air Force after he had once again become its chief.

I am certain the damage done both to buildings and personnel is very small compared to any other form of war and the energy expended. The moral effect is great – very great – but it gets less as the little material effect is seen. The chief moral effect is apparently to give the newspapers copy to say how wonderful we are, though it does not affect the enemy as much as it affects our own people.[52] Major General Sir Hugh Trenchard, Independent Air Force Headquarters

The Armistice, which came into immediate effect on 11 November 1918, recognised that the German Army had been defeated on the ground by superior forces. When news of it filtered through to the men of the RAF, it prompted a strangely muted response. Many aircrew, having come to terms with the likelihood of an early death, were overwhelmed by the sudden freedom to plan a life free from fear. But their sense of liberation was tempered by sadness for family and friends who had died or been maimed over the previous four years.

The engines were ticking over and the observers were in their cockpits stowing away the ammunition drums for their Lewis guns. Already two or three Rolls engines had roared as they were run up, when the tall figure of our C.O. was seen hurrying from the Squadron Office. His long arms were swinging and the ends of his scarf flapping as he came striding across to the hangars. 'Morning, Major!' several voices greeted him as he approached. 'Morning, lads!' he called out and waved both arms. 'Wash-out, everybody. The war's over. Hostilities cease at eleven ack emma today!' The engines were speedily switched off. For a moment there was silence, then someone raised a cheer and we all joined in. After that we talked in excited groups for a while, and then, feeling rather lost, wandered back to our huts.[53] Lieutenant Vivian Voss, 48 Squadron RAF

By the evening, spirits had lifted and, with the atmosphere of anti-climax dispelled, many squadrons organised a 'binge'.

We had a good night when the Armistice was signed. Being night flying people we have plenty of rockets and lights and so we had a real November 5, though it was a few days late. We got to bed about 4.30 a.m. feeling pretty well tails up and tired.[54] Second Lieutenant Alan Smith, 101 Squadron RAF

By the end of the war the RAF consisted of a veritable armada of 22,647 aeroplanes and seaplanes, flown and serviced by some 30,122 officers and 263,410 other ranks. Once it was apparent that the Armistice would hold, demobilisation began and redundant units were gradually disbanded. By August 1919, the ninety-nine operational squadrons on the Western Front had been reduced to twenty-four, mostly attached to the army of the Rhine. This drastic process of reduction continued until November when only one squadron remained on duty in Germany. In all 26,087 officers, 21,259 cadets and 227,229 other ranks were demobilised from the RAF between November 1918 and January 1920.

Many pilots who had come to love the thrill of flying found that they were faced with the near certainty of never again taking the controls of an aircraft. Some tried their best to stay in aviation but in the grim post-war climate the odds were against them.

When I was being demobilised from Germany, via Dunkirk and Uxbridge, a friendly officer and I talked together at the noticeboard having noticed that there was a sale of government stock to be held at Hendon. We both decided we'd like to go to this sale. So we went from Uxbridge by bus, got to Hendon and were amazed at the offers – there were literally hundreds of aircraft, engines and parts. Anything pertaining to air warfare or manufacture was for sale at give-away prices. He had been a pilot of a DH4, I'd been a pilot of an RE8 and Bristol Fighter and we both thought that it would be lovely to buy an SE5 A which were up for sale for £5. We agreed to the price, he bought one, I bought one. We had them filled up with petrol and oil, tested them

there and then for engine efficiency against chocks, then took our aircraft up and flew around Hendon for about half an hour. We landed within five minutes of one another, stopped our props, climbed out and shouted to one another in joy at having enjoyed such a wonderful flight. At that time the SE5 was the 'honey' machine of the war. We discussed things, reckoned up how much it would cost us – neither of us had a job to go to. I was 20, he was 21 and we had heard that it cost £10 to have the certificate of airworthiness. Therefore both of us became very dejected at having to realise that we couldn't possibly afford them. We'd no hangar, no reason to believe that we had any place at home where we could even house the aircraft. So we talked with the air mechanics and we agreed to sell them back for £4 10s. It took us I should think half an hour in silent tears to walk away from Hendon aerodrome realising that we had been defeated in our objective of being civil flyers.[55]
Philip Townshend

Their flying careers, and the war in the air that had spawned them, were both now a thing of the past.

CHAPTER FOURTEEN

Aftermath

Throughout the war the German Air Service adopted an essentially defensive strategy and consequently was never able to aspire towards enduring supremacy in the air. The British aerial forces aimed higher and although suffering greater pro-rata casualties – particularly during those periods when the technological advantage of superior aircraft design was held by the Germans – gained more concrete results from their painful investment in the air. Tactically the RAF and its predecessors fully vindicated their underlying *raison d'être*. During most of the decisive land engagements the British infantry and artillery commanders unstintingly received all the information and support they could reasonably expect. This allowed them, when the crunch came, to overcome the advantages that the Germans generally possessed through their well-sited and domineering defensive positions. The Western Front turned out above all to be an artillery war and, as the gunners' eyes in the sky, the unglamorous corps aircraft repeatedly sought out vulnerable targets to ensure that they were destroyed or at least grossly inconvenienced by a stream of shells. These machines formed the backbone of the flying services and without the mundane, daily toil of the BE2 Cs and RE8s, doggedly performed in the face of extreme danger, the British Army would have been unable to fulfil its part in the long struggle of attrition that was the Great War. It is to them and not the scouts in their DH2s, SE5s and Camels that the real credit of the first war in the air belongs. Although a few airmen found themselves temperamentally unsuited to the nature of air fighting from the start and had to return home in humiliation, the strain eventually took its toll on almost everyone who was exposed to it. Life in the air may not have been as immediately sordid as the miserable existence faced by the stoic infantry in the trenches, but it was a grim battle.

The glorious romance of air fighting probably stands out far more clearly on the printed page than ever it did in actual practice.[1] Lieutenant William Johns, 55 Squadron IAF

In almost five years of war the development of aerial warfare had irrevocably altered the world. But peace left the RAF in a strange and vulnerable position. Almost all its personnel were engaged solely for the duration of the war. With the cessation of hostilities they naturally clamoured to shed their uniforms and return to civilian life. Yet in the face of the increasingly severe cut-backs in military expenditure in the years which followed, the senior officers of the RAF were determined to maintain their existence as an independent third service. To emphasise their distinct identity new titles were given to every rank and following his reappointment as Chief of the Air Staff in March 1919 the now Air Marshal Sir Hugh Trenchard made great efforts to build up a unifying spirit throughout the RAF, just as he had so many years before at the Central Flying School at Upavon. A separate Royal Air Force College for officers was founded at Cranwell, while the skilled other ranks were recruited as boys and inculcated in the discipline and traditions of the service at RAF Halton. Looking for a new role to justify the independence of his position, Trenchard successfully seized upon the use of RAF units in the small-scale conflicts that arose in the realigned Middle East. Across a much troubled region aircraft offered a quick, flexible response to the localised insurrections that could blow up almost without warning upon the whim of a disgruntled tribal ruler. Economic and political necessities prohibited the maintenance of a full-time army of occupation. But one squadron could effectively 'police' a huge area and visit death from the skies on the defenceless villages which harboured insurgents and their leaders in an ironic echo of the predictions made by so much of the pre-war literature about aviation's potential.

In Britain there was a growing awareness in the 1920s and

1930s that the ever-increasing range and load-bearing capability of modern aircraft, symbolised by the first transatlantic flight made by John Alcock and Arthur Whitten-Brown in June 1919, meant that the possibility of even more devastating bombing raids on major cities by huge fleets of 'super bombers' was coming closer to reality. The RAF seized upon these fears to highlight its own capacity to carry out the same kind of large scale raids on enemy cities. Combined with the role of aggrandised imperial policeman, the RAF's senior figures came to believe that the service's future role would be predominantly strategic and, ironically, lost sight of its original purpose in providing tactical support to the army which it had achieved with such indubitable success over the Western Front. As a result, when the 'Phoney War' vigorously burst into life in May 1940 following the German Army's second, more successful attempt to thrust its way through the Low Countries, the RAF had forgotten many of its erstwhile skills and proved incapable of carrying out the multi-layered ground-to-air co-operation role it had so consummately performed during the last fighting retreat undertaken by the British following the German offensive in spring 1918. In a salutary demonstration of the need for a careful balancing act between strategic and tactical requirements to effect the successful exercise of air power, many of the basic lessons had to be painfully relearned over the next four years.

During the First World War, although relatively few had been harmed by it, the potentially deadly arm of strategic bombing had reached out to threaten everyone. By the start of the next global conflict, the benefits of modern science had conspired to bring H.G. Wells's prophesy of 1908 even closer to its grim fulfilment. Beginning in the late summer of 1940 the bombs began to rain down on London much as Wells had predicted and when *The War in the Air* was reprinted in 1941 he was able to hark back with sardonic satisfaction to his apocalyptic vision. Asking in a new preface whether there was anything new that he needed to add, he was able to answer, 'Nothing except my epitaph. That, when the time comes, will manifestly have to be: "I told you so. You *damned* fools." (The italics are mine.)'[2] Caught once again between the Scylla of reprisals and the Charybdis of desperately trying to cause serious damage to German industry, the RAF gave vent to the frustrated rage of the people of Britain through a spiralling campaign of mass bombing. Under the command of Air

Marshal Sir Arthur Harris, this reached its apogee in a series of spectacular, thousand–bomber raids on vulnerable German cities which were aimed specifically at destroying the morale of the civilian population. On the night of 13/14 February 1945, a devastating raid was launched on Dresden. The first wave of bombers smashed the buildings to the ground. A second wave dropped incendiaries to maximise the effect of the damage. A hot wind whipped mercilessly through the burning buildings and caused a 'fire storm' which killed some 35,000 people.

Whilst we were preparing some scrambled eggs and mushrooms, we heard the warning which, this time, was the real thing, and the radio said that three large formations were approaching the town from different sides. I saw the so-called 'Christmas Tree' carpet of markers that were released by the first plane and it was right above the city. My mother, my sister, a lady friend, my niece and I went into the cellar and we bent over my niece to shelter her in case something fell from the ceiling, to take that upon us, and not to let it hit the child. Then the sound of the falling bombs were heard, at first afar, then it came closer and closer. I thought, 'When will the next come?' and, 'Will it fall on to our house?' But I was told that if it is a hit then one doesn't hear it any more. It was a very strange feeling, one couldn't control oneself at all. It was a fright which shook the knees, the teeth were chattering, and one was somehow numb and couldn't do anything about it. I told myself, 'It's stupid! It doesn't help at all to have one's knees shaking!' But it was not possible. It took about three quarters of an hour and then it quietened down and we got out and saw that everything around us was on fire. The smoke started to bother the eyes and we decided to send mother and my niece to friends who lived in a big house where we thought that the cellar was stronger and better built than ours. My sister, myself and this lady stayed on. We were then surprised to hear from far away another warning. We couldn't go back into the house as it was smoking and burning so we had no other choice but to go into the trench which father had dug out in the garden before his death with pieces of wooden board and earth on top. You could sit, but not stand, inside, like in a rabbit hole. We got in there and the second raid started. It was more frightening because we were actually outside. It was so light, that I could read the time on my watch, it was something around two o'clock. It was very strange to see that about 100 metres from us was a huge crater – it could have been a fraction of a second in that the pilot released the bomb otherwise it would have hit us and of course we wouldn't have been alive. I saw corpses lying in the street. Some seemed rather small, burns can't burn bones like that, so what causes it, I do not know. I presume they were burnt by the phosphor canister bombs which were thrown the second time. I decided to go back to the place where I worked so I ran through the burning streets. They were not narrow, so there was not much chance that the burning parts of crashing houses would hit me but it was rather a strange journey. When I came to the bridge there was the sight of people walking across which reminded me of Napoleon's army after the Russian winter. Eventually I arrived at my place of work rather blackened in my face, my hair singed and my coat smelled of smoke having been burnt by sparks.[3] Sophie Satin

Aviation had added one of the most deadly and indiscriminate weapons to the arsenal of war. The cycle of destruction was finally completed six months after Dresden when the first atomic bomb was dropped on Japan.

Source References

IWM SR = Imperial War Museum, Sound Archive
IWM DOCS = Imperial War Musuem, Department of Documents

CHAPTER ONE   The War in the Air

1. H.G. Wells, *The War in the Air*, (London: Penguin Books, 1967), pp. 139–40.

CHAPTER TWO   The Dawn of Aviation

1. Quoted in Alfred Gollin, *No Longer an Island*, (London: Heinemann, 1984), p. 191.
2. *Daily Mail*, 6 November 1906, quoted in Gollin, *No Longer an Island*, p. 193, and Michael Paris, *Winged Warfare*, (Manchester: MUP, 1992), p. 66.
3. Quoted in General Sir Anthony Farrar-Hockley, *The Army in the Air*, (Stroud: Alan Sutton Publishing/Army Air Corps, 1994), p. 14.
4. IWM SR 15, E.J. Furlong, Reels 1 and 2.
5. Furlong, SR 15, Reel 1.
6. IWM SR 9, Donald Clappen, Reel 1.
7. Quoted in Sir Walter Raleigh and H.A. Jones, *The War in the Air*, 6 Vols. (Oxford: The Clarendon Press, 1922–1937), Vol. I, pp. 194–5.
8. Raleigh, *The War in the Air*, I, p. 198.
9. Raleigh, *The War in the Air*, I, p. 206.
10. IWM SR 18, Graham Donald, Reel 1.
11. IWM SR 310, Charles Tye, Reels 2 and 3.
12. IWM SR 3, Edward Bolt, Reel 4.
13. D.S. MacDiarmid, *The Life of Lieutenant General Sir James Moncrieff Grierson*, (London: Constable and Co., 1923), p. 248.
14. Raleigh, *The War in the Air*, I, p. 226.
15. Raleigh, *The War in the Air*, I, p. 237.
16. IWM SR 27, Cecil King, Reel 3.
17. King, SR 27, Reel 3.

CHAPTER THREE   1914

1. Autobiographical notes quoted in Andrew Boyle, *Trenchard*, (London: Collins, 1962), p. 115.
2. Major James T.B. McCudden VC DSO MC MM, *Five Years in the Royal Flying Corps*, (London: Aeroplane and General, 1918), p. 24.
3. IWM SR 16, James Gascoyne, Reel 4.

4. Raleigh, *The War in the Air,* I, pp. 294–5.

5. IWM SR 4208, C.E.C. Rabagliati, Reel 1.

6. McCudden VC, *Five Years in the Royal Flying Corps,* p. 29.

7. Lieutenant Colonel Louis Strange DSO MC DFC, *Recollections of an Airman,* (London: The Aviation Book Club, 1940), p. 43.

8. Strange, *Recollections of an Airman,* p. 42.

9. Rabagliati, SR 4208, Reel 1.

10. King, SR 27, Reel 8.

11. King, SR 27, Reel 8.

12. IWM DOCS, Major W.R. Read, diary, 26 August 1914.

13. Read, diary, 26 August 1914.

14. Gascoyne, SR 16, Reel 4.

15. McCudden VC, *Five Years in the Royal Flying Corps,* pp. 54–5.

16. King, SR 27, Reel 8.

17. Gascoyne, SR 16, Reel 4.

18. McCudden VC, *Five Years in the Royal Flying Corps,* pp. 54–5.

19. Read, diary, 27 October 1914.

20. King, SR 27, Reel 8.

21. King, SR 27, Reel 8.

22. King, SR 27, Reel 8.

23. Rabagliati, SR 4208, Reel 1.

24. King, SR 27, Reel 8.

CHAPTER FOUR   1915

1. Boyle, *Trenchard,* p. 128.

2. IWM DOCS, Lieutenant Colonel H. Wyllie RAF, diary, 23 January 1915.

3. IWM SR 24, Archibald James, Reel 15.

4. IWM SR 4055, Charles Chabot, Reel 1.

5. IWM SR 292, S.S. Saunders, Reel 8.

6. Saunders, SR 292, Reel 9.

7. Gascoyne, SR 16, Reel 1.

8. McCudden VC, *Five Years in the Royal Flying Corps,* p. 64.

9. Captain G.F. Pretyman, quoted in H.A. Jones, *The War in the Air,* Vol. II, p. 98.

10. Lanoe Hawker, quoted in Tyrrel Hawker, *Hawker V.C.,* (London: Mitre Press, 1965), p. 85.

11. James, SR 24, Reel 5.

12. Read, diary, 30 September 1914.

13. Read, diary, 22 October 1914.

14. McCudden VC, *Five Years in the Royal Flying Corps,* p. 61.

15. Duncan Grinnell-Milne, *Wind in the Wires,* (London: John Hamilton Ltd, nd, pp. 118–19.

16. IWM SR 87, F.J. Powell, Reel 8.

17. James, SR 24, Reel 15.

18. Saunders, SR 292, Reel 9.

19. James, SR 24, Reel 15.

20. Saunders, SR 292, Reel 9.

21. Lanoe Hawker, Combat Report dated 25 July 1915, quoted in Hawker, *Hawker V.C.,* p. 103.

22. Powell, SR 87, Reel 2.

23. A.J. Insall, *Observer: Memoirs of the RFC, 1915–1918,* (London: William Kimber, 1970), pp. 60–61.

24. Powell, SR 87, Reel 8.
25. Quoted in Norman Macmillan, *Sefton Brancker*, (London: Heinemann, 1935), p. 109.
26. Maurice Baring, *Flying Corps Headquarters*, (London: William Blackwood, 1968), pp. 105–6.
27. T.B. Marson, *Scarlet and Khaki*, (London: Jonathan Cape, 1930), pp. 160–61.
28. Marson, *Scarlet and Khaki*, p. 162.
29. Max Immelmann, letter dated 28 October 1915 quoted in Franz Immelmann, *Immelmann: The Eagle of Lille*, (London: John Hamilton, nd) pp. 142–3. Trevor Henshaw, *The Sky their Battlefield*, (London: Grub Street, 1995), p. 56, states that the pilot of the British plane was actually Captain C.C. Darley.
30. Immelmann, letter dated 20 December 1915, quoted in Immelmann, *The Eagle of Lille*, pp. 162–4.
31. McCudden VC, *Five Years in the Royal Flying Corps*, pp. 83–5. Henshaw, *The Sky their Battlefield*, p. 103, gives the name of the first pilot to be attacked as Captain Steinbach Mealing. He also reports that sixteen machines took off from Douai but none attacked them.
32. Jones, *The War in the Air*, II, pp. 156–7.
33. Letter from Trenchard to Henderson, 3 April 1916, quoted in Malcolm Cooper, *The Birth of Independent Air Power*, (London: Allen & Unwin, 1986), p. 31.

CHAPTER FIVE Training

1. IWM SR 9, Donald Clappen, Reels 3 and 4.
2. IWM SR 171, T.F. Rogers, Reel 1.
3. Clappen, SR 9, Reels 3 and 4.
4. IWM SR 3765, Arthur Harris, Reel 1.
5. Grinnell-Milne, *Wind in the Wires*, p. 16.
6. IWM SR 10409, Gordon Hyams, Reel 2.
7. Chabot, SR 8, Reel 13.
8. Grinnell-Milne, *Wind in the Wires*, pp. 26–7.
9. Donald, SR 18, additional notes in transcript.
10. Donald, SR 18, additional notes in transcript.
11. IWM SR 11376, Laurie Field, Reel 11.
12. Grinnell-Milne, *Wind in the Wires*, pp. 39–40.
13. Strange, *Recollections of an Airman*, p. 136.
14. IWM SR 7042, Gerald Livock, Reel 1.
15. IWM SR 2, C. Bilney, Reel 5.
16. IWM SR 317, F. Silwood, Reel 1.
17. IWM DOCS, Sir Robin Rowell, typescript memoir, pp. 5–6.
18. James, SR 24, Reel 15.
19. Grinnell-Milne, *Wind in the Wires*, p. 44.
20. IWM SR 14, Reginald Fuljames, Reel 2.
21. Robert Smith-Barry quoted in John Taylor, *C.F.S.: Birthplace of Airpower*, (London: Putman, 1958,) p. 79.
22. IWM SR 7, Frank Burslem, Reel 1.
23. H.H. Balfour quoted in F.D. Tredery, *Pioneer Pilot*, (London: Peter Davies, 1976,) p. 88.
24. Gwilym Lewis, *Wings Over the Somme*, (Wrexham: Bridge Books, 1994), p. 95.
25. IWM SR 301, Ronald Sykes, Reel 6.
26. Sykes, SR 301, Reel 6.
27. Sykes, SR 301, Reel 6.
28. Field, SR 11376.

29. IWM SR 320, Archibald Yuille, Reel 4.
30. Sykes, SR 301, Reel 6.
31. Powell, SR 87, Reel 8.
32. Powell, SR 87, Reel 8.
33. IWM SR 47, J.C.F. Hopkins, Reel 6.
34. IWM SR 17, C. Gordon-Burge, Reel 4.
35. Hopkins, SR 47, Reel 1.
36. IWM SR 984, Howard Andrews, Reel 1.
37. IWM SR 171, T.E. Rogers, Reel 1.
38. W.J. Harvey, *Rovers of the Night Sky*, (London: Greenhill Books, 1984), pp. 17–18.

CHAPTER SIX   1916

1. Jones, *The War in the Air*, II, p. 165.
2. Grinnell-Milne, *Wind in the Wires*, p. 96.
3. Saunders, SR 292, Reel 9.
4. IWM SR 307, Harold Taylor, Reel 1.
5. Powell, SR 87, Reel 8.
6. Powell, SR 87, Reel 8.
7. Powell, SR 87, Reel 8.
8. Lewis, *Wings Over the Somme*, p. 33.
9. Wyllie, diary, 31 May 1916 and 21 June 1916.
10. Wyllie, diary, 8 June 1916.
11. Henderson, quoted in Cooper, *Birth of Independent Air Power*, pp. 45–6.
12. IWM DOCS, Lieutenant T.McK. Hughes, diary, 1 May 1916.
13. Hughes, diary, 4 July 1916.
14. IWM SR 23, Alan Jackson, Reel 3.
15. Wyllie, diary, 30 June 1916.
16. Rowell, memoir, pp. 27–8.
17. IWM SR 4162, Cecil Lewis, Reel 2.
18. Lewis, SR 4162, Reel 2.
19. Lewis, SR 4162, Reel 2.
20. Lewis, SR 4162, Reel 2.
21. *RFC Communiqués 1915–1916*, ed. Christopher Cole, (London: Kimber, 1969), pp. 298–9.
22. Jones, *The War in the Air*, II, pp. 253–4.
23. Roderic Hill quoted in Chaz Bowyer, *Albert Ball, VC*, 2nd edn, (Wrexham: Bridge Books, 1994), p. 81.
24. Rowell, additional papers, 'Comments by Captain Ball on a lecture on Aerial Tactics from the point of view of a single-seater pilot'.
25. Rowell, 'Comments by Captain Ball on a lecture on Aerial Tactics etc.'
26. Alan Bott, *Cavalry of the Clouds*, (New York: Doubleday Page and Company, 1918), p. 50.
27. Bott, *Cavalry of the Clouds*, pp. 57–60.
28. Bott, *Cavalry of the Clouds*, pp. 62–3.
29. Hughes, diary, 2 July 1916.
30. General von Below quoted in Jones, *The War in the Air*, II, pp. 270–71.
31. IWM DOCS, J.O. Evans, letter to mother, 1 August 1916.
32. IWM DOCS, Captain A. Gibbs, copy of letter to mother, 22 August 1916.
33. Manfred von Richthofen, *Red Air Fighter*, (London: Greenhill Books, 1990), pp. 93–4.
34. Lewis, *Wings Over the Somme*, pp. 75 and 78.

35. Trenchard quoted in Jones, *The War in the Air*, II, pp. 283–4.
36. Haig quoted in Jones, *The War in the Air*, II, pp. 296–7.
37. Baring, *Flying Corps Headquarters*, p. 189.
38. McCudden VC, *Five Years in the Royal Flying Corps*, pp. 118–19.
39. von Richthofen, *Red Air Fighter*, pp. 100–101.

CHAPTER SEVEN   Zeppelins

1. Winston Churchill, *The World Crisis, 1911–1918*, (London: Odhams Press, 1938) Vol. I, pp. 264–5.
2. Churchill, *The World Crisis*, I, pp. 268–9.
3. Raleigh, *The War in the Air*, I, pp. 375–6.
4. IWM SR 14914, Eric Beauman.
5. IWM DOCS, Miss W.L.B. Tower, extended transcript of journal for 1914–1915, p. 18.
6. Quoted in IWM DOCS, Misc. 89 (1294), John Hook, unpublished book, 'They Come! They Come!', 2nd ed. (1989), p. 16.
7. Donald, SR 18, Reel 6.
8. IWM DOCS, Captain H.C. Meysey-Thompson, diary, April 1915.
9. IWM DOCS, Holcombe Ingleby MP, letter from his wife Jane to his son Clement, 12 August 1915.
10. Reginald Warneford, Combat Report, completed 8 June 1915, quoted in Mary Gibson, *Warneford VC*, (Yeovil: Friends of the Fleet Air Arm Museum, 1979), pp. 99–100.
11. Alfred Muller quoted in Gibson, *Warneford VC*, p. 89.
12. Quoted in Misc. 1294, Hook, 'They Come! They Come!', pp. 35–6.
13. Quoted in Misc. 1294, Hook, 'They Come! They Come!', p. 47.
14. Quoted in Misc. 1294, Hook, 'They Come! They Come!', pp. 47–8.
15. Quoted in Misc. 1294, Hook, 'They Come! They Come!', p. 47.
16. IWM DOCS, W.A. Phillips, letter, 9 September 1915.
17. IWM DOCS, J.H. Stapley, letter, 5 October 1915.
18. A. Rawlinson, *Defence of London: 1915–1918*, (London: Andrew Melrose Ltd, 1923), pp. 23–4.
19. Rawlinson, *Defence of London*, pp. 27–8.
20. Quoted in Misc. 1294, Hook, 'They Come! They Come!', p. 63.
21. Sir John Slessor, *The Central Blue, Recollections and Reflections*, (London: Cassell, 1956), p. 11.
22. Slessor, *The Central Blue*, p. 12.
23. Kapitanleutnant Breithaupt quoted in Jones, *The War in the Air*, II, p. 133.
24. Slessor, *The Central Blue*, p. 13.
25. IWM SR, John Slessor, SR 3176, Reel 3.
26. IWM DOCS, R.J. Smith, letter from his sister Christine, 14 October 1915.
27. IWM DOCS,, Lieutenant D.Y. (Denis) Wheatley, letter from Charles De Lacy, 18 October 1915.
28. Quoted in Jones, *The War in the Air*, VI, p. 118.
29. Harris, SR 3765, Reel 1.
30. IWM DOCS, Mrs M. Dayrell-Browning, letter, 4 September 1916.
31. William Leefe Robinson, quoted in Jones, *The War in the Air*, II, pp. 224–5.
32. IWM DOCS, Lieutenant W. Leefe Robinson VC, transcription of letter to parents, 22 October 1916.
33. Dayrell-Browning, letter, 4 September 1916.
34. IWM DOCS, Misc. 186 (2804), letter from Patrick Blundstone to his father, 3 September 1916.

35. W.J. Tempest, quoted in Jones, *The War in the Air*, II, pp. 237–8.
36. Leefe Robinson VC, letter, 22 October 1916.
37. IWM SR 331, Sybil Morrison, Reel 3.
38. IWM SR 4048, Egbert Cadbury, Reel 1.

CHAPTER EIGHT   Naval Aviation

1. IWM SR 7255, Hugh Burroughes, Reel 3.
2. IWM SR 38, J.S. Middleton, Reel 2.
3. IWM SR 998, Thomas Elmhurst, Reel 1.
4. IWM SR 311, Frederick Verry, Reel 1.
5. IWM SR 303, Victor Goddard, Reel 14.
6. Verry, SR 311, Reel 1.
7. Goddard, SR 303, Reel 14.
8. Goddard, SR 303, Reel 14.
9. Goddard, SR 303, Reel 14.
10. Goddard, SR 303, Reel 14.
11. IWM SR 313, Thomas Williams, Reel 1.
12. Verry, SR 311, Reel 1.
13. Williams, SR 313, Reel 1.
14. Williams, SR 313, Reel 1.
15. IWM SR 298, George Stubbington, Reel 3.
16. Donald, SR 18, Reels 7 and 8.
17. Donald, SR 18, Reel 9.
18. F. Silwood, SR 317, Reel 1.
19. Thomas Thomson, SR 309, Reel 6.
20. Silwood, SR 317, Reel 1.
21. Silwood, SR 317, Reel 1.
22. Stubbington, SR 298.
23. Goddard, SR 303, Reel 14.
24. IWM SR 19, William Hawkins, Reel 2.
25. IWM DOCS, Admiral Sir Richard Phillimore, papers include Combat Report written by Captain William Dickson RAF, 19 July 1918.
26. Phillimore, Combat Report written by Captain Bernard Smart RAF, 19 July 1918.
27. Phillimore, Combat Report written by Captain W.D. Jackson, 19 July 1918.
28. Phillimore, Combat Report written by Captain William Dickson, 19 July 1918.
29. Donald, SR 18, Reel 10 and additional notes in transcript.
30. Donald, SR 18, Reel 10 and additional notes in transcript.
31. Donald, SR 18, Reel 10 and additional notes in transcript.
32. Donald, SR 18, Reel 10 and additional notes in transcript.

CHAPTER NINE   1917

1. Rowell, memoir, pp. 22–3.
2. William Bishop VC, *Winged Warfare*, (London: Hodder and Stoughton, 1918), p. 33.
3. Bishop VC, *Winged Warfare*, pp. 43–5.
4. Bishop VC, *Winged Warfare*, pp. 63–4.
5. W.A. Molesworth, letter quoted by Alan (Jack) Scott, *Sixty Squadron, RAF: 1916–1919*, (London: Greenhill Books, 1920), pp. 50–3.

6. IWM DOCS, Wing Commander N. Macmillan, extensive papers concerning First World War aviation, including transcribed notes of Frank Courtney.
7. Scott, *Sixty Squadron, RAF*, p. 45.
8. IWM SR 4060, H.N. Charles, Reel 1.
9. T.B. Marson, *Scarlet and Khaki*, (London: Jonathan Cape, 1930), p. 144.
10. Marson, *Scarlet and Khaki*, pp. 143–4.
11. RAF Museum, Edward Mannock VC, diary, 20 April 1917.
12. Mannock VC, diary, 3 May 1917.
13. Mannock VC, diary, 9 May 1917.
14. Mannock VC, diary, 14 June 1917.
15. Mannock VC, diary, 7 June 1917.
16. Mannock VC, diary, 20 July 1917.
17. Mannock VC, diary, 19 August 1917.
18. William MacLanachan, *Fighter Pilot*, (London: Newnes), pp. 223–4.
19. Hugh Trenchard quoted in Jones, *The War in the Air*, IV, pp. 133–4.
20. Hughes, diary, 18 June 1917.
21. Donald, SR 18, additional notes in transcript.
22. Yuille, SR 320, Reel 4.
23. IWM SR 13, George Eddington, Reel 5.
24. IWM SR 7462, Frederick Winterbotham, Reel 1.
25. IWM SR 5, Leslie Briggs, Reels 1 and 2.
26. IWM DOCS, Lieutenant J.S. Walthew RFC, letter, 31 July 1917.
27. Eddington, SR 13, Reels 5 and 6.
28. IWM SR 9470, H.N. Wrigley, Reel 2.
29. IWM SR 6, Charles Burne.
30. IWM SR 4173, Norman Macmillan, Reel 1.
31. McCudden VC, *Five Years in the Royal Flying Corps*, p. 194.
32. McCudden VC, *Five Years in the Royal Flying Corps*, p. 195.
33. Arthur Rhys Davids quoted in H.A. Jones, *The War in the Air*, IV, p. 189.
34. McCudden VC, *Five Years in the Royal Flying Corps*, p. 195.
35. Arthur Gould Lee, *No Parachute*, (London: The Adventurers Club, 1969), pp. 162–3.
36. Gould Lee, *No Parachute*, pp. 162–3.

CHAPTER TEN   Dawn Patrol

1. Macmillan, SR 4173, Reel 1.
2. Arthur Rhys Davids, letter to mother, 22 April 1917, quoted in Alex Revell, *Brief Glory: The Life of Arthur Rhys Davids*, (London: Kimber, 1984), pp. 138–9.
3. McCudden VC, *Five Years in the Royal Flying Corps*, p. 175.
4. Lewis, SR 4162, Reel 1.
5. Bishop VC, *Winged Warfare*, pp. 72–3.
6. King, SR 27, Reel 8.
7. IWM SR 15736, Ernest Tomkins, Reel 5.
8. Macmillan, SR 4173, Reel 1.
9. Lewis, SR 4162, Reel 1.
10. IWM SR 11308, Gwilym Lewis, Reel 4.
11. Macmillan papers, extract from the diary of R.J. Brownell, 9 September 1917.
12. Macmillan, SR 4173, Reel 1.
13. Bishop VC, *Winged Warfare*, pp. 231–2.
14. Cecil Lewis, SR 4162, Reel 1.
15. Macmillan, SR 4173, Reel 1.
16. Cecil Lewis, SR 4162, Reel 1.

17. MacLanachan, *Fighter Pilot*, pp. 25–6.
18. Sykes, SR 301, Reel 6.
19. Sykes, SR 301, Reel 6.
20. IWM SR 9463, George Jones, Reel 1.
21. Ira Jones, *King of Air Fighters*, (London: Greenhill Books, 1989), p. 150.
22. Ira Jones, *Tiger Squadron*, (London: White Lion, 1972), p. 84.
23. James, SR 24, Reel 15.
24. Elliott Springs, *Diary of an Unknown Aviator*, (London: John Hamilton, [1927]), pp. 235–6.
25. IWM SR 10387, Sardar Malik, Reel 1.
26. Verschoyle Cronyn quoted in Alex Revell, *High in the Empty Blue*, (Mountain View: Flying Machines Press, 1995), p. 166.
27. Jones, SR 9463, Reel 1.
28. Grinnell-Milne, *Wind in the Wires*, p. 138.
29. IWM SR 308, Herbert Thompson, Reel 1.

CHAPTER ELEVEN   Gothas

1. Chabot, SR 8, Reel 13.
2. Quoted in Misc 1294, Hook, 'They Come! They Come!', p. 119.
3. Quoted in Misc. 1294, Hook, 'They Come! They Come!', p. 124.
4. Quoted in Misc. 1294, Hook, 'They Come! They Come!', p. 120.
5. McCudden VC, *Five Years in the Royal Flying Corps*, pp. 151–2.
6. Hopkins, SR 47, Reel 6.
7. McCudden VC, *Five Years in the Royal Flying Corps*, pp. 154–6.
8. Douglas Haig, quoted in Jones, *The War in the Air*, V, pp. 38–9.
9. Sir William Robertson quoted in Jones, *The War in the Air*, V, pp. 39–40.
10. IWM DOCS, A.T. Wilkinson, memoir, pp. 3–4.
11. Jan Smuts, quoted in Cooper, *Birth of Independent Air Power*, p. 103.
12. IWM DOCS, Mrs C.G. Knollys, letter, 25 September 1917.
13. IWM DOCS, Sir Clive Morrison-Bell, letter from his wife, 3 October 1917.
14. IWM DOCS, Lady Burford-Hancock, notebook recording her experiences 1917–18.
15. Anon., 'In a German Airship over England', (*Journal of the Royal United Services Institute*, Vol. LXXI, London, 1926).
16. Anon., 'In a German Airship over England', (*Journal of RUSI*, Vol. LXXI).
17. IWM SR 4223, Karl Schutz.
18. Anon., 'In a German Airship over England', (*Journal of RUSI*, Vol. LXXI).
19. Anon., 'In a German Airship over England', (*Journal of RUSI*, Vol. LXXI).
20. Schutz, SR 4223.
21. Chabot, SR 8, Reel 13.
22. Rawlinson, *Defence of London*, pp. 222–3.
23. Cadbury, SR 4048, Reel 1.

CHAPTER TWELVE   On the Ground

1. IWM SR 4081, Percy Douglas, Reel 1.
2. Cecil Lewis, SR 4162, Reel 1.
3. Jackson, SR 23, Reel 3.
4. Wyllie, diary, 19 June 1916.
5. Macmillan papers, article by Stauton Waltho, 'Dud Day'.

6. Walthew, letter, 31 August 1917.
7. McCudden VC, *Five Years in the Royal Flying Corps*, p. 199.
8. W. E. Johns quoted in Peter Ellis & Jennifer Schofiel, *Biggles! The Life Story of W E Johns*, (Godmanstone: Veloce, 1993), p. 58.
9. Arthur Rhys Davids, letter to Mother, 22 April 1917, quoted in Alex Revell, *Brief Glory*, p. 91.
10. Charles, SR 4060, Reel 1.
11. Arthur Rhys Davids, letter to Mother, 18 April 1917, quoted in Alex Revell, *Brief Glory*, p. 89.
12. A. R. Kingsford, *Night Raiders of the Air*, (London: Greenhill Books, 1988), pp. 142–144.
13. Macmillan papers, Waltho article, 'Dud Day'.
14. Elliott Springs, *War Birds*, p. 210.
15. Cecil Lewis, SR 4162, Reel 1.
16. F. T. Nettlingham, *Tommy's Tunes*, (London: Erskine Macdonald Ltd, 1917), p. 76.
17. Jones, *King of the Air Fighters*, p. 208.
18. Baring, *Flying Corps Headquarters*, p. 231.
19. Grinnell-Milne, *Wind in the Wires*, pp. 234–235.
20. Powell, SR 87.
21. Field, SR 11376, Reel 11.
22. Jones, *King of the Air Fighters*, p. 206.
23. Hughes, diary, 3 October 1917.
24. Macmillan papers, extract from diary of R. J. Brownell, 16 November 1917.
25. Elliott Springs, *War Birds*, p. 179.
26. Elliott Springs, *War Birds*, pp. 188–190.
27. Gwilym Lewis, SR 11308, Reel 2.
28. Rogers, SR 171, Reel 2.
29. Walthew, letter to his mother from Reverend P. H. Wilson.
30. Powell, SR 87, Reel 8.
31. Saunders, SR 292, Reel 1.
32. Eddington, SR 13, Reels 5 & 6.
33. Eddington, SR 13, Reels 5 & 6.
34. Verschoyle Cronyn quoted in Alex Revell, *High in the Empty Blue*, p. 166.
35. Sir Gordon Taylor, *Sopwith 7309*, (London: Cassell, 1968), p. 85.
36. Saunders, SR 292, Reel 6.
37. King, SR 27, Reel 8.
38. Taylor, *Sopwith 7309*, pp 3–4.

CHAPTER THIRTEEN   1918

1. McCudden VC, *Five Years in the Royal Flying Corps*, p. 240.
2. McCudden VC, *Five Years in the Royal Flying Corps*, p. 235.
3. McCudden VC, *Five Years in the Royal Flying Corps*, pp. 240–2.
4. Lewis, *Wings over the Somme*, p. 103.
5. Lewis, *Wings over the Somme*, p. 99.
6. McCudden VC, *Five Years in the Royal Flying Corps*, pp. 254–6.
7. McCudden VC, *Five Years in the Royal Flying Corps*, pp. 264–5.
8. McCudden VC, *Five Years in the Royal Flying Corps*, p. 254.
9. McCudden VC, *Five Years in the Royal Flying Corps*, pp. 256–7.
10. McCudden VC, *Five Years in the Royal Flying Corps*, p. 271.

11. McCudden VC, *Five Years in the Royal Flying Corps*, p. 274.
12. IWM SR 4151, Gustav Lachman, Reel 1.
13. Vivian Voss, *Flying Minnows*, (London: Arms and Armour Press, 1977), p. 136.
14. Fritz Nagel, '*Fritz*', (West Virginia: Der Angriff Publications, 1981), p. 77.
15. Hopkins, SR 47, Reel 4.
16. Hopkins, SR 47, Reel 1.
17. IWM SR 3167, Aubrey Ellwood, Reel 1.
18. Wilfred May, letter, 9 March 1950, quoted in Peter Kilduff, *Richthofen: Beyond the Legend of the Red Baron*, (London: Arms and Armour, 1993), p. 203.
19. Joachim Wolff, quoted in Kilduff, *Richthofen*, p. 201.
20. Roy Brown, Combat Report, 21 April 1918, quoted in Kilduff, *Richthofen*, p. 203.
21. IWM SR 9468, Jack Treacy, Reel 2.
22. Edward Mannock quoted in Peter Vansittart (ed.), *Voices from the Great War*, (London: Penguin Books, 1963), p. 230.
23. Gwilym Lewis, SR 11308, Reel 3.
24. Jones, *Tiger Squadron*, p. 65.
25. Jones, *King of the Air Fighters*, pp. 163–4.
26. Jones, *King of the Air Fighters*, pp. 195–6.
27. Jones, *Tiger Squadron*, p. 93.
28. Jones, *Tiger Squadron*, p. 108.
29. Gwilym Lewis, SR 11308, Reel 3.
30. Donald Inglis, Combat Report quoted in Ira Jones, *King of the Air Fighters*, pp. 252–3.
31. RAF Museum, Edward Naulls, Letter to Editor of *Strand* magazine, 1 November 1943.
32. James Van Ira quoted in Ira Jones, *King of the Air Fighters*, pp. 251–2.
33. Malcolm McGregor quoted in G.H. Cunningham, *Mac's Memoirs*, (Wellington: A.H. and A.W. Reed, 1937), p. 63.
34. Rudolf Stark, *Wings of War*, (London: Arms and Armour Press, 1973), p. 81.
35. Hopkins, SR 47, Reel 3.
36. Hopkins, SR 47, Reel 3.
37. Hopkins, SR 47, Reel 5.
38. Yuille, SR 320, Reel 4.
39. Yuille, SR 320, Reel 4.
40. Sykes, SR 301, Reel 5.
41. Burslem, SR 7, Reel 2.
42. Sykes, SR 301, Reel 6.
43. IWM SR 4233, Ralph Silk, Reel 1.
44. Gascoyne, SR 16, Reel 3.
45. Gascoyne, SR 16, Reel 4.
46. Strange, *Recollections of an Airman*, pp. 187–9.
47. IWM SR 9466, Frank Roberts, Reel 1.
48. W.E. Johns quoted in Peter Ellis and Jennifer Schofiel, *Biggles!*, p. 88.
49. IWM SR 4224, Roy Shillinglaw.
50. Shillinglaw, SR 4224.
51. IWM SR 4122, Herbe Haase, Reel 1.
52. Diary, 18 August 1918, quoted in Cooper, *Birth of Independent Air Power*, p. 136.
53. Voss, *Flying Minnows*, p. 289.

54. IWM DOCS, Captain O. Smith, letter to his parents from his brother, Second Lieutenant A. Smith, 12 November 1918.
55. IWM SR 14910, Philip Townshend, Reel 1.

CHAPTER FOURTEEN   Aftermath

1. W.E. Johns quoted in Ellis and Schofiel, *Biggles!*, p. 70.
2. Wells, *The War in the Air*, p. 8.
3. IWM SR 6833, Sophie Satin, Reel 3.

Bibliography

The authors would like to thank all of those who have given permission for these sources to be used. In particular they would like to acknowledge those individuals who hold the copyright of the collections of unpublished papers held in the Imperial War Museum. Every effort has been made to obtain permission from the relevant copyright holders. But where this has not been possible, the authors would be pleased to hear via the Museum from anyone with whom contact has not been established.

Published sources

Anon., *A Short History of the Royal Air Force*, (London: Air Ministry, 1929).

Anon., *In a German Airship over England*, (Royal United Services Journal, Vol. LXXI, London, 1926).

Anon., *War Flying: The intimate record of a pilot*, (London: John Murray, 1917).

Baring, Maurice, *Flying Corps Headquarters, 1914–1918*, (Whitstable: Blackwood, 1968).

Barker, Ralph, *The Royal Flying Corps in France: From Mons to the Somme*, (London: Constable, 1994).

Barker, Ralph, *The Royal Flying Corps in France: From Bloody April 1917 to Final Victory*, (London: Constable, 1995).

Bickers, Richard, *The First Great Air War*, (London: Coronet, 1989).

Bishop VC, William, *Winged Warfare*, (London: Hodder and Stoughton, 1918).

Bishop, W. Arthur, *The Courage of the Early Morning: The story of Billy Bishop*, (London: Heinemann, 1966).

Bott, Alan, *Cavalry of the Clouds*, (New York: Doubleday Page and Company, 1918).

Bowyer, Chaz, *Albert Ball, VC*, 2nd ed., (Wrexham: Bridge Books, 1994).

Bowyer, Chaz, *Handley Page Bombers of the First World War*, (Bourne End: Aston, 1992).

Boyle, Andrew, *Trenchard*, (London: Collins, 1962).

Bruce, J.M., *Britain's First Warplanes*, (Poole: Arms and Armour, 1987).

Castle, H.G., *Fire over England: The German Air Raids of World War One*, (London: Leo Cooper, 1982).

Churchill, Winston, *The World Crisis, 1911–1918*, (London: Odhams Press, 1938) Vol. I.

Cole, Christopher, *McCudden VC*, (London: Kimber, 1967).

Cole, Christopher, ed, *RFC Communiqués 1915–1916*, (London: Kimber, 1969)

Cooper, Malcolm, *Birth of Independent Air Power*, (London: Allen & Unwin, 1986).

Cunningham, G.H., *Mac's Memoirs*, (Wellington: A.H. and A.W. Reed, 1937).

Dudgeon, James, *'Mick': The story of Major Edward Mannock*, (London: Robert Hale, 1981).

Ellis, Peter & Jennifer Schofiel, *Biggles! The Life Story of W.E. Johns*, (Godmanstone: Veloce, 1993).

Farrar-Hockley, General Sir Anthony, *The Army in the Air*, (Stroud: Alan Sutton Publishing/Army Air Corps, 1994).

Gibson, Mary, *Warneford VC*, (Yeovil: Friends of the Fleet Air Arm Museum, 1979).

Gollin, Alfred, *No Longer an Island*, (London: Heinemann, 1984).

Grinnell-Milne, Duncan, *Wind in the Wires*, (London: John Hamilton Ltd, nd).

Harper, Harry, *My Fifty Years in Flying*, (London: Associated Newspapers, 1956).

Hartney, Harold, *Wings over France*, (Folkestone: Bailey Brothers, 1974).

Harvey, W.J., *Rovers of the Night Sky*, (London: Greenhill Books, 1984).

Hawker, Tyrrel, *Hawker V.C.*, (London: Mitre Press, 1965).

Henshaw, Trevor, *The Sky their Battlefield*, (London: Grub Street, 1995).

Heydemarck, Haupt, *Double Decker C666*, (London: John Hamilton, nd).

Immelmann, Franz, *Immelmann: The Eagle of Lille*, (London: John Hamilton, nd).

Imrie, Alex, *Pictorial History of the German Air Service, 1914–1918*, (London: Ian Allen, 1971).

Insall, A.J., *Observer: Memoirs of the RFC, 1915–1918*, (London: William Kimber, 1970).

von Ishover, Arnanad, *The Fall of an Eagle: The life of Fighter Ace Ernst Udet*, (London: Kimber, 1979).

Jones, Ira, *Tiger Squadron*, (London: White Lion, 1972).

Jones, Ira, *King of the Air Fighters*, (London: Greenhill Books, 1989).

Jones, Ira, *An Air Fighter's Scrapbook*, (London: Greenhill Books, 1990).

Kilduff, Peter, *Richthofen: Beyond the Legend of the Red Baron*, (London: Arms and Armour, 1993).

Kilduff, Peter (trans. and ed.), *Germany's Last Knight of the Air: The memoirs of Major Carl Degelow*, (London: Kimber, 1979).

Kingsford, A.R., *Night Raiders of the Air*, (London: Greenhill Books, 1988).

Layman, R.D., *The Cuxhaven Raid*, (London: Conway Maritime Press, 1985).

Layman, R.D., *Before the Aircraft Carrier*, (London: Conway Maritime Press, 1989).

Lee, Arthur Gould, *No Parachute*, (London: The Adventurers Club, 1969).

Lewis, Cecil, *Sagittarius Rising*, (London: Penguin Books, 1985).

Lewis, Gwilym, *Wings Over the Somme*, (Wrexham: Bridge Books, 1994).

McCudden, Major James T.B., VC DSO MC MM, *Five Years in the Royal Flying Corps*, (London: Aeroplane and General, 1918).

McInnes, I. and Webb, J.W., *A Contemptible Little Flying Corps*, (London: London Stamp Exchange, 1991).

MacLanachan, William, *Fighter Pilot*, (London: Newnes, nd).

Macmillan, Norman, *Into the Blue*, (London: Jarrolds, 1969).

Macmillan, Norman, *Sefton Brancker*, (London: Heinemann, 1935).

Marson, T.B., *Scarlet and Khaki*, (London: Jonathan Cape, 1930).

Mead, Peter, *The Eye in the Air*, (London: HMSO, 1983).

Meijering, Piet Hein, *Signed With Their Honour*, (Edinburgh: Mainstream Publishing, 1987).

Middleton, Edgar, *The Great War in the Air*, (London: Waverley, 1920).

Morris, Alan, *Bloody April*, (London: Jarrolds, 1967).

Morris, Alan, *First of the Many*, (London: Jarrolds, 1968).

Morris, Joseph, *The German Air Raids*, (Dallington: Naval and Military Press, 1993).

Morrison, Frank, *War on the Great Cities*, (London: Faber, 1937).

Muddock, J. Preston, *All Clear: The Story of the London Special Constabulary, 1914–1919*, (London, 1919).

Nagel, Fritz, *'Fritz'*, (West Virginia: Der Angriff Publications, 1981).

Nettlingham, F.T., *Tommy's Tunes*, (London: Erskine Macdonald Ltd, 1917).

Norris, Geoffrey, *The Royal Flying Corps*, (London: Frederick Muller Ltd, 1965).

Oughton, Frederick and Vernon Smyth, *Ace with One Eye: The Story of Mick Mannock*, (London: F. Muller Ltd, 1963).

Paris, Michael, *Winged Warfare*, (Manchester: MUP, 1992).

Powers, Barry D. *Strategy Without Slide-Rule*, (London: Croom Helm, 1976).

Raleigh, Sir Walter, and H.A. Jones, *The War in the Air*, 6. Vols (Oxford: The Clarendon Press, 1922–1937).

Rawlinson, A., *Defence of London, 1915–1918*, (London: Andrew Melrose Ltd, 1923).

Revell, Alex, *Brief Glory: The Life of Arthur Rhys Davids*, (London: Kimber, 1984).

Revell, Alex, *High in the Empty Blue*, (Mountain View: Flying Machines Press, 1995).

von Richthofen, Manfred, *Red Air Fighter*, (London: Greenhill Books, 1990).

Rochford, Leonard, *I Chose the Sky*, (London: Kimber, 1977).

Scott, Alan (Jack), *Sixty Squadron, RAF, 1916–1919*, (London: Heinemann, 1920).

Sheffield, G.D., *The Pictorial History of World War I*, (London: Bison Books, 1987).

Slessor, Sir John, *The Central Blue, Recollections and Reflections*, (London: Cassell, 1956).

Springs, Elliott, *Diary of an Unknown Aviator*, (London: John Hamilton, [1927]).

Stark, Rudolf, *Wings of War*, (London: Arms and Armour Press, 1973).

Strange, Lieutenant Colonel Louis, DSO MC DFC, *Recollections of an Airman*, (London: The Aviation Book Club, 1940).

Taylor, John, *C.F.S.: Birthplace of Airpower*, (London: Putnam, 1958).

Tennant, J.E., *In the Clouds above Baghdad*, (London: Cecil Palmer, 1920).

Tredery, F.D., *Pioneer Pilot*, (London: Peter Davies, 1976).

Voss, Vivian, *Flying Minnows*, (London: Arms and Armour Press, 1977).

Whitehouse, Arch, *The Fledgeling*, (London: Nicholas Vane, 1965).

Whitehouse, Arch, *Fire over England*, (London: Robert Hale, 1968).

Wilson, Trevor, *The Myriad Faces of War*, (Cambridge: Polity Press, 1988).

'Wing Adjutant', *The Royal Flying Corps in the War*, (London: Cassell, 1918).

Woodman, Harry, *Early Aircraft Armament*, (London: Arms and Armour, 1989).

Wynn, Humphrey, *Darkness shall cover me: Night bombing over the Western Front, 1918*, (Shrewsbury: Airlife, 1989).

Unpublished Manuscript Sources

1. Imperial War Museum, Department of Documents

Burford-Hancock, Lady

Dayrell-Browning, Mrs M.

Evans, J.O.

Gibbs, Captain A.

Hughes, Lieutenant T. McK.

Ingleby, Holcombe, MP

Knollys, Mrs C.G.

Leefe Robinson VC, Lieutenant W.

Macmillan, Wing Commander N.

Meysey-Thompson, Captain H.C.
Morrison-Bell, Sir Clive
Phillimore, Admiral Sir Richard
Phillips, W.A.
Read, Major W.R.
Rowell, Sir Robin
Smith, Captain O.
Smith, R.J.
Stapley, J.H.
Tower, Miss W.L.B.
Walthew, Lieutenant J.S., RFC
Wheatley, Lieutenant D.Y.
Wilkinson, A.T.
Wyllie, Lieutenant Colonel H., RAF
Misc. 89 (1294): John Hook, unpublished book, 'They Come! They Come!', 2nd ed. (1984).
Misc. 186 (2804): letter from Patrick Blundstone.

2. Royal Air Force Museum

Mannock VC, Major Edward (Diary, 1917)
Naulls, Edward, Letter to Editor of *Strand* magazine, 1 November 1943.

Unpublished Oral Sources

Imperial War Museum, Sound Archive

Allan, Agnes 517
Andrews, Howard 984
Argent, William 12346
Arthur, John 13875
Bates, Norman 10262
Beard, Charles 10642
Beauman, Eric 14914
Beeton, Arthur 8323
Berry, William 1
Bilney, Christopher 2
Bolt, Edward 3
Boon, John 9476
Bremner, Donald 4
Brice, George 10266
Briggs, Leslie 5
Bristow, Philip 13718
Burne, Charles 6
Burroughes, Hugh 7255
Burslem, Frank 7
Cadbury, Egbert 4048
Chabot, Charles 8
Chabot, Charles 4055
Chadwick, Albert 9654
Charles, H.N. 4060

Chitty, John 11114
Clappen, Donald 9
Collins, F. Adams 10
Coombes, Laurie 9460
Coryton, William 3190
Cross, Arthur 12255
Dickson, William 3168
Donald, Graham 18
Douglas, Percy 4081
Eastgate, Charles 11343
Eddington, George 13
Ellwood, Aubrey 3167
Elmhirst, Thomas 998
Field, Laurie 11376
Frey, Richard 4109
Fuljames, Reginald 14
Furlong, Eric 15
Gascoyne, James 16
Gedge, William 15251
Goddard, Victor 303
Gordon-Burge, C. 17
Haase, Herbe 4122
Haig, Fred 9461
Haire, Ernest 10401
Hallam, Grace 3160
Hancock, Ernest 8950
Harris, Arthur 3765
Harrison, Hubert 10916
Hawkins, William 19
Hillman, Charles 9462
Holdstock, Henry 20
Hopkins, J.C.F. 21
Humberstone, Ernest 22
Hyams, Gordon 10409
Jackson, Alan 23
James, Archibald 24
Jones, George 9463
Joubert de la Ferté, Philip 4143
Kemp, Leslie 26
Kidd, Dixie 15714
King, Cecil 27
Lachman, Gustav 4151
Leigh, Humphrey 37
Lewis, Cecil 4162
Lewis, Gwilym 11308
Lewis, Gwilym 14912
Livock, Gerald 7042
Long, Francis 4799
Lubbert, Friederich 4167
MacDonald, Doris 14916
Macmillan, Norman 4173
Malik, Sardar H.S. 10387
Mann, Conrad 28
Mapplebeck, Thomas 9857

Middleton, J.S. 38
Morrison, Sybil 331
Murton, Leslie 15252
Ostler, Walter 39
Pentland, Jerry 9464
Pope, Edwin 8272
Powell, F.J. 87
Rabagliati, C.E.C. 4208
Rickner (Mr) 4213
Roberts, Eric 9465
Roberts, Frank 9466
Rogers, T.E. 171
Salmon, Donald 15250
Sanders, Henry 4648
Saunders, S.S. 292
Schutz, Karl 4223
Shaw, C.K. 4226
Shepherd, Dolly 904
Shepherd, Dolly 579
Shillinglaw, Roy 4224
Silk, Ralph 4233
Silwood, F.D. 317
Stowell, L.H. 319
Stubbington, Henry 298
Sutherland, Colin 9467
Sykes, Ronald 301
Tapp, Russell 9627
Taylor, Harold 307
Thompson, Herbert 308
Thomson, Thomas 309
Tomkins, Ernest 12197
Tomkins, Ernest 14227
Tomkins, Ernest 15736
Towler, T.S. 4251
Townshend, Philip 14910
Treacy, Jack 9468
Tripp, Leonard 13546
Tye, Charles 310
Verry, Frederick 311
Wardrop, W.E.D. 29
Whitehouse, Arthur 7036
Wilkinson, John 12967
Williams, Richard 9469
Williams, Thomas 313
Winterbotham, Frederick 7462
Woolley, Edgar 316
Wright, Ernest James 4891
Wrigley, H.N. 9470
Yuille, Archibald 320

Index

Aboukir, HMS, 176
'aces', 125, 242–3, 314, 326, 328
Addison, 1st Viscount, (Minister of
   Munitions), 269
Admiralty: airship research and development,
   6, 175; conflict for resources, 64; aircraft
   design, 110; relationship with War Office,
   134, 141, 162; aerial defence plans, 141;
   relationship with Air Board, 163–4;
   merchant shipping policy, 260
Advisory Committee for Aeronautics, 9, 15
Aerial Navigation Sub-committee, 6, 9, 175
Aeroplane Company, RE, 13–14
Africa, HMS, 184
ailerons, balanced, 17
Air Battalion, RE, 12–14, 16, 22
   Airship Company, 22
   2(Aeroplane) Company, 13–14
Air Board, 162, 164, 261–2, 269, 273–4
Air Committee, 15, 161
Air Council, 274
Air Force (Constitution) Bill, 274
Air Ministry, 307
Air Organisation Committee, 273
air-raid warnings, 270
aircraft: burning, 254–5; carriers, 191–6, 199;
   construction, 58; design, 17, 42–3, 70,
   103–7, 202; losses, 33–4; production, 202;
   trainer, 82; wind dangers, 34–5
Aircraft Manufacturing Company, 106
Airship Company, RE, 22
airships: Admiralty and War Office research
   funding, 6–7; 'blimp' nickname, 182;
   bomb capacity, 183–4; British naval, 175–7;
   British research, 8–9; German threat,
   19–20; recruits, 177–8; training, 178–82;
   Zeppelin's work, 4, 6, 140
Aisne: German retreat to (1914), 33; Battle of
   the, 46, 55; 1917 offensive, 200, 209
Albatross aircraft: first RFC encounter, 29;
   RFC encounters, 126, 217, 235, 252, 314;
   superiority of, 131, 204
Albatross D I, 131–3, 135, 202
Albatross D II, 202
Albatross D III, 211, 219
Alcock, John, 350
Aldis sight, 253

'All Clear', 270–1
Amiens: aircraft park, 24, 25; German
   advance (1918), 319
Amiens, Battle of (1918), 330
Ancre, 1917 assault plans, 201
Andrews, Howard, (RFC), 98–9
anti-aircraft guns: 'Archibald', 55–8; coastal
   batteries, 260; German, 55–8, 129–30, 317,
   331–2; home defence, 144–5, 146, 147,
   169–70, 260, 281, 285; mobile, 146, 154,
   159–60, 164
Antoinette Monoplane, 17
Antwerp, Zeppelin base, 143
'Archibald', *see also* anti-aircraft 55–6
Armistice, 344, 345–6
Army Aircraft Factory, (later Royal Aircraft
   Factory), 10, 15, 18
Army Council, 64, 261
Army Estimates, 22
Army Manoeuvres (1912), 48
Arras, 1917 offensive, 201, 206, 207, 209,
   211, 219
artillery: aerial observation, 44, 48–50,
   68, 99, 113, 138, 225, 348; Somme
   bombardment, 117
Ashmore, Lieutenant Colonel (later Brigadier
   General) Edward, (First Wing, RFC, IV
   Brigade, RFC), 43, 65, 116, 270
Asquith, Herbert (British Prime Minister), 6,
   11, 14, 159, 161–2, 164
Astra-Torres airship, 176
Aubers Ridge, attack on (9 May 1915), 53
Australian Flying Corps (AFC), 231, 339,
   254, 259, 322, 339–40
Aviatik aircraft, 63, 108
Avro aircraft, 24, 38, 90
Avro 504 K, 90

Balfour, Sir Arthur, (First Lord of the
   Admiralty), 163–4
Balfour, Harold, (RFC), 91
Ball, Captain Albert, VC, (60 Squadron
   RFC): combat technique, 123–5, 207,
   212–13, 218; reputation, 214, 240;
   decorations, 125, 214, 328; improvements
   to SE5, 212; death, 213–14
Balloon Establishment, 7

Balloon Factory, 7–10, 175
Balloon School, 9, 13
Balloon Sections, 7
balloons: airship training role, 178–80; defence role, 278; history of army use, 7; kite balloons, 102, 117, 174–5, 207–8
Bannerman, Lieutenant Colonel Sir Alexander, (OC Air Battalion, RE), 13
barbed-wire, 113
Baring, Captain (later Lieutenant Colonel) Maurice, (RFC Headquarters), 65–7, 135, 295
Barker, Captain William VC, (28 Squadron RFC), 256
Barlow, Air Mechanic Keith, (3 Squadron RFC), 25
Barrington-Kennett, Lieutenant B.H., (Military Wing, RFC), 20
Barrow-in-Furness, dirigible development, 175
Battlecruiser Fleet, 184, 187
battleships, 199
BE2 aircraft, 18, 24, 25
BE2 A aircraft, 29
BE2 C aircraft: success, 18; stability and manoeuvrability, 42, 71, 230; adopted as standard RFC machine, 42–3; Fokker contests, 71, 108, 136; bombing raids, 122, 131–2; anti-Zeppelin duties, 156, 173; SS Airship construction, 176; obsolescent, 202; role, 348
BE2 E aircraft, 202, 282
BE8 aircraft, 24
BE9 aircraft, 104
BE12 aircraft, 134
Beardmore engines, 105
Beatty, Vice Admiral Sir David, (Battlecruiser Fleet), 187
Beatty School of Flying, 82
Beauman, Flight Sub Lieutenant Eric, (Hendon Flight, London Air Defence, RNAS), 144
Begbie, Lieutenant S.C.H., (74 Squadron RAF), 254–5
Bell, Gordon, 33
Below, General Fritz von, (Headquarters, German Second Army), 129
Bertrab, Leutnant von, Iron Cross, (German Air Service), 217
Bilney, Christopher, (RFC), 84
Bishop, Lieutenant (later Major) William VC, (60 Squadron RFC, 85 Squadron RFC): formation flying, 204–5; first dogfight, 205–6; escort duty, 206–7; flying skill, 218; reputation, 240; marksmanship, 243; combat technique, 248, 326; command of 85 Squadron, 298, 298–9, 326–7; drinking, 298–9, 326
Black, Sir John, (Director of Contracts, Admiralty), 176

Blair Atholl, test flights, 8, 9
Blériot, Louis, 5
Blériot aircraft, 24, 35, 45
Blériot Experimental (BE), 10
'blimp', 182
Blomfield, Major, (56 Squadron RFC), 212, 294–5
Blundstone, Patrick, 169
Bocker, Kapitanleutnant, (Zeppelin L14), 158
Boelcke, Leutnant Oswald, (German Air Service), 71, 131, 132, 135, 137
Bolt, Air Mechanic Edward, (Military Wing, RFC), 18
bombing: accidents, 50–2; air-raid warnings, 270; airships, 183–4; bomb racks, 50; bomb-sights, 69; bombing methods, 37–8; bombing raids, 68–9; close escorts, 121–2; Cooper bombs, 233, 338, 339; detonators, 50; development of, 44; devices for dropping bombs, 19; distant escorts, 121–2; equipment, 29; formations, 121–2; German bombing of Britain, 140, 146–60, 262–6; grenades, 36–7; long-distance bombing raids, 162–3; night raids, 115–16; petrol bombs, 37; phosphor bombs, 339; scope of, 114–15; Smuts Report, 271–3; strategic raids in France, 162, 261; strategic raids in Germany, 162–4, 261, 344; tactical, 330, 332; targets, 50, 68–9, 122, 138, 340; training, 99–100; Zeppelin raid casualties, 284
Bott, Lieutenant Alan, (70 Squadron RFC), 126–8
Bourdillon, Lieutenant Robert, (Central Flying School, Upavon), 69
Bourlon Ridge, 238
Brancker, Major (later Brigadier General) Sefton: Assistant-Director of Military Aeronautics, 41, 42–3, 64, 67, 77; Third Wing command, 65; Director of Air Organisation, 111
Brandon, Lieutenant Alfred, (39 Squadron RFC), 169
Breithaupt, Kapitanleutnant, (Zeppelin L15), 155, 157
Breslau (Turkish/German light cruiser), 196–7
bridges, 50
Briggs, Wireless Operator Leslie, (RFC), 227
Bristol Bullet, 33, 96
Bristol Company, 11
Bristol Fighter, 202, 339, 346
Bristol Fighter F2 A, 210–11
Bristol School of Aviation, 11
Bristol Scout, 60–1
Britain: aviation research, 4–6; research funding, 6–7, 9; balloons, 7; aeroplane development, 7–8, 9–10; airships, 8–9; aviation industry, 11, 41–2, 110, 112; Zeppelin bombing raids, 146–60, 260, 278–85; Gotha

bombing raids, 262–6, 274–8, 283, 285
British and Colonial Aeroplane Company, 11
British Army: use of balloons, 7; Chief Kite Instructor, 8; formation of Air Battalion, RE, 12–14; aviation funding, 22; Somme (1916), 101; anti-Zeppelin defences, 148, 164; Home Defence role, 164; Mobile Anti-Aircraft Brigade, 164; importance of aerial observation, 348
British Expeditionary Force (BEF): RFC's Military Wing plans, 15–16, 22, 23; deployment plans, 23; First Army and Second Army, 40, 68; Third Army, 62, 309; role in 1916, 101; Somme (1916), 101, 116; General Headquarters, 102; Fourth Army, 116–17; air cover, 175–6; Fifth Army, 201, 307, 309, 315
Brooke-Popham, Major H.R.M., (RFC), 33
Brooklands, 10–11, 41, 80
Brown, Captain Roy, (9 Squadron RNAS, 209 Squadron RAF), 94, 252, 321
Brownell, Second Lieutenant R.J., (45 Squadron RFC), 246–7, 298
Bruges, German submarine base, 201
Buckingham bullets, 207
bullets, incendiary and explosive, 166
Burford-Hancock, Lady, 277
Burke, Lieutenant Colonel, (Second Wing, RFC), 43, 65
Burne, Sergeant Charles, (5 Squadron RNAS), 231–2
Burroughes, Hugh, (Director, Aircraft Manufacturing Company, Hendon), 176
Burslem, Lieutenant Frank, (RFC, 218 Squadron RAF), 90, 335

Cadbury, Lieutenant Egbert, (Yarmouth Station, RNAS), 173, 283–4
Calshot aerodrome, 142
Cambrai, German counter-attack, 306
cameras, 46–7, 68
Campania, HMS, 186, 191
Canadian Air Force, 327
Capper, Lieutenant Colonel John, (Superintendent of the Balloon Factory), 7–8, 9, 10, 13
Caudron Biplane, 83
cavalry, 236
Cave Brown Cave, Commander T.R., 176–7
Central Flying School: establishment, 15, 16; instructors, 18, 91; Trenchard's appointment, 20, 65, 349; expansion, 41; bomb-sight development, 69
CFS bomb-sight, 69
Chabot, Second Lieutenant (later Lieutenant) Charles, (4 Squadron RFC, 39 Squadron RFC), 47, 81, 263, 282
Chalmers, Kitty, 264
Charles, Engineering Officer

H.N., (56 Squadron RFC), 212, 291
Chemin des Dames, 200
chivalry, 240–1
Cholmondley, Captain Reginald, (3 Squadron RFC), 51
Churchill, Winston (First Lord of the Admiralty), 20, 141–3, 161, 174
Clappen, Donald, 13, 77, 78–9
Clipper of the Clouds, The, 5
clock code, 48–50, 68, 226
Coastal Airships, 182
Cobby, Captain A.H., (4 Squadron Australian Flying Corps), 339
Cody, Charles, 18
Cody, Leon, 18
Cody, Samuel Franklin, 8, 9, 16–18
Collins, Jose, 294
Cologne, Zeppelin base, 143
combat techniques, 108, 123–5, 248, 309–13, 324–6
Committee of Imperial Defence, 6, 14, 16
communications: between pilots, 247; clock code, 48–50, 68, 226; flares, 44, 114, 119, 227; headphones, 89; klaxons, 119, 227; maroons, 270; Morse, 44, 49, 99, 225; pigeons, 190; signal lamps, 44; sirens, 270; telephone wires, 53; umbrellas, 114; wireless, 44, 48, 190, 203–4, 225–7
Compiègne, landing ground, 32
Constantinesco interrupter gear, 211, 212, 242, 250
contact patrol, 54
Cooper, Second Lieutenant H.A., (11 Squadron RFC), 62–3
Cooper bombs, 233, 338, 339
Courtney, Second Lieutenant Frank, (45 Squadron RFC), 210
Courtrai, railway junction, 52
Cowdray, 1st Viscount, (President of the Air Board), 261, 272, 274, 307
Cranwell, Royal Air Force College, 349
Crean, Captain T., (4 Squadron RFC), 36
Cressy, HMS, 176
Croft, Celia, 275
Cronyn, Lieutenant Verschoyle, (56 Squadron RFC), 257–8, 303
Crossley tenders, 31
Crystal Palace, airship landing, 8
Curzon of Kedleston, 1st Marquess, (President of the Air Board), 162, 163–4, 261, 273
Cuxhaven Raid (1914), 143–4, 195

Daily Mail, 5, 76, 160
Dardanelles: expedition, 175; Goeben, 196–8
Darley, Captain C.C., (11 Squadron RFC), 71
Dawes, Major George, (11 Squadron RFC), 62

Dayrell-Browning, Muriel, 167, 169
de Havilland, Geoffrey, 10, 105, 106
De Lacy, Charles, 159
Derby, 17th Earl of, 161–2
Derby Committee, 161–2, 273
DH2 aircraft, 106–7, 108, 133, 135–7, 348
DH4 aircraft: in combat, 198, 231; arrival on Western Front, 202, 211; Arras air offensive, 211; anti-Zeppelin action, 284; bombing raids, 340–1; postwar, 346
DH9 aircraft, 339
Dickson, Captain William, (HMS *Furious*), 194–5
Directorate of Military Aeronautics, 15, 64, 111
dirigibles, 22
Dobson, Second Lieutenant G.M.B., (Central Flying School, Upavon), 69
dockyards, defences, 145
dogfights, 248–55, 320
Donald, Lieutenant (later Captain) Graham, (RNAS): Cody encounter, 17; training, 82–3; anti-Zeppelin duty, 148; seaplanes, 186–7; bombing the *Goeben*, 196–9; opinion of Sopwith Camel, 221–2
Dormer, Second Lieutenant F.A., (6 Squadron RFC), 229–30
Douai aerodrome, 74, 75, 213, 214
Douglas, Lieutenant Percy, (11 Squadron RFC), 286
Dover: German seaplane raids, 145; Zeppelin raids, 150
Dresden, bombing (1945), 351–2
duels, aerial, 29–31, 108–10, 137–8
Dunkirk, RNAS base, 151, 188
Dunne, Lieutenant John, (Balloon Factory), 7–8, 9, 10
Dunning, Squadron Commander E.H., (RNAS), 192–3
du Peuty, Commandant Paul-Fernand, (French Air Commander), 102
Dusseldorf: British bombing raids, 162–3; Zeppelin base, 143

Eastchurch aerodrome, 11, 16, 19, 142–3
Eddington, Sergeant George, (6 Squadron RFC), 230, 302
Ellins, Corporal, (66 Squadron RFC), 305
Ellwood, Lieutenant Aubrey, (RNAS), 320
Elmhurst, Midshipman Thomas, (HMS *Indomitable*), 178
Empress, HMS, 185
Engadine, HMS, 185, 186, 187
Engel airfield, 231
engines: Beardmore, 105; British industry, 111–12; capacity, 112; fitters, 303; French, 110, 111; Gnome Monosoupape, 61–2, 106; Hispano-Suiza, 212, 312; in-line, 111–12; Le Clerget, 221; Le Rhone, 110, 221; manufacture rate, 261–2, 266;

Maybach, 140, 312; Mercedes, 126, 131, 218, 262; quality control, 112; RAF1, 43; Rolls-Royce Eagle, 211; Rolls-Royce Falcon, 210; rotary, 111; supply, 42, 111–12; Wolseley, 175
English Channel: air threat, 4–5; first air crossing, 5
Epehy, railway junction, 122
Evans, Private Oswald, (2/16th London Regiment), 130

Falkenhayn, General Erich von, (Chief of the German General Staff), 130
Fampoux, railway, 115
Farman Experimental (FE), 10
Farnborough: Balloon Sections, 7, 8; workshops, 16; headquarters stock of machines, 24; size of establishment (1914), 40–1; headquarters restructuring, 43
FE2 B aircraft: production, 105; features, 105–7; formation flying, 106, 136; contests with Fokkers, 106, 108–10; contests with Albatross, 131–2; photographic reconnaissance, 206–7; night bombing raids, 330–1; replacement, 341
FE8 aircraft, 107
Festubert, Battle of, 53, 54
Field, Lieutenant Laurie, (40 Squadron RFC), 83, 94, 297
Fisher, Admiral of the Fleet Lord, (First Sea Lord), 176, 178, 192
Fitzgerald, Flight Sergeant, (1 Squadron RFC), 104–5
Flanders, Allied offensive (1917), 219, 236
flares, 44, 119, 167, 227
Flesquières, 238–9
Flying Certificate test, 87
Fokker, Anthony, 70
Fokker aircraft, 70–6, 103, 106, 108–9, 334, 339
Fokker D VII, 252, 336
Fokker E1, 70–1, 136
Fokker Triplane, 234–5
Folkestone, German air raid, 263
formation flying, 106, 204–5, 218, 244, 247, 324–5
Foster, Sergeant R.G., (11 Squadron RFC), 105
France: aeroplane development, 4, 9; research funding, 9; aero industry, 42, 111, 112; aircraft design, 110
Frankfurt, air raid, 343
French, General (later Field Marshal) Sir John, (C-in-C BEF), 27–8, 40, 68, 274
French Air Service, 69, 70, 103
French Army: Battle of Loos, 67–8; Verdun, 101, 103, 116, 130–1, 200; Somme, 116, 200; command, 200; 1917 offensive, 200–1
Friedrichshafen, 4
'friendly fire', 26, 36

Fuljames, Reginald, (RFC), 89
Furious, HMS, 192–5
Furlong, Eric, 12

G-plane, 140
Gallipoli: aerial detachments, 65; Churchill's removal, 161; end of campaign, 196
Garros, Lieutenant Roland, (French Air Service), 70
gas, 52, 53
Gascoyne, Air Mechanic (later Lieutenant) James, (3 Squadron RFC, 92 Squadron RAF), 26, 33, 35, 51, 338
Geddes, Sir Eric, (First Lord of the Admiralty), 274
German Air Service: air duels, 29–31; aircraft markings, 36, 74; reconnaissance, 58, 102; Fokker's work, 70–6; Somme (1916), 129–30; Jagdstaffeln (Jasta), 131, 135, 202, 219; Albatross aircraft, 131–3; bombing plans, 140; reorganisation, 202; Jagdgeschwader No.1, 219–20; Gotha bombers, 262; Kampfgeschwader 1, 262; bombardment (1918), 315–17; pressures on (1918), 329; Fokker DVII, 336; defensive strategy, 348
German Army: trenches, 45–7, 53; use of gas, 52, 53; anti-aircraft guns, 55–8, 129–30; 1916 strategy, 101; Somme (1916), 129, 131; airship development, 145–6; Hindenburg Line, 201, 205; Second World War, 350
German Navy, airship development, 145–6
Germany: aeronautical research, 4; research funding, 9; Schlieffen Plan, 23; British air raids, 162–4, 261, 344
Giant bombers, 274, 332–3
Gibbs, Captain Arthur, (1st Battalion, Welsh Guards), 130
gliders, British research, 7
Gnome Monosoupape engine, 61–2, 106
Goddard, Victor, (RNAS), 179–82, 191–2
Goeben (Turkish/German battlecruiser), 196–9
Gonneham aerodrome, 34
Gordon-Burge, C., (RFC), 97
Gosport, 1 (Reserve) Squadron, 89
Gosport tube, 89
Gotha G-IV: production and delivery, 140, 262; bombing raids on Britain, 221, 262–6, 283; defences against, 270, 278; Western Front bombing, 332–4
Grahame-White, Claude, 11
Grahame-White School of Flying, 84
Grand Fleet: Aircraft Committee, 175; airship cover, 184
grenades, 36–7
Grider, Lieutenant John, (85 Squadron RFC), 256, 293, 298–9
Grierson, Lieutenant General Sir James, (GOC Eastern Command), 18–19

Grinnell-Milne, Second Lieutenant (later Lieutenant) Duncan, (16 Squadron RFC, 56 Squadron RFC): response to anti-aircraft fire, 57; opinion of Longhorn, 80; training, 80–2, 88; opinion of 'The Pulpit', 104; on thrill of combat, 259; on 56 Squadron's band, 295–6
Grosskampfflugzeug, 140, 262
ground crew, 243–4, 302–5

Haase, Herbe, 343
Hague Conference (1907), 141
Haig, General (later Field Marshal) Sir Douglas, (GOC First Army, later C-in-C BEF): manoeuvres (1912), 18–19; use of aviation, 28, 44–5, 67, 133–4, 138–9, 202, 268, 273; First Army command, 40, 68; Battle of Neuve Chapelle, 44, 49, 67; relationship with Trenchard, 44, 67, 133–4, 307–8; Battle of Loos, 67–8; C-in-C BEF, 68; attrition strategy, 101; Battle of the Somme, 116, 121, 138; Flanders offensive (1917), 201, 236; Cambrai plan, 236; Ypres preparations, 268, 273
Hainault Farm, landing ground, 144
Halberstadt Fighter, 198
Haldane, Richard (Secretary of State for War), 9, 11
Halton, RAF, 349
Handley Page aircraft, 341
Handley Page Aircraft Company, 18
Hanover aircraft, 314
Harris, Lieutenant (later Air Marshal Sir) Arthur, (RFC), 79–80, 165, 351
Hart, Sydney, 156
Harvey, W.J., (RFC), 100
Harvey-Kelly, Lieutenant Hubert, (2 Squadron RFC), 25
Harwich Force, 185
Hawker, Captain (later Major) Lanoe, VC, (6 Squadron RFC, 24 Squadron RFC), 53, 54, 61, 108, 120, 136–8
Hawkins, Armourer William, (RNAS), 193
Hazebrouck, German offensive (1918), 320
headphones, 89
Henderson, Brigadier General (later Major General Sir) David, (Director-General of Military Aeronautics): Director of Military Training, 15; Director-General of Military Aeronautics, 15, 64, 111–12, 272; RFC command, 24, 40–1, 42, 64–5; Trenchard's complaints, 75–6; Smuts Report, 269; Chief of Air Staff question, 307
Hendon: establishment, 11–12; flying displays, 11, 95; Beatty School of Flying, 82; Aircraft Manufacturing Company, 106; defence role, 142–3; RNAS flight, 144; sale of government stock, 346–7
Henri Farman aircraft: RFC stocks, 24; in combat, 29–30, 56; armaments, 29–30, 37,

43, 60; landing, 32; lightweight, 35; petrol bombs, 37; performance, 43, 61–2:
Hermes, HMS, 184–5
Higgins, Major (later Brigadier General) Josh, 39, 43, 102
Hill, Second Lieutenant Roderic, (60 Squadron RFC), 124
Hindenburg, Field Marshal Paul von, (Chief of the German General Staff), 130
Hindenburg Line, 201, 205, 237, 330, 334
Hobbs, Second Lieutenant Alan, (3 Squadron RFC), 72–4
Hogue, HMS, 176
Holt-Thomas, George, 176
Home Defence, 164, 260, 270, 285
Hopkins, Second Lieutenant J.C.F. (83 Squadron RFC), 97, 98, 267, 319, 331–2
Hosking, Lieutenant C.G., (4 Squadron RFC), 36
howitzer shells, 118
Hughes, Sergeant H.F., (3 Squadron, Australian Flying Corps), 231
Hughes, Recording Officer Lieutenant Thomas, (1 Squadron RFC, 53 Squadron RFC), 114, 129, 221, 297
Hull, Zeppelin raid, 149
Hunaudières, Wright demonstration, 3
Hurlingham Club, balloon training, 178
Hyams, Gordon, (RNAS), 81

Immelmann, Max, Leutnant, (62 Section, German Air Service), 71–3, 75, 110
Immelmann Turn, 230
Independent Air Force (IAF), 290, 292, 308, 340–4, 349
Indomitable, HMS, 178, 191
Ingleby, Jane, 149
Inglis, Lieutenant Donald, (85 Squadron RAF), 327–8
Insall, Second Lieutenant A.J., (11 Squadron RFC), 62–3
intelligence, use of, 27

Jackson, Lieutenant (later Captain) Alan, (5 Squadron RFC), 115, 288
Jackson, Captain W.D., (HMS *Furious*), 193, 194
James, Lieutenant (later Major) Archibald, (16 Squadron RFC, 6 Squadron RFC), 47, 54, 58, 59, 88, 255
'jamming', wireless, 113
Janie, Elsie, 294
Jellicoe, Admiral Sir John, (Grand Fleet C-in-C), 174, 187–8
Jillings, Sergeant Major David, (2 Squadron RFC), 26
Jilly, landing ground, 32
Joffre, General Joseph (C-in-C French Army), 101, 116, 200
Johns, Lieutenant William, (55

Squadron, IAF), 290, 340–1, 349
Joint War Air Committee, 161–2
Jones, Lieutenant George, (4 Squadron, Australian Flying Corps), 254, 259
Jones, Lieutenant Ira, (74 Squadron RAF), 254–5, 294, 297, 323–6
Joubert de la Ferté, Captain Philip, (3 Squadron RFC), 26, 29
Joyce Green, landing ground, 144
Joynson-Hicks, William, 161, 260
Jutland, Battle of (1916), 187

Keen, Captain, (40 Squadron RFC), 214–16
Kenwood House, mobile anti-aircraft base, 159–60
King, Air Mechanic Cecil, (Central Flying School, Upavon, later 5 Squadron RFC, 3 Squadron RFC): Trenchard's orderly, 21; recruitment to RFC, 21–2; on German advance (1914), 31–2; on night duty, 35; on roundels, 36; on grenades, 37; on commanding officer, 39; on start-up procedure, 243–4; on flight sergeant, 304
King's Lynn, Zeppelin bombing raids, 146
Kingsford, Lieutenant Reg, (100 Squadron, IAF), 292
Kinkead, Captain S.M., (9 Squadron RNAS), 252–3
Kitchener, Horatio Herbert, Field Marshal Lord, (Secretary of State for War), 40, 42
kite balloons, 102, 117, 174–5, 207–8
kites, man-lifting, 7
Kitty Hawk, North Carolina, 3
klaxons, 119, 227
Kolle, Kapitanleutnant Waldeemar, (L45) 279–80

L1, 146
L2, 140, 146
L3, 146
L4, 146
L6, 146
L12, 150–1
L13, 152
L14, 158–9
L15, 155–8
L21, 172–3
L31, 169–70
L32, 169
L33, 169
L34, 172
L45, 278–81
L54, 194
L60, 194
L70, 283–4
La Boiselle mines, 118–19
Lachman, Leutnant Gustav, (German Air Service), 317
La Fère, landing ground, 32

landing fields, surfaces, 17–18, 34
Larkhill, 11, 13, 22
Lateau Wood, artillery batteries, 237
Law, Andrew Bonar, (Chancellor of the Exchequer), 274
Le Cateau: withdrawal to (1914), 31; retreat from (1914), 32
Leckie, Captain Robert, 284
Lee, Lieutenant Arthur, (46 Squadron RFC), 237–8
Leefe Robinson, Lieutenant William, VC, (39 Squadron RFC), 167–8, 171, 211
Leggett, Elsie, 147
Leggett, May, 147
Le Prieur rockets, 207
Levy, Esther, 264
Lewis, Second Lieutenant (later Lieutenant) Cecil, (3 Squadron RFC, 56 Squadron RFC): on artillery bombardment, 117–20; on Vickers gun, 242; on patrolling, 245; on dogfights, 249; on machine guns, 250–1; on stress, 287; on music, 293
Lewis, Second Lieutenant (later Lieutenant) Gwilym, (32 Squadron RFC, 40 Squadron RFC): flying instruction, 91–2; on DH2, 108; on Albatross, 133; on patrolling, 245–6; on drinking, 299; on McCudden, 311; in action, 312; on Mannock, 322–3, 327
Lewis gun: aircraft mounting, 29–30, 60, 61, 104–5; in combat, 74, 106, 235, 311–12; Ball's technique, 123–4; use of incendiary and explosive bullets, 166; Bristol Fighter mounting, 210; SE5 mounting, 250
Leyland lorries, 31
Linnarz, Hauptmann Karl, (LZ38), 147
Livock, Gerald, (RNAS), 84
Lloyd George, David (Chancellor of the Exchequer, later Prime Minister), 6, 159, 164, 261, 269, 307–8
London: aerial defences, 144–5; Zeppelin raids, 147, 149, 151–8, 160, 166–72, 278–83; German aeroplane raids (1917), 263–5, 266–8, 275–8, 283, 340; Second World War bombing, 350
London Air Defence Area, 270
Longmore, Lieutenant Arthur, (RN), 18–19
Loos, Battle of, 67–8, 101
Loraine, Robert (3 Squadron RSC), 11, 25, 56
Loraine, Violet, 294
Ludendorf, General Erich von, (German C-in-C), 306–7
Lusitania, 188
Luxeuil, RNAS base, 162
LVG biplane, 62–3
LZ1 (Luftschiff Zeppelin), 4
LZ4, 4
LZ37, 149
LZ38, 147, 149

McCubbin, Second Lieutenant G.R., (25 Squadron RFC), 110
McCudden, Air Mechanic (later Major) James, VC, (3 Squadron RFC, 29 Squadron RFC, 56 Squadron RFC, Home Establishment, RFC): career, 25, 314; first experiences in RFC, 25; on early armaments, 29; on landing sites, 34; on ground crews' life, 35; on bomb accident, 51; on shrapnel shells, 56; flying skills, 97; on dogfights, 135–6, 234–6; reputation, 240; attention to detail, 241–2; marksmanship, 243; home defence role, 264–5, 267–8; ping-pong championship, 289–90; class prejudice against, 293; combat technique, 309–13; temperament, 313–15; decorations, 315, 328; death, 315, 327
McElroy, Captain G.E.H., (40 Squadron RAF), 327
McGregor, Lieutenant Malcolm, (85 Squadron RAF), 329
machine guns: aircraft mounting, 20, 29–30, 60, 61, 104–5, 210, 250; alignment, 242–3; anti-aircraft force, 146; development of, 44, 59–60; Lewis, see Lewis gun; malfunctions, 242, 311–12; Vickers, see Vickers machine-gun
MacInnes, Major (later Brigadier General) Duncan, (Director of Aircraft Equipment), 15, 111
MacLanachan, Second Lieutenant William, (40 Squadron RFC), 219, 251
Macmillan, Lieutenant Norman, (45 Squadron RFC), 233, 241, 245, 246, 248, 250
Major, Miss I.A., 264
Malik, Lieutenant Sardar, (28 Squadron RFC), 256–7
Manica, SS, 174
Mannheim, planned raid (1917), 268
Mannock, Second Lieutenant (later Major) Edward VC, (40 Squadron RFC, 85 Squadron RAF): temperament, 214–16, 218–19, 322, 326; reputation, 216, 240, 322, 329; marksmanship, 216, 243; combat technique, 217–18, 324–5; influence, 297, 322–6, 329; 85 Squadron Command, 299, 326–8; lectures, 323–4; death, 328–9; decorations, 328
Marcoing, railway junction, 122, 131
Marix, Flight Lieutenant Reginald, 143
markings, aircraft, 36, 74
Marne, retreat to (1914), 28, 33
maroons, 270
Marson, Recording Officer T.B., (56 Squadron RFC), 66–7, 213, 295
Martinsyde aeroplanes, 11, 17, 122
Martinsyde Scout, 60, 109
Mathy, Kapitan Leutnant Heinrich,

(German Air Service), 149, 152–3, 169, 280
Maubeuge, BEF, 23, 24, 26, 29
Maurice Farman 'Longhorn', 54, 80, 86, 105
Mauser pistol, 30
May, Lieutenant Wilfred, (209 Squadron RAF), 320–1
Maybery, Captain R.A., (56 Squadron RAF), 290, 295
Mayfly, 175
mechanics, 243–4, 302–5
medals, 25, 52, 61, 125, 150, 315, 328
Melun, landing ground, 32
Merville, landing ground, 52
Messines: trenches, 45; Ridge, 219; Battle of (1917), 220, 232
Meteorological Office, 331
Meysey-Thompson, Captain H.C., (2/4th Battalion, Berkshire Regiment), 148
Middleton, Chief Petty Officer Engineer J.S., (Kingsnorth Station, RNAS), 177
Military Aeroplane Trials, 16
mines, 197, 219
Ministry of Munitions, 261, 269, 274, 344
missiles, explosive, 19
Molesworth, Captain W.E., (60 Squadron RFC), 208
Mons (1914), 28–9, 318
Montagu of Beaulieu, 2nd Baron, 161–2, 260
Moore-Brabazon, Lieutenant J.T.C., (Photographic Section, RFC), 46–7
Morane aircraft, 50, 104, 119
Morane Parasol, 51
Morane Saulnier, 70
Morrison, Sybil, 172
Morrison-Bell, Lady, 275–7
Morse code, 44, 49, 99
Muhler, Coxswain Alfred, (LZ37), 150
munitions factories, 145, 285
Myers, Mrs T., 264

Nagara Point, German Seaplane Station, 198
Nagel, Leutnant Fritz, (Kraftwagen Flak 82), 317–18
Naulls, Private Edward, (2nd Battalion, Essex Regiment), 328
Naval Flying School, 16
navigation, 13–14
nerves, 55, 84, 215–16, 258–9, 348–9
Netheravon aerodrome, 22, 25, 41, 43
Neuve Chapelle: Battle of, (10–12 March 1915), 44, 49–50, 53, 101, 113; German trenches, 47
Newall, Lieutenant Colonel Cyril, (OC Forty-first Wing, RFC), 340
Nieuport Scout: features, 110; in combat, 123, 131, 229; contests with Albatross, 204; replacement machines, 210; escort patrol, 223
night flying, 97–8, 165, 332–3

Nivelle, General Robert, (C-in-C French Army), 200–1, 219
Nordholz Zeppelin station, 143–4
North Hinder light vessel, 188
North Sea Airship, 182
Northcliffe, Alfred Harmsworth, 1st Viscount, 5, 76, 308
Northern Training Squadrons, 95
Nulli Secundus airship, 8
Nulli Secundus II, 8–9

observation: balloon history, 7; artillery, 44, 48–50, 68, 99, 113, 138, 225, 348
Ochy, bombing squadron base, 340
O'Gorman, Mervyn, 9, 10
Ostend: German Air Service base, 140, 143, 149–50, 262; German submarine base, 201

parachutes, 255
Parliamentary Air Committee, 161
Passchendaele, 220, 228, see also Ypres, Third Battle of
patrol leaders, 245–6, 252
Pemberton Billing, Noël, 160–1, 260
Penn-Gaskell, Lieutenant, (5 Squadron RFC), 29
Pétain, General Philippe, (C-in-C French Army), 201
Peterson, Oberleutnant, (German Air Service), 150
Pezarches, landing ground, 32
Pfalz aircraft, 314
Phillips, W.A., 153
phosphorous bombs, 339
Photographic Section, 46
photography: Arras reconnaissance, 206–7; artillery bombardment, 117–18; box camera plates, 46–7; 'C' Type camera, 68; Cambrai raid reconnaissance, 236; detailed reconnaissance, 203; interpretation expertise, 113; training, 98–9; use of, 138
pigeons, 190
pilots: 'aces', 125, 242–3, 314, 326, 328; airship recruits, 177–8; airship training, 178–82; combat techniques, 108, 123–5, 248, 309–13, 324–6; communications between, 247; drinking, 296–9; flying clothes, 341; losses, 73, 210, 287, 299–300; morale, 286–9; nerves, 55, 84, 215–16, 258–9, 348–9; officers and NCOs, 293, 301–3; postwar life, 346–7; recreation, 291–9; recruitment, 21–2, 41; scout, 107–8, 138, 240–3, 290; training, 73, 77–100
Player, H.W., 152
pom-poms, 55, 146
Powell, Lieutenant (later Major) F.J., (5 Squadron RFC, 41 Squadron RFC): response to anti-aircraft fire, 57; on Monosoupape engine, 62; combat

technique, 63–4, 108; fighting instruction, 95; flying skills, 96–7; on scout pilots, 107; on notifying next-of-kin, 301

Pozières Ridge, 116

Pretyman, Captain G.F., (3 Squadron RFC), 52

provisions, dropping, 335

'Pulpit, The', 104

Purfleet, anti-aircraft battery, 166

Pyott, Second Lieutenant I.V., 172

Rabagliati, Lieutenant C.E.C., (5 Squadron RFC), 28, 31, 39

RAF1 engine, 43

railways: bombing targets, 50, 52, 115, 122, 138, 330, 340; bombing success rate, 69; photographic reconnaissance, 203; effects of bombing, 285

Rawlinson, Lieutenant Commander (later Lieutenant Colonel) Alfred, (Mobile Anti-Aircraft Section, RNAS, West Sub Command, Royal Garrison Artillery), 154–5, 159, 283

Rawlinson, General Sir Henry, (GOC Fourth Army), 116

RE8 aircraft: introduction, 202; vulnerability, 222–3; in action, 227, 336; stability, 230–1; role, 348

Read, Lieutenant William, (3 Squadron RFC), 32–3, 36, 55–6, 62

reconnaissance: airships, 184; Battle of Jutland, 187–8; first flights, 26–7; ground fire, 35–6; Haig's use of, 44–5; importance, 309; of trenches, 45–6; photography, 46–7, 113, 203, 206–7, 236; sketch maps, 45–6

Reconnaissance Experimental (RE), 10

Red Cross, 277

Rees, Major Lionel, (32 Squadron RFC), 108

revolvers, 58–9

Reynolds, Lieutenant H.R.P., (2 Company, Air Battalion, RE), 14

Rhodes-Moorhouse, Second Lieutenant William, VC, 52

Rhys Davids, Second Lieutenant Arthur, (56 Squadron RFC), 234, 235–6, 241, 290–1, 295

Richthofen, Freiherr Manfred von, Leutnant, (later Rittmeister, German Air Service): in action, 89, 211; first combat action, 131–2; duel with Hawker, 137–8; influence, 219–20; status, 235; death, 320–2, 328

rifles, 58–9

Riviera, HMS, 185

Roberts, Lieutenant Frank, (2nd Squadron Australian Flying Corps), 340

Robertson, General Sir William, (Chief of Imperial General Staff), 269, 274

Robey, George, 294

rockets: Le Prieur, 207; maroons, 270

Roe, A.V., 11, 17

Rogers, Lieutenant T.E., (6 Squadron RFC), 78, 99, 300

Roland aircraft, 122, 133

Rosser, Milton, 156

Rothermere, 1st Viscount, 308

roundels, 36

Rowell, Lieutenant (later Captain) Robin, (8 Squadron RFC, 12 Squadron RFC), 87, 116, 203

Royal Aero Club, 13, 47, 87

Royal Air Force (RAF): formation, 65, 274, 307, 308; response to Armistice, 345–6; strength, 344, 346; World War II, 350–1

Royal Air Force units, see under Royal Flying Corps units

Royal Aircraft Factory, (earlier Army Aircraft Factory): role, 10; RFC relationship, 15; BE series, 18, 42–3; RAF1 engine, 43; 'The Pulpit', 104; FE2 B, 105; FE8, 107; War Office policy, 110

Royal Artillery, 50, 113, 138

Royal Engineers, 13

Royal Flying Corps (RFC): formation, 14–15, 272; Naval Wing, 15, 16; Military Wing, 15–16, 18–22; BEF plans, 15–16, 22, 23; recruitment, 21–2, 41; BEF mobilization, 23–6; reputation, 39; expansion, 40–3, 67; aircraft standardization 42–3; Photographic Section, 46; first VC, 52; command (1915), 64–7; size of force (1915), 67, 111; role, 68, 174; cooperation with French Air Service, 69; losses, 73, 130; pilot training, 73, 77–100; effects of Fokker opposition, 75–6; public image, 77; size of force (1916), 101, 111–12; reorganisation (1916), 102; relationship with army, 102, 130; defensive/offensive strategy, 102–3, 128–9, 209; relationship with RNAS, 112, 134–5, 162–4, 261, 272–3, 274; relationship with Royal Artillery, 113–14, 138; status, 138–9; aerial defence plans, 141; anti-Zeppelin action, 156–7; strategic bombing raids, 162–4, 261, 344; Home Defence role, 164–6, 260; size of force (1917), 201–2; pilot losses, 210; Third Battle of Ypres, 222; expansion (1917), 266; amalgamation with RNAS, 319–20; ground-attack operations (1918), 334

Royal Flying Corps (and RAF) units:
I Brigade, 102, 116
II Brigade, 102
III Brigade, 102
IV Brigade, 116
VIII Brigade, 340
Administrative Wing, 43
First Wing, 43–4, 46, 47, 52, 65, 68, 102
Second Wing, 43, 65, 69, 102
Third Wing, 52, 62, 65, 69, 102, 116
Fourth Wing, 43

INDEX

Ninth Wing, 102, 116, 201–2, 340
Tenth Wing, 102
Eleventh Wing, 102
Twelfth Wing, 102
Fourteenth Wing, 116
Twenty-second Wing, 301
Forty-first Wing, 340
Eightieth Wing, 338–9
Home Defence Wing, 166
1 Squadron, 22, 43, 48–9, 50, 59, 60,
    89–90, 105, 114, 129, 302, 304
2 Squadron, 22, 24, 25, 26, 43, 52
3 Squadron, 22, 24–5, 26, 29, 33–6, 51–2,
    55–6, 75, 118–20, 244
4 Squadron, 22, 24, 46–7, 228, 289
5 Squadron, 22, 24, 25, 28, 30–2, 35–9,
    57, 62, 64, 107–8, 115, 287–8, 304
6 Squadron, 22, 53, 61, 223, 230, 255,
    300, 302, 336–8
7 Squadron, 22, 43, 52
8 Squadron, 52, 116
11 Squadron, 62, 63, 105, 123, 131,
    206, 286
12 Squadron, 131, 203
16 Squadron, 47, 54, 57–9, 104, 259
20 Squadron, 105
22 Squadron, 120–1
23 Squadron, 109, 115, 157–8, 289
24 Squadron, 120
25 Squadron, 106, 110
27 Squadron, 122–3
28 Squadron, 257
29 Squadron, 135–6, 225
32 Squadron, 108, 133, 135, 311
39 Squadron, 166, 167–8, 169–71,
    263, 282
40 Squadron, 214–19, 246, 251, 296–7,
    299, 311–12, 322–3, 327
41 Squadron, 296, 301
42 Squadron, 297
45 Squadron, 209–10, 233, 241, 245,
    246–8, 250, 298
46 Squadron, 237–8, 339
48 Squadron, 211, 317, 345
53 Squadron, 221, 297
54 Squadron, 202
55 Squadron, 211, 290, 340
56 Squadron, 66–7, 211, 212–13, 221,
    234, 235–6, 241–2, 245, 249, 251,
    257–8, 266, 287, 290–1, 294–6, 303,
    310–11, 313–15
60 Squadron, 123–4, 204–8, 210, 234,
    243, 248
66 Squadron, 221, 266, 303, 305
70 Squadron, 122, 127–8
74 Squadron, 254–5, 294, 297, 323–6, 329
83 Squadron, 319, 331–2
85 Squadron, 256, 293, 298–9, 326,
    328, 329
88 Squadron, 339

92 Squadron, 338
100 Squadron, 341
101 Squadron, 346
103 Squadron, 339
151 Squadron, 333–4
201 Squadron, 335, 336
209 Squadron, 321
218 Squadron, 335
Royal Naval Air Service (RNAS): origins 16;
    seaplane development, 19; public image,
    77; aircraft design, 110; relationship with
    RFC, 112, 134–5, 261, 272–3, 274; aerial
    defence role, 141–2, 146, 156, 164; coastal
    stations, 146; 'strategic' bombing raids
    (1916), 162, 261; role, 174; airships, 175;
    seaplanes, 184–8; anti-submarine patrols,
    188–90; anti-Zeppelin action, 188
Royal Naval Air Service units:
    Hendon Flight, London Air Defence, 144
    Mobile Anti-Aircraft Section, 154–5,
        159, 164
    Third Wing, 162
    1 Squadron, 149–50
    5 Squadron, 231–2
    8 Squadron, 134–5, 202
    9 Squadron, 95, 252–3
Royal Navy: invasion protection, 4; airship
    research 6; aeroplane development, 10;
    Eastchurch base, 11, 16; RNAS formation,
    16; aerial defences, 144, 164; Grand
    Fleet Aircraft Committee, 175; airship
    recruits, 177–8; wireless direction-finding
    stations, 184, 188; role of airships, 184;
    amalgamation with RFC, 319–20
Rumpler aircraft, 310, 312
Russia, collapse of, 306
Rutland, Flight Lieutenant F.J., (HMS
    Engadine 187

Saar, bombing raids, 162
St Julien, British position, 53
St Louis Exhibition, 7
St Quentin, landing ground, 32
Salmond, Major (later Major General) John
    M., (3 Squadron RFC, later Second Wing,
    RFC), 51–2, 65, 308
Samson, Lieutenant (later Commander)
    Charles, (RN), 11, 19, 143, 184, 189–90
Sandy, Lieutenant J.L.M., (3 Squadron,
    Australian Flying Corps), 231
Satin, Sophie, 352
Saulnier, Raymond, 70
Saunders, Air Mechanic/Observer (later
    Sergeant) S.S., (1 Squadron RFC), 49, 50,
    59, 60, 105, 302, 304
Scarpe, 1917 assault plans, 201
Scheer, Vice Admiral Reinhard von, (High
    Seas Fleet), 187–8
Schlieffen Plan, 23, 140
Schneider Seaplanes, 191

School of Special Flying, Gosport, 91
Schutz, Leutnant Karl, (Second in Command, L45), 279–81
Scott, Major Jack, (60 Squadron RFC), 210
Scott, Admiral Sir Percy, 154
scout pilots, 107–8, 138, 240–3, 290, 348
Scouting Experimental (SE), 10
SE5 aircraft: introduction, 202, 211–12; features, 211–12, 221; in action, 234–5, 317, 339; McCudden's engine tuning, 309; Mannock's work, 323; postwar sales, 346–7; role, 348
seaplanes: carriers, 184–6; development, 19; German raids on Britain, 145; RNAS bases, 141; take-off conditions, 185–6, 191
searchlights, 144, 146, 331–2
Senlis, landing ground, 32
Serris, landing ground, 32
Shaw, Air Mechanic James, (5 Squadron), 63
Sheerness: German seaplane raids (1914), 145; German air raids (1917), 263
shelling, 117–18
shells, high-explosive, 160
Shillinglaw, Lieutenant Roy, (100 Squadron, IAF), 342–3
Shoreham-by-Sea, training, 81
Shorncliffe Camp, German air raid, 263
Short Brothers, 11
Short Folder Seaplane, 185
Short Pusher Biplane, 184
Short Seaplane, 187
shrapnel, 56
Shutte-Lanz airships, 146, 167
Siegert, Major William, (German Air Service), 140
signal lamps, 44
Silk, Lieutenant Ralph, (6 Squadron RAF), 336–8
Silwood, F., (RNAS), 85, 189, 190
sirens, 270, 343
Skene, Second Lieutenant Robert, (3 Squadron RFC), 25
SL2, 146, 151
SL11, 167–9
Slade, Lieutenant R.J., (11 Squadron RFC), 71
Slessor, Second Lieutenant (later Marshal of the Royal Air Force Sir) John, (23 Squadron RFC), 156–8
Smart, Captain Bernard, (HMS Furious), 194–5
Smith, Second Lieutenant Alan, (101 Squadron RAF), 346
Smith, Christine, 159
Smith, Mrs C., 147
Smith, Mrs F.W., 151
Smith-Barry, Major (later Colonel) Robert, (1 (Reserve) Squadron, Gosport), 88–92, 100
Smith-Dorrien, Lieutenant General Sir

Horace, (GOC Second Army), 28, 40
Smuts, Lieutenant General Jan Christian, 269–74, 278, 307, 340, 344
Somme, Battle of the (1916), 101, 116–30, 138–9, 162, 200, 203, 319
Sopwith, Tom, 110
Sopwith aircraft, 186, 187
Sopwith Camel: pilot training, 93, 94; aircraft carrier experiments, 191; Tondern bombing raid, 193–4; Goeben pursuit, 196, 198; on Western Front, 202; instability and manoeuvrability, 221–2, 277; in action, 252–3, 256, 317, 320, 339; role, 348
Sopwith Pup, 97, 202, 248, 267
Sopwith Tabloid, 24, 143
Sopwith Triplane, 202
Sopwith '1½ Strutter', 110, 122, 126, 192, 209, 201
Sowery, Lieutenant Frederick, (39 Squadron RFC), 169, 171
Special Schools of Aerial Fighting, 95
Springs, Lieutenant Elliot, (85 Squadron RAF), 293
SS Airship, 176–7, 180–2
SS Zero, 182–3
Stapley, J.H., 154
Stark, Lieutenant Rudolf, (German Air Service), 330
Sterling radio, 48
Strange, Second Lieutenant (later Lieutenant Colonel) Louis, (5 Squadron RFC, Eightieth Wing RAF), 29–30, 43, 59, 60, 338–9
Strasser, Peter, 146, 283–4
Stubbington, Air Mechanic George, (HMS Campania, RNAS), 186, 191
stunting, 91, 92
Submarine Scout Airship, 176–7
submarines (and U-boats), 175, 176, 184, 188–90, 201, 260
Sudan, balloon observation, 7
'Surplus Aircraft Fleet', 272, 344
Sykes, Captain (later Major General Sir) Frederick, 15, 22, 24, 65, 308, 344
Sykes, Sub Lieutenant (later Lieutenant) Ronald, (9 Squadron RNAS, 201 Squadron RAF), 93, 94–5, 252–3, 335–6

Tank Corps, 236
Taylor, Lieutenant Gordon, (66 Squadron RFC), 303, 305
Taylor, Sergeant Harold, (25 Squadron RFC), 106
telephone wires, 53
Tempest, Second Lieutenant W.J., (39 Squadron RFC), 169–70, 171
Templer, Major (later Colonel) James, (Superintendent of the Balloon Factory), 7
Thomson, Thomas, (RNAS), 190

INDEX

Tomkins, Lieutenant Ernest, 244
Tondern, Zeppelin base, 193–5, 279
Tower, Winifred, 145
Townshend, Philip, 347
tracer bullets, 170, 207, 331
training: accidents, 81–2; advanced training, 87–91; aerial manoeuvres, 92–7; basic training, 80–7; Flying Certificate test, 87; landing, 83–4; night flying, 97–8; public image of aerial warfare, 77–8; recruits, 77–80; School of Special Flying, 91–2; solo flights, 84–7; take-off, 81–2 reconnaissance, 98–9; aerial observation, 98, 99; bombing, 98, 99–100; photography, 98–9
transport of equipment, 31–2
Treacy, Lieutenant Jack, (3 Squadron, Australian Flying Corps), 322
Trenchard, Major (later Air Marshal Sir) Hugh (RFC Headquarters, later Chief of the Air Staff): Central Flying School, 18–21; temperament, 20; Military Wing command, 24; RFC recruitment, 41, 77, 78–9; First Wing command, 43–4; relationship with Haig, 44, 67, 133–4, 138–9, 307–8; on RFC's role, 52, 163; RFC command, 65; relationship with Baring, 65–7; response to Fokkers, 75–6; escort policy, 122; offensive policy, 125, 128, 134, 209, 220; response to Albatross, 133; RNAS relations, 134–5; RFC expansion, 202; SE5 design, 212; concern for resources, 220–1, 266, 273, 340; parachute policy, 255; bombing policy, 278; 'no empty chairs' policy, 299, 328; Chief of the Air Staff, 307–8, 349; IAF command, 308, 340; attitude to strategic bombing, 344–5
trenches: discomforts, 77; German system, 45–6, 53; mortar-emplacements, 113; reconnaissance of, 45–6, 113, 203
Truscott, Second Lieutenant F.G., (45 Squadron RFC), 209–10, 217n
Tudor-Hart, Lieutenant W.O., (22 Squadron), 121
Tudor-Jones, Second Lieutenant Charles, (3 Squadron RFC), 72–4
Tunbridge Wells, Zeppelin raid, 158–9
Turko-Italian War (1911), 140
Tye, Coppersmith Charles, (Handley Page Aircraft Company), 18

U-boats, see submarines
UC 36, 188
Ultra code-breaking organisation, 225
umbrellas, 114
United States of America: aeroplane development, 3–4, 7, 9; industrial resources, 266, 306
Upavon, see Central Flying School

Usher, Second Lieutenant R.H.C., (27 Squadron RFC), 123

Valenciennes: engine sheds, 69; long-range reconnaissance, 72, 74
Van Ira, Lieutenant James, (74 Squadron RAF), 329
Vaucour, Lieutenant A.M., (70 Squadron RFC), 126–8
Velu, railway junction, 122
Verdun, Battle of (1916), 101, 103, 116, 130, 138, 200
Verne, Jules, 5
Verry, Frederick, (RNAS), 179, 183
Very lights, 48, 167, 247, 297
Vickers, 11
Vickers, Son & Maxim, 175
Vickers Fighter (FB5, 'Gunbus'), 61–2, 63, 71, 106
Vickers machine-gun: Sopwith mounting, 110, 221; Bristol Fighter mounting, 210, 317; SE5 mounting, 211, 250; RE8 mounting, 223; in action, 235; problems, 242, 311–12
Victoria Cross, 25, 52, 61, 150, 214, 315, 328
Vimy Ridge: French offensive (1915), 53; Canadian capture (1917), 208
Voss, Lieutenant Vivian, (48 Squadron RFC), 317, 345
Voss, Leutnant Werner, (German Air Service), 235–6, 257, 303

Waller, Corporal J.H., (25 Squadron RFC), 110
Walthew, Lieutenant Jack, (4 Squadron RFC), 227–8, 289, 300–1
Waltho, Lieutenant Stanton, (RFC), 289, 292
War Cabinet, 262, 266, 268, 269, 271, 340
War Committee, 112
War in the Air, The, 1, 6, 350
War Office: Military Aeroplane Trials, 16; RFC expansion, 40; Henderson's role, 64; aircraft design, 110; relationship with Admiralty, 134, 141, 162; aerial defence plans, 141; Home Defence role, 164; airship development, 175
War Policy Committee, 269
Warneford, Lieutenant Reginald, VC, (1 Squadron RNAS), 149–50
weapons: anti-aircraft guns, 55–8, 129–30, 144–5, 146, 147, 169–70, 281; bombs, 19, 29, 36–7, 50–2; explosive bullets, 166; grenades, 36–7; gun-mountings, 103–5; incendiary bullets, 166; inflammable fish-hooks, 156–7; machine guns, 29–30, 44, 59–60, 146; missiles, 19; Lewis gun, 29–30, 60, 61, 104–6, 123–4, 166, 210, 235, 250, 311–12; Mauser pistol, 30; petrol bombs, 37; pom-poms, 55, 146; revolvers, 58–9; rifles, 58–9; shrapnel, 56; Vickers

machine-gun, 110, 210, 211, 235, 242, 250, 311–12, 317
Weir, Sir William, (later 1st Baron) (Controller of Aeronautical Supplies, Secretary of State for Air), 261–2, 266, 272, 308, 344
Wells, H.G., 1, 4, 350
Whitten-Brown, Arthur, 350
Wilhelm II, Kaiser, 146, 162
Wilhelmshaven, High Seas Fleet base, 174
Wilkinson, Boy Scout A.T., 271
Williams, Captain Billy, (School of Special Flying, Gosport), 91
Williams, Florence, 152
Williams, Thomas, (RNAS), 183–4
Wilson, Reverend P.H., (22nd Wing RFC), 302
Winchester, Clarence, 12
Winterbotham, Lieutenant Frederick, (29 Squadron RFC), 223–5
wireless: early efforts, 44, 48; spark radio, 48; Sterling radio, 48; 'jamming', 113; on seaplanes, 190; central wireless stations, 203–4; RFC operators, 225–7; direction-finding stations, 184, 188
Wobesser, Hauptmann von, (SL2), 151
Wolff, Leutnant Joachim, (German Air Service), 321

Wright, Orville, 3–4, 7–8, 9, 259
Wright, Wilbur, 3–4, 5, 7–8, 9, 259
Wright Biplane, 82
Wrigley, Lieutenant H.N., (3 Squadron, Australian Flying Corps), 231
Wyllie, Captain Harold, (4 Squadron RFC, 23 Squadron RFC), 46, 109, 115, 289

Yarmouth: RNAS base, 173; Zeppelin bombing raid, 146
Ypres: BEF position (1914), 33–4; First Battle of, 45; German gas attack, 52, 53; Second Battle of, 120, 306; Third Battle of, 220, 222, 227–36, 273
Yuille, Lieutenant Archibald B., (RFC, 151 Squadron RAF), 94, 222, 333–4

Zeebrugge, German submarine base, 201
Zeppelin, Count Ferdinand von, 4
Zeppelins: early, 4; British defences against, 20, 141–5, 147–50, 260; German naval orders, 140; bombing raid casualties, 284; raids on Britain, 64, 146–60, 166–73, 260; Tondern base, 193–5 (for individual Zeppelins, see under 'L' and 'LZ')